MW01485346

CROSSROADS OF FATE

CADICLE: VOLUME 5

A K DUBOFF

CROSSROADS OF FATE
Copyright © 2016 A.K. DuBoff

All rights reserved. This book is protected under the copyright laws of
the United States of America. No part of this publication may be used or
reproduced in any manner without written permission from the author,
except in the case of brief quotations embodied in critical articles,
reviews or promotions.

This is a work of fiction. Names, characters, organizations, places,
events, and incidents are either the products of the author's imagination
or are used fictitiously.

Published by Dawnrunner Press
Cover Illustration: Copyright © 2016 Tom Edwards

ISBN: 1-954344023
ISBN-13: 978-1954344020
Copyright Registration Number: TXu002017394

0 9 8 7 6 5 4 3

Produced in the United States of America

CONTENTS

CHAPTER 1

A WARNING SIREN blared, echoing through the hangar on the lower level of H2. Unfortunately for Deena Laecy, such occurrences were all too common in the TSS headquarters within the Rift. "Shite, what now?" she muttered to the three members of her crew presently working in the engineering lab.

"Fok! This manifest can't be right," Nolan, the lead bioelectric engineer, exclaimed as he scrolled through the holographic projection on the lab's display console.

Laecy dashed over to review the list of incoming TSS ships. *This is a fifth of our entire fleet!* "We don't have enough docking capacity."

Becca gasped. "These damage reports… We can't address all of this!"

"Why the sudden influx?" Aram asked, crossing his arms.

Laecy breathed out a slow breath to calm her racing heart. "We don't have a choice. Becca, go to fleet control to get damage assessment triage set up. Nolan—" She cut off when she saw High Commander Taelis approaching. *What's he doing here?*

"I trust you received the manifest," Taelis stated, his face drawn.

"Yes, sir," Laecy replied. "I was just delegating—"

"We'll take care of triage in fleet command. Finishing the *Conquest* is your priority," the High Commander cut in.

"But—"

"The fleet repairs can wait," he told her. "We need that ship finished."

Orders are orders. Laecy nodded. "Nolan, go with Aram to finish up the wiring in the podiums. Becca, run through the Mainframe connections again; we need to solve the lag issue. I'll continue the propulsion tests here."

The three engineers inclined their heads to Taelis and then jogged out of the lab toward the central elevator.

"Sir, what's going on?" Laecy asked the High Commander once they were alone.

"We lost Kaldern."

"Stars!" Laecy breathed. She was used to losing TSS ships on a regular basis, but whenever the Bakzen attacked a planet with a civilian population, it was way more personal. "That explains the arrival list."

"Most of the ships were able to jump out before the port was destroyed." Taelis shook his head. "That was the staging ground for the reserve fleet. If we'd lost them…"

"It'll be okay, sir," Laecy assured him. "We'll find a way to make the repairs."

"We can't wait for Wil any longer," Taelis murmured.

"I'm sure he'd come now if you asked."

"He hasn't yet mastered simultaneous observation," the High Commander replied. "If he doesn't soon, we might not have another choice but to bring him in, anyway."

—   —   —

The Rift beckoned to Wil at the edge of his consciousness. For three weeks he had denied its call, ever since meeting with the Aesir. His new knowledge about the true nature of the Rift—a fray created in the fabric of space by the Bakzen, marring the natural structure—had driven him from the one location where he had once felt free.

Around him, Wil's Primus Elite trainees sulked with a mixture of weariness and annoyance in the center of the zero-G spatial awareness practice chamber. Even his wife, Saera, was floating to his right side with her arms crossed and lips pursed with frustration.

These last few weeks have been a total waste and they know it. Simple spatial dislocation isn't enough. Yet, Wil couldn't bring himself to even reach out toward the Rift to attempt simultaneous observation. The extra strength the Rift gave him in any telekinetic feat wasn't worth the reminder of how it was formed by the Bakzen in an attempt to find a haven from their Taran creators. However, without accessing the Rift, he would never be able to achieve simultaneous observation—a critical component of his role in the Bakzen war, where he would perceive events in normal space, the Rift, and subspace at the same time so the TSS could finally outmaneuver the enemy.

Ian groaned, tousling his light brown hair. "Oh, come on! You're not even trying."

There was no sense in Wil denying the truth. "It might not be necessary. Now that we have the independent jump drive—"

"Everything we've practiced requires a telepathic link," Michael interrupted. "You need the amplification from the Rift if it's going to cover the distance we need, simultaneous observation or not."

Wil searched for a suitable rebuttal, but his friend was right. *I do need the Rift. Running away from what it represents won't win the war.*

Maintaining a telepathic link in close proximity was easy after years of training together. Communications were instantaneous and effortless, even across the span of the massive Headquarters structure deep within Earth's moon, but the connection wavered beyond that distance. The entire purpose of honing their telepathic communications was to bypass the need for traditional subspace comm relays, which were comparatively slow and unsecured. Except, the Primus Elites and TSS fleet would be spread out across the Rift, and possibly even in more distant star systems. To maintain any level of efficiency, the telepathic link would need to cover that whole spectrum. Only the unique environment of the Rift could supply enough energy for Wil to maintain a telepathic network that extensive without degradation.

Wil sighed inwardly. "All right, let's go again."

"For real this time?" Michael asked, an eyebrow raised with skepticism.

"You can't let the truth about the Rift and the Bakzen hold you back. We need you," Saera added telepathically in private.

"Yes, for real," Wil replied aloud. *She's right; I have to.* He began to clear his mind in preparation for the simultaneous observation attempt. "Form up."

Saera and the Primus Elites drifted through the dim room into their standard circular formation around him, gripping the tablets used for practicing manual control inputs while within the trance-like telepathic link.

Wil took slow, even breaths—losing himself in the simulated starscape. Next to him, he telepathically reached out to Saera as his anchor. Her presence steadied him as he began to drift outward, giving him a solid tether so he would always be able to find a way back to his physical self from the depths of subspace. *"Fleet?"* Wil asked telepathically.

"Fleet check," replied Michael first, as Wil's second-in-command.

"Tactical?"

"Tactical check," replied Ian, lead for special tactical assaults.

"Pilots?"

"Primus team check," replied Ethan, the Primus Squad pilot team lead.

"Pilot command check," replied Curtis, the communications hub for relaying precision strike orders to the larger TSS fleet.

The verbal exchange with its conditioned responses served as a cue for the team to initiate their telepathic link, branching from Wil through Saera and his four officers, then on to the members of each specialty unit. His skin tingled as the network materialized around him. The energy of the telepathic bonds formed an invisible web connecting each individual, with the strongest corridors between Wil and his officers and through Saera as his anchor to the physical world. Wil habitually tested all the connections before proceeding, viewing the bonds as silver threads in his mind.

Satisfied that the links were secure, he reached out toward the Rift.

Pure energy within the Rift beckoned him, drawing him into a full state of spatial dislocation. He pierced the dimensional veil, fueled by the Rift's power to push himself further. *I saw the pattern when I looked into the void with the Aesir. Simultaneous observation is no different. I can do this.*

Energy within subspace swelled to meet him, but all he could sense was the overwhelming force of the Rift in the distance. He tried to extend himself further, but the tie to his physical self held him back. Fear welled in the inner recesses of his consciousness. *I could lose myself here.* He shoved the thought aside, determined to succeed. *No, I'm not alone.* Before he could hesitate again, he let go—placing full trust in his wife and friends.

For a moment, he floated freely. Subspace was boundless. He could finally test his limits. Exhilaration surged through his unrestrained consciousness. There was so much to explore—

Then, tethers reformed around him. He fought against the restraints, still thirsting for freedom.

"We have you." It was Saera's voice in his mind.

Wil relaxed, remembering what he had set out to do. He probed the new ties around him, finding that they were only a gentle net to keep him from drifting too far while still allowing him to move without constriction. Nothing was holding him back.

The vastness of subspace spanned before Wil, but that was only one layer. Rather than outward, he reached through—grasping for the physical plane of his reality. As he pierced the dimensional divide, subspace appeared to shatter around him. He started to fall, thrown against the boundary of the tethering net. Gripped with sudden apprehension, he withdrew into the safety of the net, desperate to remain connected. The dizzying sense of freefall ceased, replaced by the call of a power source just beyond his sight.

As Wil tried to get his bearings, he realized that he hadn't actually fallen, but had instead zoomed outward. The fabric of space unfolded before him—layers of energy, of planes—woven together in an intricate pattern.

He brushed against the layers, calling each one into perfect focus as he seamlessly passed from one plane to the next.

There were too many layers to take in at once, so he turned his attention to the familiar. His home physical plane stood out most brightly in the cross-section, framed by a subspace band to either side. In the great distance, sandwiched between the upper subspace band and the physical plane, was the scarring Rift amid tatters of the underlying spatial fabric. Wil positioned himself at the horizon between physical reality and subspace—searching for the balance that had always eluded him.

Everything came into focus. Wil saw his friends floating around him, overlaid by the energy flowing through subspace. He let his consciousness drift, pulling out from the room, passing through Headquarters, beyond the moon, and viewing Earth from afar. As he had glimpsed before, in the great distance, he sensed the border of the Rift—but touching it was farther than he wanted to venture. Yet, he was sure that if he was closer, he would be able to see everything within the Rift, too. In the state of simultaneous observation, his consciousness was free to roam, to pick up details within the physical realm, Rift, and subspace planes all at once.

Wil grinned with giddy excitement. *This is it! We have all the tools we need to win.*

As much as he wanted to continue exploring the world around him with a new perspective unlike any other, he withdrew back to his physical self. With a gasp, he opened his eyes—seeing reality again through his corporeal eyes. It seemed so dull and narrow by comparison.

He disconnected from his friends, breaking the telepathic network.

The Primus Elites hovered perfectly still, stunned.

"Well, that was different," Saera broke the silence.

"Did you…?" Michael began.

"Simultaneous observation," Wil confirmed.

"Stars! You actually did it," exclaimed Ethan.

Wil ran a hand through his chestnut hair. "Yeah… that was weird."

"What did you see?" Saera asked.

"I can't quite describe it. At first, it was like seeing a cross-section of the different planes, and then some sort of composite image between the physical world and subspace."

Everyone's eyes widened.

"So, an actual overlay of the two planes at once?" Curtis clarified.

"With the ability to focus on each independently to get better detail," Wil responded. "But yes, I could hold the perception of both planes at the same time."

Michael tilted his head. "How far could you see?"

"As far as I wanted," Wil replied. "It was like using a jump drive, but with consciousness. Traveling through subspace doesn't have the same physical limitations."

Ian lit up, his amber eyes wide. "We really will be able to maintain the telepathic link across whole sectors!"

"Yes, I believe so," Wil affirmed.

Saera let out a long breath. "That's a relief."

"However, we do have a slight problem," Wil continued. "The Rift isn't here at Headquarters, so we can't really practice properly."

"What are we supposed to do now, then?" questioned Michael.

"We work on relaying commands while I'm that far extended. I've always been 'here', more or less, when we've tried before."

His men nodded, and Saera gave him a supportive smile.

"That's for another time, though," Wil said, knowing they shouldn't push too far in one day.

"Quit while we're ahead, right?" Ethan grinned.

Wil rolled his cerulean eyes. "We never quit, but taking well-deserved breaks is always a good policy."

"I'll support that," Ian said. "Dibs on the main viewscreen!"

"Not fair!" Tom, one of Ian's best pilots, interjected with a slight flush showing through his dark complexion. "You've been monopolizing it with that stupid game of yours for the last two weeks." He folded his lean arms across his chest.

"Hey, I happen to have an incredibly high score and can't stop until I crush that tough guy from Urulan VIII at the end of the tournament tomorrow," Ian shot back.

Ethan laughed. "We all know that 'tough guy' is actually a thirteen-year-old girl, so…"

Ian's face reddened. "That's beside the point—"

Wil threw up his hands, suppressing an amused grin. "Rights to the entertainment system are beyond my purview. Enjoy your afternoon." He began to draw himself telekinetically toward the door.

Before he'd gone a meter, most of his men dove for the door, brushing past Wil and Saera in one dark blue mass. Only Michael hung back, always the most composed of the group.

"Can't have the viewscreen if I get there first!" Tom declared as he hurled himself through the doorway into the gravity lock.

"But I called dibs!" Ian protested, vaulting in after him.

The rest of the men quickly slipped inside before the door sealed shut, leaving their three senior leaders still floating in the center of the training chamber.

Saera giggled. "All right, then."

Wil shook his head, resuming his slow pull toward the door. It would take two minutes for the lock to be prepared for them to exit; no need to rush. "Maybe I didn't instill enough 'no one left behind' message in the training."

"They're aware of others when it matters," Michael said in his comrades' defense.

Wil touched down on the wall, grabbing a handhold. "I know. They should enjoy this relaxation time while they can."

Michael's brow furrowed as he gripped the wall next to Wil. "Simultaneous observation was the last step, wasn't it? We can't really train anymore away from the Rift, despite what you said."

"No," Wil confessed. "It won't be long now before we go."

"Why the hesitation? We're ready," Michael said.

"Yes, you are, but…"

"Ever since you got back from the Aesir, you've been different. Today is the first time you've actually attempted to observe since then. Now, I don't want to say it seemed easy for you—since it's not something I can do, so it's not my place to pass judgment—but it certainly didn't seem like you were straining. It was almost like you'd done it before." Michael searched Wil's face. "What happened with the Aesir? Why have you been avoiding the Rift?"

Wil cast his gaze down. "Nothing for you to worry about."

Saera tensed next to him. "The important thing is that now we know that observation *is* possible. We need to be a team, just like we've trained to do."

Michael's blue eyes flitted between them. "You both know something you're not telling the rest of us."

"It's my job as a commander to evaluate the facts. I've told you all the critical information," Wil replied.

"What about as your friend?" asked Michael.

"As your friend, trust me when I say you're better off not knowing what I know."

The gravity lock chirped that it had returned to zero-G.

Wil released the hatch, and it slid open with a hiss. "I know it's maddening to have things kept from you, but all the shite happening behind the scenes is not an inner circle you want to be in."

Michael hesitated before climbing into the gravity lock. "I trust you."

"Likewise." Wil swung into the gravity lock, followed by Saera. "I promise, I'll tell you everything when the time is right." *Assuming I make it until then.*

His friend nodded. "Understood."

The gravity lock silently activated, drawing Wil and his companions toward the floor. After a minute, the outer door slid open when the gravity had equalized with the passageway outside the lock.

"I'd like to go over the logs from the session," Wil said. "For now, let's keep this new development between us, okay?"

"Of course," Michael replied. "I'll tell the others to keep their mouths shut."

"Thanks."

"Now, I should probably make sure that Tom and Ian haven't locked each other in some sort of telekinetic death-vise." Michael glanced down the hall toward the central elevator.

Wil cracked a smile. "Sometimes I'm thankful for the telekinetic dampening effect of subspace."

"I'll see you tomorrow." Michael gave a parting wave and jogged down the hall.

"I should get to work," Saera said with a huff, tugging on her auburn braid. "I have some assignments to grade."

"I'm still surprised you volunteered to instruct that class."

She shrugged. "Someone needs to teach the next generation. So few Agents are left around here."

Wil couldn't argue that point. Many of the Agents he'd been around his whole life had recently been deployed to the Rift's Jotun division in preparation for the final battles of the war. Headquarters was eerily empty. *Soon we'll be gone, too.* He returned his thoughts to the present. "I'll need the viewscreen in the living room to go over the data."

"Is there any chance you can use the one in your office?" his wife asked with pleading jade eyes. "I was hoping to get in some quality couch time with a glass of wine. It's the only thing that takes the edge off of poorly constructed navigation proofs."

Wil's chest constricted. "I guess I could work in a study room—"

Saera crossed her arms. "So, you're still avoiding the administrative wing?"

"Just one specific place, and unfortunately my office happens to be nearby."

"Avoidance isn't healthy, especially when it's an old friend and superior officer."

Wil sighed. "I know."

"Good. Now get to work!" Saera shooed him playfully with a wave of her hand.

Not so easily swayed, Wil pulled her in for a quick kiss, capitalizing on their few private moments together.

She kissed him back and relaxed into his arms.

"I shouldn't be too long," Wil murmured as he pulled back.

"All right. I'll see you for dinner." She squeezed his hand as they parted at the elevator lobby, taking separate cars to their respective destinations. Wil put his tinted glasses back on and gathered his thoughts. Achieving simultaneous observation would certainly fast track the rest of his officers' training. They could be pulled into the war at any moment.

Once on the destination floor of Level 1, Wil darted from the elevator lobby to his office down the same corridor as the High Commander's office. He'd been avoiding Banks since their last conversation following Wil's revelations with the Aesir three weeks prior. While Wil understood the High Commander's reasons for keeping so much from him, he had opted to avoid any further confrontations for as long as possible. He just needed to slip into his office and close the door before anyone spotted him.

Of course, the best-laid plans didn't always work out.

Just as he was about to duck through his office door, Wil spotted his father approaching in a hurry.

"Wil, CACI said you were headed this way. I just saw the raw logs from the training session this afternoon. Did you—?" Cris started.

Shite! I wasn't even thinking about the automatic data upload to the Mainframe. Over the years, Cris had asked enough questions about daily training activities that Wil had shared the logs with him so he could avoid filing a formal daily report. The upload included automatic flags when new benchmarks of telekinetic intensity were achieved. It was no wonder his latest feat had triggered an alert. "Not here," Wil muttered under his breath and dashed into the comparative safety of his office.

Cris followed Wil before he had a chance to close the door. "This is the last place I expected to find you."

"Saera needed our quarters to herself." Wil kept his gaze down.

"Wil, did you achieve simultaneous observation?" Cris pressed.

Wil took several seconds to respond, weighing his options. Lying would only delay the inevitable. "I think so. The Rift doesn't extend this far so I can't be sure, but I saw normal space and subspace."

His father looked him over, his awe visible even through his tinted glasses. "What changed?"

"I stopped trying to resist."

Cris' brow knitted. "How long have you been resisting?"

"I've been holding back ever since I met with the Aesir."

"Why?"

"The Rift isn't a good place to be."

"As you've said," Cris said under his breath. "I don't know what happened out there—since you refuse to talk about it—but we have to move forward."

"I am. I'm doing what you told me to do."

Cris frowned. "In that case, you know that you have to meet with Banks about this development."

"Yeah."

His father groaned. "It's been weeks, Wil. What did he say that upset you so much?"

"Like I told you before, it's not anything I can discuss." *There's no need to make others endure the truth about the Bakzen's origins.*

"That's not a satisfactory explanation."

"This is between me and Banks. I'll talk to him when I have something productive to say."

Cris sighed. "I'm pretty sure that achieving simultaneous observation warrants an immediate discussion."

Wil slumped into the chair behind his desk. "Except, I know that conversation is the beginning of the end. No more hypotheticals—the start of real actions with real consequences."

His father eased down onto the front of the desk. "The sooner we start, the sooner it will be over."

"I can't picture an 'after'. My entire life has been building to what's now right around the corner."

"If there's one thing I've learned over the years, it's that the future never works out quite like you imagine," Cris replied. "We'll get through the coming months—helping each other, like we always do—and then we'll deal with the rest."

Wil grimaced. "You make it sound so straightforward."

"No, it won't be. But it can be done."

The words of encouragement had little substance, but somehow Wil was comforted. "I think I'll need a few more of these pep talks before all this is over." He cracked the hint of a smile.

"Whatever you need, I'll be here."

"Thanks." Wil took a deep breath and let it out. "I should start reviewing the logs from this afternoon's session."

His father rose and stepped toward the door. "I'll leave you to it. Hang in there, Wil."

CHAPTER 2

FEW ACTIVITIES WERE duller than proofreading sample contracts, as far as Michael was concerned. How such activities were pertinent to his training as a TSS officer in the Bakzen war had never been explained to his satisfaction, but the assignment was due later that afternoon so he wasn't in a position to argue.

He flipped over to his back with his head propped up on a pillow and his tablet resting vertically on his chest. A quick glance to his left revealed that the two other Junior Agents currently in the room appeared equally enthused with their own assignments. Bran occupied the farthest of the three beds on the same wall as Michael's, and Cameron was on the leftmost of the two opposite them, which framed the entry door. The three of them and the two additional members of their unit had shared the room since their first day in the TSS. Wil had offered them an upgrade to Junior Agents' housing after two years, but the Primus Elites had unanimously declined; the quarters were their home, and sharing the same space offered the best opportunity for collaboration.

"Is it just me, or are these assignments getting more and more tedious?" Bran commented when he noticed Michael stir.

Michael sighed. "It's not just you."

"Maybe Wil is running out of things to teach us?" Cameron speculated. "Before the breakthrough with simultaneous observation yesterday, things had been pretty slow for a while."

That might not be far from the truth. Michael leaned his tablet back on his knees, looking over at his friends. "It may seem pointless now, but we're getting valuable skills that'll come in handy one day or another."

Bran shrugged. "Well, I'm anxious to kick some Bakzen ass."

"Same here," Cameron agreed. "Being awesome at reading supply logs won't win a space battle."

"I know," Michael yielded. "For whatever reason, Wil seems to be delaying our deployment."

"It's not like we're going on vacation. I can understand why he'd want to put it off," Bran said.

"That doesn't change the sense of urgency," Michael countered.

Cameron nodded. "That's true. All these years, it's been motivational talks about how we don't have time to waste and everyone's counting on us to swoop in and end the fighting. Then Wil meets with the Aesir, and now he's done nothing but drag his feet for weeks."

"Something happened out there," Michael murmured.

Bran frowned. "I don't like that he's been so quiet about it."

Michael shook off the doubt. "He's still the same leader we've always trusted. He'll step up, like he always does."

Shouts of dismay erupted in the common room of the Primus Elite quarters.

What now? Michael set down his tablet and rose from his bed to investigate. "Is the tournament still going on?"

"I think so," Cameron replied. "Sounds like it's not going well for Ian." He and Bran got up to follow Michael to the common room.

Their bedroom was situated on the front left of the adjoining common area, closest to the shared viewscreen. A dozen of the Primus Elites were gathered on the two innermost plush couches oriented toward the screen. Ian stood in front of the black couches in the space normally occupied by the coffee table, which had been propped on its side against the front wall. His eyes were fixed on the screen—knees bent and arms extended, poised for action.

A three-dimensional hex grid displayed on the viewscreen depicted a fantastical battlefield with a party of five characters on each side. One of Ian's characters, which looked to be some sort of troll, was kneeling on the ground panting. Above it, a massive barbarian was shaking a club victoriously above its head.

"Fok!" Ian swore under his breath. "Don't fail me now, Morg." He brought up a character menu for the troll with an upward swipe of his hand, scouring the item list.

"Just use Galinda to cast Cure," Curtis suggested while he played with a short strand of his curled, dark hair between his thumb and forefinger.

"No, I need her Gale attack to knock back the archers," Ian dismissed, his eyes never leaving the screen. He selected a medpack and used it on the fallen troll.

Ian then swept his hand to activate a tall, female figure with blue skin and pointy ears. He mimed raising a staff above his head and fanned his arms outward, causing the onscreen character to release a wind blast toward a group of enemy soldiers holding longbows. The enemy archers all stumbled backward two hexagonal spaces.

"Ha!" Ian declared triumphantly.

In retaliation, the barbarian standing over Ian's troll readied its club for another blow.

"Not so fast." Ian jumped up and to the side, causing his newly healed troll to dart out of the way before the barbarian could strike. He spun around and swung the troll's ax in an arc over his shoulder to strike the barbarian's ankles.

The barbarian cried out with surprise while Ian simultaneously activated his three dormant characters to launch an assault on the opponent player's combat units. Within moments, the battlefield was ablaze with fireball attacks cast by a sorceress on the enemy team.

Michael leaned against the doorframe, taking in the action as Ian and his opponent slowly wore down each other's forces. The other Primus Elites gasped and cheered with each attack, completely captivated by the game as it unfolded before them. In time, the battle came down to Ian's caster—Galinda—and the sorceress in the opponent's party.

"How is the game won, anyway?" Michael whispered to Bran.

Bran didn't take his eyes off the viewscreen. "One of the

players needs to collect the Essence from the other team's slain characters."

Like absorbing their souls? Michael scowled. "Sounds kind of morbid."

"It's just a game. Shh," Cameron hissed.

Ian continued to wave his hands in a throwing motion as Galinda cast her spells onscreen. "Ah ha!" he declared. "Power attack is ready." He cupped his hands in front of his chest and an orb of energy began to form in front of Galinda, radiating purple sparks.

When the orb was the size of her torso, Ian thrust his hands forward and the orb shot directly for the remaining enemy character. The sorceress opponent fell to her knees, then all the way to the ground.

An orchestral fanfare sounded. The Primus Elites burst into exuberant cheers.

"Now *that* is how it's done!" Ian directed Galinda on a path through the battlefield to collect tiny white orbs that appeared above each of the fallen enemy characters. When all the orbs had been collected, the music swelled and the Essence orbs combined into one sphere, which merged into Galinda's chest. A white halo appeared around her, and the staff in her hand transformed into a new weapon with intricate carvings and a glowing white orb on the top. The fallen characters from Ian's party rose and turned to Galinda. She victoriously thrust her staff into the sky.

Ian grinned. "Thank the stars that's over!"

"Now you just have to defend your title next year," Curtis said with a smirk.

"Oh, I will!" Ian declared.

Hopefully, we're done battling the Bakzen by this time next year and we can get this life back. Michael inched back into the bedroom, remembering his unfinished contract review assignment. "Congratulations, Ian."

"Thanks!" Ian replied, his eyes radiant with victory. "Glad to see you finally joined in."

"Sorry, I've been pretty preoccupied with another fight."

Ian nodded. "I guess we all will be soon enough."

Michael withdrew the rest of the way into his bedroom.

Though he had remained on the outskirts of some of the group's social activities, there was an unquestionable bond between them. Seeing them become so enthralled and connected with one of their own playing a game, he liked to think that was a good indication they would make it through the war to come. Except, when lives were on the line, there would be no safety net—no chance to try again next year, or revert to a previous save and try again.

He shook off a sudden chill. *We're about to enter into the unknown. I hope we really are ready…*

— — —

After weeks of avoidance, Wil finally found_himself sitting across the desk from Banks in the High Commander's office. On a rational level, he knew they needed to find a way to work together—somehow. But the wound was still raw. *He lied to me about the Bakzen for my whole life. How am I supposed to trust him again?*

"So," Banks broke the awkward silence following their forced pleasantries, "you're making progress with simultaneous observation."

"I can do it now, if that's what you're asking," Wil replied, keeping his gaze fixed on the wall behind the High Commander's shoulder.

"Consistently?"

"It's more of an 'all or nothing' thing. I'm past the threshold now."

Banks folded his hands on the desktop. "Congratulations."

Wil held in a scoff. *It's hardly the accomplishment I dreamed it to be.*

The High Commander searched his face. "Are you okay, Wil?"

I don't know anymore. Wil swallowed. *It's really not fair for me to be upset with him. He didn't start the war… He was only trying to protect me.* He straightened in his chair. "I've had a lot to think about since I got back."

"I know." Banks paused. "I never wanted you to find out about the Bakzen like that. I should have told you sooner."

"What's done is done."

"Still…"

Wil finally met the High Commander's gaze. "Dwelling on past regrets won't get us anywhere."

"You're right."

"Regardless," Wil continued, "as much as I wish I didn't know that the Bakzen started out like us, in some ways, it's a good thing to know. Their faults, their desires—it was all born from the same place as our own motivations."

Banks nodded. "A fair point."

"I don't know how others would react if they knew the truth. I've told Saera, but anyone else…"

"I agree that it's best to keep it confidential."

"My men know I'm keeping something from them. They keep pushing me."

"They're a perceptive group," Banks replied, cracking a slight smile.

"Yes. Annoyingly so, sometimes."

Banks examined him. "How close are you to completing their training?"

Wil cast his eyes down. *That's not what he's really asking… I'd never engage them in this battle if I had a choice.* "They've honed their skills, but a lot of what they know is still only theory."

"Then we'll need to get them some real-world experience."

"How? There's no facility here that could possibly help us prepare any more than we already have."

"Not here, perhaps," the High Commander replied, "but H2 is set up for that very purpose."

"It's that time, isn't it?" *I can't avoid the war any longer.*

"Everyone will be here to help you, Wil. We'll win."

—   —   —

While the conversation had been strained, Banks was relieved that at least Wil was talking to him again. He had enough to worry about without the added concern of infighting within the TSS.

Events were once again converging, as so often seemed the case. Wil's new ability marked a turning point in the war, necessitating that the Primus Elites be deployed as soon as possible. That would leave Banks with some time to investigate the other matter that had been bothering him for the past few weeks.

The words of the Aesir Oracle were still fresh in his mind—a cryptic message about a Dainetris heir who had survived the Dynasty's fall more than one hundred years prior. A legitimate heir could have immeasurable influence on the future of Taran politics, shifting the balance of power. As long as the Priesthood remained in their position of absolute control over communications among the Taran worlds and had the final say in all policy decisions, there would be no way to make any meaningful changes without the added influence of a seventh High Dynasty. However, the return of the Dainetris Dynasty would not only remove the Priesthood from its present position as a tie-breaking vote, but the reemergence might also unveil what had brought about the Dynasty's downfall. If Banks' instincts were correct, the Priesthood was to blame, but he knew them well enough to be certain they would protect their secrets at any cost. If a Dainetris heir had survived, the Priesthood must have a reason for permitting it.

Unfortunately, hunches weren't useful. Banks still had a job to do. Before anything else, there was a war to win.

The latest report from High Commander Taelis at H2 in the Rift suggested a new Bakzen offensive. Wil's recent mastery of simultaneous observation had come just in time.

Banks set aside his thoughts about the Dainetris Dynasty and instructed the computer to call Taelis via the viewscreen.

The other High Commander answered after a minute, appearing agitated, as usual. "Jason, hi. Do you need something?"

"No, I wanted to give you some good news."

Taelis grunted. "I could use it."

"I just got confirmation from Wil that he was finally able to observe."

Onscreen, Taelis froze with surprise. "He did it?"

Banks nodded. "Just yesterday. It's hard to believe this day has finally come, but I've reviewed the training log myself."

"We really needed this. Now more than ever."

"Yes... it sounds like conditions are deteriorating."

Taelis slumped. "We don't know what's causing it, Jason. A whole group of people on Kaldern spontaneously started voicing support for the Bakzen and attacked the planetary shield generators."

"Civilians?"

"Yes, and a whole lot of them. People who should hate the Bakzen after what they've been through—their homeworlds destroyed."

That's concerning, indeed. "People snap sometimes," Banks speculated.

"No, this was more than that," Taelis countered. "The video footage is unnerving. It was like they were in a trance."

"Brainwashing?"

"Or telepathic influence. Except, we have no way to stop it until we know the root cause."

"All the more reason to move forward with our end strategy."

Taelis inclined his head. "Yes, Wil and his officers should come here as soon as possible."

"Agreed, but they need some field experience before they're sent into battle," Banks cautioned. "Everything is all out of sequence."

Taelis narrowed his eyes. "What are you hung up on—an internship?"

Banks nodded. "In part. And completion of the other Junior Agent testing protocols."

Taelis gave a dismissive flip of his wrist. "Just promote them. We don't have time to waste on all that."

"Is it wasting time to make sure they won't break under the pressure?"

"Even seasoned Agents can break."

"I'm just not sure they should be in the field yet," Banks insisted. "They're untested and can make mistakes. Are we really willing to take that risk?"

"Jason, I don't think you understand what we're facing here.

We need to end this now. Promote them."

Banks sighed. "It will require approvals. I'll let you know as soon as I get confirmation." He ended the transmission. There was no doubt that the Priesthood would heartily agree, but it was the perfect conversation starter for the question related to his other research.

Without delay, Banks instructed CACI to contact the Priesthood. He paced in front of the viewscreen as he waited for the call to connect.

The lifelike image of the Priest robed in black appeared onscreen. "Do you have news?"

"More of a question," replied Banks. "We have reached a pivotal time. Do we bring in the Primus Elite group now, or wait until they have had a chance to complete the formal training program?"

"What still remains?"

"Internships and formal CR testing, mostly."

The Priest shook his head. "Protocol means little now. The war must end, through whatever means necessary. You know your task—there's no need for our approval."

Just as I suspected. Now time for the real question. "Understood. Since I have you, there is one other matter on an unrelated topic."

"Yes?"

"Were there any survivors to the Dainetris Dynasty?"

The Priest's red eyes widened, but he quickly returned to his typical stoic composure. He took a moment to respond. "The Dainetris Dynasty fell."

That wasn't a very conclusive answer. "But were there any survivors after the fall?"

The Priest's eyes narrowed. "We have far too many urgent matters in the present to think about the past. Finish preparing the TSS forces and end the war." He terminated the video feed.

Banks had known the Priest for far too long to misinterpret the abrupt end to the conversation. There was at least one Dainetris survivor, and the Priesthood didn't want them found. *So, they keep secrets even from me.* Banks knew all about secrets— after all, knowing how to keep his own was the first step toward uncovering the secrets kept by others. And he had learned from the best.

— — —

The resourcefulness of the Bakzen never ceased to amaze Arron Haersen. Turning Tarans into Bakzen drones—it was nothing short of brilliant. Refugees from Aleda and Grolen had so easily been transformed into the Bakzen's tools on Kaldern, saying and doing anything their telepathic commands demanded. The latest demonstration was only a test, but it made for a powerful example of future possibilities. With the first phase complete, they could now move on to the real test with the Kaldern survivors.

"That was entirely too easy," Tek said through his smirk. He paused the video playback of the riot on Kaldern prior to the Bakzen invasion. The viewscreen on the side wall of the Imperial Director's office dimmed.

"It's no doubt the procedure works," Haersen replied. "The question is, how do we get enough individuals under the influence of our neurotoxin to converge on Tararia? We need to take out their central government before we can execute the next stage on a broad scale."

"We will have to cut a path to Tararia—one they won't notice until it's too late." Tek rose from his desk and turned around to stare out the broad window along the back wall overlooking the plaza outside the primary administrative building for the Bakzeni Empire.

His response could only mean one thing. "They're ready?"

Tek nodded. "Right on schedule."

A slow smile spread across Haersen's angular face. It had taken nearly a decade to mature and train the Bakzen hybrid clones spliced with Wil's genetic code; they were free of the natural ability inhibitor found in all others. If their conditioning was complete, then the Bakzen would finally have the necessary means to rip covert rift corridors directly to Tararia, giving them a direct route that would bypass the need for navigation beacons, and thereby make their approach undetectable.

"Perfect timing," Haersen informed his new commander. "The TSS is on the move."

General Tek perked up with interest. "What news have you heard?"

"There are rumors that the TSS is about to bring the Dragon into the war. We will finally get our chance."

"How easy it will be to bait him," agreed Tek. "I can only imagine he's still reeling from his meeting with the Aesir, after the truth he must have discovered when he looked into the void."

"He'll be distracted and eager to latch onto any hope he can find."

Tek nodded. "But if our first plan doesn't work, we will simply exploit his sympathetic Taran mind—have him deliver us Tararia."

Haersen clenched his fist, strengthened through years of gene therapy to mold him into a new version of himself. "Such weakness."

Tek's eyes narrowed. "Don't forget, not so long ago, you were one of them."

"I saw the true way," Haersen countered. Since joining the Bakzen, it had been a constant struggle to affirm his loyalty. The failed assassination of Wil had been an enormous setback, and he knew that it was only his detailed understanding of TSS procedures that continued to keep him alive. He hoped that knowledge would enable the Bakzen to win the war.

"Words are hollow. What more can you give us now?"

Haersen looked down. "I have no more details at this time, sir."

"Then be gone." Tek made a dismissive wave of his hand.

Haersen bobbed his head and turned to leave. Tek wasn't a gracious leader, but he was fair—not subject to the domineering and favoritism found in the TSS. He had remained true to his word with Haersen, and that spoke for itself. Though Haersen hadn't yet achieved equal footing with the Bakzen, it was almost time to make a new future where anything was possible.

CHAPTER 3

W ̲IL ̲ ̲BOLTED ̲ ̲UPRIGHT ̲ in bed, gasping. The horrific images were already fading from his mind, but his heart still raced from what only moments before had been a vivid reality.

Saera roused next to him. "Wil, are you okay?"

"Yeah, it was just a dream."

"You haven't been sleeping well." The concern on Saera's face was evident, even in the subtle light cast from her jade eyes.

"Ever since I got back from meeting the Aesir. Something similar happened after my first encounter with the Bakzen. I don't know if it's just stress dreams, or a premonition." *Envisioning the destruction of the Bakzen by my hand... All my fears and doubts.*

"Either way, you should try to get back to sleep. I'll be right here with you." She lay down and placed a reassuring hand on Wil's arm.

If only that were still enough to help me sleep through the night. "I know." Wil stayed upright.

After a moment, Saera sat back up. "What's on your mind?"

"It's all about to start. My entire life has been looking toward the future, but now it's almost time for action."

"You're ready. You've been ready for a long time."

"Maybe for too long. There's been so much anticipation and build-up, I'm afraid I'm going to overthink everything and fail."

"No, Wil, you're prepared to face whatever comes."

If only success didn't come at such a high price. "Thank you for standing by me."

"Of course. Always."

"Having you with me these last few years… it's given me a reason to keep going."

"We have a lot more to look forward to."

Wil lay down and put his arm around her. *If I only have a few moments left to myself before the war begins, this is how I want to spend them.*

—

It had been a good practice session, but Wil was tired and anxious to be finished for the day; the lack of quality sleep was taking a toll.

As he exited the gravity lock from the zero-G practice chamber with his trainees, Wil's handheld buzzed in his pocket. *Ugh, what now?* There was a message from Banks, with instructions to meet him in his office. *Great.*

"Have a good night. I'll see you tomorrow," Wil said to his men and then headed toward the central elevator.

He took his time in transit, dreading what the meeting could be about. After their last conversation the previous afternoon, it was only a matter of time before he would be called upon to fulfill his duty. He wanted to savor every final moment of freedom.

Wil's fears were confirmed as soon as he stepped into Banks' office. The High Commander was standing at the back of the room, staring at a holopainting of a mountain landscape. He turned as Wil entered, his expression tense—almost sad.

Wil closed the door. "It's time, isn't it?"

Banks nodded.

Wil took a deep breath. "When do we leave?"

"Two days."

Wil leaned against the back of the couch at the center of the office. "What about my men? They haven't completed the training protocol."

Banks came forward a few steps to stand across from Wil. "They'll participate in a working internship, then graduate in the field under the auspice of a senior officer."

"Yes, sir." *We're going to war. All the formality doesn't matter anymore.*

"Saera will accompany you, of course. And your parents will be on the *Vanquish*."

"The *Vanquish* is going, too? You've already dispatched the other warships. Doesn't that leave Headquarters rather exposed?"

"We have to go all in."

"But—"

"Wil, you have to focus on the frontlines. Let me worry about what happens here."

"Okay." Wil pushed off the couch.

"Try to take some time to get rested up over the next couple days. You'll be thrown into the middle of things when you arrive at H2."

The headquarters beyond the Rift... it's been so long. "It's bad over there, isn't it?"

Banks nodded. "They've been suffering heavy casualties. We would have given the Elites normal internships, if we could, but..."

They're desperate. "I'll do what I can."

"Taelis has saved the last wave of resources for you." Banks swallowed. "However, if things don't go well, there's not a lot of backup."

"I always knew I'd be part of the endgame. We'll do our job as quickly as possible."

"I have absolute faith in you and your team."

"You always have." Wil paused. "How does it feel now to be giving this order? Your entire career has been for this."

Banks came around the couch. "I'm so very proud of you, Wil. I know what you've been through over the years, and the truth you bear over the nature of the war and what we're up against. You have taken it all with such strength and grace. You embody everything a leader should be, and if you can't navigate us to an end of this war, then no one can. I'm just honored to have had the privilege of knowing you."

Wil's throat tightened. "I couldn't have become that kind of person without you." In one motion, Wil stepped forward and embraced Banks—something he hadn't done since he was a child.

Banks was caught by surprise, but hugged him back. "Take care of yourself."

"You too." *He's watching over the only home I've ever had. If I make it through this, I'll want it waiting for me.*

With a resolute nod, Wil left Banks' office and trudged to his quarters. He found it empty and dark; Saera's class must have run late. He let out a slow breath and eased down onto the couch in the living room.

For nearly twenty-five years—his entire life—he had been coached and trained for an event in the distant future. It had all started to feel much more real once he had begun training his officers, but now, having a tangible departure date a mere two days away, changed his entire perception.

He sat in the dark, trying to come to terms with what lay ahead. As his mind wandered, he lost track of time and was startled by a flood of light when the front door opened.

Saera paused in the doorway when she saw Wil blinking in the sudden brightness. "Hey. Did I wake you?" She closed the door behind her.

"No, I was just sitting here."

"Tough day?"

Wil took a deep breath. "I just talked to Banks. We depart for H2 in two days."

Saera dropped onto the couch next to Wil. "So soon?"

"Desperate times."

"Are you doing okay?"

"No."

"Wil—"

"No, please, don't. There's nothing you can say." Wil fought against the burn in his eyes for a moment but then submitted to the emotion.

Saera held Wil's head to her chest as the tears silently rolled down his cheeks and soaked into her shirt. The years of stress and anticipation streamed away in the quiet moment. Wil relished in the warm comfort of Saera's embrace, thankful for a safe place where he could be vulnerable and didn't need to put on a strong front. For a few moments, he could just be a young man who was scared of going to war.

When his tears were dry and his breathing was easy again, Wil sat back up on the couch. "On the plus side, this means we can finally crack into the stash of pomoliqueur left over from the wedding." *Hardly consolation, but I'll take it.*

"Finally!" Saera smiled, but Wil could feel her worry.

She'll put on a brave face for me, but I wonder how long she'll be able to keep up the façade once we're in the thick of battle. "I need to go break the news to my men."

"Do you want me to go with you?"

"No, it's all right. Besides, their share of the pomoliqueur should make the news more palatable."

Saera nodded. "That should do the trick. Well, I'll figure out whatever food goes with pomoliqueur and get us some dinner. Maybe I'll even procure a real wax candle for some proper mood lighting."

"That would be lovely." Wil kissed her—just a peck at first, then long and deep. "I'll see you soon."

It was nearing dinnertime, but Wil anticipated his men were still in their quarters winding down after the afternoon practice session.

Wil hit the buzzer on the entry door, and Ian answered. "Hey," Wil greeted him with a somewhat forced smile. "Is everyone around? I need to talk to you."

Ian nodded. "Yeah. A few people are still in the showers, but we're all here. What's up?"

"It can wait a few minutes. May I come in?"

"Of course." Ian stepped aside.

Two rows of sectional couches faced the broad viewscreen on one wall and a few lounge chairs were scattered around the perimeter of the spacious common room. At the back center of the space was a round table surrounded by twenty-one chairs; the touch-surface and integrated holographic projector made it perfect for the group's strategy discussions. The entire quarters felt lived in after housing the same group for nearly five years, made more personal by several scrappy collages documenting team activities plastered on some of the otherwise blank walls.

A few men rose from their seats around the common room as Wil entered, and several more emerged from the bedrooms. Wil closed the door but stayed in the entryway, attempting to avoid direct eye contact with anyone. *How are they going to take it?*

After an awkward minute, Michael and a handful of other men walked out from the bathroom. They were dressed in their dark blue loungewear, but their hair was still wet. "What did you want to see us about?" Michael questioned.

"Make yourselves comfortable," Wil said as he gestured toward the round table at the back of the room.

The men took seats around the table in their specialist groups. Wil sat down in his usual seat between Ian and Michael. All eyes were on Wil, anxiety evident on every face.

"We're shipping out in two days." Wil gave them a moment for the statement to sink in.

The men looked at each other, particularly to their Captain. The anxiety turned to stoicism for some and outright worry for others.

"I know you haven't finished the formal training program," Wil went on, "but we decided that it's time you get some hands-on experience."

"What does that mean, exactly?" asked Michael on behalf of the group.

"We're going to H2. While I get acquainted with the command systems, you'll continue to practice using their training center. Supposedly, they have a more advanced setup than we have here."

"For how long?" Ian asked.

"However long they'll give us."

Most men let out a shaky breath and leaned back in their chairs, staring at the blank tabletop.

Ethan broke the silence. "Then we go to battle?" The flush on his face stood out against his blond hair.

"Yes. We've trained for this. We're ready." The group seemed unsure. Wil looked to his Captains for support, but they avoided his gaze.

I need to have everyone with me. We can't be fragmented. "This isn't a time for second-guessing and doubt. We have a job to do."

"You just dropped some pretty heavy news on us. Give us a break," Curtis replied.

"This was coming for a long time."

"It just felt like it was still a long ways off," Ethan added.

I know the feeling. Wil looked around the table, catching a few bewildered stares. *They're looking to me for reassurance. I need to give them something, even though I'm barely holding it together myself.* "Look, this is tough for me, too. I've had the war looming in front of me for my whole life, and now that it's right around the corner, I feel… lost. I wish I had some magical words of encouragement to make this easier for you, but I don't. All I can say is that we're in this together. We've trained and practiced—countless hours, running through as many scenarios and crazy strategic plans as I could think of. We work together seamlessly, and that's our strength.

"The Bakzen may be daunting to face alone, but together we're far stronger than they can ever be. We know what it is to care about others, to stand strong as an individual and still be part of a team. We each have a role to play, and we know our parts inside and out. I've pushed you, harder than I should have at times, but now you're so in tune with yourselves and each other that you can beat even the toughest simulations while half-asleep with your eyes closed. Yes, those may just be simulations, but why doubt what you can do in real life? We're the elite of the elite. When someone tries to stand in our way, we rise to the occasion. We always do. And while the next few months will test us more than ever, I'm confident we'll come out ahead." Wil swallowed. "More than all that, we're brothers. We have to take care of each other, like any family would. I promise you, I'll do whatever I can to make sure you all get home safely."

After a few moments, the hardened faces of the men around the table softened.

"Your impromptu speeches are never required but are always appreciated," Curtis joked.

"We know we're prepared," Ian said. "It's just a lot to take in."

Michael looked around the table, and everyone nodded. "Tell us what you need and we're there."

Wil flashed a heartfelt smile, his nerves beginning to settle. "Thank you. I'm grateful to have all of you by my side."

Beneath the dedication, though, he could tell they were still on edge. They needed some time to decompress, and he did, too. There was no knowing when they might get another break. "Let's cancel practice for the next two days. You deserve some R&R." *Besides, there's nothing we can go over now that will make any difference.*

Curtis and several others looked shocked. "No practice for two whole days? What are we supposed to do?"

"I don't care," Wil replied. "Sleep, get drunk, get laid. Whatever you want. We leave here with no regrets."

"What about you?" asked Michael.

"I'm going to focus on being an attentive husband, for once. I trust you'll be able to fend for yourselves."

Ian, for one, was having no difficulty getting behind the prospect of free-time. "Maybe," he said with a devious glint in his eyes.

As much as I want to think we'll get through the war just fine, there's no knowing what sacrifices we might need to make. "All joking aside, make this time count. These are the last two days of freedom we may get."

"—For a few months, or even years," Michael clarified. "Then we can have all the free-time we want. No more war hanging over our heads."

He's right, I can't show any doubts that we'll win. "We just have to commit and get through this. All of us. Together."

There were determined smiles and nods around the room.

"Now, go relax and have some fun. Just try not to go too crazy."

"Us? Never," Ethan said with a playful smile.

There were more than a few other mischievous grins, but Wil had no real concerns. *Their sense of duty is as strong as mine. They'll be rested and ready when I need them.* "Now if you'll excuse me, I have a beautiful woman waiting for me with a bottle of Tararia's finest liqueur."

Curtis exchanged glances with Ethan. "How do we get in on that?"

Wil cracked a slight smile. "I thought you might ask. I'm afraid you're on your own with finding a partner. But the high-class booze I stashed in the supply closet down the hall might help with that. Locker P-0187." That prospect perked up even the most serious men in the group. "It's so good that it might just be illegal on a few planets. Enjoy."

"Oh, we will!" Ethan exclaimed.

"Let it never be said that I don't take good care of you."

"We'd never think of it," Michael said.

Now I just have to take care of you when it matters most.

— — —

Most of the Primus Elites had retreated to their own personal corner of Headquarters to process the transition—some following Wil's advice, and others contemplating their own thoughts and their place in the fight to come. For Michael, it was a time of quiet reflection.

After ensuring the equitable distribution of the pomoliqueur, he'd headed for the spaceport on the surface of the moon. Though he couldn't look down on Earth, he enjoyed taking in the familiar star constellations.

The presence of someone approaching pulled him from his thoughts. He glanced over and was surprised to see Saera's former roommate and longtime friend, Elise, heading over. He had rarely spoken to her since Wil and Saera's wedding, but she had a combination of self-confidence and humility that Michael found to be good company.

"I thought I might find you up here," she greeted after a moment.

"Looking for me?" Michael asked.

"Saera told me about the deployment," Elise replied, casting her dark eyes down. "I doubt I'm far behind you."

"We'll need everyone in their own way."

Elise came to stand next to him, placing her arms on the railing in front of the panoramic viewport. "We're living in crazy times."

"I'll say."

They stood in silence for a few minutes.

"Are you scared?" Elise asked at last.

"I'm not sure," Michael replied truthfully. "On the one hand, I'm apprehensive about heading into a dark unknown and know that we'll be putting our lives on the line every moment we're out there. On the other hand, I'll still be with my best friends. I have complete faith in them and know we'll be successful."

"I wish I felt so confident."

"Oh, you'll be fine." Michael gave her a playful nudge.

"Yeah, yeah." She cracked a smile, keeping her eyes on the starscape.

Michael examined her profile, finding her quite striking in the starlight. "Really, why did you come find me up here?"

Elise took a slow breath, finally glancing up at him. "You'll look after Saera, won't you? She's my best friend. I'm going to miss her like crazy, but it'd be easier knowing that someone has her back."

"I think that's Wil's job as her husband."

"I know, but he'll be busy leading everything. You and Saera knew each other from before, right?"

Michael tensed. "Yeah, since we were little kids."

"So, you care about her, too. You know where I'm coming from."

"I do, but things are a little more complicated when it comes to us." Michael returned his attention out the viewport.

"She's always dodged my questions when I've asked about you two," Elise said slowly.

"That doesn't surprise me."

"Did you have a falling out?"

Michael let out a short breath through his teeth. "Not exactly."

"What then?"

"She was going through a rough time. I wanted to be there for her, but instead she ran away. It took me a long time to come to terms with why she did that," he admitted.

Elise nodded. "You cared about her as more than just a friend."

"We were kids," Michael said with a shrug.

"And now?"

"Now I have a lot more important things to worry about than my childhood crush."

"I guess we all do," Elise murmured.

"Don't worry," Michael continued. "I'll be looking out for her, just like I'll be looking out for the rest of my friends."

Elise relaxed against the railing and smiled. "Thanks."

"Who's going to be looking after you?"

Elise flushed. "I guess I'm on my own."

"I find that hard to believe."

"Well, apparently, hanging out as the sidekick to a secret dynastic heir isn't a great way to get noticed as an individual."

"Tell me about it."

She laughed. "Oh, right! I guess you've been down that road, too."

"I knew who Wil was from the start. He told all the Primus Elites on our first day."

"Lucky you, being in the inner circle."

"I'm far from that." *Who knows what it is Wil and Saera are keeping from us.*

"Well, regardless, Wil is lucky to have you as a friend. Based on what Saera has relayed to me, he counts on you."

"The Primus Elites are a team. We try not to let each other down."

"For what it's worth, I don't think the Bakzen stand a chance." She grinned.

He smiled back. "Thanks."

Elise pushed off from the railing. "Now, if you don't have anything better to do, I heard they were going to open up a special dessert buffet. No better send-off to a deployment than a proper sugar high, right?"

"Was that an invitation to join you?"

She gave him a sheepish shrug. "I figure us sidekicks should stick together."

"Okay, deal."

— — —

"Can you believe we head out in two days?" Cris asked his wife. The news from Wil and Banks about the expeditious deployment was more of a harsh reality than a shock.

Kate linked her arm around his as they situated themselves on the couch in their quarters. "It's all so surreal."

Leaving their familiar and comfortable home was going to be difficult, despite the time they'd spent on the *Vanquish* over the years. This trip was different.

"How's Wil holding up?" Kate asked after a pause.

"Well enough. He wants all this to be over."

"I can relate."

Cris leaned back. "But I wonder if it really will be over once the Bakzen are gone."

Kate brought her head to his chest. "There'll still be another enemy out there. It won't truly be over until they're gone, too."

The Priesthood will bury evidence of the war and then move on to their next scheme to perpetuate their control. We'll never be truly at peace until they no longer rule the Taran Empire. "I'll do everything I can to accomplish that in my lifetime. After what everyone has been through with the war, we need to look toward a better future."

"I'll be right there alongside you through it all."

Cris held his wife close. "I couldn't do any of this without you."

She smiled up at him. "You lucked out, then, because you don't have to."

— — —

"I have to say, the liquor stash was a great idea," Saera commented as she took another sip of her pomoliqueur.

Wil smiled back at her. "You can thank my dad for that one."

"Best in-laws ever! Sorry you got stuck with my family."

"It's not all bad."

Saera sighed and patted his leg. "That's nice of you to say. At least we don't have to see them often." *It helps that we're literally not living on the same planet.*

"Do you ever miss Earth?" Wil asked.

"I may have lived there, but it was never a real home—at least not with that family."

"Then the TSS came along…"

"At that moment, my entire perspective changed. I *really* didn't know what I was getting into!" Saera chuckled to herself, thinking back on how out-of-place she'd been in the TSS at first, when things that she now took for granted had seemed like magic. "But this is where I found the family I always wanted. I wouldn't have done anything differently."

Wil wrapped his arm around her. "I can't believe how far we've come."

Saera snuggled up to him. "I know, right? It's hard to believe there was a time before we knew each other."

"Not just that," Wil clarified, "but how things were for the first few years. Sneaking around just to see each other…"

"That was exhausting!" Saera exclaimed. "And for *years*! How did we manage to keep it secret for so long?"

"We're just that good."

She laughed. "I guess we are."

Wil disentangled from Saera just long enough to top off their glasses with more pomoliqueur. He handed her glass back to her.

"To better times," Saera said, raising the drink for a toast.

"To better times." Wil clinked his glass against hers and they both took a sip.

She sat in quiet contemplation for a few moments. "How long do you think it will take before we can get back to this?"

Wil slumped back on the couch. "I have no idea."

"I guess we don't even rightly know what we're walking into, huh?"

"No, we really don't."

Saera felt him tense next to her, and she took his hand. *That wasn't the right thing to bring up.* "We need to enjoy these times while we can."

The anxious worry evaporated from Wil under her gentle

touch. "Thank you for keeping me grounded."

"Always. I'd do anything for you."

"And I you."

Saera polished off her drink and set down the empty glass. "No more heavy talk." She climbed onto Wil's lap, straddling him. "We have two days to ourselves. We need to make the most of it."

Wil placed his hands on her hips. "How do you propose we do that?"

"For starters, I'm going to consume an inadvisable amount of chocolate."

"Your phrasing makes me hesitant to endorse that plan, but okay."

"Also, no checking email or anything work-related for the next two days."

"Agreed."

"Good. Now, I believe we have a backlog of terrible movies to watch." Saera pressed herself closer to Wil, drawing him in for a kiss.

"Do I have to pay close attention?" He slid his hand up the back of her shirt.

"Absolutely not."

CHAPTER 4

IT WAS TIME.

Wil looked out over the empty TSS spacedock above the moon. Only the *Vanquish* and a handful of shuttles remained. The fleet was deployed, committed to the war. His fleet. *I can't believe we're leaving.*

But reality was sinking in. A place that was once so filled with life was now barren, grim. When Wil and Saera had been married on that same spacedock two years before, the war had still seemed so far off. Even with the TSS backdrop and Banks as the officiant to serve as reminders for his other duties, the wedding had highlighted a commitment in Wil's life that transcended anything to do with the Bakzen and impending war. Yet, as much as he wanted that love to be the driving force in his life, he had to focus on his responsibility to the TSS—a purpose he was born to fulfill.

"Ready?" Saera's voice pulled Wil back to the present.

He turned to see that all the Primus Elites had gathered behind him at the dock. Saera was standing a few paces in front of the group.

"Yes, let's go." Wil led his team up the gangway onto the *Vanquish*, with Saera by his side.

Cris, as captain of the *Vanquish*, met them at the top of the gangway. "Welcome aboard," he said as Wil crossed over the threshold.

"Reporting for duty, sir."

"You and Saera can accompany me in the Command Center. We have the officers' lounge reserved for your men during the trip over." Cris gestured down the hallway.

Wil nodded. "Thank you. Michael, make sure everyone gets settled in."

"Yes, sir. See you on the other side." Michael led the Primus Elite trainees away.

Wil, Saera, and Cris were left alone in the hallway. "How are you doing?" his father asked.

"Ready to get to work," Wil replied.

Cris smiled. "I know that feeling."

Wil glanced in the direction of the Command Center. "We should get going."

"Right." Cris led the way down the hall.

Saera grabbed Wil's hand and gave it a squeeze. *"I'm here for you,"* she said telepathically.

"Partners, just like always."

The Command Center was abuzz with final systems checks in preparation for departure. Wil's mother, Kate, was in the First Officer's chair directing the cross-checks. She smiled at Wil and Saera when they entered, but quickly resumed her duties as Cris made his way to the captain's chair next to her.

Wil and Saera took seats at the back of the Command Center by the main door. The spherical room curved overhead and below the transparent floor, wrapped in a massive viewscreen that gave a 360-degree view of the surrounding space. The two command chairs were in the center of the room, and the pair of consoles in front were occupied by the ship's pilot, Alec, and the tactical officer, Kari. They had been a part of the crew for almost Wil's entire life, and he couldn't imagine the *Vanquish* without them.

After a few minutes, Kate nodded to Cris. "Everything is in order."

Cris took a deep breath. "Okay. Alec, lay in a course for the Prisaris rift gate to H2."

"Aye." Alec made the necessary inputs on his console. "Ready."

"Take us out," Cris commanded.

Anxiety washed over Wil as the *Vanquish* pulled away from the dock, a knot starting to form in his chest. *Keep it together.* He reached over the armrest and took Saera's hand; her soft touch gave him the reassurance he needed. *I'm not in this alone.*

The *Vanquish* pulled away from the spacedock and into open space beyond the moon.

"Make the jump to subspace when ready," Cris instructed Alec.

"Initiating jump sequence." Alec made the final inputs.

A low vibration emanated from the floor and soon filled the air. The space surrounding the vessel changed to shifting blue-green as it made the jump to subspace. The *Vanquish* followed the set course through the SiNavTech navigation beacons. Wil held Saera's hand and sat in silence for the duration of the travel, trying to keep his mind from wandering too far into thoughts of what would come next.

The *Vanquish* dropped out of subspace near the Prisaris shipyard. As a key production facility for TSS ships, it was a familiar location for Wil. Five years ago, he and his father had brokered the arrangement that allowed the TSS full use of the shipyard in exchange for licensing his independent jump drive design to SiNavTech. The shipyard had enormous production capacity, but lack of TSS resources had caused production to begin winding down several months prior, and most of the finished ships had already been sent through the rift gate.

On the far side of the shipyard, the rift gate was suspended in open space. The ring dwarfed even the largest of the vessels at the shipyard, designed to accommodate several carriers in one transfer to the other dimensional plane. It had replaced the smaller rift gate located several star systems closer to Bakzen territory, which had previously linked H2 with the rest of the Taran worlds. Traditional rift gate designs required the entry and exit points to be at an identical place relative to normal space, but Wil had consulted with some of the TSS' other engineers to successfully link the new gate to the existing gate at H2, despite the relative physical distance in corresponding normal space. The innovation had enabled more effective transportation of the new vessels from the Prisaris shipyard, and had also allowed for a greater buffer between the vulnerable mid-production vessels and the encroaching enemy.

Wil surveyed the remaining ships throughout the production yard as they passed through. *If these are the only reserves, then I need to make sure to limit losses. We couldn't begin to replenish the fleet with so few.*

As the *Vanquish* neared the giant ring, Alec initiated the start-up sequence for the rift jump. The ring lit up, and components along the inner track began rotating around the ring's circumference. The rotation accelerated until the movement was soon a complete blur. The space at the center of the ring began to take on the familiar blue-green hue of subspace. With a flash, the subspace portal became a fully formed tunnel to the other dimensional plane. It was difficult to see the portal, but Wil's trained eye detected the bending of light around the surface of the event horizon where light was being reflected back.

"Gate is stable," Alec announced.

"Take us through," commanded Cris.

The *Vanquish* slipped through the event horizon at the center of the ring. A shudder ran the length of the ship as it made the transition to subspace. For a moment, everything was still. Then, the ship dropped into the Rift on the other side of the gate.

Wil shifted in his chair. The energy on the other side of the Rift felt different from his home plane, and it always took a minute or two to adjust. Looking around the Command Center, it was apparent that the other Agents felt uneasy, as well. *Better get used to it. We'll be here for a while.*

Gazing out the front of the spherical viewscreen, Wil was struck by the changes around the headquarters structure. When he had last visited H2 five years before, to test the prototype IT-1 fighter, the cylindrical structure and rift gate ring were the dominant features in the echoed starscape. To his relief, Wil saw new spacedocks branching in all directions from the core H2 structure, hosting several massive carriers and fleet support vessels for medical, food, and repairs. In his limited view, the combat fleet had multiplied by at least twenty-fold. *This is more than I was expecting.*

"They've been busy!" Cris commented from the captain's chair.

"I can't believe this is all here, just out of view," Saera said with audible awe.

"There's a lot we can't normally see." Wil rose from his seat at the back of the Command Center and stepped forward to stand next to his father's command position. "I wonder where they want us to dock."

"I already sent out a docking request," Alec said. "It looks like we're being directed to one of the outer platforms. They're full up."

Cris frowned, his brow knitted with confusion. "Bomax."

They knew we were coming, right? "I'll take one of the shuttles over. That way, I can begin getting oriented as soon as possible. I hope it's okay if my men remain here for a few hours, until I know where we're staying."

Cris nodded. "Yes, of course."

"Thanks. Saera, want to come along with me?"

"Sure." She rose from her seat. *"Where is it we're going?"* she asked him telepathically.

"I'm working on that." At the door, Wil turned back to give a parting wave to his parents and the rest of the Command Center crew. "See you soon."

"Good luck!" Kate called out as Wil led Saera from the Command Center.

They made their way to the shuttle hangar several decks below, and Wil selected one of the smallest transport vessels. *They'd better find room for this.*

Wil initiated the start-up sequence. "This is ridiculous. How could they not have berthing set aside for the *Vanquish*?"

Saera buckled into the passenger seat next to Wil. "No kidding. I thought they were expecting us."

"Me too. Banks made it sound like they're pretty desperate for backup." Wil completed the pre-flight check and pointed the shuttle toward the bay exit.

Saera smiled playfully. "I don't blame them for wanting you here. I mean, you *are* pretty great—not that I'm biased, or anything. I'm not surprised you're so in demand."

Wil's heart warmed. *She always knows just what to say.* The shuttle passed through the force field, and Wil swung it around toward H2. "Thanks for coming with me."

"Thank *you* for taking me! I've been curious to see this Taelis guy in action."

"He is amazingly dedicated to his job, that's for sure." *Knowing what I know now, his matter-of-factness makes a lot more sense. I definitely misjudged him when we first met.*

The command console chirped with an incoming message. Wil opened the audio channel.

"This is fleet command," said a weary female voice. "What is your destination?"

"This is Agent Wil Sietinen. I'm en route to see High Commander Taelis."

A pause. "One moment." The comm channel muted.

Wil rolled his eyes.

Saera's brow knitted with exaggerated sympathy. "They need your logistical skills more desperately than we ever imagined," she joked.

The comm channel reconnected. "So sorry, sir. The docking coordinates have been sent to your nav computer. The High Commander will meet you at the gangway."

"Thank you." Wil ended the transmission. "I wonder what all that was about." *They should be far more organized than this— something is definitely off.*

"We'll find out soon enough."

Wil piloted the shuttle to the designated docking coordinates. They passed by dozens of vessels of various classifications. Some looked brand new, but others had charred sections, or were even missing components. He suppressed another wave of anxiety. *We're in a war zone now. This will be a common sight.*

When the clamps were securely on the hull, Wil powered down the shuttle and exited with Saera.

They had walked half the distance down the gangway when Wil spotted Taelis and some of his officers coming to greet them. He recognized the Lead Agent, Connor Ramsen, and several of the other officers from his previous visits, but there were also some new faces. They all looked tired and distraught, but they smiled with genuine happiness at the sight of Wil.

"Hi, Wil. It's good to see you again," Taelis said as they approached.

"Hello, sir. You, as well." Wil placed his hand on the small of Saera's back. "This is my wife, Saera."

"Yes, of course. It's a pleasure to meet you." Taelis raised his hand in greeting, in the traditional Taran custom. "It's great to have someone with your skill joining us."

Saera bobbed her head. "Thank you, sir."

Taelis sighed, deflating a little. "Please forgive the modest welcome for you and your men."

"Well, the Elites are still on the *Vanquish*," Wil replied. "There didn't seem to be a docking space for anything larger than our transport shuttle."

"Yes, sorry about that." Taelis sighed again. "It's been a tough few days."

Looking closer at the faces of Taelis and his officers, Wil noticed a deep weariness. *Something definitely happened.* "What's going on?"

Taelis hesitated and looked at Ramsen.

"I'm here now. For you," Wil reminded them.

Taelis nodded. "Four days ago, there was an uprising on Kaldern, one of the border worlds we use as a TSS outpost. The planetary shield was disabled by the time the Bakzen attacked. We were completely outnumbered and had to retreat. A quarter of the vessels here are those that survived the attack, and we can barely accommodate the influx. We've been trying to reestablish our position, but resources are limited."

They didn't want to reassign anything they had set aside for me, Wil realized. "I'll assess the situation as soon as I'm briefed on the details."

Taelis nodded. "Well, we don't have a lot of time. Let's get you up to speed." He gathered himself. "We have a lot to go over, but I'd like to start out with a bit of good news. We have a flagship for you."

"Oh?" *I would have liked to be involved in the design.*

Taelis' lips parted in a slight smile. "It's easier if I just show you. The engineering team is very excited."

"All right, let's see it."

"We'll meet you in the War Room," Taelis told his officers. "This way," he said to Wil and Saera, leading them down the hall toward one of the elevators.

They took the elevator up several levels and then followed the corridor around to another section of the spacedock. As they came around a bend in the hallway, a ship came into view. Wil immediately recognized the distinctive telekinetic relay band around the perimeter of the ship—a design he had toyed with and then dismissed due to concerns over its potential destructive power. "You built it?"

Taelis nodded. "I recognize that you had passed over the design, but I knew you would need something beyond our current fleet. I put Laecy to work. It took a lot of trial and error, but the engineering team eventually figured out how to make it come together."

Saera initially lit up in response to the High Commander's excitement, but she looked to Wil for an explanation when he didn't share their enthusiasm.

They went behind my back. Don't they know what this ship can do? "I had no idea you continued to work on it. You should have told me."

Taelis swallowed. "I didn't want to press the issue and distract you from training your officers. We realized that it could be a game-changer if we could make it work. The engineering team picked away at it until they finally had a breakthrough about a year ago. We only finished preliminary testing last week."

It's done now. I guess it's up to me how it gets used. "All right. Let's see the inside."

"Of course." Taelis held out his arm to let Wil be the first up the gangway.

Wil felt an immediate resonance with the ship when he passed through the entry port. The soothing energy washed over him, setting him at ease. *It's like the Aesir ship—it must have a similar biofeedback system.*

Saera's tense expression faded as soon as she stepped off the gangway next to Wil. "It feels different here."

"Amazing, isn't it?" Wil closed his eyes and released himself to the vessel, feeling it pulse in response to him. When he opened his eyes, he noticed the TSS emblem opposite the entry portal. *The TSS* Conquest. "A fitting name as any."

Saera nodded. "It is."

"Come on, let's go to the Command Center." Wil walked with Saera down the corridor.

The hallway was more utilitarian than most of the TSS ships Wil was used to, but the design was still inviting enough to make the vessel comfortable for an extended voyage. Warm hued lights inset in the ceiling and side panels cast a pleasant glow across the viewscreens mounted at logical intervals along the length of the corridor. The screens currently displayed neutral images of starscapes, but Wil touched one of the panels as he passed by and it brought up a menu for the Mainframe.

The Command Center was precisely where Wil hoped it would be. His breath caught as he glimpsed the design through the open doorway. He flashed an excited grin to Saera behind him, his initial reservations about the ship fading.

A transparent platform extended from the entry door into the center of the spherical room. Five standing-height, minimalist black chairs were arranged in the middle of the room on the main platform, with four around the perimeter and one at the center. Each one was mounted on a swivel base, with an adjustable handhold in front mounted to the same rotating platform. Based on seams and some mechanics in the transparent floor panel, it appeared that the chairs could fold down into the floor for the operators to stand at the handholds as a podium. A step down from the main platform, two consoles faced outward toward the front. Likely, the consoles controlled navigation, weapons, and communications like standard TSS ships.

As Wil entered the Command Center, the dimmed lights rose to full brightness. He looked around in wonder. "This is just like I imagined."

He strolled to the center chair and ran his hand along the top arch of the back, then brushed his fingertips on the podium in front of the chair. The telescoping base was bent slightly toward the chair for easier access, with a cylindrical grip to either side at the top of the arm. When Wil's fingers touched the handhold grip, the viewscreen wrapping the walls and ceiling illuminated in vivid color, displaying the surroundings of the *Conquest* with holographic depth unlike anything Wil had seen in a Command Center before.

"It's amazing," Saera breathed as she came to stand beside Wil.

"It really is." He gripped one side of the handhold, feeling the ship respond to his presence. "Take one of the other stations."

Saera tentatively grasped one side of the handhold to Wil's left. "Whoa."

A tingle ran through Wil's arm as he sensed Saera's presence through the ship. He reached out to her through the biofeedback system, and the ship automatically entwined their energies. *It's effortless.*

"Do you approve?" Taelis said from behind.

Startled, Wil and Saera let go of their respective handholds. "Yes, very much so," Wil replied.

"I see you've discovered the neural link in the central podiums," Taelis continued. "The consoles up front have it, as well."

"Yes. I've never felt anything like it." *What will I be able to do with such a link?*

Taelis nodded. "That's what took the engineering team so long to work out. We knew that you would need an anchor during simultaneous observation. It will need to be calibrated to you and your Seconds, but our hope is that you will be able to project your vision of the activities in both dimensional planes on the viewscreen."

The Bakzen's movements in real-time for everyone to see. "I had never thought about serving as a visual conduit. I suppose it could work. I'd need to play around with it."

"We've never been able to properly test it, of course, since you're the only one with the ability. The biofeedback systems for mental visualization have passed all field tests, though, so it's just a matter of the spatial translation between the Rift and normal space. None of our computers have been able to reconcile those inputs."

"I'll see what I can do." *It very well may be possible. And more.*

"Is there an assigned crew yet?"

"No," Taelis replied. "I can provide recommendations for some engineers and tactical officers, but the crew is fully at your discretion."

"Excellent. I'll review your nominations." Wil felt the pull of the ship. "Unless you have other quarters in mind, I'll stay here with my men."

"That was our intent."

Now, we have more pressing matters to discuss. "Saera, will you get the Primus Elites oriented here while the High Commander briefs me on the latest developments with the Bakzen?"

She nodded, a bit reluctantly. "Will do."

Wil turned to Taelis. "I'm at your disposal. Let's get started."

CHAPTER 5

SAERA WATCHED WIL depart with the weathered High Commander. It was unnerving to see the leader of H2 so drained and disheartened. *I can only imagine what he's been through over the years. Anyone would get worn down eventually. I hope I can keep Wil from feeling that way.*

Though she wouldn't admit it aloud, Saera wished she were attending the briefing with Wil. She knew the lack of invitation wasn't meant personally, or as a means to sideline her, but it was uncomfortable to be left out of the action. Even harder to admit, part of her felt like if she were away from Wil, he would somehow be lost to her. His words from early in their relationship had always gnawed at the back of her mind over the years—that winning the war might take everything he had to give, and he might not make it through alive. She wasn't sure Wil remembered that admission, but she had taken it upon herself to make sure it didn't come to that. While she felt always being by his side was the best way to fulfill her silent promise, she would be there for her partner in any way he needed. *Right now, that means taking care of his closest friends.*

Saera wandered over to the consoles at the front of the Command Center. She was well versed in TSS craft after so much time helping Wil with spec reviews, and the *Conquest* appeared to follow conventional design principles, despite the flashier finishes. It only took her a few moments to locate the communications system. She was just about to activate a comm channel to the *Vanquish* when she sensed a presence behind her.

"Be careful with that," a male voice warned.

Saera spun around to see a man dressed in a gray work jumpsuit, perhaps in his late-thirties. She didn't detect strong telekinetic ability from him, so he was likely Militia division. No rank was visible on his outfit. "I know my way around ships."

"This one happens to be very sensitive," the man countered.

Rather brazen, talking to an Agent that way. "I'll be spending a lot of time here, I imagine. I need to become acquainted."

The man frowned. "A crew hasn't been decided."

"Well, it has a captain. Given that he's my husband, I'm pretty sure I'll be assigned."

The man was silent for a moment, connecting the dots. He looked Saera over. Then, there was a spark of recognition. "Are you Agent Alexander?"

"Yes."

"Where is Agent Sietinen?"

"He went for a briefing with the High Commander. You just missed him."

His eyes narrowed. "Why are you still here?"

I could ask you the same thing. "I have been tasked with getting the Primus Elites settled on the ship. It seems you're a little short on quarters, so we'll be staying here."

"All the quarters are on the lower levels."

"I figured as much." It was becoming difficult for Saera to hide her irritation. She took a slow breath. "I was about to send a message to the *Vanquish* so they could begin shuttling the Primus Elites over here."

"Why were you using the ship's communications?"

That's enough. Saera crossed her arms. "Why the barrage of questions? Who are you?"

"My name is Aram Laensir. I helped design the *Conquest.*"

"Well, Aram, it's a very nice ship. Now, if you'll excuse me, I have some logistics to manage." She turned back to the communications console.

"Wait."

Saera looked back at him expectantly.

"I was supposed to give Agent Sietinen and his team an orientation. I guess I should just start with you," Aram said, looking a little apologetic for his initial behavior.

"All right, go ahead."

Aram nodded. "Okay. The *Conquest* follows the basic prototype for the cruiser-class TSS ships, as you probably noticed."

"Yes."

"The interior layout and overall structure are the same, with some cosmetic modifications. The internal systems, however, are quite unique. The main feature is the neural interface."

"These podiums in the middle." Saera stepped up onto the center platform.

"That is the primary interface, yes, along with the front consoles. From here, an Agent can connect to any system in the ship."

Any system? "Even navigation? Weapons?"

"Based on the early sketches we were working from, that was the whole point."

So, Wil designed a giant amplifier for his abilities. This isn't just for simultaneous observation—it's weaponized telekinesis. Saera felt a sudden pang in her chest. *All this time I've been thinking of Wil as a leader and strategist, but if he designed something like this ship... he sees himself as a living weapon. Is this what has always weighed so heavily on him? Why wouldn't he talk to me about it?*

Aram cocked his head. "Did you want me to continue?"

Saera returned from her thoughts. "Yes, please."

"You may have noticed the band around the exterior perimeter of the ship. That's the relay for the telekinetic input. It focuses the telekinetic energy from any of the access points throughout the ship. It can support the shield generator, or even the jump drive."

"Spatial dislocation?"

"In theory. We haven't been able to test it—none of the Agents working on the project were a high enough CR to even make an attempt."

Only Wil is powerful enough to dislocate a vessel this size. Maybe some of the Primus Elites could dislocate a fighter, but nothing like this. "I guess we'll have to test it out, then."

"I'd love to have the chance to observe, when you do," Aram said. There was a hunger in his gaze.

Saera examined him. "I find it interesting that you were working on a project with such focus on telekinetic energy relays, given that you aren't an Agent."

Aram's face darkened. "I can't help that I was born without such abilities."

"I'm sorry, I didn't mean to offend."

Aram walked over to the console at the front left of the Control Center. "You were about to send a message, right?"

"Yes. Was there anything else you'd like to tell me about the ship?"

"It can wait. I'll just have to go over it with Agent Sietinen again." Aram accessed the communications menu on the console and made some inputs. "Which ship was it you wanted to contact?"

"The *Vanquish.*"

Aram made some additional inputs. "The comm channel is ready for you to initiate."

"Thank you."

Aram headed for the door.

I don't think this guy likes me... "Thank you for the overview. Knowing about those features is helpful."

"Sure." Aram left without so much as a glance.

Saera shrugged off the strange meeting. *Can't please everyone.* She initiated the comm link to the *Vanquish.*

After a moment, a rectangular video feed appeared on the front of the room's domed ceiling, displaying the *Vanquish's* Command Center. Cris and Kate were in the center chairs. They seemed surprised to see Saera.

"Hi," Cris said. "Where are you? CACI couldn't identify the source of the call, only that it was TSS."

Saera held out her arms to either side. "This is the *Conquest.* It's brand new and very fancy."

Cris smiled back. "Clearly. That's an interesting setup for the Command Center."

"Wait until you see what it can do." *It's impressive, even if it is terrifying.*

"I bet. What can we do for you?" Cris asked.

"Wil requested that I get the Primus Elites settled in on the *Conquest*. Can you send them over on some shuttles?"

"Of course. Anything else?"

"Not at the moment. Wil is getting briefed by Taelis right now."

Cris' expression turned serious. "Okay. I'll tell the Primus Elites."

"Thanks. See you soon, I'm sure."

Cris nodded. "Talk soon."

Saera ended the transmission. *Now to find the hangar.*

True to Aram's word, the interior layout of the *Conquest* was identical to other TSS cruisers Saera had toured. She made her way slowly, taking in the design details of the ship. It lacked some of the finer finishes found on the *Vanquish* and other vessels intended for longer-duration missions, but it was aesthetically pleasing and had just enough artwork and padded seating to echo the comforts of home.

As Saera passed by the corridor leading to Engineering, she noticed a slim woman with a light brown braid studying a control panel down the hall. If she wasn't mistaken, it was H2's Lead Engineer, Deena Laecy. "Deena, right?" Saera called out with a wave of her hand.

The engineer was caught by surprise. "Everyone calls me by my last name, Laecy. Have we met?"

"No, I recognized you from your personnel file. I'm Wil's wife, Saera."

Laecy's brown eyes sparked with recognition. "Of course! Sorry, I'm bad with faces. Is Wil here?"

"He's meeting with Taelis now. I'm on my way to meet the Primus Elites and get them settled in."

"I guess that shouldn't be a problem…" Laecy murmured.

"What do you mean?" Saera asked.

"Well, I have system reports for the *Conquest* routed to my handheld, since we're still in testing," Laecy replied. "I'm checking out some strange heat readings in some of the wiring conduits."

"Did you find the cause?"

The engineer frowned. "No. The temperatures have returned to normal operating ranges, and there's no record of overheating in the ship's logs."

Tampering? Saera came to full attention. "Who has access to the *Conquest* now?"

"A couple of my team members are down in Engineering so the ship isn't completely unattended, but otherwise it's just us."

"What are those engineers' names?" Saera asked.

"Nolan and Becca. Why?"

Saera's stomach knotted. "What about Aram Laensir?"

"Aram? No, he's working back in the lab."

"Well, he stopped by when I was in the Command Center a few minutes ago."

Laecy crossed her arms. "He shouldn't have been up there without a senior engineer. He's apprenticing in bioelectric engineering, working on the neural interface with the ship."

Trespassing and mysterious performance readings was a concerning combination. "How long have you known him?"

"He's bounced around to a few different positions over the past three years or so. He used to be a pilot."

Saera tilted her head. "He's not an Agent."

"Many of our pilots here aren't."

"Why the career change?"

The engineer slumped. "There was an accident. His squad landed in the H2 hanger and there was an explosion. Killed one of my best friends. A few of the pilots were never the same afterward, him included."

Saera took a step toward the nearest access terminal on the wall. "What was the cause of the explosion?"

"A Bakzen weapon. Silver goop stuff—we call it Detno. We've only ever seen it out on the battlefield before and since then. Normally it detonates on impact, but this one didn't go off until the fighter was back at H2. Never did identify what triggered it." Laecy's brow knitted. "Why?"

"Time to reopen the investigation." Saera activated the terminal and navigated toward the inter-ship communication system.

Laecy's eyes widened with shock. "You don't think Aram…?"

"Two strange circumstances and one person present for both. I'm not taking any chances around Wil."

"Becca and Nolan were present for both, for that matter,"

Laecy countered.

Saera brought up the *Vanquish* on the comm menu. "Then we'll question all of you." The call connected after a moment. "Cris, hold off on sending the Primus Elites over. We have a situation."

— — —

Wil surveyed the War Room. It was completely interior to the Headquarters structure, with no viewports. An oblong touch-surface table with polished metal legs was in the middle of the room, equipped with a holographic projector and surrounded by a dozen chairs upholstered in dark blue fabric with a slightly iridescent sheen.

Five officers sat around the table. All of them had been at Wil's hasty welcome from the transport shuttle.

Taelis took a seat near the middle of the table and gestured for Wil to sit at the head by the door.

"What did you think of the *Conquest*?" Ramsen, the Lead Agent, asked.

"It's perfect," Wil replied. "I can't wait to perform a detailed inspection."

The officers nodded with satisfaction. They then looked between Taelis and Wil, not sure who was going to take the lead.

Wil broke the uncomfortable silence. "I know it's strange, finally having me here." No one said anything, but a couple people looked down at the smooth tabletop. "The last time you saw me, I was still more or less a kid. I hope I made a decent impression on you, but I was totally out of my depth. I've learned a lot since then. I know what you need from me, and I'm here to lead."

Taelis relaxed into his chair. "Good."

"Now, tell me everything."

A grimace passed across Taelis' face. "Where to begin?"

Wil folded his hands on the tabletop. "For starters, what's the state of the TSS fleet?"

"We have the numbers we hoped to have for you, but the fleet isn't positioned well at the moment. We have far too many ships bunched up here around H2." Taelis activated the holographic projector at the center of the table. "Here's a schematic of our current positions."

Wil studied the map. Red dots indicated offensive vessels, such as cruisers and battleships, green were supply carriers, and blue were field medical stations. Most of the red dots were either at the frontlines or clustered around H2 and the nearby planets. "Do all of these represent vessels only within the Rift?"

"Yes, since we lost Kaldern, we have barely any ships subscribed in normal space aside from a few remaining planetary outposts," Ramsen replied.

"Why?"

"The Bakzen typically like to fight battles in the Rift because of the telekinetic benefits," Taelis clarified.

They can strike us on either front. We need to cover both. "High Commander Banks indicated that you're at the limits of production—that what we have now is all there is to work with."

"More or less," Ramsen responded.

"We can activate ships that are standing guard near some of the populated planets," Taelis added, "but doing so would leave the worlds exposed. It'd be a last resort."

Let's hope it doesn't come to that. "What about supplies for the crews—food?"

"We're fully stocked," said a man in his late-thirties, whom Wil recalled was Simon Elari, the Agent responsible for fleet supply management. "We have almost a year's supply, if we were to be cut off from the main Taran distribution network."

At least there's some good news. "Okay. How about the Bakzen fleet? What do we know about their numbers and capabilities?"

Taelis shook his head. "They can hit us fast and hard. No one has seen too far into Bakzen territory since your encounter with them nearly a decade ago. Based on everything we've been able to see, it's going to come down to a numbers game—which one of our fleets can deliver the most damage, the quickest, before our supplies run out. At the rate things are going, we're in a bad position. We know you'll change that.

"We have run as many simulations as we can, and all

indicators are that the TSS needs to make a big move first, before the Bakzen can make theirs. And the sooner, the better. Though the Bakzen have largely been keeping to this side of the dimensional Rift and have stayed close to the planet that they claimed as their homeworld, they have recently started venturing to the outer reaches of the Rift. Those explorations seem to be expanding. We know that the Bakzen have ramped up production, but we don't know of what exactly. They have taken over some worlds that are rich in metal ores and minerals. Our greatest fear is that they have been manufacturing additional rift gates—or worse, ships with standalone jump drive functionality—and that they are gearing up for an all-out assault. Best we can tell, the Bakzen are positioning for a single, massive invasion campaign."

Back when I met Carzen and Tek, it seemed like they were gearing up for something. Is this all part of the same plan? "What's their target?"

"We don't know," replied Taelis, a hint of defeat in his tone.

"What aren't you telling me?" Wil asked, sensing that the High Commander was holding back.

"The Bakzen also now have some sort of remote telepathic control for use on civilian populations," Taelis revealed. "That's how the shield was brought down on Kaldern earlier this week, near as we can tell."

"Shite," Wil muttered under his breath, thinking through the implications for such a capability. No one could be trusted; no world would be safe.

"Kaldern was the first time we've witnessed it," the High Commander continued. "If it's happened before, it was never on a large enough scale for us to notice, though we have seen the Bakzen use a neurotoxin in the past."

Wil examined the worried expressions of the officers around the table. "Do you know how they're exerting the telepathic control now?" *Direct control would take enormous focus. If it were biological...*

"That's unclear," Taelis said. "We've increased our surveillance to keep watch for the initial signs, based on what happened on Kaldern, but until we have access to an affected subject to study, we can't prepare counter-measures."

Another unknown threat. I'm losing count. "Okay. What about positioning of the Bakzen fleet?"

Ramsen scowled. "The distribution of the Bakzen forces seems random. We haven't been able to extrapolate any likely targets or timing based on our mapping of the Rift and TSS positions."

Wil came to full attention. "Wait, you have a map of the Rift?"

Taelis looked taken aback. "Yes." He glanced at Ramsen, then back to Wil.

Unbelievable. "Why did no one ever share that with me?"

"I'm sorry, it didn't seem important to send to you while you were still training."

Wil took a calming breath. "Show me." *Anything related to the Rift is important. Or, maybe looking into the void with the Aesir changed my perspective, seeing how the Bakzen continue to tear apart the fabric of space.*

A new holographic map projected over the table. Wil examined the image, seeing the weak points between subspace and regular space portrayed as dark spots across the map. The dark areas were clustered around the main Rift, but others branched outward. Not all were connected, but small tears radiated well beyond the war zone. *It's almost like subspace pathways...* "Has this map been cross-referenced against normal space?"

"We did," Taelis said, "but there's no correlation."

You need to know what to look for. "Did you account for subspace movement in your analysis?"

Taelis looked ashamed. "We tried but haven't been able to. This is one of the many reasons why we couldn't wait any longer to bring you here."

"Let's see..." Wil accessed the map library on the touch-surface table. He found the most recent subspace scan and overlaid it with a map of normal space, with labels for the Taran-occupied worlds. The two images were a jumbled mess suspended over the table. Wil stood up and began manipulating the images by hand, aligning some key points to account for the common movement patterns in subspace. He made a few adjustments to the inputs via the touch-surface table and then refreshed the composite map.

When the new image resolved, Wil's stomach sank. Expressions of horror spread across every face around the table. Hovered above them, the map showed all the micro-rifts forming direct pathways to the major Taran colonies, including multiple pathways directly to Tararia.

Taelis paled. "How could we have missed this?"

Wil swallowed. *The Aesir were right—the Bakzen want all of us gone.* "We can't waste any time."

"No." Taelis looked drained of hope. "Tell us what to do."

It's all on me now. "Our first order of business is to attack the Bakzen supply lines. Their forces aren't yet sufficient to make a full assault from the Rift, or they would have made a move already."

"Agreed," Ramsen said.

Taelis nodded faintly.

I wasn't expecting to break up my team right away, but I don't see another option. "My Primus Elite trainees and I can communicate faster and more securely than subspace comms. They'll move into the field as officers at some of the key TSS outposts and on the lead tactical vessels so I can instantaneously relay secure orders to the fleet. They have also been highly trained with battle strategy, and can advise on tactics even when I'm not directly involved. That way, I can focus on one key battle at a time while they handle the rest of the coordination."

Taelis pulled himself together. "Of course. Just tell us where you need everyone and we'll arrange the transportation."

Wil mentally ran through each of his men and weighed several scenarios. *I need to keep my Seconds with me. Ethan's pilots will be an invaluable strike force. The rest all have the skills and autonomy to function without direct supervision.* He typed a list of twelve names on the tabletop and the specific position for each to assume in the fleet. "Ramsen, please take these men and acquaint them with the TSS forces. I'd like them positioned at these locations." Wil highlighted a dozen points on the holographic map above the table with the person assigned to each.

"Understood," Ramsen acknowledged.

But the pilots... I can't throw them out into battle quite yet. "On a related matter, High Commander Banks mentioned that you have some training facilities here that are more advanced than what we had back home."

Taelis nodded. "Yes, we have a flight testing course and several amplifier chambers for telekinesis conditioning."

"I'll need use of the flight course. My pilots have to log some more hours in actual spacecraft. Too much training has been done in simulators."

"Yes, anything you need," Taelis replied. "We have other pilots that will need some time on the course, but we'll work around your pilots' schedules."

"Have the second generation of IT-1 fighters completed testing?" *That's where they really need to practice—right-angle turns while simultaneously executing a jump to the Rift. No amount of simulator practice can prepare for the real thing.*

"Almost," said Agent Faerin, liaison working with Laecy's engineering team. "We're in the final trials to work out a few bugs, but the first wave will be ready within the week."

"Excellent, thank you. We'll only need four. Please be sure to include my pilots in your final calibrations so they can start tuning to their fighters."

"I will," she confirmed.

Wil nodded. That only left Michael, Ethan, Curtis, Ian, and Saera. He would need to review Taelis' list of recommendations for additional crew on his own ship. "That's all for now. I need to start reviewing specifics and calibrating the *Conquest*. Talking won't get us any closer to victory."

Taelis nodded and stood. Everyone around the table rose, as well. "You have your orders. Meeting adjourned."

Wil inclined his head to Taelis and immediately left the War Room. *Things are worse than I thought. This is going to put us all to the test.*

As soon as he exited to the hallway, his handheld chirped. The message was from Saera: >>Meet us in Laecy's lab. There's a problem.<<

CHAPTER 6

CRIS COULDN'T DECIDE if he was furious or petrified. Since receiving the message from Saera, an icy vise had latched around his chest. *An hour in and there's already a crisis. What's next?*

He took a deep breath as he stepped into the hangar on the bottom level of H2. The cavernous room housed what few backup fighters remained of the TSS fleet. Situated between two rows of craft, the engineering lab was a freestanding island wrapped in translucent windows. The door was cracked open enough to reveal Saera and Laecy huddled around a terminal inside.

Saera glanced over her shoulder as he approached. She slumped forward against the console. "This is bad."

"What is?" Cris asked, sliding the door closed behind him.

Laecy sighed. "I got a strange heat spike from the *Conquest*, which happened to correspond to one of my engineers being somewhere they shouldn't have been, so we started digging deeper as a precaution. The events today may be unrelated, but it's a good thing we went to investigate. It turns out that select telekinetic relays in the *Conquest* have been lined with Detno."

Friendly name. "What's that?"

"It's highly explosive," Saera explained. "The placement in the ship is such that it would create a chain reaction. One trigger at the right intensity would take out the whole ship and anything around it."

"To the naked eye, the material is virtually indistinct from ateron, which we repurposed from the cracked testing sphere to use for the main relay conduits," Laecy added. "Both transfer electromagnetic energy, so the wiring passed at the basic connection tests. We've only run low-level currents—around a CR 5 in intensity. The Detno doesn't trigger until a 7."

"It's possible the heat spike was caused when Wil and I interfaced with the ship for the first time," added Saera.

Cris' heart sank. "So, the entire ship needs to be scrapped."

"No," Laecy quickly cut in. "I've run a full diagnostic, and the Detno is only in four specific locations. We can extract it. Everything else checks out, from the structure to the software."

"It's repairable?" Cris clarified.

Laecy nodded. "An easy fix, really. It'll only take a few hours."

"That's not the issue," Saera continued. "The bad part is that we don't know who did it—the out-of-place engineer today may have simply been coincidence. If there's sabotage on this vessel, there's no telling if there are other bombs throughout the fleet."

"Who has access?" Cris asked Laecy.

"Me, Becca, Nolan, and Aram on my team are the only ones with both the knowledge and the opportunity to pull this off. Lacing in the Detno could be done quickly, but identifying the right placement for optimum explosive amplification took serious skill."

"I've already vetted her," Saera said with a sympathetic glance toward Laecy. "We couldn't start investigating until I knew she could be trusted."

Laecy frowned. "I hope I don't need another one of those mind probes any time soon."

Regret flitted across Saera's face. "I'm sorry. It was necessary."

"Yeah, I know." The engineer shook it off. "Anyway, what I don't understand is why anyone would go to these lengths. If they have that kind of access, why not take everything out?"

Cris thought for a moment. "I suspect because they were waiting to make the most impact."

"So, they were after Wil," Saera said.

"Most likely," Cris replied. "Every act of sabotage increases the chance of being discovered, so each attack needs to maximize results. It's common knowledge that the TSS has been waiting for Wil—how critical he is to our strategy. May as well wait until they can take out not just him, but his officers, too. Everyone would be on the *Conquest* during a practice session when they'd access the telekinetic relays—it's the perfect opportunity."

"That does make sense, in a twisted way," Saera muttered.

Laecy's face paled. "I can't picture anyone on my team doing that."

Cris felt Wil approaching before he heard the knock on the door. "Come in."

Laecy flashed Wil an apologetic smile. "I should have known everything was going too well."

"What's the problem, exactly?" Wil asked, looking around the group.

They filled him in on the critical information. He took it in silently.

"The culprit's actions may not have been their own," Wil said after a few moments. "The Bakzen seem to have some new method for remote telepathic control. It's been witnessed in the civilian population, but there's no telling if anyone within the TSS is affected."

Cris froze. "For one individual at a time, or...?" *If they could turn all our Militia...*

Wil shook his head. "Large groups, but we don't know its limits."

Saera tossed up her hands. "Great, that's all we need."

"If the Detno is triggered by use of telekinesis," Wil continued, "doesn't that mean an Agent was behind the explosion in the hangar years ago? It couldn't have been a member of your engineering team."

"Not necessarily," Laecy replied. "Electromagnetic energy transfer occurs at specific frequencies. Perhaps the Detno trigger is an ultrasonic or infrasonic frequency rather than the intensity of telekinetic energy itself."

"What type of equipment could produce that frequency?" Wil asked.

Laecy glanced at the console in her lab used for ship performance simulations. "What we have right here."

Wil took a deep breath. "Okay, first things first. Laecy, can you personally tend to the Detno removal?"

"Yes, it'll take a little longer, but I can work alone," she confirmed.

"Good. Get started as soon as you can and seal off the *Conquest*," Wil instructed. "Meanwhile, we need to have serious conversations with Becca, Nolan, and Aram."

—   —   —

The faces in front of Wil were not those of guilty individuals. Except, surface appearances were often misleading. *Haersen fooled me before. We don't have the luxury of being polite.*

Under normal circumstances, diving into another's mind was strictly forbidden. Agents lived by a code of respect for others' autonomy, especially regarding those without telepathic abilities. Such individuals had no way to block their thoughts from a random encounter—no chance to maintain privacy. Agents were conditioned to ignore others' thoughts, as though they didn't exist. To tune into another's consciousness took focus and a deliberate disregard for the respect that was critical to everyday existence.

The present situation was different. They were at war, and one of the individuals seated before Wil had been compromised by the enemy. There was no time for a traditional investigation using questions and clues. He needed to know who and why. Immediately.

Behind him in the windowless room, Wil could feel Cris and Saera readying their own telepathic probes. A combined assessment would be the most reliable way to determine the guilty party.

Though only Saera had examined Laecy, Wil was certain it wasn't her. She didn't ever leave H2 and had never given Wil any reason to doubt her, aside from perhaps being too willing to bend to Taelis' whims. The others, though, had occasionally traveled to the Outer Colonies on relief missions. Any one—or all—of them may have been turned at any time.

Wil took a step forward, pausing to make eye contact with each of the suspects as he looked down the line. "I'm sorry to do this. I know you've trusted me as a friend—that's why I didn't want to leave the interrogation to a stranger. But we need to know the truth. You may not even know that truth yourself."

"I have nothing to hide," Becca said as she straightened in her chair. Her hazel eyes darted between Wil, Saera, and Cris—anxious and tense.

There's only one way to find out for sure. Wil focused in on her mind, causing Becca to become rigid in her chair. First, he only skimmed the surface of her consciousness, sensing her fear and resistance to the invasion of her inner thoughts. He paused to let her acclimate, then dove deeper.

Surprising calm resided beneath the surface. Her thoughts were logical and organized—the mark of a true engineer. None of the fear from the outer thoughts was present, only a deep sense of dedication and purpose. She was committed to the TSS, to fulfilling her duty.

Wil examined the deepest layers of her consciousness, but it was pure and intact.

He withdrew, glancing at Saera and his father. *"Did you find anything?"* he asked them in unison.

They shook their heads.

Wil returned his attention to the young engineer. "You're free to go, Becca. Thank you."

She rose to her feet, slightly unsteady. "I'd like to help Laecy with the repairs," she stated after a moment. "That way, you can get settled in faster."

He nodded his consent. "Thank you, I'll let her know you're cleared to board."

Becca bobbed her head and rushed out of the room.

Wil took a moment to send Laecy a message confirming that Becca was trustworthy. At least two of the key engineers were on his side.

Aram was up next. "Let's get this over with," he muttered.

"You don't seem concerned at all," Wil commented.

"I don't expect someone else to know my mind better than I know my own," Aram retorted.

Saera took a step forward. "You don't have much respect for Agents, I've noticed."

He scoffed. "Why should I—because you have abilities the rest of us don't? That doesn't make you special."

"It doesn't change that we're your superior officers," Cris stated, stepping forward, as well.

"You're not as powerful as you think you are. I've seen way too many people die. You're no more invincible than the rest of us," Aram sneered.

How did he last this long in the TSS? "Are you conspiring with the Bakzen?" Wil asked bluntly.

"No," Aram replied. "Not that I don't see the appeal."

On the surface, the statement appeared to be the truth. However, Wil wasn't about to take anything at face value.

He dove into Aram's mind, searching for evidence of deceit or manipulation. Thoughts of the present filled the outer levels of his consciousness—envy of Wil for his effortless mastery of engineering and telekinesis alike. Except, that envy had been twisted into hatred that ran deep into Aram's subconscious.

Anger and resentment seared within. Aram yearned for the power of an Agent—the very abilities the Bakzen could grant him. He wanted to feel the power course through him, to stand above others and be admired. He'd show the Agents what it really meant to be powerful. They'd all see one day what they had been missing—what he was and they could only dream of becoming.

But he'd never acted on those impulses. They were only fantasies in his inner mind.

Wil faltered. *He has to be the one. Not Nolan...?* He searched even deeper in Aram's mind, examining crevices long since sealed and buried. Even there, no true treachery was to be found.

The search complete, Wil released him.

Aram glared back. "Satisfied?"

"You may not be guilty of working with the Bakzen, but you aren't fit to be a member of the TSS." To either side of Wil, he sensed Saera and Cris bristle in response to Aram's sentiments.

"All of you elitist Agents really are the same," Aram spat. "The rest of us will never be good enough for you."

"It's unfortunate that you feel that way. If you didn't pass such superficial judgment, you may have found we have more in common than you think." Wil glanced over at his father and wife. "I recommend we suspend Aram from duty. Do you concur with that assessment?"

"Absolutely," Cris replied without hesitation.

Saera nodded. "Agreed."

"Why don't you go find a nice quiet corner for Aram to wait out the rest of the war?" Wil said to his father. "Saera and I will finish up here."

Cris beckoned to Aram. "Come on."

"You're really just going to hold me here?" Aram asked, incredulous.

"I don't see your perceptions of Agents or the TSS changing overnight. You know too much to be released as a civilian. What choice do we have?"

"I'd rather die than be held as a prisoner."

"I wouldn't make that kind of permanent decision so rashly. You can wait it out."

Cris directed Aram out the door, giving him telekinetic prods when he dragged his feet.

Nolan gaped at Wil when the door closed. "Me?" The surprise in his tone seemed genuine.

I can't imagine finding out I'd been acting without my knowledge. "Laecy said the four of you were the only ones with the necessary access and abilities. Either she's wrong about that, or…"

The engineer swallowed hard. "You've known me for years. You know I'd never—"

"Nothing is certain." Wil's stomach turned over. "We'll figure this out."

Nolan nodded, though his frown and creased brow indicated that everything was far from all right. He took a deep breath. "Do what you have to do."

Wil and Saera reached out to Nolan's mind together.

Fear and self-doubt overwhelmed his consciousness, willing for himself not to be the perpetrator. Thoughts of his TSS family flitted across the surface—the good times he'd spent building and creating were enjoyable, despite the ever-present war as the backdrop. Nothing pointed to betrayal or ill intent.

"Are you working with the Bakzen?" Wil asked him, both spoken aloud and within his mind.

"I don't know," Nolan responded, unable to speak anything but the truth.

"Where did the Bakzen find you?" Saera asked, her words echoing in Wil's consciousness as he heard them out loud.

Nolan shuddered, his eyes fluttering as a spasm wracked his body. "Lordan," he stammered.

"When were you on Lordan?" Wil asked.

"Four years ago," Nolan forced out. "Relief efforts. After Bakzen attack. So much smoke…"

"Have you heard of it?" Saera asked Wil.

"Not specifically, but I don't keep track of the individual Bakzen raids." Wil returned his attention to Nolan. "How were you contacted?"

"Not there." Nolan shook his head. "Called afterward. They found me," he punched his fists against the sides of his head, "in my mind."

Wil telekinetically pinned the engineer's limbs to his seat so he couldn't hurt himself. "How did they relay orders?"

Nolan's breath was labored. "Video communications. Told me what to do. Made me wipe record after."

Wil dove deeper into Nolan's mind, searching for evidence of the interactions. He navigated through the sea of memories, finally arriving at a vault anchored in the greatest depths. Forcing open the lock, a collage of commands poured forth—all the actions Nolan had performed under the Bakzen's influence without conscious awareness, relaying information and implementing subtle acts of sabotage.

One of the memories stood out to Wil. His gut wretched with instant recognition when he saw a video feed through Nolan's eyes, and the face staring back was a perverse mutilation of someone Wil had once known well. The last time he had seen that face was as he lay bleeding out on the floor of the secondary communications room in TSS Headquarters—the day that Arron Haersen revealed himself as a traitor. Except, this video was recent, and Haersen wasn't the same. That could only mean one thing: not only was he still alive, but he was working with the Bakzen. He was *becoming* a Bakzen.

Wil recoiled with terror, heart pounding in his ears. He released his hold over Nolan.

Saera withdrew from Nolan's mind, as well. *"What is it?"*

"That was Arron Haersen—at least, that's who he used to be. I'd recognize him anywhere after what he did to me, but he's changed..." The rest needed no explanation.

In front of them, Nolan was slumped forward, breath ragged and perspiration on his brow.

"I'm sorry!" Tears welled in Nolan's eyes. "I didn't know. I didn't have any control. I—"

"We know, Nolan. You weren't acting on your own accord," Wil assured him, stepping forward to place a comforting hand on his shoulder.

The distraught engineer searched Wil's face. "Please, don't kill me!"

Wil shook his head. "No, of course not. We can likely find a way to undo whatever control the Bakzen have over you. It's just a matter of time."

Nolan hung his head. "All I ever wanted was to help."

"You have," Wil told him. "Laecy is repairing the relay conduits right now—the *Conquest* will be fine. You still helped deliver the ship I needed."

"I'm glad," Nolan murmured, his trembling beginning to subside.

Wil beckoned him from the chair. "Now, let's get you to Medical so they can start working on a cure." *I need to tell Taelis that Haersen is with the Bakzen.* Haersen and Tek—that was a duo worth destroying.

— — —

Banks startled at the chirp of an incoming communication from Taelis. *I wasn't expecting to hear from him so soon. That's either good news or bad.*

"Hello, Erik," Banks greeted the other High Commander,

stepping toward the viewscreen on the side wall of his office.

Taelis appeared more worn than usual; definitely bad news. "It's been an eventful day so far."

Banks' heart sank. "What happened?"

"We discovered that one of the engineers had laced some of the telekinetic relays in the *Conquest* with Detno."

"Is everyone okay?"

Taelis dismissed the inquiry with a wave of his hand. "Everyone's fine—they caught it in time, fortunately. Repairs are almost complete."

"That's a relief!"

"The larger concern is that he was under subconscious influence of the Bakzen. He didn't even know what he had been doing," Taelis revealed.

"Like on Kaldern?"

"I'm afraid so. But there's more... Apparently, your former Mission Coordinator, Arron Haersen, made his way to the Bakzen. He's still with them now."

That's a name I never thought I'd hear again. "Was he also under the influence of the Bakzen when he shot Wil?"

"That's unclear," Taelis replied. "He may just be a genuine defector. Either way, it explains why the Bakzen have known so much about our supply routes and procedures in recent years."

"That it does." Banks shook his head. "Is there any record of their conversations?"

"No, Wil only found out because of a memory deep in the engineer's mind. We checked the communications logs and there aren't any records—they must have been erased immediately. There's nothing to cross-reference with other potential collaborators."

Banks wilted under the weight of the implications. It was one thing for civilians to begin acting irrationally, but TSS soldiers turning against them at any moment would be disastrous. "How many others might be acting against their knowledge?"

Taelis shook his head slowly. "It's impossible to know. Medical is trying to discern the nature of the influence. Whatever it is, we'll have to come up with some kind of detection tool and counter measures, if possible."

It could be anyone within the TSS. Or any supplier, family member... "What else can we do for now?"

"Agents will need to perform thorough mental assessments on everyone—clear a team to initiate interrogations, then have the cleared Agents perform an assessment of others."

That was fine, in theory, but it would serve as a major distraction from the work at hand. "We don't have that time or energy to spare."

"Is there another choice? It's too big of a risk to go unchecked."

Banks sighed. "It is." *We're in a terrible position either way. Unless the Bakzen's intent was to divide us?*

"I'll have all available Agents vet those around them. If there's anyone else who's been compromised, we'll find them."

"I can do the same here," Banks agreed. "The question is, what do we do if we find anyone else?"

Taelis hesitated. "We can't turn them loose into the general population. The only options are imprisonment or execution."

Banks was unwilling to compromise on one point. "I won't execute anyone just because of something they *could* do."

"Where can we possibly hold suspects?" Taelis asked, worry pitching his voice. "We barely have the resources to support our troops, as it is. Besides, putting all the Bakzen's potential drones in one place would make it a target—and one we'd have no way to defend."

"There might not be that many."

"Or maybe it's half our soldiers and we don't stand a chance." Taelis exhaled heavily, slumping against the front of his desk. "Maybe we're better off not knowing."

"There are risks either way." Banks had seen enough to know that the ripple effects of an investigation might be more difficult to manage than the hypothetical actions of a Bakzen accomplice.

The other High Commander paused to consider the counterpoint. "If we stay quiet, at least morale would remain intact. That may be the most valuable commodity we have right now. We have no way to know if the Bakzen will exert influence, or when. If someone isn't committing active sabotage, they're still a resource to us."

A cold reality, but Banks had to agree. "So, we tell everyone to keep an eye out for suspicious activity but otherwise continue normal operations?"

"It's an option. And maybe the best one, given the alternatives."

Banks frowned. "Alerting everyone to the danger might be counterproductive. We could quickly find ourselves overwhelmed with finger-pointing and mass hysteria."

"Can conditions truly deteriorate so quickly?"

"It's happened before," Banks cautioned. *Like when Tarans first ostracized the Bakzen and started the war.*

Taelis let out a slow breath as he contemplated the options. "Then we tell only the most senior officers—those who have proven level-headed in such matters. With any luck, Medical will be able to pinpoint the cause of the telepathic influence before it becomes a bigger issue."

"Yes, I agree. That's the best course." Concern continued to gnaw at the back of Banks' mind. "Except, even if we're able to address the breach within the TSS, there's still the civilian population..."

"That's too large a task for us to tackle at the moment. We must focus on the internal concern, for now."

"All right," Banks conceded.

Taelis' shoulders slumped further. "Yet another reason to end the war as quickly as possible."

"That's in Wil's hands now. He'll deliver."

The other High Commander nodded. "We're counting on it."

CHAPTER 7

SAERA WAS STILL queasy from the interrogation with Nolan. *He was innocent, despite his actions. How many others will live with that burden?*

A chirp from her handheld pulled her back to the present. It was from Wil: >>Just got the all-clear from Laecy. Can you get the Primus Elites settled in for the night?<<

Establishing some sense of familiarity and home was just what she needed. >>I'm on it,<< she wrote back.

The *Conquest*'s hangar was completely empty when she arrived. Saera milled around the cavernous space while she waited for the transport shuttles carrying the Primus Elites from the *Vanquish*. It felt wrong to just stand around idly waiting, but there was little else she could do. *Soon we'll have a clear sense of direction, once Wil has a plan.*

The minutes dragged on, and eventually Saera sat down on the floor with her back against the cool, metal wall. Bored, she pulled out her handheld and started playing a puzzle game. She had just passed Level 17 when the proximity alarm for the outer hangar door sounded. *Finally.*

Saera jumped to her feet and stretched out some of her soreness from the uncomfortable sitting position on the hard floor.

The hangar door slid open, leaving only a force field between the interior and the vacuum of space. Two shuttles outside were slowing on their final approach. The vessels passed through the force field, one at a time, and came to rest several meters from Saera. The side doors opened, and the Primus Elites filed out.

"Welcome to the TSS *Conquest*," Saera greeted as the men approached.

"Thanks," Ethan replied. "So, this is the new flagship?"

"Sure is." Saera examined the young men. They seemed a little travel worn—no wonder, after being cooped up in the *Vanquish*'s lounge for a whole day. "Let's get you situated."

Saera led the Primus Elite trainees up several decks to the residential area, requiring four trips on the lift to transport everyone. Once reunited, they made their way past a common area to a row of doors at the end of the hall, adjacent to the captain's quarters by the lift. "Go ahead and pick out your rooms," she said.

The men poked their heads into the quarters. "It looks like all of them are singles," Curtis commented.

"I don't even remember what it's like to have my own room," Ethan said.

"I'm sure you'll all adjust." *They seem a little upset about being separated. I guess if you spend enough time with a group, they can become an extension of yourself.*

It only took a couple minutes for the men to work out the room assignments. Not surprisingly, they stayed clustered in their training groups.

"What now?" Michael asked, once everyone had deposited their minimal personal possessions.

"Now we wait for Wil." *And the plan.*

—   —   —

Wil had endured enough briefings for one day. The added complications with Nolan had only lengthened an already trying afternoon. At least now there was some sense of direction.

After the final meeting for the day concluded, he found his way back to the *Conquest* in short order. When he arrived, the Command Center was empty. *Quarters, perhaps?* Wil took the lift down one deck. As soon as the doors opened, he heard voices from down the hall. Despite his low spirits after discussing the Bakzen's telepathic control with Taelis, the cheerful voices brought a smile to his face.

Wil found his men in a common room near the living quarters. Saera was with them, and she rose in greeting as Wil neared.

He looked around the expectant faces. "Hi, sorry to keep you waiting."

Michael smiled back. "We've made do."

"Good." Wil stared at his feet, torn about the news he had to deliver. "So…" he began slowly, "the developments today have revealed just how vulnerable the TSS is right now. I was fully intending for us to remain here together, but that's no longer realistic. I need some of you to integrate with the rest of the TSS fleet right away."

The smiles faded.

"What about finishing our training?" Tom asked.

"The training is over. Everything we do now is for the war."

The men nodded with understanding.

"Your new assignments will be sent to your handhelds shortly. You leave in the morning, so take tonight to say your goodbyes. It might be a while before we're all back together in person again."

After living so closely for five years, the notion of being distributed across entire star systems would make it difficult for the men to part ways from their friends. Wil beckoned Saera away so the Primus Elites could have some time for farewells without the oversight of their commander.

"Don't worry. You've trained them well," Saera said in a low voice once they were down the hall.

"It's not them I'm worried about."

"Oh, come on! You've got this." She gave him a gentle nudge with her shoulder. "I have no doubt that we're going to win this thing in no time."

He smiled back at her. "You're right. We will." *But at what cost?*

They walked hand-in-hand to the captain's quarters. The

door slid to the side, revealing panoramic viewports along the back wall. The space immediately inside the door was arranged as a sitting area with a couch and two chairs around an oval coffee table. A compact bistro table and two chairs were situated next to the left wall near a door leading into what Wil suspected was a separate bedroom.

"I already unpacked," Saera commented as they stepped inside.

"Thanks," Wil collapsed into one of the chairs across from the couch. "I guess this'll be home for the next few months, or however long it takes."

Saera took a seat across from him. "It'll go quickly, I'm sure."

"Hopefully." Wil massaged his eyes. "First, I need to pick the rest of the crew."

"Do you have a list of the candidates?" Saera asked.

"Taelis said he sent something over." Wil pulled out his handheld and located a message from the High Commander. Several personnel files were attached. "Not many options."

"He does seem to always get straight to the point."

"That he does," Wil agreed. He projected the files on the nearby wall viewscreen.

Saera smiled. "All right. Let's pick our crew."

—   —   —

Haersen followed Tek along an upper grated walkway overlooking the hanger below. Rarely would they leave the planetary headquarters, but such a momentous occasion called for the Imperial Director's presence.

The rows upon rows of matured hybrid clones beneath them in the warship's hangar made for an impressive display. Their chestnut hair was sheared to stubble, blending in with their coarse skin that appeared more Taran tanned than a distinctly orange tint like their pure-blooded Bakzen counterparts. Each drone bore a constant scowl beneath their sorrel eyes. All of them had been risen to their full telekinetic potential—ready to fulfill their purpose in the war.

It was a shame they were only made to die.

Between the center rows, a sleek barrel one meter in diameter extended the length of the hangar, with one end pointed toward the exterior door. Fitted with pods to hold one of the clones, the device would launch its payload into space. When the pod depressurized, the clone would become fodder for expanding the Rift.

"A magnificent army," Haersen commented to his commander.

"They are," Tek agreed. "Your first generation of Bakzen brothers."

That was a fair assessment, given that they were only one generation removed from their Taran origin. Haersen's own transformation would always make him an outsider, but at least he was advancing toward a more evolved state. In many ways, the hybrid clones were a step backward. The idea of willingly incorporating the inferior genetic matter of a pure Taran would have been an atrocity under any other circumstances. Except, Wil was different. Whatever selective pairings had led to his creation, it was enough to unlock a trait that the Bakzen had never been able to replicate. Though the Bakzen line would be diluted, it was to shape an even better future. When the next iteration of the hybrids was perfected, an even more powerful era for the Bakzen would begin.

Tek stepped to the railing and looked down upon the hundreds of clones who were about to be sacrificed for the greater Bakzen cause. "Such genetic potential wasted on mindless drones. We'll eventually find out what they can become, but not today." He strode down the elevated walkway toward the exit door.

Haersen jogged to catch up, cursing that the Bakzen hadn't been able to modify his small stature.

They made their way to a lift, which carried them to the Command Center at the top of the ship. Suiting its warship designation, the entire vessel was simple and utilitarian to the Bakzen extreme, lacking any form of ornamentation or more than the most basic padding on seats. Walls were either riveted metal or plastic sheeting, and lights were placed at bare minimum intervals to cast the necessary illumination. After so many years among the Bakzen, Haersen was used to only having the essentials.

As soon as they entered the Command Center, Tek took the seat at the center of the room, leaving Haersen to sit in one of the four guest chairs along the back wall, two to either side of the entry door. The two Bakzen soldiers stationed at control consoles in the front of the room bowed their heads to Tek while four others posted at stations wrapping around the side walls of the oblong room rose to greet him.

Tek waved them back to work. "Ready the first drone."

The domed viewscreen encircling the ceiling and floor shifted from a perfect rendering of the surrounding starscape to show the side of the warship and the exterior hangar door. A barely perceptible force field covered the opening, and the barrel of the launching tube thrust forward through the barrier.

"Bring up the Rift map," Tek instructed, straightening in his chair.

With a shimmer across the viewscreen, a purple overlay appeared, displaying a graphic representation of Rift pockets in the surrounding space. The warship was positioned at the edge of the purple mass representing the Rift.

Haersen gripped the armrests of his seat, his breath shallow with anticipation. If the test was successful, the new Bakzen drones without natural telekinetic ability inhibitors would be able to expand the Rift far more efficiently than their previous brethren. With the rift corridors serving as guided tunnels to their destinations, no navigation beacons would be needed—the Bakzen could travel without detection and launch their attacks on the unsuspecting Taran worlds. The faster they could complete those pathways, the better.

"Deploy when ready," ordered Tek.

The barrel of the launch assembly illuminated as a pod rocketed out into space. At the horizon of the Rift, the pod burst apart, exposing the Bakzen drone to open space.

Any other living being would quickly depressurize and freeze in the vacuum, but the drone instinctively formed a subspace distortion around itself—just enough to maintain consciousness as it clung to life. It thrashed in weightlessness, contained in the bubble that spanned the spatial planes.

Eventually, it could hold on no more. The subspace distortion began to collapse, but as it did, the drone released all of its telekinetic potential in one last vain attempt to save itself.

A burst of white light flashed across the viewscreen. When the image resolved, a new purple extension appeared on the Rift map overlay. The drone was gone.

"Two-hundred-eighty percent increase over previous benchmarks," the soldier at the front right console announced.

Tek stroked his chin. "Nearly three times the impact of our previous drones. We had hoped for four."

"Improvements for the next generation," Haersen offered.

"Indeed. This will still speed our progress toward enveloping Taran territory in the Rift." Tek gazed out at the new tendrils of the Rift extending before them. "Maybe the drones can even serve another purpose."

CHAPTER 8

TOM STARED OUT the viewport of the transport shuttle at the new temporary residence he would share with the other pilots in the Primus Squad. The cruiser was berthed next to the most advanced flight training grounds available within the TSS. Wil had talked about the facilities before, but the sporadic descriptions hadn't done the course justice.

A sea of programmable obstacles and dummy ships stretched out as far as Tom could see. Six fighters were presently weaving through the course—taking a shot before jumping to subspace and reappearing hundreds of meters away. Had he not performed such maneuvers himself before, it would have seemed remarkable. Understanding the tricks, however, he could tell that the pilots were either new or just not very good.

"They're hung up on forward momentum," Tom commented to the other members of the Primus Squad. "All of the jumps are still 'forward' compared to the previous location, even when the jump is horizontal or vertical."

"You're right," Sander agreed from the seat next to him. "Not once have they jumped behind an enemy that's trailing them."

Across the central aisle, Andy snorted. "Basic stuff."

Tom studied the pilots' movements in the obstacle course. "They're probably thinking in terms of line-of-sight."

"And they can't see behind them," Ray completed the thought, staring out his own viewport next to Andy on the other side of the ship.

"Exactly," Tom nodded. "We've spent so much time blindfolded in a spatial awareness chamber that it doesn't matter to us anymore."

Sander grinned. "That's right. And I'm betting the Bakzen don't move like us."

"I can't wait to get my hands on a real IT-1..." Andy said as he gazed wistfully out the viewport.

"I'd wager you won't have to wait long," Tom replied.

The transport ship was on its final approach for docking with the cruiser, lining up the main entry door with a temporary gangway attached to Deck 5 of the cruiser. With a slight shudder, the transport ship locked into place.

Tom jumped to his feet and grabbed his travel bag from under his chair. "Let's go."

They walked down to the central aisle past rows of empty chairs—the only four passengers on a craft designed to carry twenty. Along the back right wall, the exit door hissed open when they approached.

Beyond the door, the temporary gangway formed an enclosed, windowless tunnel to the other ship. Light shone from the open hatch at their destination five meters away. A female figure appeared in the doorway.

"Welcome. Come aboard," she called out.

Tom led the way across the gangway. As he neared the cruiser, he saw that their greeter was wearing a Militia uniform.

She appeared to be in her early-forties, and her dark hair was pulled into a short ponytail at the base of her neck. Deep brown eyes evaluated Tom and the other Primus Elite pilots. "I'm Chelsea," she greeted. "I'm the Lead Engineer here on the Concord, and I'll assist with your orientation to the IT-1 fighters."

"We're eager to get into the real thing," Sander said.

"Glad to hear it," Chelsea replied, flashing them a warm smile. Her eyes, though, spoke to a deep weariness—teetering on the brink of defeat, like so many others Tom had seen during their brief time in the Rift.

"Where should we store our things?" Tom asked, raising the

strap of his travel bag slung over his shoulder.

"We have quarters set aside for you on Deck 8." Chelsea gestured toward a lift down the hall. "Drop your bags in your rooms and then meet me in the hangar."

"See you soon." Tom set off with the others down the hall.

The corridor's metal walls were bare, and a thin industrial carpet covered the floor. Recessed lights in the ceiling cast harsh shadows as they passed underneath—a distinct contrast to the ambient illumination and decorated halls he was used to back at Headquarters.

Ray scanned the hallway with distaste. "This place is pretty bare-bones."

"It's a battleship," Andy pointed out. "No need to give a false impression that anyone would actually enjoy being here."

They found their assigned rooms in the center of a hall on the port side of Deck 8. Unlike on the *Conquest*, the rooms each held two bunks.

"Dibs on Sander as my roommate. He doesn't snore," Tom announced as soon as they'd assessed the two chambers.

"Agreed," Sander replied with a somewhat apologetic smile toward Ray. "Sorry."

Ray groaned. "I'm used to it by now."

Andy shrugged. "I don't know what you guys are complaining about." He headed into the room on the right.

"Yeah, it's a mystery…" Tom muttered as he entered the room on the left, thankful that he would no longer have to endure the equivalent of a vacuum pump operating next to him all night.

The room was tiny compared to their former quarters back home. Narrow bunks were pressed along the wall to either side of the door, and a sliding door along the back wall led to a small washroom with a sink, shower, and toilet. The dark blue linens on the beds were the only breath of color among the monotone gray of the other surfaces; clearly aesthetics hadn't been a high priority. Between the foot of each bed and the back wall was a full-length cabinet.

Tom dropped his travel bag on the left bed and went to investigate the cabinet. Inside, he found several empty hangers and a flight suit with matching helmet. "All right! Now we're talking."

Sander dropped his bag on the other bed and opened up the corresponding wardrobe. "We're heading to the hangar, right? I guess we should bring these along."

"With you one-hundred percent. I'm in the mood for some flying!" Tom gently removed the flight suit from its hanger, rubbing the silky metallic fabric between his fingers. He tucked the lightweight helmet under his arm with the clear half-dome facing forward. The nameplate on the back was still blank, awaiting an owner's moniker.

They met up with Andy and Ray in the hall and headed down to the hangar, following a directory posted in the lift.

The hangar was like any other Tom had seen over the years, with a three-story ceiling and exposed bulkheads arcing above squads of fighters. Extra parts and supplies hung overhead in racks that could be lowered near one of four service stations dotting the expansive open floor. The key difference was that rather than TX-70 fighters, the hangar was filled with a fleet of the new highly maneuverable IT-1s Wil had designed with a revolutionary neural interface. Their sleek frames were finished with matte black plating to blend in with the surrounding starscape, and the aerodynamic wings meant the craft could be equally at home in open space or in a planet's atmosphere, if necessary.

Tom grinned at his companions. "Now the real fun begins."

Chelsea was waiting for them in the middle of the hangar near four IT-1s pulled out from the main line. She waved them over.

"I see you found your flight suits," she commented.

"Seemed worth bringing," Tom replied.

"I should have mentioned them, yes," Chelsea nodded. "We'll get you lockers down here for storing the suits in the future. Please, dress and we'll get started."

Tom removed his dark blue jacket and then slipped on the new suit over his remaining clothes. The fabric automatically adjusted around him to form a pressurized barrier that conformed to his body right up to the neck collar. He kept the helmet off, waiting to connect to the air supply within the fighter.

"You're familiar with the properties of the IT-1 fighters?" Chelsea asked when the Primus pilots had finished dressing.

"Yes," Tom confirmed. "I assume you mean the neural interface."

She nodded. "Precisely. And specifically, the more time you spend with one particular craft, the stronger your bond."

"We treated the simulator the same way," Andy told her. "Not nearly as significant of a bond, but enough that we're used to the idea of syncing with a ship."

"Good. These are the second generation IT-1s," Chelsea continued. "We've made some tweaks to the interface and interior based on pilot feedback over the last couple years. I think you'll like them."

Sander smiled. "Can't wait."

Chelsea placed a headset in her ear. "Climb in and we'll get started. There isn't any live ammo on board, so fire at will. The computer is synced with the training grounds to relay targeting accuracy stats."

Tom selected the fighter on the right end of the row and approached. When he extended his hand toward the first handhold, he detected a slight energy hum emanating from the ship. As he made physical contact, the hum intensified and a spark shot up through his arm. He recoiled.

"It's just feeling you out," Chelsea assured him. "Go on."

He returned his hand to the hull of the fighter and gripped the first handhold. Another spark shot through him, but then settled into a gentle pulsing of energy. To free up his hands, Tom placed the helmet over his head but left the seal open. He climbed up the five steps on the side and peered into the cockpit.

The primary controls for the craft matched the manual setup from the simulators. A yoke was positioned in the front center for most maneuvering, and physical buttons along the front console would control the more specialized functions.

Tom swung his leg over the edge and dropped into the seat. It had virtually no give, and he found himself sitting up far too high above the controls. *Really, this is where they skimp on the finishes?* He was about to voice a complaint to Chelsea when he realized he was beginning to sink into the seat and the backrest was adjusting to his posture. He assumed a flight position and secured the flight harness as the seat continued to customize to the contours of his body. *Of course it would,* he realized, his cheeks warm.

With his comfort established, he turned his attention to the controls. He swiped his hand over the main console. Immediately, the holographic overlay and the head-up display appeared, just like the simulators he was used to. Hopefully, the handling was the same, as well. Feeling along the right side of the seat, he located the oxygen supply tube and hooked it into the port by his neck. Once in place, he twisted his helmet to lock it against the suit's neck ring. A flutter of cool air rushed across his face as the suit sealed.

"Initiating pre-flight check," Tom said into the helmet's comm.

"Keep your hands on the controls during the check," Chelsea replied over the comm. "It will calibrate to your neural patterns."

Tom gripped the yoke, and an electric tingle ran through the capacitive gloves on the flight suit. He concentrated on the ship like he'd practiced with the simulator, trying to sense the controls. The neural interface solidified in his mind's eye, complete with a visualization of the navigation, weapons, and environmental settings like a holographic wheel overlaid on his consciousness. Blue flashed across his vision as the pre-flight check concluded. "Ready," he told Chelsea.

The other Primus pilots acknowledged completion of their own checks.

"There's no better way to get a feel for the fighters than with actual flight. Just take it slow," Chelsea instructed.

A section of the hangar wall slid to the side, revealing a force field across the main door out to open space.

Tom maneuvered the fighter toward the door using the manual controls—there'd be plenty of time to test out the neural interface in a less confined space. As he neared the door, he accelerated to break through the force field. The engine hummed through the floor of the fighter as it spun up in response to his commands. With a smooth lunge forward, it rocketed out of the hangar.

The power and fluidity of the craft's controls left Tom breathless for his first several moments of flight outside the hangar. A grin spread across his face as he steered the craft in a curve to pass above the cruiser while the other Primus pilots made their exit. "It's even smoother than in the simulator!"

"Stars, this is awesome!" Andy agreed.

"Let's try some formations," Sander suggested as he popped up above the cruiser near Tom.

"Keep your distance from each other for now," Chelsea cautioned.

"We've got it. Don't worry," Tom assured her. *"Delta formation?"* he asked his friends telepathically.

In acknowledgement, the three other fighters arranged into a diamond behind him. He directed them toward open space far from the hazards of the obstacle course. *"Go!"*

The four fighters rocketed forward in formation, then Tom activated the specialized maneuvering thrusters combined with a split-second jump to subspace to execute what would appear as a right-angle turn to an outside observer. Simultaneously, Sander and Ray turned ninety-degrees to the right and left, while Andy dipped straight down from his spot at the back of the diamond. Each craft then flipped one-eighty and fired at the empty space where they had been. Without an actual target, there was no hit to verify, but the important part of the test was their end positions.

Sander cheered over the comm. "These can really move!"

"That was *not* taking it slow," Chelsea cut in. "But I have to admit, that was impressive. The simulator practice definitely paid off."

"What do you say we test out the obstacle course?" Andy suggested.

"Sounds good to me," Ray agreed.

"Have any scenarios been programmed for us to try?" Tom asked Chelsea.

"I had prepared some basic target practice, but I think you'd be bored with that after a couple seconds," she replied. "Let me find one of the advanced training modules we use with the veteran pilots."

"That's right! Advanced to pro levels on Day One!" Sander exclaimed.

Tom lined up with the course, eager for the simulation to begin. "Ready when you are."

— — —

The *Conquest* wasn't as homey as TSS Headquarters, but Michael was happy to have a room to himself after five years of sharing his personal space. Still, it felt good knowing that at least the other Captains were nearby.

His new quarters consisted of a main room with a double bed, desk, and wardrobe, and an adjoining bathroom. A single viewport above the bed provided an unobstructed view of H2, where the *Conquest* was still docked to finish Wil's inspection. They'd head out to the field for further telekinetic calibrations any day, but for the time being, the main goal was to get settled into their new residence.

Michael reclined on the bed, thankful it was an optimum firmness for his liking. As he settled into the pillows, he grabbed his handheld from its charging pad so he could check his email. As he was scanning through the message list, a notification dropped down from the top of the screen: >>New chat request from Elise Patera. Accept?<<

Michael's heart leaped. *Why is she writing me?* Their conversation his last night at Headquarters was one of the only times they'd corresponded for any meaningful length of time outside of class. Though the banter had been easy and natural, he'd figured that would be the end of it.

Curious, he opened up a secure chat exchange over a subspace relay to Headquarters. >>Hi<< he typed.

>>Hey!<< typed back Elise.

>>It's good to hear from you,<< Michael replied.

>>I've been thinking about all of you over there. I haven't heard from Saera yet. How's it going?<<

>>So far, so good. We have a new cruiser with telekinetic

relays—I'm anxious to test it out.<<

Elise took a moment to respond. >>Nice! I hate being stuck on the sidelines.<<

>>Where did you end up?<<

>>I'm still right here at Headquarters. They assigned me to teach a handful of navigation and interplanetary biology classes when the more senior Agents were called into the field.<<

She's one of the lucky ones. >>Be thankful. I have a feeling it's going to get pretty bad out here.<<

>>Still...<<

>>Besides, you're not on the sidelines,<< Michael continued. >>The trainees are lucky to have a good teacher.<<

>>You flatter me.<<

>>It's true!<< he insisted. >>Your class presentations were always some of the most entertaining.<<

>>If you say so,<< she yielded.

>>And hey,<< Michael wrote without fully thinking through the statement, >>this way I won't have to worry about you being in danger.<<

Elise didn't respond right away. >>You'd worry about me?<<

I barely know her. However, as he thought back over their limited time together, he was struck by her genuine sweetness and gentle spirit. Being in the thick of battle would ruin her; not all Agents were meant to use their power for destructive ends. >>I know you could hold your own out here, but I feel better knowing you won't have to fight.<<

>>What about you... Out there on the frontlines with Saera, Wil, and the others...<<

>>We'll be fine,<< Michael assured her. *We'll be the Bakzen's biggest target. They already tried to take us out from within once.*

>>I'll be thinking about you, all the same.<< Elise paused. >>I hope you really can end the war quickly.<<

>>We'll do our best.<<

The chat indicated that Elise entered text, but then deleted it. Eventually, another message came through, >>Will you message me, when you get the chance? It'd be nice to stay in touch.<<

To his surprise, Michael found his heart warmed with the thought. >>Gladly.<<

>>Okay, good! Now, be careful out there.<<

>>Always.<< Michael picked his words more carefully this time, >>I'm glad you wrote me.<<

>>Me too,<< Elise replied. >>I think we could all use a good friend right now.<<

— — —

Banks paced across his office. *What am I supposed to do?*

With Wil settled into H2, Banks' attention had fully shifted to his investigation into the Dainetris Dynasty. As he looked over the results of the genetic analysis again, there was no mistaking that he had finally found a match. *The only living Dainetris descendant.*

Pieces of the woman's file were fanned out over Banks' desktop. Vital statistics, known associates, occupation. Nothing about her stood out, and yet she was the sole survivor of what had once been the second most influential High Dynasty.

There's more to this than I can see. The Aesir's words had been gnawing at the back of Banks' mind for days. *Why do the Aesir want her to have a son? How am I supposed to convince her to do that?*

He examined the woman's picture. She had a sadness in her pale blue eyes that soured her expression, despite the natural beauty passed down from her genetic legacy. But it had been generations since the Dainetris name was one of power. The recent years had not been kind.

Does she know anything of who she is? Banks rubbed his eyes. *I guess it's time to take a trip.*

CHAPTER 9

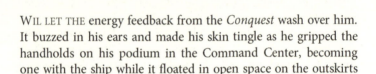

WIL LET THE energy feedback from the *Conquest* wash over him. It buzzed in his ears and made his skin tingle as he gripped the handholds on his podium in the Command Center, becoming one with the ship while it floated in open space on the outskirts of the uninhabited system near H2.

It was yet another day of practicing with his crew to calibrate the *Conquest* and learn the nuances of its operation. Though rhythm with his team was lacking, at least the ship was living up to Wil's expectations. Without fail, the ship responded to every minute shift in his attention: the weapons system charged in response to a thought of an enemy attack, extra power automatically routed to the shields with the threat of an incoming blast, and communications between the crew members effortlessly passed through the relays integrated into the ship. Yet, the fluidity from the practice sessions back home had been lost. There was a lag with his core team, some hesitation. It was subtle, but noticeable nonetheless.

I know it's not the ship. Why aren't we working well together anymore? Ever since they arrived at H2, something had been off. Wil had been trying for days to get the rhythm back, but it still wasn't right. It had been difficult to part ways with half his team, even though they were still in regular communication while they advised the fleet on tactics across the Rift—putting their leadership training to use so Wil could focus on honing in his coordination with his Seconds on the *Conquest*. However, after spending five years together with only a handful of days apart, it still felt like part of himself had been displaced.

Maybe we need to mix things up. Breaking from the standard calibration exercise, Wil focused on the beginning of a spatial dislocation wave. *Perhaps some subspace maneuvering...* The spatial dislocation wave radiated out from him, stretching slowly. The ship hummed in anticipation.

"Whoa, hold on!" Michael exclaimed. He let go of the podium at his station to Wil's right.

Wil pulled himself back from his trance-like sync with the ship. "What?" The energy dissipated.

Ian, Ethan, and Curtis also released the handholds on their podiums.

At the front left console, Saera crossed her arms with disapproval.

Next to her, the newest member of the Command Center crew, Rianne, was watching with great interest. "Just incredible," she murmured, tucking the bangs of her short red hair behind her ear. She was a seasoned Militia tactical officer and veteran pilot, and had been at the top of Taelis' list for key ship personnel. For most of the previous week she had just been in an observational role, but based on her prior performance record, Wil had no doubt that her even temperament and experience would be an asset once they got into battle.

"You can't just initiate a spatial dislocation jump without any warning." Michael's brow furrowed.

"We might have to one day," Wil countered. "You need to be prepared for anything." *Now they're outright resisting me. I never thought it would be my own team holding me back.*

Michael's eyebrows raised. "After we've been able to test that it actually works!"

"Yeah, I'd really rather not get lost in subspace..." Ian added.

"I wouldn't let you get lost in subspace." *Don't they trust me anymore?*

"Aside from that," Ian continued. "I can't compensate for the time lag from the spatial dislocation distortion if I don't have any notice. Kind of makes it difficult to execute precision tactics."

"My connection to the larger TSS fleet is at risk in the same way," Curtis interjected.

Ethan held out his hands palm-down, gesturing for them to remain calm. "We can get used to it. I deal with it when the pilots make rift jumps in their fighters, but having the dislocation on both sides of the connection will be tricky. We just need to practice."

Wil took a deep breath. "Whatever we're doing right now isn't working."

"No, it's not," Michael agreed.

The men frowned at each other.

Saera stood up and approached them. "It's been a long session. Maybe you should take a break."

"We won't have the luxury of breaks soon," Wil replied. "We need to build up our endurance."

"If endurance is the goal, then we need a different approach entirely, because this is wiping me out," Ian said.

"There are too many ties to hold." Michael shook his head wearily. "It was easy in the zero-G isolation chamber, but there's so much to keep track of now."

What can we possibly do differently? How can we stay more synced…? Wil thought for a moment. "What if I bring you into the full distortion with me?"

Michael looked puzzled. "I thought the point was for us to anchor you?"

"That's what we practiced, but that was before I knew about this ship."

"Is that enough of a tether?" Curtis didn't look convinced.

"I don't see why not," Wil replied. "The ship is a solid, fixed point. Even when executing a jump, it's still a point of reference. I can link to the ship, and you can link to me."

"It might work…" Michael mused.

"The only real way to test it is to try." *If I bring them into the distortion, will they be able to see what I see?*

Curtis looked around the group. "Right now?"

"We may as well." Wil gripped the handholds on his podium.

A crease formed between Ian's eyebrows. "Are you sure about this?"

"Just relax," Wil assured him.

Reluctantly, the four men took their respective handholds. Saera sat back down at the front console to serve as their secondary anchor point through the ship.

Wil cleared his mind and focused on his position in space. He separated from his physical reality and extended outward. The signatures of those around him were faint, but he concentrated on his connection with the ship. It was a steady pull, bonding him to his sense of self. Through that bond, he reached out to the others who had formed their own link with the ship. He worked his way through the energy pathways, finding common ties to bring them all together. Carefully, he brought his four Seconds to him, keeping them anchored to the ship through a central point. They resisted at first, then gave into his lead—placing complete trust in Wil to keep them tethered as they gave up their own connection with the ship.

With the single tether to the *Conquest*, Wil took them outward, hovering on the brink of subspace. As they approached the horizon, he centered his mind and took them through the dimensional veil.

"Fleet?" asked Wil telepathically.

"Fleet check," replied Michael.

"Tactical?"

"Tactical check," replied Ian.

"Pilots?"

"Primus team check," replied Ethan.

"Pilot command check," replied Curtis.

The responses were seamless, more instantaneous than they ever had been before.

"How are your external connections?" Wil asked.

"I just pinged Kalin at the outpost in Antaris," said Curtis. *"The timing is good."*

"And faster among us here," Michael commented.

"All right. Let's put it to the test." Wil ran his team through a series of exercises, dolling out commands for his team to relay tactical maneuvers while simultaneously testing all the *Conquest*'s battle systems. The timing was exceptional, and the ship's systems responded to their every maneuvering command. Wil

kept them tethered as he held the presence of the two dominant dimensional planes in his mind, orchestrating a scenario that seamlessly passed between the dimensional veil. The rhythm was back, and smoother than ever.

When the men began to tire, Wil returned them to normal space. "How was that?"

"You surpassed all the prior benchmarks," Rianne reported, awe in her hazel eyes.

"Saera?" Wil asked.

"Felt solid to me," his wife replied.

The ship can take it. What about the rest of my team? Wil looked to his men. "Could you see both planes?"

"All I saw was a haze of the outside world. I think I was more here than there," Ian said.

"Same," Ethan agreed.

This wasn't the full answer, then. "I need to find a way for you to see what I see. Maybe project my vision on the viewscreen."

"Then we wouldn't have to put everything into words," Michael stated.

Curtis placed a hand on his chin, pensive. "How would we keep our vision clear enough to see everything on the viewscreen?"

"This was a decent first attempt. I think we can get there." *But do we have enough time to work out the proper balance?*

Michael nodded. "Even so, I'm still concerned about the tethering."

"Why?" Wil asked.

"It's a lot for you to manage. It might be fine for these short spurts, but how quickly will you fatigue?" Michael looked Wil in the eye through their tinted glasses.

It will be easier for me to bear than anyone else. We don't have another option—this is the only thing that's worked in the way we need. "I'll be fine."

"If that's the direction we're going, then it's going to take a lot more practice to get our vision clear enough," Ian commented. "Taking in the full sphere of the viewscreen is tough enough, even when fully connected with our physical self. How are we supposed to do that while tethered through you?"

Then maybe the viewscreen isn't the answer. "What if we just used the ship as a processor. The bioelectronic interface interprets thought, right? Perhaps we can use the ship to translate my vision and relay it to you."

"Except that *you're* our tether to the ship," Ethan pointed out.

"I'm more of a mental hub. You're still physically connected through the podiums and that's all the bioelectronic relays need," Wil replied. "Plus, there's no reason I can't be a two-way conduit." *It's a lot, but I'll have to find a way.*

The men pondered the proposition. It was sound, in theory. They smiled tentatively, their enthusiasm returning.

I have my team back. Wil took the handhelds on his podium. "Ready for a test run?"

Michael grabbed his own podium. "Let's see what we can do."

—   —   —

Walking into the secured incarceration wing in the center of H2 instantly set Laecy on edge. *Nolan doesn't belong here. It's not fair.*

She understood why he needed to be kept away from the engineering operations, but she missed his expertise and companionship. With both Nolan and Aram gone, there was too much for Laecy to handle with Becca alone, and almost none of the engineering support staff knew enough details about the newest fleet upgrades to be of much use in her lab.

A Militia guard was posted outside of Nolan's cell door. "Credentials," he demanded.

Laecy activated the ID badge integrated into her jumpsuit.

The guard nodded and stepped aside from the door. He entered in a passcode and the door slid to the side, revealing a force field across the opening.

Inside, Nolan was lounging on a bunk along the back wall. He was reading on a rudimentary tablet without network connections, mitigating security risk. When he noticed movement outside the cell, he set down the tablet and swung his legs over the edge of the bunk. "Laecy!"

"Hi, Nolan," she greeted through the comm system into the room. "Sorry it took me so long to come visit you."

"I wasn't expecting any visitors. This is a pleasant surprise." He stepped up to the edge of the force field.

"How are you?"

Nolan shrugged. "Bored. I wish I could help you out. I hate being stuck in here."

Laecy nodded. "I could use you. Have they made any progress toward identifying a way to counter the telepathic influence?"

"The medical staff won't say much when they come in to examine me, but I think they're onto something. They started getting all excited the last time they came in—saying something about a 'counteragent to the neurotoxin.' "

"That sounds promising." *I need him back. We have so much to do...*

"I feel fine," Nolan murmured. "I just don't understand how they got to me."

"The Bakzen have always been crafty," Laecy replied, "but we'll find a way to stop them."

Nolan cracked a smile. "I'll get back to the fight as soon as I can. In the meantime, can you get me some better reading material? I can't endure another mediocre detective story where I figure out the twist halfway through."

"I'm envious that you actually have time to read something other than fleet reports and engineering diagrams."

"Down time isn't all it's cracked up to be." Nolan sighed.

"All right, I'll see what I can do." Next to her, the guard shifted restlessly on his feet. "I should get back to it."

"Thanks for stopping by."

"Of course. I'll see you soon." Laecy waved goodbye to her friend and retraced her path down the hall toward her lab. *Back to work.*

—   —   —

Cris strolled through the administrative wing of H2. There had been far too many meetings over the last few days.

He checked the calendar on his handheld. At last, he was free for the evening. *Finally, I can get some downtime with Kate.*

Just as he was about to head for the lift, Cris heard someone approach from behind. He turned to see Taelis.

"Hi, Cris. May I speak with you?"

Not that I have the option of declining. "Sure, what is it?"

"Walk with me." Taelis began striding down the hall.

Cris followed him through several corridors with expansive viewports giving an unobstructed view into space. It still felt strange to Cris, being exposed after spending so many years in the hidden Headquarters within the moon.

Taelis led them to a small conference room. The back wall was entirely glass, looking out over one of the many spacedocks around the perimeter of the massive H2 structure.

The High Commander sat down on the far side of the table, and Cris took a seat across from him.

"How strong is Wil?" Taelis asked.

Cris was caught off-guard. *This guy really doesn't care for pleasantries.* "What do you mean?"

"To be perfectly frank, we've backed ourselves into a corner. All of our strategies hinge on Wil's ability to execute, but there's no assurance that he'll come through. Don't get me wrong—I acknowledge that he's brilliant. What he was able to piece together with those subspace maps is incredible, and I can't believe we didn't see it before. Then, from an engineering perspective, he's strengthened the fleet tenfold. And, of course, I've heard the story about how he broke the CR testing sphere."

Cris' eyes narrowed behind his tinted glasses. "What are you asking?"

"I want to know if he'll break under the pressure. Honestly." Taelis folded his hands on the table.

"Why are you asking me?"

"Because you're his father, primary trainer, and supervising officer. I'd say that makes you the most qualified person to make an informed assessment."

Cris looked past Taelis, out at the spacedock. "I'm not sure."

Taelis frowned. "That's not a satisfactory response."

"Fine, you want my honest opinion? I think we've trained

him and pushed him, and he could have snapped at any time. Somehow, he's gotten through it all. It's not fair for me to place a wager on how much longer he'll continue bearing the pressure. I've watched him bounce back from even the most devastating experiences, but I also acknowledge that even the strongest people have a breaking point. What you need to understand is that he's the kind of person that will give all of himself to see this war through to the end. Beyond where others would have given up, he'll make sure we win, even if it's the last thing he does. So, to answer your question, he's the strongest person I know. If I had to count on someone to come through, it'd be him."

Taelis nodded and let out a slow breath. "Would Wil tell me the same thing?"

What kind of a question is that? "Wil has always been his own harshest critic. He'd tell you he still has a lot to learn, but that he'll do his best." Cris straightened in his chair. "I ran out of things to teach him a decade ago, but somehow he's continued to teach himself new abilities and trained his men to become the most gifted group of soon-to-be Agents we've ever seen. It's no coincidence that he's never reached a limit to his power, even though he's maxed out the scales."

"Our existing equipment might not be able to measure his full potential, but the months ahead will push him to his limit," Taelis replied.

"None of us knows what he's capable of doing. Push too hard and..." Cris couldn't finish the thought. *I like to think that he'd only use such power for good, but some of the enemy lines have blurred over the years.*

Taelis sighed. "That's the thing—we don't have another choice. We're counting on Wil to do things that we never dreamed were possible. Stars! The entire notion of simultaneous observation seemed ludicrous when I first heard it—a crazy theory invented by desperate tacticians. Now, that's the foundation of our entire strategy."

An act only one person in all the Taran worlds can perform. No backup plan. "Why wait for Wil all these years? Everything I've heard is about how you can't hold out much longer. Why not just send a bomb to the Bakzen homeworld?"

Taelis let out a bitter chuckle. "You think we didn't try that?"

"Well, I—"

Taelis leaned forward. "We started with diplomacy—dead end. We tried blockades—overrun. We tried leaving the Bakzen alone—they came for us. And when we threw enough firepower at them to wipe out the whole system, it all just disappeared."

"Disappeared?"

"Bombs, ships. They just wink out of existence midway to their target." Taelis rubbed his eyes. "Cris, I can tell you don't care much for my demeanor, but I've been dealing with the reality of this war for nearly forty years. I've seen my friends die, seen entire worlds destroyed. As a commander, it's been my responsibility to hold it all together. But our enemy is infinitely stronger than us—it hasn't been a matter of winning or losing battles, but of how heavy the casualties will be on any particular day. Simply put, the Bakzen can move faster than we can attack. Simultaneous observation isn't for precision strikes or tactical efficiency, it's a hope for finally making any headway."

Cris swallowed. "Without that insight, the Bakzen will just move any of our weapons, or bury them in subspace?"

"Yes. That is the grim reality."

That would wear down anyone, seeing an endless string of failures. Cris cast his gaze down at the tabletop. "It's difficult for me, as Wil's father… knowing what's being asked of him."

"I know." Taelis softened. "I saw that protectiveness when I first met you years ago. At the time, I thought it was counterproductive, but I realize now it was that consideration and caring that's gotten Wil this far. Without it, he might not be able to trust others in the way that it's now so critical for him to trust his officers."

"It's important to be able to lean on others sometimes." *Things might have been different for Taelis if he'd let others in.*

The High Commander nodded. "Banks was always clear about how tight-knit the Primus Elites are as a group. Much of the technology we've developed for Wil relies on that connection with his team. Through their collective ability, we should be able to visualize where the Bakzen are moving on either side of the Rift, before the move is complete, so we can preempt their attacks."

"I've gone over the stats from Wil's practice sessions with his officers," Cris replied. "If they can achieve even half the speed from those test runs under real-world conditions, it'll be quite a sight to behold."

"I hope so. We practically need to fight two wars simultaneously." Taelis wilted. "As taxing as the battles have been so far, it will only get worse once the Bakzen realize we have officially brought the Cadicle into the war."

"At least we know what they've been planning, now that we've seen the subspace map."

"Indeed."

"But it also means we need to be deliberate and aggressive if we're going to successfully head off their plan," Cris said.

"Which is why the TSS has been grooming Wil. If there's anything we've learned, it's that the Bakzen rely on calculations and reason, even if their movements are too quick for us to anticipate. We need their precise calculation ability, combined with something less predictable if we're to get ahead. What Wil can see through simultaneous observation surpasses the capabilities of any computer, and he also brings the element of intuition. Our good old fashioned Taran heart and gut instinct is what sets us apart."

"Is that enough?"

"It has to be. We've tried everything else."

All the TSS' hopes rest on Wil, and he knows it. "Wil won't let you down. You asked me how strong he is, but that doesn't really matter. He has incredible determination and heart. If that's what we're counting on to win this fight, then you're in good hands."

Taelis looked as though a weight had been lifted. "That's what I needed to hear."

CHAPTER 10

A WARM BREEZE off Lake Tiadon swept across Banks' face as he strolled down the residential street in Sieten. *How long has it been since I felt the sun?*

Rarely was he ever able to leave TSS Headquarters, and the timing of this trip was far from ideal. But he couldn't ignore the Aesir's message. He had to speak with the Dainetris heiress.

She was under the assumed identity of one of the longstanding families in the Dynasty's former service. It was entirely possible that her ancestors were illegitimate children, but as long as both parents were Taran citizens, the default heir was the firstborn child, unless officially named otherwise by the parents. If she stepped forward and made a claim to her rights as a Dainetris Dynasty heir, the balance of power on Tararia would shift. Seven High Dynasties would once again have voting rights and the Priesthood would no longer be the tiebreaker, greatly undermining their ability to constrict the flow of information and undermine the social standing of those with abilities, as was currently the case.

Banks wound his way through the streets, taking in the bustling city life with parents walking their children to school and shopkeepers tending storefronts. It was a neighborhood of administrative staff and laborers, the sort of people Banks would rarely see under other circumstances. He found himself enjoying the window into their day-to-day lives. These were the people the

TSS protected—the people behind the population statistics—and each one of them was deserving of a peaceful, safe existence.

For being a poor neighborhood by Tararian standards, the streets were impeccably maintained—well-swept and no litter in sight. Trees planted along the roadway added a dash of color to contrast the white-washed stone and concrete walls.

His destination address was located in a block of government housing on the outskirts of the city, reserved for those in the employ of the Sietinen Dynasty or other administrative offices. Banks found the employment program somewhat questionable, walking a fine line between assistance and indentured servitude. Though room and board was covered in addition to a small salary, the income wasn't enough to ever break free from working for the employer, aside from the rare instance where the right contacts could lead to a new position with another company, or an opportune marriage. The life was certainly better than homelessness, but it was far from freedom.

He located the correct building and took the stairs up to the third of six stories. The door was dark green, like all the others in the white-washed building. He hit the buzzer.

A muted chime sounded on the other side of the door. After several seconds, footsteps approached. An intercom crackled. "Who are you?" asked a female voice.

"My name is Jason Banks. I'm an officer with the Tararian Selective Service. I'm looking for Elaine Pernelli," he stated, following the cover story he'd concocted for the visit.

"Show me your credentials," the woman requested.

Banks spotted the security camera and pressed his jacket lapel to display his ID.

The door lock released with a click and swung inward, revealing a woman in her mid-thirties. With her light brown hair loose around her shoulders, she evaluated him with pale blue eyes. "My name is Marie. Elaine was my mother. I'm sorry, but she passed away many years ago."

"When was that?" Banks asked, already knowing the answer.

"I was very young," Marie replied. "Around five years old. I spent my childhood as a Ward."

It's likely she really doesn't have any idea who she is. He proceeded with the lie, "This may sounds strange, but would you mind if I spoke with you about your mother? We were childhood friends. Anything you can tell me about who she grew up to be would be wonderful."

"I don't remember much, but I'll help in any way I can, Agent Banks."

"Please, call me Jason," he said.

She bobbed her head and stepped aside. "Come in."

Banks followed her into the apartment and she re-bolted the door behind him.

The government housing came furnished with generic, modest accommodations in the compact living space. From the couch's squared lines and neutral gray upholstery to the black countertop and white walls, all the materials were monochrome and utilitarian. The only color in the room was a holopainting of some exotic red flowers that was displayed on the end table next to the couch. It was only the height of Banks' hand, but it captivated him from across the room.

"I know this isn't much," Marie said as she stepped away from the door, noticing that Banks was evaluating the room. "But I'm happy to have my own place."

"I'm in quartered housing, too. I know how it is," he replied. "That's a lovely image," he gestured to the holopainting of the flowers.

Marie lit up. "That was my mother's. She left it to me when she passed."

"It's nice you have something to remember her by."

"Yes, the only thing, really. And I never met the rest of my family," Marie murmured. "I've often wondered what they were like."

"Based on what I recall from my childhood, they were good people."

She bowed her head. "That's kind of you to say." She glanced at the couch. "I don't have much to offer for refreshments. Would you like anything?"

"No, I'm fine," Banks responded, knowing that anything besides water would be cutting into her rations.

"Well, please have a seat." She directed him to the couch a few steps away. "What brings you here?" she asked when they were seated.

"Like I said, I was a childhood friend of your mother's. When I tried to find her, I came across you instead."

Marie looked down. "I'm sorry you won't get the chance to see her again."

"Her daughter is the next best thing, I guess." Banks paused, weighing how best to find out what she knew about her lineage. "It must have been difficult being a Ward. Did they treat you well?"

"The Sietinen Dynasty is very generous," Marie hastily replied.

"I wasn't suggesting they mistreated you," Banks clarified. "I just imagine you felt alone, with only memories of your parents."

"Of my mother, at least. I never knew my father."

"What about your grandparents?" Banks pressed.

"I wouldn't have ended up a Ward if they were still around."

Fair point. Banks looked around the room for any other personal effects, but nothing stood out. "Besides the painting, do you have anything of your mother's? Documents, jewelry?"

Marie inched away from him. "This is all I have. If anything else of hers was left, it was seized when she died. The painting is the only thing that's mine. Please don't take it, too."

"No, no!" Banks held up his hands above his lap to set her at ease. "I didn't mean to alarm you. Your mother and I had exchanged some little trinkets as children—that's all. I was only wondering if anything remained."

"No." Marie relaxed the slightest measure.

"What about yourself? Did you ever have interest in applying for a scholarship with the University, or…?"

She laughed. "Me? I was never a good student. Working as a nanny is fine by me. Nothing like a fancy Agent, such as yourself."

"Being a nanny is good, honest work. I'm glad to hear you enjoy it."

Marie wrung her hands. "I never wanted anything special for myself. A comfortable home, a nice dress or two. I'm content."

Banks released a slow breath. *Taran politics would eat her*

alive. I understand what the Aesir meant about her. But a child...
"Working as a nanny, did you ever want a family of your own?"

Marie blushed. "I'd thought about it. Having a little baby to spoil. It'd be good."

"Why didn't you?"

She shrugged. "Never met the right person, I suppose. And I'm on an assistance program so I could never qualify for a donor."

Shite, I have no right to meddle in someone's life like this. But if a child with abilities were born to a lost Dainetris heir, it would give the Sietinen Dynasty everything it needs to unseat the Priesthood. Banks took a slow breath. "Would you still want one now?"

"Are you serious?" she asked, incredulous.

Banks blocked out the rational part of his brain yelling at him to stop the madness. "Things never really worked out for me, either. I can't offer you companionship, but I can provide the other things you need."

Marie's eyes widened with surprise and she let out a little laugh. "Bold, aren't you!"

Slow down! That isn't why you came here. Banks hurriedly rose to his feet and took a step toward the door. "I'm sorry, that was highly inappropriate." *There has to be another way.*

Marie shook her head. "Talking about babies within five minutes of meeting. Maybe you do things differently in the TSS."

It isn't fair to use her like this. "We in the TSS are outsiders in many ways, yes, but I overstepped my bounds by any standard. Apologies."

She studied him for a few moments. "To be honest, I am intrigued by your offer."

Banks sat back down, stunned that she hadn't thrown him out the door. "It was a rash suggestion. I suppose I've been doing a lot of thinking about family and legacies recently."

"Me too, actually," Marie admitted. "I love the children I care for, but I never get to really live life, you know? It's always about duty and caring for others."

"Being a parent is no different."

"Still, that care would be for a part of me. All the effort would have meaning in my own life—being able to mother someone, like my mother wasn't able to be there for me."

Banks swallowed hard. *If we strike an agreement, there's no turning back from this path. The Priesthood would not take kindly to this intervention.* "Marie, maybe we should forget I said anything. I spoke without thinking through the implications. I'd be leaving you alone as a single mother."

She searched his face with her pale eyes. "Do they pay you well in your position?"

"By most measures, yes."

Marie clasped her hands in her lap. "I'm willing to have the conversation. We might be able to come to a mutually beneficial arrangement."

I doubt this is what the Aesir had in mind. Banks took a slow breath. "Before we go too far, we should at least verify compatibility."

"Yes, of course," Marie hesitated. "How?"

"I'll need a blood sample," he requested. *What I really need to check is what's so special about this genetic line.*

Marie rose from her seat and walked over to the kitchen area. She grabbed a knife and used the tip to prick her finger. She wiped a bead of blood onto a tissue and placed it in a clear plastic bag. "Here."

Banks hurried over to take the bag from her. "This won't take too long."

Marie wrapped a bandage around her finger. "Call me if you'd like to move forward. The direct contact info is next to the door."

"I'll be in touch soon." He paused at the exit to swipe his handheld over the contact details to save it to the device.

Marie came up behind him and brushed her fingertips against his hand. "This isn't what I expected when you showed up at my door, but I'm glad you came."

"Maybe it was meant to be." Banks quickly dismissed himself. *So much for my plan of slowly gathering information. I can't believe I'm considering this.*

He headed back toward the TSS shuttle he'd borrowed for the trip. The onboard lab facilities were minimal, but the bioscanner would be sufficient for inputting the blood sample so he could perform a genetic analysis.

Carefully, he removed the tissue from the plastic bag and placed the bloodied spot on the bioscanner. The machine sent a flash of white light through the sample and began sequencing the genetic material.

On its own, the sample wouldn't tell Banks anything aside from unfortunate genetic anomalies that might impact the health of the subject or their offspring. He needed to compare the sample to his own genetic profile on record in the TSS database to see if their pairing would compound any negative recessive genetic traits.

The initial sequencing of Marie's sample completed in ten minutes, finding no concerning code segments. That wasn't surprising, given the High Dynasties' level of refinement over countless generations. And, sure enough, Marie was most certainly of Dainetris descent.

Next, Banks compared her code with his own genetic sample to verify that they were a strong enough match. To his surprise, the result came back at ninety-four percent compatibility—well above the seventy percent threshold used for reproduction approvals. With his TSS clearance and some forged documents, he could certainly receive almost instantaneous approval for the application to disable their contraceptive implants while keeping his involvement concealed from the Priesthood's prying eyes.

After answering the basic compatibility question, Banks decided to cross-check the Dainetris sample against the genetic profiles for Wil and his family. There had to be some connection between Dainetris and the manipulation around the creation of the Cadicle.

Two more minutes passed while the computer ran the analysis. The screen illuminated with the results.

Banks' breath caught in his throat. Aside from the most minute variations, the Dainetris sample bore the same markers as Vaenetri for compatibility with Sietinen. *That's why they kept her alive! This was the backup genetic line.* Before the Dainetris Dynasty fell, it must have been an even chance of which dynasty match would ultimately produce the Cadicle—leaving the final decision up to the nanoagent directing the resonance connections between individuals. With all but one pairing eliminated, no wonder the Priesthood had gone to such lengths to ensure Kate and Cris ended up together. All the same, the Priesthood couldn't eliminate their only backup; however, they could leave her to live a quiet life ignorant of her birthright.

Banks' heart pounded in his ears. With that magnitude of compatibility, it wouldn't matter if a pairing was one or two generations removed. A union between Dainetris and Sietinen would be too much for the Priesthood to combat—not to mention, the best chance for cracking the genetic anomaly causing the Generation cycle of telekinetic abilities. *That's what the Aesir are after.*

All of that would be lost if Marie never bore a child—she was the only chance of the Dainetris line continuing, and Banks was the only person who had uncovered her lineage, as far as he knew. For her own safety, he couldn't tell her. Moreover, the Priesthood couldn't suspect she knew. Her child must appear to have been born from love, without any motivation for political advancement. *Fok! I can't believe this is happening.*

Hand shaking, Banks opened an encrypted communication to Marie's apartment.

"Hello," she greeted. "What were the results of the analysis?"

"A fine match," he replied. "Two million. I can offer you two million credits in a lump payment, but the child would be grown before we could ever speak again. I'll provide legal documentation of parental lineage, but I can't be involved in your lives." *I'll fabricate a narrative to rival the Priesthood's greatest lies... Perhaps make the father on record a wealthy, childless merchant who fell in love with a nanny while visiting Tararia and decided that life wouldn't be complete without an heir to inherit his business. It's just plausible enough that it might keep the Priesthood from suspecting outside intervention.*

Marie considered the offer in silence. "Meet me at Café Marscel." The call ended.

Heart still racing, Banks moved to the pilot's chair and brought up directions for the café. *Stars! Please forgive me.*

CHAPTER 11

WIL COULDN'T HELP but smile. The practice session had gone exceptionally well.

Everything was coming together. The new telekinetic tethering technique with the ship was working perfectly, and the calibrations were almost complete. Soon, it would be time to run full-scale scenarios with a test fleet. *I need to start working on overall strategy.*

Wil settled into the workstation in his quarters. The corner desk had a touch-surface with an integrated holographic projector, and a viewscreen curved around the two walls above the desk. He brought up the fleet manifest for a more thorough review. *I need to know what I'm working with.* He displayed a written list on the desktop and projected a map of the fleet positions via the holographic display.

The quantity of ships was limited, but workable. However, as Wil dove deeper into the specifications, he was alarmed to see that only half the fleet possessed independent jump drives. *That's going to complicate matters.*

Wil was pulled from his thoughts by the sound of the door opening. He felt Saera's presence. "Hey," he greeted without turning from the workstation.

"Hey." Saera came over and hugged Wil from behind. "Is that the fleet manifest?"

"Yes, it is."

"You don't look happy."

I'm not. "Only half the fleet can make jumps to and from the Rift without a gate."

Saera's brow furrowed. "Wait... I thought the fleet had been retrofitted with your new rift drives?"

"So did I."

"That changes things, doesn't it?"

"I'm just trying to work out by how much."

Saera looked over the manifest. "Is there anything you can do to upgrade the jump drives?"

"Not at this point. They barely have the resources to keep the current fleet intact, let alone make upgrades." Wil pivoted in his chair to face Saera.

She frowned. "So, we're stuck."

"Well, not necessarily."

"What do you have in mind?" Saera leaned against the side of the desk.

"I'm wondering if there's anything we can do to the navigation systems."

"Isn't it the jump drives that generate the subspace distortion field?" his wife asked.

"Yes, but I'm not talking about enabling travel across the planes. Just better communication."

Saera perked up. "How so?"

"If we upgrade the navigation systems on the other ships to interpret location data within the Rift, we could still coordinate battles on both planes. All the ships would be able to track the relative location of TSS and Bakzen vessels, regardless of which plane they're on—and extrapolate trajectories to avoid collisions."

She nodded. "It's not ideal, but it would mitigate many of the logistical challenges."

Wil let out a heavy sigh. "However, one of the reasons for implementing the independent jump drive in the first place was to avoid pinging the navigation beacons, since the Bakzen know how to use that information against us."

"Oh, right..."

Still, there might be a way. "If we could network the

navigation systems to communicate directly with each other without pinging the beacons, it might solve our problems."

Saera considered the suggestion. "I could see that."

"Most importantly, I think it's just a software upgrade."

"Really?"

Hopefully. "Well, I need to run it by someone who knows a little more about the stock SiNavTech systems. Almost all of my work has been with the modified designs."

"Your dad?"

"That's what I was thinking."

Saera smiled. "Let's call him up."

Wil pulled out his handheld from his pocket to contact his father.

Cris picked up right away. "Hi, Wil. I haven't talked to you in a while. How are you?"

"I'm fine. Are you still at H2?"

"Yes, I was just about to grab a shuttle back to the *Vanquish.* What's up?"

"Saera and I were just talking over some potential modifications to the fleet's navigation system. I wanted to get your thoughts."

Cris paused ever so slightly. "Sure, of course."

I know SiNavTech systems aren't his favorite topic, but he knows them better than anyone else here. "Meet us on the *Conquest* in the Strategy Room by the Command Center."

"Okay, see you soon." Cris ended the call.

Wil stood up. "Let's go. I want to put together some mock-ups before he arrives."

The conference room was set up for collaboration. Across the hall from the entrance to the Command Center, it provided a workspace for discussion between officers or for tactical planning with a small group. The oval table was surrounded by eight chairs and touch-viewscreens lined the walls. A holographic projector over the main table and secondary projectors at either end of the room facilitated group strategizing. The screens and touch-surface table illuminated when Saera and Wil entered.

Wil grabbed a stylus clipped next to the viewscreen by the door. "The trick will be to mathematically express the relationship between normal space and subspace. Obviously, it will be a variation on the coding used for the independent jump drives. However, that model only accounts for the movement over the time needed to execute a jump. The navigation systems will need to monitor subspace drift in real-time." He made a few notations on the viewscreen.

Saera nodded. "Can we use a real-time feed from the navigation beacons?"

Perhaps, but not alone. "That would require having a beacon that's close enough for the readings to be accurate."

"Is there any way to extrapolate?"

Wil thought for a minute, running through the options. "It would never be precise enough. To be useful, we need to have accuracy within two meters or less."

Saera contemplated. She gave a little jump of excitement. "Hold on..."

Wil was still deep in his own thoughts, staring at the viewscreen. "Hmm?"

"The rift drive maps the subspace course a moment before the jump, right?" Saera asked.

"Yes."

"So, we need to do a fake jump. In intervals—say, once every five seconds or so."

Wil brought his full attention on her. *That's an interesting thought.* "Go on."

Saera began to pace. "We've always known there was excess processing capacity, so we could put that to use. Every envoy will have at least one ship with a rift drive. That's all it would take."

"That's true," Wil mused. "Each of the nav systems is scaled with the capacity to calculate two jumps at once, because of the need for an emergency abort in subspace. However, that only comes into play during an active jump—most of the time, the secondary system is idle."

"Exactly. We could rig the system to scan subspace in preparation for a jump, but never execute," Saera said triumphantly. "Like a background ping."

"And just disable the ping during a jump when it wouldn't be needed, anyway," Wil concluded. "We could probably even network the nav systems for ships in the area to corroborate data and share the load."

"Sounds reasonable to me."

As usual, she has a brilliantly simple solution. "It's not quite the direction I was originally going, but I think this would be more accurate."

Saera grabbed a stylus from next to another viewscreen. "We'll need to program some background code for the nav systems and rewrite the jump protocol."

"That's easy enough, but the coding for the networking functionality is another story. We could possibly use the existing relay protocol with the navigation beacons for starter code, but based on the number of ships in the area, there will be a variable number of data points to reconcile. That's a whole other protocol." *What a programming nightmare. When am I going to find the time for all this? So much for an easy fix...*

Saera tapped the stylus between her fingers. "Do we need to use data from every available ship, then? What if we placed a cap?"

Wil shook his head, starting to feel overwhelmed. "Inconsequential, from a coding perspective. Even if we capped it at five, the system would still need to know how to handle four if one jumps away. Yes, we could program a separate scenario for each—but with all that effort, we may as well do it correctly. After all, the more ships, the higher the accuracy. The variability is variability, regardless of scale."

"Okay, then that's what we'll do." Saera looked over her notes on the viewscreen. "That means..." She started jotting down a list of required code components.

Wil did the same. He glanced over at Saera's work to make sure they weren't duplicating efforts, and they soon had an outline worked out for the new nav system operations.

They were putting the final touches on the outline when Cris arrived. "Wow, what are you up to?" He looked over the scrawlings on the viewscreens.

"Perfect timing," Wil said as he finished his notes. "We need to reprogram the nav systems for the TSS fleet."

Cris' eyes widened with alarm behind his tinted glasses.

"Come again?"

"Only half the fleet is equipped with rift drives. We need a workaround, and I think we have a serviceable solution." Wil went over the outline of the nav system changes.

His father took it in. "So… what's your question for me?"

"Will it work?"

After a few moments of contemplation, Cris said, "Most of your assumptions about the stock SiNavTech system are correct, but the relay protocol from the navigation beacons won't be of any use for what you're proposing. You may as well just start from scratch."

Great, so even more work. "Anything else?"

"No, the rest of this should integrate fine," Cris replied. "The logic all aligns with the system architecture."

Awesome. So, we have a workable plan, with no time to execute. Wil looked over the outline with open concern.

"I can lead the re-programming," Saera offered.

"Are you sure? This is a lot to take on," Wil said, though he knew full well that she was one of the few people other than himself who understood it well enough to do the work.

She nodded. "Absolutely. You have enough to think about already. Let me help you."

I need to be willing to delegate. He nodded. "That would be great."

Saera smiled. "Then consider it done."

"I'm happy to assist," his father added. "Let me know if you need anything."

"I'm sure I'll have some questions," Saera replied. "I'll reach out as things come up."

"Great. Is that everything for now?" Cris glanced toward the door.

It's late. We've all had long days. "Yes, thanks for sanity checking this for us. Have a good night. Say hi to mom."

"Of course. Good night." Cris left them alone in the conference room.

"Well, I should get to it," Saera said through a sigh.

"It can wait until tomorrow." *We need a break, too.* Wil pulled Saera in for a kiss and she leaned against him. "I want to forget about the war for a night."

Saera grabbed Wil's hand and pulled him toward the door. "I can help with that, too."

CHAPTER 12

BANKS STIFLED A yawn. He checked the clock next to his bed—it was already time to get up and resume his duties as High Commander. *Not yet.*

The last few days had been a blur, and he still felt like his head was in a fog even after returning to Headquarters. Banks' stomach turned over with another wave of doubt. His trip to Tararia had been life-changing, even if those changes weren't directly to his own life. As much as he was driving himself crazy thinking through alternatives, he had already set a plan in motion that could not be retracted. He had committed to the course.

An unwelcome chirp sounded in the bedroom, indicating an incoming communication. *Ugh, it's too early to talk to anyone.* Banks dragged himself out of bed and stumbled to the viewscreen in the adjacent living room. He saw the call was from Taelis in H2. *Shite, bad news at this hour?*

Banks accepted the incoming video call. "Hello, Erik." It took everything for him to return his focus to the TSS.

The viewscreen illuminated with the image of the other High Commander. "Good morning, Jason. I hope I didn't wake you."

Banks pawed at his tousled hair. "No worries. I was just getting up." He cleared his throat. "What's going on?"

Taelis flashed a faint smile. "I thought it might be time to discuss our progress over the last couple of weeks, and the next steps."

"Yes, of course." Banks rubbed his eyes. *Pull yourself together.* Taelis hesitated. "Is this a bad time?"

I can't think about it anymore. She has everything she needs. "No, sorry. Just getting my thoughts organized." Banks got settled on the couch.

"Okay. I trust you've read the most recent briefing?" Taelis asked.

I knew I was forgetting something. "I must apologize. I was traveling the last few days and haven't had the opportunity."

Taelis didn't bother to hide his annoyance. "Traveling? What for?"

Banks swallowed. *This is not business I can share.* "To Tararia. It was a political matter."

"Tararian politics... Always such urgency, and for no reason." Taelis scowled. "Matters of the war must come first. Traveling or not, you have a responsibility to review—"

"Lecturing me won't change the situation."

The other High Commander yielded, "You're right." He shook his head. "I've just been pretty on edge with everything going on."

"I understand." *I'm doing nothing to help—letting myself get distracted by other matters while we have a war to win.* Banks suppressed a wave of guilt. "Cris has been checking in with me every day, so I'm familiar with most of the activities covered in the briefing report. What did you want to discuss?"

Taelis gathered himself. "First off, Medical was able to identify the underlying neurotoxin that was affecting Nolan. They've synthesized a counteragent to distribute within the TSS—we shouldn't have to worry about any other rogue Bakzen accomplices, at least not any working unconsciously."

"That's excellent news."

"Unfortunately, that doesn't help us with the broader population at the moment. We've handed over the formula to the Priesthood to address the impacted civilians."

Banks frowned; it was a powerful weapon to hand over with the assumption it would be used responsibly. *Can we trust the Priesthood with that task?*

"I know what you're thinking," Taelis continued. "It's our

only option for now."

"All right," Banks conceded.

"In other news, we're almost ready to begin field trials with the fleet for the new nav system."

So soon? "That's great to hear."

"The upgrade should be completed within the next few days, and then Wil intends to test it out with his pilots in the training grounds. However, that introduces the matter of jurisdiction."

Banks nodded. "All of the rift jumps."

"Precisely." Taelis crossed his arms. "What are your thoughts?"

"I don't think it's either of our places to claim oversight. That's why we have Wil." *If we want him to lead us, it's time we give him the proper authority.*

"Well yes, his strategic insight and leadership is invaluable."

"Without question. It's the very reason we need to name him Supreme Commander."

Taelis looked unsure. "Now?"

Is there a right time? "We can't keep calling him a leader without the proper title. It's our responsibility to set a chain-of-command example for the rest of the TSS."

"It is," Taelis agreed, "but I think the naming of Supreme Commander would carry more weight as a formal ceremonial gesture. With the necessity to upgrade the nav systems, we're still weeks away from Wil heading to the frontlines. It makes more sense to name him on the eve of that departure."

This was always the plan, but now he's afraid to give up control—as much as he knows he has to rely on Wil. Banks knew better than to press the issue. "You know the state of morale better than I do. I'll defer to your judgment."

Taelis shook his head. "It's not just the morale of the soldiers. I don't want to throw too much at Wil at once."

"He's been expecting it for a long time."

"But while he's still so involved in the minutia of calibrations?" Taelis challenged.

Banks stood his ground. "And much broader issues of fleet distribution, if I understand correctly."

"Yes, some of the strategic groundwork has been laid."

We can't forget what all of this is about. "Official title or not, I'd urge you to show your full support of Wil to the other officers. We need their complete trust, with no hesitation."

"Agreed." Taelis paused in thought. "I recommend gradually handing over control of key functions to Wil over the next few weeks, as he expands his field tests. We can schedule a formal handoff of command to correspond with the conclusion of the exercises."

A fair compromise. "I support that approach."

"Very well. Regarding jurisdiction for the rift jump tests, I move that it be under my purview."

"That's fine." *I have no claim to it, anyway. It's Wil's show now. Taelis will see that soon enough.*

"What about the relocation of battle cruisers?" asked Taelis.

"Matters of the war have always been up to you. I'm here to support all of you in any way you need—I make no claim to jurisdiction."

Taelis nodded. "Thank you for your willingness to accommodate."

"I gave up control as soon as Wil left here."

"Don't think your role in this is over yet."

"I have no such illusions."

Taelis was silent for a few moments. "I'll be in touch about the command hand-off."

"Talk to you soon," Banks said, feigning a friendly smile.

Taelis ended the transmission.

Banks leaned back on the couch. Arguments over jurisdiction were a waste of energy. He had more important things to do—like figure out what other secrets the Priesthood may be keeping from him. For years he'd thought he was an insider, but learning about the hidden Dainetris heir had called into question his underlying assumptions about the Priesthood's relationship with the TSS. With Taelis and Wil leading the charge in the Rift, it was time to do some digging.

—   —   —

"Reporting for duty!"

Laecy jumped up from her desk in the engineering lab at the sound of Nolan's voice, swiveling around to see him grinning at her from the doorway. "They found a cure?"

Her friend nodded. "I'm good as new."

She ran forward to give him a hug. "Thank the stars!"

Nolan patted her back. "Now *please* give me something to work on. My brain has started to go stale from lack of use."

"The timing couldn't be better," Laecy replied, returning to her desk. She gestured toward a holographic projection. "We're working on a patch to the nav network. Some of the older ships require a minor update to prepare for the overall system upgrade."

"Let me guess—it requires manually loading the interim update onto each and every one of those older ships?"

Laecy smirked. "Yep. And I think I know just the guy to go through the fleet of TX-70s…"

Nolan groaned. "Clearly I got out of solitary confinement at the perfect moment."

"Welcome to the land of freedom." Laecy clapped him on the shoulder. "It's good to have you back."

—   —   —

Saera's eyes were bleary after staring at lines of code for days on end. She reviewed the protocol she'd just written. It was solid.

Is that it? She checked the list of components for the navigation system upgrade. The recently completed module was the only outstanding item. "Finally!" She smiled to herself and scratched it off the list.

When Saera stood up, it took a moment for her back and legs to adjust. She did a few stretches, loosening the muscles that had tightened after a week hunched over a computer console. *Glad that part's over! Time to go show off.*

She loaded a copy of the code onto a portable drive for backup and logged out of the computer in one of the H2 conference rooms where she'd been holed up. The location had worked well for bringing in consultants on various aspects of the coding, but she had led the project. She felt a great sense of accomplishment with the work, since it was a tangible contribution to Wil's larger efforts. While she often acted as a sounding board for Wil's ideas, it was rare for her to have the chance to take a leadership role in bringing those concepts to fruition.

The conference room was near the docking location for the *Conquest*, and Saera quickly made her way back to the ship. It was late into the evening, so she headed straight for the residential quarters. The common room was empty. *Everyone must have already turned in for the night.*

She found Wil at the workstation in their quarters. He seemed absorbed in whatever he was reviewing, but he turned around when she entered. "Hey you," he greeted. "How's it coming?"

"Done." Saera grinned.

"Done?" A cautious smile spread across Wil's face.

She nodded. "I've completed all the quality control checks, and every scenario you gave me checked out."

Wil jumped up from the chair and embraced Saera. "Thank you so much. This wouldn't have been possible without you."

She hugged him back. "Oh, please. I'm hardly the only one who could have done it." She pulled away slightly and looked him in the eye. "I'm happy I was able to help."

"Maybe others could have done it, but you're the only one I could trust to do it right without me having to constantly check up."

He never would have given up control before. As if I needed more evidence that he's stressed out. "Well, the final package still needs your approval."

"Let's take a look. I'm anxious to get it in the field."

CHAPTER 13

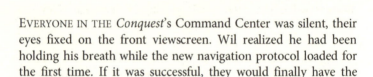

EVERYONE IN THE *Conquest*'s Command Center was silent, their eyes fixed on the front viewscreen. Wil realized he had been holding his breath while the new navigation protocol loaded for the first time. If it was successful, they would finally have the coordination tool they needed to put their advanced tactics into practice.

Saera checked the network connection from her console in the front left of the Command Center. "Network relays appear to be functioning like we planned."

"I'm reading the placement of the fleet across both planes," Rianne confirmed from the station to Saera's right. While only one of the stations needed to be staffed at any given time, Rianne's participation allowed Saera to jump in as relief for one of Wil's other officers, if needed.

"I guess it's time to test it out for real," Wil said, looking around at his officers stationed at their podiums.

"May as well dive in," Michael agreed.

Ian nodded. "Test squads are standing by for your orders."

"Standing by," Ethan acknowledged.

Curtis grinned. "Let's do something fun."

Wil smiled back, encouraged by their enthusiasm. "All right. Saera, take us over to the testing grounds."

A low vibration emanated through the floor as the jump drive powered up. After five seconds, a blue-green haze formed around the ship as it slipped into subspace. Wil soaked in the energy radiating from the Rift as the ship reemerged within a particularly energized spatial pocket used for training pilots. The enhanced potency of the natural energy field made it the perfect place to hone skills that were difficult for beginners.

The testing grounds were arranged like a battlefield, with mock Bakzen ships represented by remote controlled wireframes equipped with dummy weapons and damage indicators. In this case, Wil had instructed that the field be staged in both the Rift and normal space so they could test their skills while he was in a state of simultaneous observation.

Four fighters sped out of the battlefield toward the *Conquest*. Notice of an incoming communication request illuminated on the front viewscreen.

"Answer," Wil instructed.

Tom appeared on the viewscreen, the image relayed from inside his fighter. "It's about time you came for a visit."

"We could hear you whining from all the way back at H2," Ethan quipped. "I hope you've improved even without me hounding you all the time."

"Oh, we're ready," Tom replied with exaggerated arrogance. "The question is, do you have what we need?"

"That's what we're here to find out," Wil told him. "Either way, get set to try something crazy."

—   —   —

Tom ended the subspace comm link with the *Conquest*. The rest of the battle practice would need to be handled via telepathic commands.

Maintaining the telepathic link was far more tiring than normal verbal communication, but its effectiveness couldn't be argued. If the new nav system worked anything like Wil had promised, their maneuverability was about to get a major upgrade.

"Stand by for orders," Ethan told the Primus Squad.

In preparation, Tom and the others arranged their fighters

into the diamond-shaped delta formation off the port side of the
Conquest. Waiting stationary so close to the ship, Tom got a true
sense of scale for the imposing vessel—three hundred meters
long and armed for battle through and through. The custom
band of telekinetic relays around the horizontal circumference of
the ship intrigued Tom the most; focusing energy through a
fighter was one thing, but using an entire cruiser as a conductor
for multiple Agents at the same time would be a sight to behold.

"*Target identified,*" Ethan said, solidifying their telepathic
network in preparation for the mock battle. "*Precision strike on
enemy propulsion. Warship.*"

"*Acknowledged,*" Tom replied. The team avoided the use of
specific target coordinates, since ships could move so quickly
through the planes during battle. Visual identification of a
specific craft was far more reliable until they could lock their
weapons on the craft's unique energy signature. He referenced
the head-up display on his fighter that translated the signals from
the plain blocks on the mock battlefield into a visual
interpretation of enemy craft and obstacles. There was no
warship. "*I don't see it here,*" he said to the other pilots.

"*Must be in normal space,*" Sander stated.

"*Interdimensional jumps are what we're testing, after all,*"
Andy pointed out.

Tom burrowed through his telepathic link with the ship to
bring up the fleet position in normal space, as relayed through
the new navigation protocol. The head-up display morphed to
show the position of rift ships in purple and the ships within
normal space in orange. Sure enough, an orange warship
appeared at a relative position of nine hundred meters at thirty-
degrees to starboard. "*There it is!*"

"*I see what they're testing…*" Ray interjected. "*Look at all those
friendly shuttles.*"

The TSS shuttles were so dwarfed by the signature of the
warship that they'd be easy to miss—tiny orange dots scattered
throughout the most obvious jump zone for transitioning from
the Rift to normal space. Such shuttles didn't have a jump drive,
and with the previous navigation protocols would have been
completely invisible to the Primus Squad when making a

dimensional jump. Though hard to spot, at least their presence was known with the new system.

"Time to dance," Tom said as he readied his jump drive. He visualized the destination within the scattered TSS shuttles— there'd only be five meters of clearance to either side, which was barely outside the spatial distortion from the jump. The placement had to be precise.

"This is a little crazy, right?" Andy said.

Sander laughed maniacally in their minds. *"We thrive on crazy!"* He initiated the jump.

Tom followed as soon as his fighter sent a blue flash across his vision to confirm the course lock. The jump drive hummed as blue-green light swirled around the fighter. He slipped into subspace.

Reality re-formed through the swirling light—objects coming into focus all around Tom, far too close to seem safe. He resisted the urge to panic and abort, trusting the nav system and his instincts. When he fully emerged from subspace, he was right on course. He targeted the mock warship's propulsion system using the head-up display. *"Locked!"* he told his squad when they appeared in their own empty pockets around him.

"Fire!" they declared in unison.

The dummy blasts struck the target, illuminating the target box in red.

"Pull back," Ethan instructed.

Tom jumped back into the Rift and returned to the original position by the *Conquest*. *"I think it's safe to say the new nav system works."*

Wil stepped forward in the telepathic network. *"Good. Now let's see what we can really do."*

— — —

Banks scanned through the web of files displayed on the holographic projector he'd erected in the center of his office. There had to be something he'd been missing all of those years. The Priesthood was involved in something far deeper than the genetic manipulation of the High Dynasties he'd discovered as a green Agent—something that traced back as far as the original conception of the plan to create the Cadicle.

Is it all really about overcoming the ability gap across Generations? That was the only reasonable explanation with far enough reaching impacts to the rest of the Taran population. Otherwise, there would have been no need for the Priesthood to embrace and dismiss telekinetic abilities to suit their priorities at any given time. *But the Priesthood keeps such close tabs on the TSS... What are they watching for?*

He stared at the data repository, hoping that something would jump out at him. *Let's see... Where does the general population interact with the TSS?*

The pieces fell into place. *Of course! Applications.*

Banks dashed over to the visual representation of the corresponding files for application records and accessed the directory. The TSS actively recruited for the Agent division, but every candidate still needed to submit a formal application. The approved applications were always forwarded to him—there was never a reason to examine the original source files under normal circumstances.

At first glance, all the files seemed to be in order. Each of the directories for the individual application cycles was organized by Accepted, Review-Rejected, and Auto-Reject. The Auto-Reject saved time by eliminating anyone with an unfavorable performance history based on predetermined factors. Banks was about to skip over the files entirely, but he noticed the unusually large folder size—a factor of five above the Review-Rejected and Accepted, even though it should have been the smallest, by far.

He picked a random year and opened up the profiles of the rejected candidates. Almost every single candidate was a woman. *That doesn't make any sense.*

Closing out of the directory, he opened up the Auto-Reject files from another year. Again, almost entirely women. It was the same for every other year he checked.

The evidence was clear: at least seventy percent of the female Agent applicants had received an auto-rejection without any review.

He sank onto the couch. *Why would they dismiss all of those candidates?* There was no innate reason to choose men over women. Certainly, there were far fewer women enrolled as Agents, but based on the application records, it should have been close to an even split.

Has the Priesthood intentionally been keeping women out of the TSS? Banks dismissed the idea. If that were the case, none would have ever been admitted. There had to be something more.

Suddenly, the big picture came into focus—the relationship between the Priesthood and the rest of the Tarans. It wasn't that they had been keeping women out of the TSS, but rather were keeping them in the general population.

Banks shook his head with disbelief. It had been right in front of him for years, a conversation he'd had with numerous Agents, including Cris as a young man. Agents rarely entered into enduring relationships—few marriages and even fewer children. If all the people with strong telekinetic propensity ended up in an organization where few would reproduce, the telekinetic potential in the broader population would greatly diminish after only a few generations. By keeping at least the women out of the TSS—those who would ultimately birth a child, regardless of the father—the chance of continuing the propagation of telekinetic-potential lines was greatly increased.

What about those that do make it into the TSS? Banks brought up the files of Kate, Saera, and a handful of other female Agents that came to mind. With the exception of Saera, absolutely every one of the others had a sister who was not in the TSS.

He let out a short laugh of disbelief. *How did I miss this before?*

A chill set in as the initial shock wore off. The Priesthood's involvement in the affairs of the TSS stretched into depths he didn't even know existed. If they would go to such extremes to keep mothers for future telekinetic children out in the reproducing population, did it go any deeper?

"CACI, take a random sampling of twenty female candidates from the Auto-Reject category over the past ten years. Display current whereabouts and familial statistics."

"Searching," the computer replied, the viewscreen on the wall of Banks' office transitioning to a placeholder for the search results. "Three of the selected candidates have no known current whereabouts," CACI reported, displaying the seventeen other records.

"For those with missing records, are they deceased?" Banks tried to clarify.

"No death certificates are on file. Current address is unknown."

So where did they go? Banks had no idea where to begin his search, but after what he'd just discovered, he had no doubt the Priesthood was involved.

CHAPTER 14

"ALL RIGHT, PRIMUS Squad, move into position. Prepare for a dimensional jump on my mark," Wil ordered, holding the three planes in his mind. Around him, his officers were telepathically linked, seeing Wil's visualizations through the *Conquest's* interface.

"Primus Squad in position," Ethan confirmed, both out loud and in Wil's mind.

Wil focused on the Rift in his visualization of the planes. Suspended at a distant vantage, he watched the mock Bakzen ships darting around the TSS targets. Two squadrons of enemy fighters were en route to the simulated TSS base.

"They're going to emerge any second," he relayed to Ethan. *"Hold your position... Jump, now!"*

In an instant, the Primus Squad passed through the dimensional veil and opened fire on the Bakzen fighters. Caught off-guard, the Bakzen fighters broke formation. The second wave of TSS forces was waiting. The team relayed their precision commands, quickly eliminating the final Bakzen ships.

"End simulation," instructed Wil. He withdrew from the state of simultaneous observation.

Everyone removed their hands from the interface podiums.

"I may be speaking too soon, but I think we have the hang of this," Ian commented.

"We do," Wil agreed. "Rianne, take us back to H2."

"Aye," she acknowledged.

The two weeks of practice had certainly paid off. Commands and reactions were seamless, and every member of the team trusted the others. All that remained was putting their skills to the test in a real battle setting.

I hope we can hold it together when it's not just pretend anymore. Wil focused on the satisfied expressions of those around him—so much optimism and eagerness. With any luck, there would be enough to carry them through to the end.

The *Conquest* completed the short jump from the training area to H2 and docked in its reserved berth connected to the central ring of the massive space station.

Wil stretched his arms and back as soon as the docking clamps locked onto the hull. "Good work today, everyone."

"Same drill tomorrow?" Michael asked.

"I think we're now to the point that it would just be more of the same. I'll send you a message later once I figure out how to proceed."

His friend inclined his head in acknowledgement and exited the Command Center with the other officers.

Saera hung back with Wil. "There's nothing more to practice."

"No, there really isn't." He held out his arm, and she came toward him for a hug. "It's been so much anticipation—"

"We'll all do just as well with the real thing," Saera assured him. "Come on, let's go get some rest."

They secured the Command Center and headed toward their quarters. As they neared the door, Wil's handheld buzzed. There was a text message from High Commander Taelis: >>Meet me in my office.<<

Wil groaned and showed the message to his wife. "Sorry. Hopefully, this won't take long."

"See you soon."

The trek from the *Conquest* to the High Commander's office was frustratingly long due to the scale of H2. *Why can't he ever come to me?* When Wil finally arrived, he found Taelis was seated behind his desk.

"Hello, Wil."

"Sir, what can I do for you?" Wil took a seat across from the High Commander, thankful to be in a chair where he could recline a little to rest his back.

"Your reports over the last couple of weeks look promising."

"Yes, we've made good progress. The new interface works just like we wanted."

Taelis paused in thought. "What more do you need?"

"Nothing," Wil admitted. "We're ready." He had to force the words, knowing what came next.

"Then I'll make the final preparations. You'll move to the frontlines next week."

"Well, there is one more thing."

The High Commander tilted his head with expectation.

"I'd like my men to officially graduate. They need to hold the proper authority over the veterans."

Taelis nodded. "We can do that."

"Are the facilities here sufficient?" Wil asked.

"We'll need to borrow the testing sphere from the main Headquarters, but our simulation chamber has all the necessary measurement capabilities."

"Good, so it won't be too disruptive."

The High Commander folded his hands on the desktop. "Testing that many in rapid succession will be a logistical challenge, but we'll make it work."

"Thank you, sir."

"I'm not your superior, you know," Taelis said after a moment. "The 'sir' is unnecessary."

"I didn't want to be too informal or impolite," Wil replied.

"Wil, you're in charge now. You can call me whatever you'd like."

"Okay." *He might not like some of the nicknames that have occurred to me over the years.*

"You did very well with them—the Elites," Taelis continued. "They're fine officers."

"They are."

"I appreciate everything you're doing for us."

Wil shrugged. "It's my job."

"But you do whatever needs to be done without hesitation.

That's the mark of a true leader."

"I'm glad you think so."

Taelis pushed back from his desk. "Anyway, I'll see to it that we have an official graduation for your men before you all head to the frontlines. Relay your strategic preparation needs to me."

"I will, thank you." Wil rose.

"Good luck."

—   —   —

"I'm glad to hear everything is going well," Banks told the other High Commander over the viewscreen. Hearing promising reports from the Rift was one positive after his own unsettling discoveries of late.

Taelis nodded. "So well, in fact, that Wil has requested a formal graduation for his officers."

"I don't disagree with his sentiment. I think it would send a strong message."

"I concur. I've made arrangements for a make-shift CR test using one of the spatial awareness chambers."

Banks nodded. "Excellent." *I'm curious how they'll score. After the surprise with Saera, I can only imagine their abilities have been elevated, as well, after spending so much time with Wil.*

"The only equipment that we can't readily provide is the testing sphere," Taelis continued.

"The most important part."

"It's nice to know the other benchmarks, but you're right—that straight measure of raw power is what we really want to know."

"I'll make arrangements to have it sent over right away," Banks told the other High Commander. "I'll come later for the graduation. It's a good opportunity to tend to some other overdue administrative business."

"The matter of command?" Taelis asked.

"Indeed. It's a fitting occasion." Banks paused, the end of the conversation in sight. He didn't want to let another opportunity slip by. "Erik, if you have a moment, there is something else we should discuss."

Taelis tilted his head. "Yes?"

"What do you know about the TSS application procedure?" Banks asked.

The other High Commander raised his eyebrows with surprise. "Not very much, to be honest. That's your domain."

"Well, apparently, I know far less about it than I realized."

"What do you mean?"

Banks took a deep breath. "A large percentage of Agent applicants have received an auto-rejection."

Taelis frowned. "With our staffing so tight? There has to be a mistake. We've needed every person we could possibly get."

"My thinking, as well," Banks said. "I've completed a thorough investigation, and I can draw no conclusion other than that the Priesthood has been intentionally keeping otherwise excellent female candidates out of the TSS with the express purpose of maintaining a higher reproductive pool of those with telekinetic abilities in the general population."

"That's completely crazy!"

"Is it, though? We both know the lengths the Priesthood goes to achieve their ends—even if we don't know what goal they are working toward."

"Just because someone doesn't express abilities in a given generation, that doesn't mean their line has lost the abilities. Only Generations 8 through 12—"

"Of course," Banks cut in. "But we also know that the abilities have completely faded from some lines. Someone expressing active abilities is the only clear indication that a line is still viable—no other genetic test is reliable during the dormant stages."

Taelis considered the position. "You have evidence of these candidate rejections?"

"Years' worth, back to well before I was High Commander."

"Then my advice to you is to forget you ever saw those files," Taelis cautioned. "No individual is in any position to stand up to the Priesthood. They have their reasons, I'm sure. Leave well enough alone."

"How can you say that? They've been keeping people from

you that could have turned the tide in the war long ago."

Taelis shook his head. "That's in the past. Now we have Wil and the war will end either way. You have to look out for your own well-being."

"This can't continue!"

"The Priesthood will continue on in whatever foking manner they want. Let it go, Jason."

Banks stared at the side wall and tried to keep his inner frustration from boiling over. *I shouldn't have expected any other reaction from him.*

"No talk of this while you're in H2, understood?" Taelis said. "The Agents have enough to worry about here."

"This stays between us," Banks agreed.

Taelis nodded. "I'll see you soon."

Banks ended the transmission and disabled the jammers that prevented the Priesthood from listening in on his private calls. Now more than ever, he couldn't be too careful.

—   —   —

For being a rushed exercise, the CR testing of the Primus Elites had gone quite smoothly, as far as Wil was concerned. One of the spatial awareness chambers in H2 had been equipped with the necessary holographic projectors and sensors for the main test, and the sphere from his home Headquarters had been brought over for the definitive strength assessments. It had taken two days, but all the examinations were finally complete and the results synthesized.

Wil examined his men's aggregated scores on the viewscreen in the observation room, and he couldn't be more proud of the results. He beamed at Saera. "All above 9.0. It's hard to believe."

"You really do have an effect on people," his wife replied after completing her own review of the results. "But they always were supposed to be the strongest."

"Not nearly as strong as you."

Saera flushed. "Well, I'm bonded to you. I'm sure that had more impact than just spending a lot of time with you."

It's strange to think that just being in my presence could change how someone else's abilities are expressed. "Either way, they've all justified placement in senior officer positions."

"Without a doubt."

The door to the observation room slid open. Taelis entered.

"Hello," Wil greeted. "The testing is complete."

"I just finished going over the results in my office. Impressive," the High Commander replied.

"I'll sign off on whatever documents are required to make the graduation official," Wil said.

Taelis nodded. "Yes, my assistant is working on that now. No need to avoid all the formalities, though—we have arranged for a brief ceremony."

Wil's eyes narrowed behind his tinted glasses. "I appreciate the gesture, but is that really the best use of resources?"

"It isn't just for them. Don't forget the morale component," Taelis countered.

"I won't argue that," Wil yielded. "But when? We're heading to the frontlines in the morning."

"Now," Taelis revealed. "We were just awaiting the final results. Come with me."

Wil tried to shake off his shock. "Where?"

"The main mess hall. This way." Taelis set off into the hallway.

Saera flashed Wil a look of surprise, and they followed the High Commander.

The mess hall was in the second ring from the bottom of H2, above the hangar. To Wil's relief, it was clear from the moment he walked through the door that little time had been allocated to preparing for the event. The rows of tables and benches were still in place, but a podium had been placed near the right wall of the room. Crowds of soldiers were filing into the room and taking seats at benches built into the tables, all facing the podium. Behind the tables, equipment was set up for what appeared to be a live video feed.

Why would they broadcast this graduation? Is it for back at Headquarters? Wil was about to ask Taelis, but he was distracted by the Primus Elites, still dressed in dark blue, waving at him from the front benches. To his surprise, he noticed that High Commander Banks was seated with them. "Banks came all the way here?"

"We thought it fitting," Taelis responded. "Please, take a seat up front."

I don't think this is just a graduation... Wil realized. He took Saera's hand and followed Taelis toward open seats in the front row facing the podium.

"Hi, I didn't expect to see you," Wil said to Banks as they passed.

Banks smiled back. "This was well worth the trip."

Wil and Saera sat down in the two open spaces at the center of the front row, with half the Primus Elites to either side.

Michael, next to Wil, was examining everyone like there was about to be some major revelation. "Why are we here?"

"Impromptu graduation ceremony, I think," Wil replied.

"Attended by this many senior officers?" Michael asked. "Either we're way more special than I thought, or there's something else going on."

The speculation was cut short as Taelis moved into position behind the podium. All attendees in the room immediately ceased their conversations and gave the High Commander their full attention.

"Thank you all for joining us on such short notice," Taelis began. "For as long as any of us can remember, we have been at war. Generations before us fought the Bakzen, and there has never been an end in sight. All of that changes tomorrow. The Cadicle—our first Primus Elite Agent—will move to the frontlines and finally bring an end to the fighting. We need to rally for this one final push, and then we will have peace.

"For the last five years, a group of twenty officers have trained under the Primus Elite designation. Today, every one of them graduates with a CR above 9.0—an achievement unrivaled by any previous cohort. Under the Cadicle's leadership, this group, combined with our veteran forces, will make the TSS unstoppable. We *will* defeat the Bakzen, and the victory will be swift."

Taelis took a step to the side, and Banks rose to join him.

"As the war comes to an end, the TSS needs to be united," Banks declared. "For years, we have had a divide between the Headquarters in Earth's moon and the Jotun division here in the Rift. With two High Commanders bearing equal authority, we have never been able to act as one."

Wil tensed in his chair. *This is it…*

"So," Taelis continued, "we will now declare a Supreme Commander of the TSS: Williame Sietinen."

Even though he had braced for the announcement, Wil's heart leaped. He'd been acting in a leadership role for years, but somehow the new title made it more real. *Everyone is looking to me. I need to end the war.*

After a moment, Wil realized that the two High Commanders were staring at him expectantly. He got up to join them by the podium, his heart pounding in his ears.

"Wil, do you accept the position as Supreme Commander and the responsibilities it entails?" Taelis asked.

I have no choice. "Yes, I do."

"Will you lead the TSS to the best of your ability until we are no longer at war?"

"Yes, I will," Wil stated. *Or until I die in the process of trying.*

"I grant you command of the TSS forces under my jurisdiction in the Jotun division," Taelis declared.

"I grant you command of the TSS forces under my jurisdiction throughout the Taran colonies," Banks echoed. "With this transfer of authority, you are now Supreme Commander of the TSS. We await your instruction."

Wil wished he could shrink back from the hundreds of eyes watching him from within the room and the thousands more certainly viewing the events over the video feed. *Of course it wasn't just going to be a graduation. But that's why they called me here, so that's what I'm going to do.* Suppressing his nerves, he stepped up to the podium. "Thank you for placing your trust in me. However, I wouldn't be here without the support of my colleagues, my wife, and my parents. We have always faced past trials together, and so we will again as we embark on the most challenging battles of them all.

"I would like to take a moment to acknowledge the graduates

today. Not only were their scores unprecedented, but they completed the training program in just five years. I am honored to have had the chance to train with them, and I am confident that they will serve as fine officers in the coming battles. I ask that you trust each of them just as you place your trust in me. Thank you." Wil took a step back from the podium, and Banks inclined his head with approval.

Applause spread throughout the room, initiated by the Primus Elites. Wil motioned for his trainees to join him up front.

Some of the men shook their heads bashfully at first, but the Captains took the initiative to heed Wil's direction and the others followed. The applause swelled as the young men lined up along the wall.

Banks and Taelis moved to the left of the line and began working their way to the right, shaking each Primus Elite's hand in turn with various expressions of "Congratulations."

When they were finished, Wil returned to the podium. "Thank you for your time. I look forward to joining the frontlines in the morning."

The clapping ceased almost at once as the attendees filed out of the room.

Wil took a deep breath. *Tomorrow is the big day.*

"So, what are our scores?" Ian asked as soon as the spectators were gone.

"They ranged from 9.0 to 9.3," Wil replied. "I'll send your individual results to your handhelds. I'd caution you to avoid direct comparison—each of you know the others' strengths far more than this test captures. Rely on your history together."

"We will, *Supreme Commander*," Curtis said.

Wil cracked a smile. "Hey, now, I didn't pick the title."

" 'Almighty Supremely Awesome One' is more like it," Ethan joked.

"One Commander to Rule Them All," Saera added, to which Michael laughed.

"All right, all right," Wil cut in when he noticed a growing expression of horror on Taelis' normally impassive face. "You're Agents now—the image of poise and dignity."

Ian grinned. "Uh, I think we may have skipped over that part on our accelerated timeline."

"Bomax! I knew I missed something," Wil jested back.

Just outside the group, Taelis crossed his arms. Next to him, Banks observed the antics with reserved amusement.

"All right, let's head back to the *Conquest* for the night," Wil suggested. "Get in a little relaxation before we get down to business."

There were enthusiastic nods and cheers all around.

"Go ahead. I'll be there soon," Wil told them before turning his attention to the High Commanders. Saera accompanied the Primus Elites toward the ship.

As Wil approached, Taelis uncrossed his arms. "They treat you like one of them."

"The best friends I could ever hope for," Wil replied. "They're serious when it matters."

"We're counting on you," Taelis said.

"We'll deliver," Wil assured him, then focused on Banks. "Are you sticking around?"

"No, I was just here to hand over command. I'll be back at Headquarters—the facility is short-staffed enough as it is."

Wil nodded. "I appreciate you coming. I know it must have meant a lot to the Elites to see you here."

"Yes, I wouldn't want to let them down," Banks said, but Wil sensed the unspoken meaning to the words—that Banks didn't want to let Wil down, and that he never would.

"Thank you," Wil replied to the hidden statement.

"Now," Banks continued, "I believe you have some celebrating to do."

CHAPTER 15

MORNING CAME TOO swiftly for Wil's liking. The afterglow of the night's festivities faded as he and Saera approached the Command Center of the *Conquest* to report for duty. No more practicing, no more margin for error—his commands would be binding and the results permanent.

"Good morning," he greeted the other officers, who were already at their posts. Each of the Primus Elites wore new black uniforms.

"Good morning," Michael replied. "All systems check out. We're ready to head out on your order."

Wil took his seat in the center of the room while Saera situated herself at the front control console next to Rianne. He gripped the handholds on his podium to access the scan results for verification, as was his obligation as captain. Everything looked good in his secondary review. "Okay, this is it. Any final comments before we head out?" he asked his friends.

"'Go team?'" Ian suggested.

"Works for me," Michael agreed.

I hope they'll always be able to find the light side of a situation. "All right, then. Go team!" Wil rallied.

"Go team!" the crew repeated in unison.

"Now, our first task will be to disrupt the Bakzen supply line through the transit corridor near Scilla. Do we have the go-ahead from the *Vanquish* and *Nova*?" he asked.

"Yes," Rianne confirmed, "the *Vanquish* and *Nova* are standing by, along with the complement of tactical attack vessels under their commands."

Wil took a moment to let the battle scenario play out in his head. His father on the *Vanquish* and Lead Agent Ramsen on the *Nova* would be important backup firepower if the rest of the fleet got into trouble. It would be best to have them hang back to catch the Bakzen by surprise. "Have them accompany us to the remote observation site at Scilla II."

"Aye," Curtis acknowledged.

"Saera, prepare to jump," Wil ordered, getting to business. "Ethan, have the Primus Squad wait near Scilla IV."

Ethan's eyes became distant as he relayed the telepathic command.

"The jump path is laid in," Saera announced.

Wil took a deep breath. "Let's go."

The *Conquest* was enveloped by the shifting blue-green shroud of subspace. The ship floated in the ethereal light for nearly a minute before dropping back into the echoed starscape of the Rift.

Next to the ship, the gravity signature of an orange planet formed a mirage in the blackness of space. The *Vanquish* and *Nova* appeared from subspace just beyond the gravity well of the planet.

"Bring up the map of the corridor," Wil instructed Rianne.

A holographic map appeared around the front of the domed viewscreen, illustrating the beacon network connecting three planets with Bakzen territory. Just beyond the Defense Barrier, a Bakzen-controlled outpost was illuminated in red.

"This supply outpost is one of five gateways into Bakzen territory," Wil stated. "It's their most direct link to the ore mines in the Utan Belt."

"Eliminate the outpost, slow the supply?" Michael filled in.

"And, eventually, cut it off entirely," Wil confirmed. "Now, two of our cruisers and a carrier are already waiting here to jump in for a surprise attack," he pointed to the edge of the mining zone in the Utan Belt. "I'll observe the setup of the Bakzen defenses, and then the first wave of TSS forces will jump in. Once the Bakzen are engaged, the *Vanquish* and *Nova* will jump in to draw fire while the Primus Squad takes out the target."

"Understood," Michael acknowledged.

Wil gripped the handhold on his podium. "Prepare to relay commands to the attack units." The other Primus Elites scattered throughout the fleet would make sure any orders were executed correctly.

The *Conquest*'s officers took their own handholds to establish the telepathic network.

Clearing his mind, Wil used the ship as an anchor while he slipped into a state of simultaneous observation—reaching out through the Rift to his remote vantage of the surrounding space. He floated in the nothingness, waiting for the planes to come into focus. Then, he saw himself on the *Conquest*, and the other ships nearby. He zoomed outward past the edge of the star system, passing by the waiting Primus Squad.

There it was: the Bakzen outpost. A shield surrounded the enormous storage complex on the surface of an asteroid, and a transport ship was off-loading ore onto a conveyor that carried the material down to boxy, prefabricated structures beneath the shield. The facility would have made for an easy target if there weren't four battlecruisers, a warship, and sixty combat fighters circling the asteroid.

Fok, this is more than we've practiced taking on in training. Except, in training he hadn't had access to the full resources of the TSS fleet. He pulled back into his physical self. "Change of plan."

—   —   —

Cris stared back, dumbfounded, at the image of his son on the front viewscreen in the *Vanquish*'s Command Center. "You want us to do *what*?"

There had never been a doubt in Cris' mind that the *Vanquish* would participate in its share of battles in the final stretch of the war. After all, it was the flagship for the main Headquarters and was equipped with the latest weapons and jump drive systems. However, Wil's first official orders as Supreme Commander caught Cris completely off-guard.

"Jump in between two of the Bakzen cruisers. Seriously?" Cris clarified.

"I can relay the exact jump coordinates and timing," Wil said confidently. "The *Vanquish* can withstand the bombardment—it'll be distracting for the Bakzen, and totally unexpected."

Unexpected all right. "I'm beginning to think we should have practiced with you."

"We don't have impact ratings for the Bakzen weapons," Kate protested from the First Officer's chair next to Cris.

"The *Vanquish* is the same design as the *Nova*, and that ship has faced the Bakzen plenty of times," Wil countered. "You have your orders."

He wouldn't put us—his own parents—at risk, so he must be sure. At least, I don't think he would... "All right," Cris yielded. "We're standing by to jump on your mark."

Cris sensed a consciousness reaching out to his mind. *"This is Michael,"* a voice said. *"Telepathically link to your pilot and jump on my order. The timing must be precise."*

"Understood," Cris acknowledged.

"They want us to telepathically network," Cris explained aloud to the Command Center crew. "I'll serve as a hub and keep Kari in the loop."

"This'll be interesting," Alec commented from the pilot's console.

"I'll relay orders to Matt in Engineering, if necessary," Kate offered. "You'll have enough to keep track of with us and communications with the *Conquest*."

"Okay, here we go." Cris opened his mind to the telepathic feed from Michael. For the first few moments, he saw only blackness, with a background hum of potential energy. Then, a panoramic image came into view.

The scene was blurry, like a video run through too many filters. However, the key objects were all visible and fully realized in three-dimensions. Cris could navigate through the image with the slightest thought. He took in the scene, noting four cruisers, a warship, and more fighters than he could readily count. Two of the cruisers were situated in such a way that the *Vanquish* could fit in between them and have a direct line of fire to the warship's propulsion system. *That must be our opening.*

"*Yes,*" Michael replied, though Cris hadn't meant to share the thought. Apparently nothing was hidden within the mental network.

"*Do you see the destination?*" Cris asked Alec.

"*Yes, but I can't calculate the jump coordinates based on this image alone,*" the pilot replied.

"*I'll give the coordinates when it's time,*" Michael assured him. "*Stand by.*"

"*Jump drive is primed,*" Alec confirmed.

Cris waited in silence, trying to keep his mind free of random thoughts to avoid any unnecessary distractions to his crew or the officers on the *Conquest*. The images of the battlefield relayed from Michael ceased while the Primus Elites concentrated on the remaining preparations.

Minutes passed. Cris shifted in his chair, anxious for the fight to begin. He found himself fatiguing as he tried to remain engaged but clear-headed at the same time.

Suddenly, a clear visualization of the battle returned. A series of commands filled Cris' mind—images more than specific words. Before he had fully processed the instructions, the *Vanquish* was executing a jump.

The ship slipped into subspace, bathed in light while the blue-green sea moved around it. All sense of peace shattered as the ship returned to the physical surroundings of normal space. The *Vanquish* was wedged between two of the Bakzen cruisers, with less than a dozen meters of clearance to either side. In front of them, the warship was an easy target.

"Fire!" Cris ordered, both aloud and in the crew members' minds.

— — —

Wil was tempted to watch the *Vanquish* rip apart the Bakzen warship, but there was the rest of the battle left to fight.

He extended his consciousness outward to take in the cross-section of the space around him, then called the Rift into focus. Bakzen fighters were darting between the planes, just as he'd predicted.

"Send the Nova *into the Rift,"* he instructed Michael.

The *Nova* appeared in the Rift at the relayed jump coordinates in a flanking position relative to the *Vanquish*'s place in normal space. Never before had the TSS been able to so perfectly align their fleet across both planes, to match their enemy's maneuvers. The Bakzen fighters would be under fire no matter where they ran.

Within a minute, the four Bakzen cruisers and the warship were fully engaged with the TSS onslaught, leaving the facility on the asteroid in normal space comparatively exposed.

"Take out the transport ship!" Wil ordered Ethan and his Primus Squad pilots. The TSS could use the facility if they could capture it with minimal structural damage.

"On the way!" Ethan acknowledged, his excitement radiating through the telepathic bond.

All the hard work and practice was finally coming together in one coordinated assault. The hunt was on, and it was nothing short of thrilling.

— — —

"Game time," Tom said to his Primus pilot comrades as he pulled out from their waiting place behind Scilla IV. His pulse raced with anticipation. It was their first real fight—no safety net like in the simulations.

He had a clear visualization of the battlefield—relayed from Ethan—but there were too many moving units, enemy and friendly, to track. Jumping into the center of the action was doable, but not without risk. He studied the images playing through his mind.

"We need to move," Ray urged.

"I'm looking for the right opening." Then, Tom spotted where they should go—a small pocket of open space between the main

action and the edge of the shield around the asteroid. He sent a mental image of the location to his comrades.

"Got it," they confirmed in unison.

The IT-1 fighter purred in response to his telepathic commands, charging the jump drive with an instantaneous thought. In unison, the four fighters winked through subspace and reemerged just at the edge of the battle raging in normal space.

A TSS cruiser—which Tom recognized as the *Vanquish*—was bombarding a Bakzen warship and four enemy cruisers in close quarters. The jump drives of the Bakzen vessels appeared to be damaged, based on his quick assessment of the scorch marks, but there wasn't time to take it all in.

"You heard Wil, take out the transport!" Tom rallied the other pilots.

They looped around from their forward flight path toward the shield surrounding the facility on the asteroid, arcing up toward the transport ship at an impossible angle for any other craft. As they came to the relative vertical, Tom opened fire on the connection point between the conveyor and the transport ship. The end of the fragile column shattered instantly, causing the boxy transport ship to rock until the stabilizers compensated. As the ship drifted away from the asteroid, it became a prime target for the Primus Squad to destroy, with no risk of damaging the rest of the facility on the asteroid.

Following Tom's lead, the four fighters first unleashed a barrage of energy charges to disable the vessel's propulsion. Since it was caught mid-materials transfer, the transport ship's shield wasn't deployed, and the blasts hit the engines hard and true. The rear of the ship exploded under the fighters' fire.

A dozen of the nearby Bakzen fighters immediately changed course toward the Primus Squad after the explosion, launching globs of Detno toward the IT-1s.

The Primus Squad rolled to avoid the explosive goop.

Tom's fighter shuddered as the Detno exploded in open space behind him. *"Now, another pass at the transport ship. Make it count,"* he told his friends.

With trained precision, they released a second round of blasts along the key structural points of the Bakzen transport ship, buckling the hull. The ship depressurized in a brief explosion.

The Bakzen fighters released their own energy weapon charges and another volley of Detno in retaliation for their destroyed asset, but the Primus Squad was too quick.

Tom and the other Primus pilots jumped to subspace. While in transition, he initiated the IT-1 fighter's trademark right-angle turn. *I bet they haven't seen it done like this.* Before the enemy knew what happened, they'd be in his sights.

—   —   —

Wil watched as the Primus fighters completed their seemingly impossible right-angle turn mid-jump. The Bakzen fighters' assaults met only empty space.

Without any time for the Bakzen ships to reorient, the Primus fighters appeared behind them and opened fire on the entire Bakzen assault line. The shields staved off the initial blasts, but it was too much, too fast for the enemy vessels to counter.

"Finish them off," Wil instructed Curtis, who relayed tactical orders to the TSS support ships based on his perception of the battle.

Wil held the precise battlefield movements across both the planes in his mind, relaying the visualization through the ship for his officers to observe. Their plan was working.

The Bakzen warship finally buckled under the relentless blasts from the TSS contingent, but the rest of the Bakzen were still fighting strong.

At the edge of his consciousness, Wil detected another Bakzen ship in the Rift—heading straight for the *Vanquish.* *"Jump!"* he instructed his father, only a moment before imminent impact.

The *Vanquish* faded into a blue-green cloud just as the new Bakzen ship appeared behind the TSS ship's former location, opening fire along its intended suicide course. Except, with the *Vanquish* gone, the Bakzen ship was now heading straight for one of the other Bakzen cruisers. The new ship initiated a jump away, but its weapons barrage had already been sent.

Blasts erupted along the length of the other Bakzen cruiser, breaking through the already compromised shields. Flames fanned out briefly from the breaches while the atmosphere vented, but soon the fire extinguished in the vacuum.

Wil waited for the new Bakzen ship to reemerge and then relayed jump coordinates to the *Vanquish*. The TSS flagship appeared behind the enemy vessel and launched a volley of hull-piercing missiles.

Almost there... Wil brought a broader view of the battlefield into focus for his officers to assess the enemy positions.

On Michael's order, the *Nova* and other TSS support vessels surrounded the remaining Bakzen forces. Within moments, the Bakzen ships were reduced to scrap floating through the vast battlefield.

Next to the ships, the ore processing facility on the surface of the asteroid appeared to be intact. Without a doubt, the extra materials would come in handy for fleet repairs after the coming battles. For once, the TSS salvage crew would receive good news.

Wil took a deep breath, overwhelmed with relief. *We did it!* "Damage report."

Rianne projected battle statistics aggregated from the other ships' reports. "Two fighters from the *Nova*'s complement were destroyed by Detno, but otherwise only minor damage," she concluded.

"Not too bad," Wil said. *Except there was a person in each of those fighters, not just a computer simulation like in practice.* "Good job, everyone. First battle down—and a solid victory."

"We just have to do that a few dozen more times and we'll be done," Ian grinned.

"The Bakzen won't make it that easy for us," Wil cautioned. *But that did go well. We really can do this.*

"What are your orders?" Saera asked from the front station.

Wil took in the vast map of their enemy's strongholds. "Now we plan our next battle."

CHAPTER 16

"IT'S TIME WE go after something bigger," Wil commented after studying the map of their progress. With four skirmishes down, he was confident in his team's ability to perform. They may as well try to gain more ground while they were still comparatively fresh. It would only become more difficult from there on out.

"But what?" Michael asked.

"A planet," Wil replied. "Specifically, Raenor." He projected a map on the domed viewscreen for illustrative purposes.

The planet was situated at the edge of the Kaldern sector, deep into what had become Bakzen territory. Before its capture, Raenor had served as a major trade post for the Outer Colonies, and it would offer an advantageous staging ground for TSS forces in the push toward the Bakzen homeworld.

His Captains, Saera, and Rianne assessed the map.

"That's definitely a bigger target, all right," Saera said on behalf of the group.

Ian raised an eyebrow. "Are we ready for that?"

"I don't see why not. We'll need more ships than we've brought to previous skirmishes, but the principles are the same," Wil replied. "Besides, we went over plenty of planetary captures in practice."

"Yeah, but those were fought against red dots, not people..." Ethan said.

Wil couldn't let that reality hold them back. "It's no different than what we've done over the last few days. Fortunately, the planet is fully Bakzen, so we don't have to worry about civilians."

"What about Bakzen civilians?" Curtis ventured.

I guess we never stopped to think if there was such a thing. Regardless, the Aesir said total elimination—no exceptions. "All Bakzen are the enemy."

The officers nodded with grim understanding.

"Now," Wil returned his attention to the map, "let's plan out our strategy."

They spent the next three hours going over various approaches to the attack. With such a large surface area to cover and numerous blind spots, their telepathic coordination and simultaneous observation would be more important than ever. In the end, they decided that eight cruisers, three battleships, and a carrier with one-hundred-twenty combat fighters would be sufficient to capture the planet while not drawing too many defensive units away from other TSS-controlled sites.

The more positions we win, the more we'll have to defend, Wil realized. Resources might be even tighter by the end.

With the plan set, Wil's officers went about making the necessary communications to the other Primus Elites and their contacts throughout the fleet.

While they worked, Wil scoped out the planet through simultaneous observation, making note of potential obstacles. Only a single space station was in geosynchronous orbit of the planet, situated above the largest city—which, to Wil's eye, was little more than a small town. Two Bakzen cruisers were on patrol in orbit, though more ships would certainly come as soon as the Bakzen realized they were under attack. The planetary shield appeared to be the original Taran model from before the planet's capture, powered by five generators situated at equidistant points around the planet's circumference. It was a challenging target, but Wil was confident they could bring down the shield and level the city before too many enemy reinforcements arrived.

Should we really destroy it all? He dismissed the thought. The Bakzen had firebombed the original Taran colony when they captured the planet, so all current structures were of purely

Bakzen design. Based on what he'd seen of Bakzen facilities as a teenager, there was nothing worth salvaging.

After an hour, all members of the attack fleet had reported their readiness to jump.

"This is more than I'm used to tracking at once," Wil reminded his crew, "so you'll be on your own with tactics. I'll try to give you a heads up if I see anything major."

"We have it under control, don't worry," Michael replied.

"One-hundred percent," Ian agreed. "Well, at least ninety-nine point nine. Gotta leave a little room for the crazy—it's what makes us so good." He grinned.

"Yeah, yeah. Save the cockiness until after we win," Wil shot back, but the hint of a smile broke through. "Let's go." He gripped his handholds and extended his consciousness outward through the ship.

Raenor came into focus, marbled with blue oceans, desert plains, and rocky mountain ranges throughout the southern hemisphere. The city, situated in one of the open expanses on the north continent, glowed with white light in the shadow of night. Lights in the viewports of the space station were dimmed; perhaps the attack would come during the night watch.

Wil dove his consciousness through the dimensional layers to assess the Bakzen forces in the Rift. The echo of the planet distorted the surrounding space, but no ships or structures were visible. It was quite unlike the Bakzen.

"How long have the Bakzen held Raenor?" Michael asked in response to Wil's confusion.

"Several years," Wil replied. "More than enough time to develop."

"Maybe the planet didn't have enough resources to make it worthwhile," Michael offered.

Wil accepted the possibility; just because the planet held strategic importance to the TSS, there was no reason for it to carry the same weight in the Bakzen's endeavors. "Regardless, this shouldn't be too difficult. Commence when ready."

He held the two planes in his mind, stretching his consciousness around the entire planet so his officers would have no blind spots. Saera steadied him from afar, a constant link to his physical self through the ship.

Orders swirled in his mind as his officers doled out commands across the distance. Cruisers and warships darted into place through subspace—surrounding the planet in a matter of seconds.

The Bakzen launched their defensive immediately, with their cruisers targeting the nearest TSS ships in sight. However, the space station was slow to respond. Lights flicked on, but soon the station was a mass of broken, twisted metal destroyed by precise shots from the *Vanquish*.

Electric sparks zagged along the shimmering surface of the planetary shield as the three warships tried to overwhelm the generators with energy feedback. There was nothing Wil could do but wait and watch as they slowly wore down the defenses.

At the edge of his mind, Wil perceived three new Bakzen cruisers en route through subspace. He sounded the mental alarm to his officers.

"Break through before they arrive!" Michael urged.

Two of the TSS cruisers halted their melee with the Bakzen ships to focus energy weapon's fire on the shield—giving everything they could to bring it down before the enemy reinforcements arrived.

The shield sputtered and dissolved into silvery dust. The TSS had broken through.

With the path clear, all TSS ships targeted the inhabited areas of the planet. They needed to take the cities and reestablish the shields under their own occupation.

Explosions appeared around the planet as the Bakzen cities were leveled with single blasts. Black smoke dotted the atmosphere like signal fires of the destruction.

The TSS warship released six landing vessels embedded in the skeleton of its underbelly, each carrying Militia soldiers to take out any remaining Bakzen foot soldiers. One ship headed for each of the shield generator sites, and another to the ruins of the main city.

Just as the landing party's ships entered the atmosphere, the three Bakzen cruisers dropped out of subspace, triangulating the bulk of the TSS fleet near the former site of the space station. The landing ships were still exposed, vulnerable to a well-aimed attack.

"*Hold the line!*" Wil ordered, wishing he could do more, but he was too far away to act. He struggled to maintain the clarity his officers needed to fight back.

A flurry of commands flitted through Wil's mind from his officers, relaying coordinates and targeting instructions. Four of the TSS cruisers disappeared for a split second before reappearing outside the triangle of enemy ships. The TSS fleet bombarded the Bakzen ships from both sides with energy weapons to overwhelm their shields. Just as the shields reached the point of collapse, four squads of TSS fighters—each led by one of the Primus Squad's members—darted into the combat zone. They made quick work of the Bakzen ships' propulsion systems and left the stranded vessels for the larger ships to finish off.

The TSS transport ships touched down on the surface. Details were too small to see from his vantage, so Wil had to trust the landing parties' commanders to see them through the capture of the former Bakzen facilities. The planetary shield needed to be restored as soon as possible.

An explosion drew Wil's attention to the far side of the planet. Horrified, he realized he'd neglected to keep track of the enemy vessels outside of the main group.

"*We lost the* Triumph,*"* Michael revealed.

Scorched and barely recognizable, the Bakzen attack ships in the second wave no longer posed a threat. The *Vanquish* and one of the other cruisers jumped to the other side of the planet to take out the Bakzen vessel that had destroyed the *Triumph*. Wil pivoted his viewpoint to gain a better vantage as the TSS vessels unrelentingly tore into the enemy craft. A precision shot took out the propulsion system, leaving the ship to be battered into mangled scrap.

Eventually, nothing but twisted metal remained of the enemy forces.

"*Anything else on the horizon?*" Curtis asked.

Wil pulled back from the planet and fanned through the dimensional planes. No additional Bakzen ships were en route.

"All clear," he declared.

"Ground units have control of the shield generator sites," Michael confirmed.

"How long until the shield is restored?"

"Twenty minutes."

Wil checked the surrounding space again; still clear. *"They still might come to reclaim the planet."*

"We'll be waiting for them," Michael replied.

Though exhausted, Wil wasn't about to let them get surprised—losing one ship was enough. He maintained the state of simultaneous observation, keeping vigilant lookout for any approaching enemy units.

It wasn't until the silvery shimmer of the planetary shield once again encased the planet that he allowed himself to return fully to his physical body. His fingers and toes tingled—he'd never remained disconnected for so long before.

"That was quite a fight," Michael said, letting go of his podium handholds.

"A whole planet!" Ian exclaimed. "That was some top-grade coordination there."

Wil couldn't share his same level of enthusiasm. *We lost a cruiser. I should have been paying closer attention. Thirty-five people...* "Damage report," he requested from Rianne, hoping the *Triumph* was the only significant loss.

Rianne projected the report on the viewscreen. "One cruiser destroyed, three cruisers reporting hull damage and minor crew injuries, eleven fighters destroyed," she summarized.

Forty-six deaths. Wil couldn't allow himself to dwell. "Good work."

"Orders?" Michael asked.

"Send the cruisers needing repair back to H2 and leave two others here as lookouts in case the Bakzen return. The rest should prepare for another battle."

"Acknowledged." Michael prepared the necessary communications.

Wil took a deep breath. "On to the next."

— — —

Banks smiled back at the other High Commander. "He's really doing it."

"We haven't made this much headway in years," Taelis said, awe audible in his voice. "In only a week, he's managed to take out two of the supply lines and reclaim one of the most strategic outposts."

"I told you to trust him."

Taelis nodded. "Your faith was not misplaced."

"However," Banks began, searching for the best words to change the topic, "there is still the other matter."

Taelis frowned. "I thought we agreed to put that issue to rest."

"It was more of a declaration on your part, which I'm choosing to ignore."

"I'll have no further part in your investigation," the other High Commander insisted. "Again, I'd caution you to move on."

I'm in far too deep now to give up. "I appreciate your concern."

"I understand what you're trying to do, Jason. Some questionable decisions got us into a bad spot in the past, and you want to make sure history isn't repeated."

"That's part of it," Banks replied. "What concerns me more is the well-being of our people. Doesn't it alarm you that talented individuals have disappeared without a trace? It's too much for me to ignore."

"I maintain that I cannot participate, but I won't stand in your way," Taelis said at last.

"I understand."

"But I do hope you find answers, Jason. For all our sakes."

CHAPTER 17

HAERSEN QUICKLY STEPPED to the side to avoid a tablet hurtling toward him from Tek's outstretched hand, thankful for his improved reflexes from the Bakzen gene therapy. The device shattered when it hit the concrete wall of the Imperial Director's office, raining components onto the smooth, gray floor.

"Stop them!" Tek spat.

"It's not that straightforward," Haersen tried to explain again. The most unfortunate aspect of his position was that he was often the bearer of bad news. Other Bakzen soldiers had resisted his presence for years, but when they realized that they could funnel the less favorable messages through him, he'd suddenly had a new purpose.

Tek's sorrel eyes flashed with seething anger. "You assured me the Dragon's presence in the war would not alter our momentum."

Haersen gulped. "I'll admit, the TSS has been far more successful in the three weeks since he's taken command than I'd anticipated."

The Imperial Director slammed his fist on the touch-surface desktop, causing the display to flicker. "There has to be a weakness. How do we exploit their Taran ideals?"

It had been so long since he'd been among Tarans, Haersen was starting to forget what life had been like. His mind raced, trying to invent a plausible answer to tell his commander, even if it would lead to another dead-end strategy. He just needed to buy some time to give Tek the opportunity to calm down. In his current state, Haersen didn't expect to make it out of the room in one piece.

"Relationships," Haersen said at last. "Tarans are driven by their relationships. If you want to get to Wil, you need to go after those he cares about."

Tek shook his head, his face twisting into a sneer of disgust. "Family. I'll never understand why Tarans feel such loyalty to others that are no more than imperfect genetic copies of themselves. I'd never stand to see such variation from one generation to the next."

"It's more than just genetic relations," Haersen continued. "Their love relationships run even deeper. Wil has a wife."

"That's right. He does..." Tek mused. He leaned against his desk. "But how do we use that to our advantage?"

Sensing he was out of immediate danger, Haersen stepped forward from his sanctuary by the exit door. "He keeps her close. We would need to scatter the TSS. We need to catch them by surprise."

Tek flicked his wrist. "Reactions to surprises are unpredictable. No, we need to present an immediate threat—something that would force them to divide in order to overcome."

"The expansion of the Rift?" Haersen offered.

"That's still too localized." Tek stroked his chin. "We need something that will threaten their very connection to each other."

Haersen perked up. "An interruption to communications?"

"Or more. I have an idea, but we'll need to stage a distraction to mask its deployment."

"The new hybrids would make for quite a spectacle—the TSS has yet to see them in action," suggested Haersen.

"Yes, good," Tek sat back down at his desk. "Track the fleet movement and give me your projections for their next targets. I'll make the other arrangements."

Haersen bobbed his head. "Of course, sir." Whatever Tek had in mind for the TSS, they wouldn't see it coming.

—   —   —

Tom pierced the dimensional veil into normal space just in time to avoid another blast from a Bakzen combat fighter. *"They're getting feisty,"* he commented to the other Primus Squad pilots.

"It's because we've been kicking their asses for the last three weeks," Sander replied.

Indeed, the TSS was in the dominant position. Veterans couldn't stop commenting how the tide had turned—the TSS was finally making a meaningful dent in the Bakzen forces. Tom knew he and his friends were good, but he wasn't sure they were *that* good. It was entirely possible the shift in momentum was just due to improved morale. Regardless, he wasn't about to turn down his share of the congratulations.

Their current assignment had taken them on yet another assault to take out a Bakzen supply line. Such missions were becoming routine after a few dozen variations. They had learned just how to strike the freighters and disable their jump drives without damaging any cargo; after all, the supplies were a valuable resource to the TSS, as well.

"Heads up, the Bakzen launched a probe or something," Ray alerted as they made their final approach toward the target freighter.

Tom spotted the object in question. It was plain and oblong, heading at high velocity—almost like a coffin. Two more identical objects shot out after the first. Simultaneously, the cylinders blew apart, revealing three bodies. Except, the Bakzen didn't bury their dead in space. *"Stay clear. It could be a—"*

The three Bakzen soldiers each detonated in a blinding flash.

Instantly, the subspace comm and nav locks in Tom's fighter cut out, and deafening buzzing consumed his senses—blurring his vision and vibrating within his skull until he felt like his head was going to explode. He couldn't think, couldn't breathe. He had been somewhere, but the sense of place was gone.

Reality restored around him. The fighter's control panel was flashing red, mirroring the warning images at the edge of his vision. Maneuvering thrusters were non-responsive.

"Shite! What happened?" Tom asked his friends.

"I blacked out for a second. Fok!" Sander's fighter weaved to the side just in time to avoid an enemy missile.

Tom realized his own course was leading directly into enemy combat. Instinctively, he dove the fighter down to avoid a barrage of weapon's fire and found that the craft was under his control again.

"I've still got the shot. Going in," Ray said.

Tom swung his fighter around to see Ray's craft take out the cargo freighter's jump drive. A clean hit—the ship wouldn't be going anywhere.

"Pull back!" Tom ordered. *"I don't want to risk encountering another one of those things."*

He headed back toward the hangar of their accompanying cruiser ship. The fighter's controls seemed to be back to normal, but he didn't want to take any chances. As soon as he landed, he powered down the fighter and scrambled out of the cockpit.

The other Primus pilots seemed equally eager to get out of their fighters, based on their hasty movements.

Sander slipped off his helmet. "What the fok was that?"

"It looked like people." Tom's stomach turned over.

"People?" Andy asked as he removed his flight gloves. "Why would the Bakzen eject their clones into space with a bomb?"

"No concern for life," Sander muttered.

"I don't think that's it," Tom replied. "I think the people *were* the bombs. It was like they detonated. The shockwave spanned the dimensional planes—I think that's what messed with each fighter's neural interface, since it reads telekinetic energy."

Ray frowned. "Wait... an inter-dimensional bomb. Is that how the Bakzen formed the Rift?"

"I don't know. Maybe." Tom found himself even more unnerved by what he'd just witnessed.

"Stars!" Sander exclaimed. "If that's the case, I can't even imagine how many clones it would have taken to create the Rift—it's massive! Hundreds of thousands, at least."

"What disturbs me more is that we're past the edge of the Rift," Tom pointed out.

Ray caught on. "So, they're still expanding it."

"Living inter-dimensional bombs to expand the Rift…" Andy shuddered.

"I can't imagine using a person like that," Sander said, his face twisted with disgust. "Just when it seemed like the Bakzen couldn't get any worse."

Tom shook his head. "How much better is the TSS, really? There have been plenty of suicide runs over the course of the war."

"At least that's voluntary," Ray countered.

"Are you sure the Bakzen's actions aren't?" Tom shot back.

The communication console in the hangar chirped before he could add more.

Andy, who was standing closest to the console, opened the comm channel. "Hi, Wil."

"Is everyone okay?" their commander asked over the speaker.

"Yeah, we're fine," Tom replied. "The subspace disruption from the explosion just messed with the telepathic link for a few seconds."

Wil let out a slow breath. "It took out subspace communications, too. We just got the network back online right before I called."

"My head's still a little fuzzy," Tom admitted. "Is the battle over?"

"Yes, we captured the cargo freighter. Good work," Wil replied.

"Did you see the subspace explosion?" Tom asked.

Wil paused. "Yeah, I saw it. Felt it, too."

"Were those Bakzen clones?" Sander asked.

"I'm afraid so," their commander replied. "I didn't think they'd resort to using them in battle like that."

"What else do they use them for? Expanding the Rift?" Ray asked, seeking confirmation for his previous hypothesis.

"Near as I can tell," Wil responded. "It's a shame they only use their power to destroy—it could just as easily be used to mend…" He cleared his throat. "I'm glad you're all okay. We'll regroup in the morning. Nice shooting." The call terminated.

"More mysterious knowledge he gleaned from the Aesir?" Tom speculated.

Sander sighed. "He always seems to know more than he's telling us."

"No matter now." Tom rubbed his temple, trying to ease a lingering echo of the explosion. "Let's get some rest." The next fight could wait for another day.

—   —   —

Michael collapsed on his bed with a groan. He attempted to massage the small of his back with his knuckles, but it did little to relieve the cramps from hours spent in the same position at the podium in the Command Center of the *Conquest*.

The weeks of battles had long since blurred together. Skirmishes fought in monotonous progression, supply lines cut off only to have others formed. The Bakzen were quick and adaptive, but the TSS did have the upper hand. As much as Michael wished he could take a break, he knew he had to continue pushing forward with his comrades.

All the same, he was worn down. Lack of sleep, a poor meal schedule, and little exercise were a wearying combination that was exacerbated by constant telepathic exertion. *How much longer can we keep it up before we start making critical mistakes?*

He dismissed the thought and rolled to his side, trying to quiet the replay of the day's events churning at the back of his mind. Even with his eyes closed, sleep was still elusive.

Rather than lay uselessly in the dark, he decided to start a puzzle game with the hope that it would distract him enough that he could unwind for the night.

Michael opened up his handheld and was about to launch the game when a chat message from Elise dropped down from the top of the screen: >>Hi!<<

His heart leaped unexpectedly. They'd exchanged a handful of emails over the last month, but real-time chatting never seemed to work out due to his grueling schedule. The correspondence was his one escape from the day-to-day reality of the war, and he was thankful they'd stayed in touch. He eagerly opened up a secure chat exchange over a subspace relay to

Headquarters. >>Hey! Sorry I haven't written for a while.<<

>>I figured you've been busy,<< Elise wrote back. >>Am I disturbing you?<<

>>No, it's good to hear from you,<< Michael replied.

>>I didn't expect to find you online.<<

He sat up on the bed so he could write better. >>You caught me in a rare moment of down time.<<

>>How are things going?<< Elise asked.

>>Making progress.<< Though a true statement, it was hardly the whole story. *We'll be out here for years, at this rate. This isn't how I thought it would be.*

>>How are you holding up?<<

>>Well enough,<< he deflected. >>It's a grind.<<

Elise paused. >>Is Saera doing okay? She hasn't written for two weeks.<<

>>She's been busy in the Command Center with us. We've been going for eighteen- or twenty-hour shifts.>>

>>I don't know how you do it.<<

>>Take it one minute at a time.<<

>>Not even hour-to-hour?<< Elise quipped. >>It *must* be bad!<<

Michael cracked a much-needed smile. >>We're making do. As long as we have our team together, we'll be fine.<<

>>I have no doubts.<<

>>But enough about the war. What's been going on with you?>> he asked, hoping for a temporary escape back to the mundane.

>>It's been pretty quiet over here. We only have about a dozen Agents holding the training program together. Most of the younger Trainees are wondering why they're even here.<<

>>That's still about work. How are you otherwise?<<

>>Honestly? I'm taking it minute-by-minute, just like you.<<

Michael frowned. >>What's wrong?<<

>>It's just… Headquarters is lifeless compared to how it used to be. This has been my home for the better part of a decade, and it's so empty now. All my friends are gone—and in constant danger—while I'm back here teaching some classes. It seems so pointless compared to what you're doing.<<

>>Elise...<< *It's not difficult to read between the lines.*

>I know what you're going to say,<< she continued, >>I'm doing my part and all that. But we should be out there helping!<<

>>I know,<< Michael started to write, but a string of messages from Elise streamed in before he could finish.

>>I don't even think they want to keep Headquarters functioning. Students are at about half course-load, since there are so few instructors. We can't do any proper training. And, with so few of us here, they don't even serve dessert anymore! What I wouldn't do for a cookie...<<

>>Actually,<< Michael finally managed to interject, >>I was just going to say that I miss being with my friends, too. And you're one of my friends now.<<

The statement must have caught Elise off-guard, because it took several seconds for her to respond. >>Sorry. It's silly of me to complain about anything, compared to what you must be going through out there.<<

Michael smirked. >>No, it's kind of refreshing to hear about a travesty like a cookie shortage, for a change.<<

>>Admittedly, that has made for a pretty bleak scene. People waiting in the buffet line for a dessert tray that will never come...<<

He laughed. >>The poor Trainees! They must be so lost and confused.<<

>>I can see it in their eyes. The devastation... No words can possibly describe it.<<

They jested back and forth about life for a while longer before a wave of tiredness finally overtook Michael. He suppressed a yawn. >>Hey, I should really get to sleep. I need to be back on duty in six hours.<<

>>Of course. Sorry to have kept you up!<<

Michael smiled. >>I'm happy we had the chance to chat properly.<<

>>Me too. I hope you're able to come home soon.<<

>>And have a proper face-to-face conversation,<< Michael ventured.

>>I'd like that,<< Elise responded, to his relief. >>Good night—and take care.<<

>>I will. Good night.<<

To have Elise seek his company was a foreign feeling, but he was grateful to, for once, have someone looking out for him. Her small bit of support from afar moved him more deeply than he anticipated; in all his years with the TSS, no one else had ever made such a gesture. As he drifted off to untroubled sleep, he took comfort knowing that Elise was thinking about him, too.

—   —   —

All the skirmishes were starting to feel like the same, never-ending battle. Wil held in a yawn as he finished his review of the morning report about fleet positions.

TSS forces were advancing toward the Bakzen Defense Barrier at a steady pace, and all but three of the known Bakzen supply lines had been cut off from the Bakzen's main planetary base. They were getting close, but victory wasn't assured. They needed to stay focused.

"What's on the agenda for today?" Ethan asked, pulling Wil from his thoughts.

"Another border post assault," he replied. He set aside the report, seeing that his officers were already done with their own reviews.

"Thrilling," Saera commented from her station with thick sarcasm.

"Oh, so Saera," Michael began, "I got a message last night from—"

The alarm sounded a single shrill chime.

Wil jumped to attention. "Report!"

"We lost our connection to the SiNavTech network," Rianne replied. "Signal corruption, no apparent cause. I'm trying to reestablish—"

"Wait," Wil cut in. "The system is programmed to disconnect automatically if there's an anomaly. Stay disconnected and run a network diagnostic."

"I'm on it," Saera confirmed.

Preliminary results from the scan appeared on the front of the viewscreen overlaid on the surrounding starscape. Red error indicators flagged at least a quarter of the beacons.

Shite, what's going on? Wil frowned. "Overlay the errors on the network map."

Saera complied. A moment later, the viewscreen morphed into a map of the SiNavTech network for the surrounding sector. The errors were localized around Bakzen territory, but some beacons connecting to distant colony worlds along major transportation routes were also registering errors.

"Fok! Tell the entire fleet to disconnect from the network," Wil ordered.

"Yes, sir," Rianne confirmed while the others glanced at Wil with sudden alarm.

"Whatever the error, it looks like it's spreading like a virus," he continued. "Notice the distribution pattern—it's along the routes that have registered a beacon ping in transit."

"What's it doing?" Ethan asked.

Wil shook his head. "Saera, any thoughts?"

She looked up from her analysis at the front console. "I can't be certain, but I think it's rewriting the beacon lock protocol, preventing any ship from being able to get a fix. There's some kind of cipher running in the background."

"Can't get a lock unless you know the secret password," Wil muttered.

"Fok, the Bakzen hijacked our nav network!" Ian exclaimed.

"That's my best guess right now," Saera confirmed, her face drawn. *"That was the flaw in our workaround for the independent jump drive. The fleet can't coordinate without the beacon network,"* she added telepathically.

"I should have anticipated this contingency." Wil rubbed his eyes. As he pulled his hands away, he noticed that everyone was looking at him, awaiting his orders. *What can we do? Half the fleet already can't move without risking getting trapped in subspace. We need to act before the whole network is down.* "Do we have any ships currently engaged in combat?"

"Two cruisers and their complement are assisting defense of a border post," Michael replied.

"How strategic is the position?" Wil asked.

His friend frowned, anticipating where he was going. "It's a significant supply cache. And, Cameron is with them."

An unacceptable loss. "All right. Saera, calculate a manual jump. We'll give them backup. Tell everyone to stay put and keep a low profile until we figure out a solution." His officers telepathically relayed the messages to their contacts throughout the fleet.

"I have the coordinates," Saera stated after a minute. "Do you want to check—"

"No time." Wil grabbed the podium and telepathically reached out to the ship. The jump drive charged in response to his unspoken command.

A blue-green cloud overtook the *Conquest* as the ship slipped into subspace. Wil bolstered his connection with the ship, ready to draw it back into subspace if they emerged in the wrong place. The vibrations softened as the ship arrived at the destination. Objects began to take shape on the viewscreen through the cloud. He spotted the asteroid well out of harm's way, but one of the cruisers was directly in their path.

Wil extended himself in an instant, enveloping the ship in a subspace bubble to prevent it from materializing inside the other ship. At the edge of his consciousness, curses sounded around the Command Center as the others realized what had happened. He felt his officers coming to his aid. Together, they sustained the subspace bubble as they drew the *Conquest* away from the ships around the asteroid. Once clear, they released the ship into normal space and took in their surroundings.

The two TSS cruisers formed an inverted V around the outpost on the asteroid, which was protected by a shield. fighters deployed from the cruisers were engaged with three squadrons of Bakzen fighters, along with a heavily armored warship and four battlecruisers.

"Shite!" Ethan breathed.

They were completely out-gunned any way Wil looked at it. Further, without witnessing the preceding action, he was blind to the Bakzen's strategy and behavior patterns for the battle. Brute force was the only option.

"Let's take them out!" Wil declared.

He gripped the podium and established his link with the ship. His officers followed his lead. *"Time to see what kind of damage the telekinetic amplifier can do. This'll be our one chance to catch them by surprise with it,"* he told them.

"Ready," they confirmed in unison.

Together, they channeled telekinetic energy through the relays within the ship. The podiums hummed and warmed to the touch as the ship charged. A buzz filled the air as energy swelled in the relays. They released the charge—aimed directly for the warship.

A beam of white light shot from the bow of the *Conquest*, striking the warship almost instantaneously. The target was enveloped by the white light, each feature of its hull standing out against the blackness of the starscape. For a moment, it shone brighter. Wil squinted against the light replicated on the viewscreen, noticing that the TSS fighters had fallen back toward the TSS cruisers. Then, the Bakzen warship disintegrated in a spectacular flash, as though each molecule vaporized from the center outward. A shockwave radiated from the destroyed vessel, hurtling the two Bakzen cruisers closest to the warship and their fighters to the side.

The TSS fighters darted behind their cruisers just in time to avoid the wave of debris as it collided with the shields protecting the TSS cruisers.

"Don't give them time to regroup! Finish them off," Wil ordered.

He sensed Ian connect directly with the *Conquest* and target the ship's weapons on the stunned enemy cruisers. The Bakzen ships' shields were disabled in the blast, and the *Conquest*'s rail guns sent fatal shots cleanly through their hulls. The TSS fighters reemerged from behind their cruisers and opened fire on the Bakzen fighters drifting through the scraps of the former warship.

Though the TSS fleet made quick work of the two cruisers that had been next to the warship, the two remaining cruisers were relatively unscathed.

"Again!" Wil commanded. He poured energy into the *Conquest*, charging the telekinetic relays. The air hummed with

the stored force waiting to be released.

His officers joined him in the charge—filling the ship near capacity.

"*Divide,*" he instructed.

Two beams shot from the ship, one heading for each of the Bakzen cruisers. Both ships disintegrated on impact, releasing a burst of white light.

Wil let go of his handhold, his breath labored and heart racing. Next to him, his officers let go of their own podiums, looking equally fatigued.

"I don't think we'll be able to do that too often," Wil said as his heart rate settled.

"No joke," Ethan replied. "But talk about effective!"

Michael surveyed the destruction on the viewscreen. "I never thought I'd see anything like it."

Saera studied Wil from her position at the front console. "*Are you okay?*" she asked telepathically.

"*Yeah, I'll be fine. Just a little more exertion than I'm used to at once,*" he assured her.

"Incoming communication from the *Victory,*" Rianne announced as a chirp echoed through the Command Center.

Wil turned his attention to the viewscreen. "Accept."

A holographic image of a middle-aged Agent appeared on the screen. Her face was tense below the tight bun of blonde hair on top of her head. "I'm Agent Drenda, in command of the *Victory,*" she said.

Next to her, Cameron sat in the First Officer's chair, representing the Primus Elites. "Thanks for stopping by! That telekinetic amplifier is really something."

"Yes, it is," Wil replied. "Captain, is your ship damaged?"

"No, nothing more than cosmetic. You showed up just in time. All the jump drives in our unit were acting up."

"Unfortunately, the issue is network-wide," Wil told her. "Everyone is to hold their current location until we can identify the cause of the issue."

"I got the order after we were already engaged," Cameron said. "Is it something the Bakzen did?"

"Most likely," replied Wil. "We'll stay here with you, for now.

I don't want to make any unnecessary manual jumps."

Agent Drenda nodded. "Happy to have your company, sir. Let us know if you need anything."

"Thank you." Wil ended the transmission. "All right. Any other distress calls, Michael?"

"We're good for now. I've been able to account for the entire fleet. We were really lucky."

"Good thing we programmed in those failsafes." Wil exhaled with relief. "Okay, now let's figure out what's going on."

Saera pulled up the network map again. "Your initial assessment of a virus seems pretty spot-on. The origin was this beacon near the Defense Barrier, as far as I can tell," she said, highlighting the beacon in question. "It's targeting the nav computers in the TSS fleet and seems to transmit from ship to ship as soon as a course is locked in."

"So, the more jumps, the faster the whole network will go down," Wil realized. "What about civilian transit?"

"For now, it appears to be limited to the TSS fleet. It was calibrated to our long-range jump systems. I can't say whether or not it could spread."

"Bomax." Wil groaned. *If the civilian network goes down, we're foked.* "Ideas? I'm open to anything."

"System reset?" Saera offered.

"Won't do any good if the underlying code is corrupted," Wil replied. "The backups are located at specific hubs rather than in each individual unit; the resets are designed to just reboot the beacons."

"So, we need to write our own protocol to push an update to the network—our own virus to restore the original functionality," Curtis suggested.

"Yes, closer. But what do we need that update to do?" Wil asked. "Ideal scenario."

"Restore the ability for our ships to maintain a beacon lock, obviously," Ian said.

"Create a firewall to prevent further hijacking," Curtis added.

"And *ideally*," Saera interjected, "prevent the Bakzen from piggybacking off of our beacon signals, like we know they do."

"That might be too ambitious. We've never been able to stop

them before," Wil countered.

"Except, we didn't know how they did it before. They inadvertently gave us the key to their kingdom." She grinned as she pulled up a snippet of highlighted code on the front viewscreen.

Wil examined the code. *Stars, she's right!* "The cipher controls the lock, but the communication protocol between the ship and beacon is right there in the open."

"All we have to do is a little extrapolation," Saera continued. "I never would have thought to put a cipher on that part, myself—it's innocuous enough on its own, but it's the last missing piece we needed to understand how they read our fleet movements."

"Do you have enough now to code a lockout?" Wil questioned.

She nodded. "Ninety-nine percent sure, anyway. The rest of the code repairs are an extension of the work I did earlier."

Good thing I was willing to delegate before. I couldn't possibly deal with all of this on my own right now. "Great, get going on it as soon as possible. Grab any help you need. This is top priority."

"I'm on it," Saera acknowledged. "Except, I think it would be best to work directly at one of those hubs you mentioned. I'll need to study how it sends the update signal."

Wil hesitated. He disliked being separated from the Primus Elites, let alone sending Saera off on her own. "It's not safe—"

"It's safer than the whole fleet being trapped in their current locations," Saera replied. "I can look after myself."

"I know you can, but—" he started to protest telepathically.

"I'll see you in a few days," Saera stated with a clear tone of finality.

Reluctantly, Wil nodded. "Okay. Just there and back."

She smiled. "I've got this."

CHAPTER 18

THE BAKZEN HAD thoroughly screwed up the SiNavTech network, that was for sure. Saera let out a heavy sigh as she massaged her eyes, taking a break from the tedious coding.

She glanced over at the beacon hub station attendant, a stocky man in his fifties. Based on his tepid reception of Saera, it had been clear he'd taken the remote assignment due to a profound disinterest in having company.

"Stan, have you finished the—" Saera started to ask.

"Yes, the relay protocol is already uploaded. I'm just waiting on you," Stan replied with a dour expression.

Saera doubted that his tone would be any different even if he knew she was married to a SiNavTech heir. "I'm almost done with the new firewall." She turned back to the viewscreen, steeling herself for the final push.

Situated in a completely unpopulated sector, the hub was a standalone station tethered by a subspace anchor, like any other navigation beacon. Its compact form barely had enough amenities for one inhabitant, let alone a visitor. Saera had been camping in her transport shuttle for power naps every night, but the circular control room with its array of viewscreens and administrative access panels had turned into her temporary home away from home.

The last three days had been an even more intense grind than when she'd led the initial coding to interface the independent jump drive with the TSS fleet. The beacon hub had a backup of the uncorrupted navigation program, fortunately, but creating the new firewall to block out the Bakzen's piggybacking on the network had proved more difficult than she'd anticipated. After two failed attempts, she had finally isolated the sequences to enact the required countermeasures to read the fleet's movement; the Bakzen would likely still be able to use the nav beacons, but they would no longer be able to access the TSS' travel logs. All that remained was inputting the final patches to restore capabilities for the TSS ships to lock onto the beacons. If all went well, they could roll out the updates before the civilian network was impacted.

She spent the next hour reviewing the mind-numbing lines of code for the new sequences. At last, she was satisfied that the quality control checks were sufficient.

"All right, Stan, let's see if this works," Saera said.

He only grunted in response, but the touch-surface on top of Saera's console changed to a security screen. Hidden characters for the password appeared in sequence as Stan entered them via his console on the other side of the compact control room. Once logged in, an upload screen appeared.

"Activating the new lock system," Saera declared as she tapped the corresponding controls.

A holographic map depicting the beacon network appeared above her console. The beacons were presently red, indicating a failed lock. Hopefully, the patch would fix that in short order.

Saera rapped her fingers on the console while the network interface refreshed after the upload. She sensed Stan glaring at her hand, annoyed by the offending sound inside his sanctuary. After listening to him loudly clear his throat for the last three days, Saera couldn't care less that he was bothered.

Seven minutes passed. The console refreshed with an updated network graphic. All the beacons were once again displayed as pleasant gold icons.

She grinned with relief. "Good as new!"

Stan scoffed. "Be more careful next time."

"You're the one monitoring the network connections, not me," Saera shot back.

"Well, I didn't start the war."

"Neither did anyone in the TSS who's alive and fighting now, but we'll be the ones to end it."

Stan swiveled back around in his chair. "If you say so."

Saera swallowed her exasperated groan. "I guess I'm finished here. Let me know if you detect any anomalies."

The attendant let out another grunt to acknowledge her statement.

Shaking her head, Saera headed for the only door out of the tiny control room. The narrow corridor branched to either side, and she stayed to the left toward the docking bay. Less than twenty meters in length, the docking bay was overcrowded with two ships parked in tandem—her sleek TSS transport ship barely fitting behind Stan's utilitarian evacuation shuttle. A pressurized door separated the room from space, but the heating controls were set to minimum levels. Saera hugged herself as she jogged to her ship, her breath appearing as a cloud in front of her face.

Saera palmed open the door to her shuttle and hurriedly closed it again behind her. Inside was no warmer, since the shuttle had been powered down all day. She climbed into the pilot's chair, the seat frigid through her clothes. Shivering and with a cloud of breath billowing out with every exhale, she powered up the main systems. Within moments, heat radiated toward her numb face and limbs. She soaked up the warmth, flexing her fingers as the feeling returned.

Once Saera felt reasonably thawed, she pulled up the communications interface to contact the *Conquest*.

After a moment, the Command Center appeared in a holographic projection in front of her, with Wil and his men at the center.

"Hi," she greeted.

"Hi. What's the status?" Wil asked.

"Everything looks good on this end," Saera replied. "I think it's safe to boot up the nav system and see if it works."

"Would you like me to attempt a beacon lock?" Rianne asked from beyond the camera's view.

Wil nodded. "Set it for the Medea outpost, we need to regroup."

Ten seconds passed while the nav system initialized on the *Conquest.*

"We have a lock," Rianne confirmed.

"Excellent. Saera, can you meet us there?" Wil asked.

"Sure, I'm on my way."

"See you soon." He ended the transmission.

Saera checked the location of the Medea outpost on the map; it was intentionally positioned away from a beacon, but not so far that a manually calculated jump was necessary. Given that her transport ship wasn't equipped with an independent jump drive and she was fatigued enough that she didn't trust herself with manual calculations, she elected to jump to the beacon and travel the rest of the way through normal space. The extra hour of transit time was a worthwhile tradeoff for the added caution.

She relaxed back into the chair for the trip. Soon she'd be back with Wil and be able to sleep in her own bed again. They had a new system to limit the Bakzen's movement and the TSS would have the advantage. Everything was looking up.

—   —   —

"If it works like we planned, the Bakzen's navigation capabilities will be severely compromised," Wil explained over the viewscreen to the captains on the ships gathered around the Medea outpost.

"What if the Bakzen have an independent jump drive, too?" Agent Ellis asked.

"They might," Wil admitted, "but maybe not on every ship, just like with our own fleet. If nothing else, at least we'll gain some added security."

"True," Cris agreed from the *Vanquish.*

Next to him, Kate nodded thoughtfully. "We should make another pass at the supply lines from Aleda while they're caught off-guard. I'd give it a day, maybe two, before the Bakzen are in a position to retaliate against the new nav system."

"Agreed, we need to move quickly if we're to keep any advantage," Wil replied. "I know the fleet needs some time to resupply after being trapped for a few days. Let's plan a run at 09:00 tomorrow. I can observe from here."

"Yes, sir," the captains confirmed.

"Speak with you in the morning." Wil ended the transmission. He let out a slow breath.

"Somehow, I feel like the change to the nav network won't cause the Bakzen to miss a beat—just piss them off," Michael commented.

Wil frowned. "I'm afraid of that, myself."

"Worst case, it changes nothing," Ian said.

"True." Wil checked the time. "I'm going to go over the full fleet report. Let's reconvene at 08:00."

"See you in the morning," Michael acknowledged.

Wil headed into the private workspace off to the right side of the Command Center. It was just large enough to hold a couch for a quick nap and a touch-surface desk. A viewscreen next to the desk was currently set to a rotating display of colorful nebulas.

He sat down at the desk and began going through the tedious reports of fleet supplies and current positions. The downed nav network had left a few ships in a tough spot, but for the most part, all the key vessels should be well positioned for the attack in the morning. They just needed a few hours to get back in order.

Suddenly, Rianne came over the comm, "Incoming message addressed to you, sir. Unknown origin. It's marked as private."

"Unknown origin?" Wil asked. "That can't be right."

"I tried a trace, but there's nothing."

"Put it through in here," Wil instructed, unsure but intrigued.

When the video feed resolved on the screen, Wil nearly fell out of his chair. Bakzen eyes met his, glowing red under a heavy brow. The face was unmistakable. *Tek.*

It took a moment for Wil to gather himself. His pulse raced, every muscle tense. *How did he get this comm channel?* "Tek. It's been awhile."

The Bakzen examined him. "It has. My, how you've grown."

What does he want? Wil attempted a covert scan to identify the transmission origin, but he found that the signal was blocked. "That tends to happen with age."

"I see you're still as spirited as ever. You know, that wasn't very nice of you to lock us out of the beacon network."

Wil swallowed. It hadn't taken the Bakzen long to notice. "It wasn't yours to begin with."

"Wasn't it? We used to be Tarans, too, after all."

Not knowing how to reply, Wil remained silent.

"I hear they've named you Supreme Commander of the TSS," Tek continued.

"That's correct."

Tek's lips parted into a sneer. "I've received a promotion myself."

"How generous of your superiors." *What's this about? There's no way this is just a social call.* He tried to stay composed, but he knew there were cracks in the façade.

Tek seemed pleased by Wil's discomfort. "My former superiors hardly had a say in the matter. I have little tolerance for ineffective leadership, you see. I had to take matters into my own hands."

A chill ran down Wil's spine. *That can only mean one thing.* "You made yourself Imperial Director."

"You do catch on quickly, I'll give you that."

Stars! We're fighting an enemy led by a madman. "So, leader to leader, what do you want?"

"I want Cambion."

Wil almost laughed at the boldness of the statement, but he felt too ill for humor. "I may be Supreme Commander, but I'm in no position to barter inhabited planets."

"Don't underestimate the power you hold," Tek countered. "This is wartime, and you call the shots."

"Then let me rephrase. I won't hand over a Taran world to you."

"Surely, there's a price you would consider."

"Money isn't a big motivator for me."

Tek tilted his bald head. "How about your wife?"

An icy fist gripped Wil's heart. *Shite, where's Saera?* "I think she'd agree with my stance."

"Don't play dumb. That wasn't my question."

They couldn't have captured her, could they? Wil was about to bring up the route information for Saera's shuttle, but Tek's level gaze stopped him.

"Answer me. Your wife, or an entire planet?"

Wil swallowed. "An irrelevant hypothetical." *She must be okay, right? She hasn't telepathically reached out to me. I sense no distress.*

"A hypothetical for the moment, but what happens next is up to you."

"Empty threats won't win you any consideration." *Stars! Where is she?* Wil shook Tek's piercing gaze to hunt for Saera's shuttle on the desktop console. When the coordinates came up, he saw she was right on course. He breathed an inward sigh of relief.

"My threats are never empty," Tek said. "You have two minutes to make your decision. Your wife, or Cambion."

"I already told you, I won't hand it over to you." *Fok! What is he after?*

Tek smiled. "I wanted to challenge myself, to see if I could make you yield to me. Look closely, and you will see that two Bakzen scout ships are ghosting your wife's shuttle. There is no way she could escape with the limited maneuverability of her craft. We can end her at any moment."

Stars, no! Sickened, Wil confirmed the presence of two ships floating in subspace that could jump into normal space at any moment and fire. His mouth went dry. "Then why haven't you?"

"Because Cambion offers much greater short-term gains."

Wil's mind raced. "Just attack it." *They likely have telepathically controlled civilians standing by to bring down the shield generators. No matter what I do now, the planet is probably lost.*

"Why destroy a single planet when I can also bring you down in the process? The beacon virus was just a distraction to lure your wife into the open—whom else could you trust to carry out such a repair? Our educated guess that you would send her was correct. Targeting her was the perfect opportunity for Cambion's destruction to carry so much more impact."

Think! There has to be a way out of this. "How's that?"

"By making it your fault."

Wil's heart dropped. "You're insane."

"Hardly. You see, the Bakzen have been at war with the TSS for long enough to anticipate your tactics. I know exactly how long it would take for you to send reinforcements to mitigate our assault, and that window will now close in less than two minutes. You can notify the TSS about the planned attack now, but your wife will die. However, if you wait out those two minutes, your wife will live—but you will need to bear the weight of knowing you could have prevented four billion deaths, if only you weren't so weak and selfish."

Fok! Sudden rage flushed Wil's face. *They must have civilian drones. Tek knows the planet is already his. This is just a game to him—making me consciously choose not to send help.* However, realizing Tek's intent didn't change that Saera was still in immediate danger. "What assurance do I have that you won't kill her anyway, as soon as the time is up?"

"Nothing other than my word. However, her death under those circumstances would be counterproductive. Killing her then would just make you angry, if I break our deal. It's guilt that will destroy you, and her living is what will make it real for you."

"I have no reason to trust you." *Stars! There might be nothing I can do for Cambion now, but Saera... I can't lose her.*

"Maybe not, but if you choose Cambion, she will surely die. In choosing her, there is at least a chance that I will honor my word, and that she might live. What is that chance worth to you?"

Everything, but... Wil could barely breathe. *He has me, and he knows it. Fok!* "I won't negotiate with you."

"Stop pretending you don't care. You have a choice to make! Either lose the person closest to you, leaving you—and the TSS, by extension—distracted and compromised. Or, save your wife, and let your guilt eat away at you until you can no longer look in her loving eyes and see anything but the bartering pawn she has become—a reminder of your choice to let all those innocents die."

"I'm not that easy to manipulate."

"Oh, but you are. I can already see you breaking."

Wil turned away from the viewscreen. *It's an impossible choice. Cambion may already be lost, but it's still my call to not even try. How can I choose between the one person who is my world, or the entire population of a planet?*

His heart pounded in his ears as the seconds ticked on.

Wil paced the room. *Fok! What do I do?* He couldn't surrender an entire planet, especially not one so populated. Compounding the staggering loss of life would be the resource loss—a strategic position as well as some of the critical remaining rations the TSS would need to make it through the coming battles. Even if the Bakzen were bringing down defenses from the inside, TSS intervention now could help mitigate those losses. To take no action at all would result in a devastating setback.

But then there was Saera… *What will keep me going if I don't have her?* Nothing, Wil realized. To lose her would destroy him, and if the TSS' success hinged on him, self-preservation was by necessity his top priority. His eyes stung, but he kept his face composed. *I'll have to live with this decision forever.*

"Time's up."

The words were knives driven straight into his heart and gut.

"Interesting choice." Tek's surprise was audible.

Wil glared back. "Let her go."

Tek waved his hand.

On the desktop, Wil saw the two enemy ships disappear. He let out the breath he'd been holding. "You'll pay for this."

"I live with no regrets. A true leader will do anything for his people." Before Wil could reply, the call terminated.

Wil sat in shocked silence. *Did that just happen?*

Warning lights flashed. *Shite!* He ran back into the Command Center, already knowing the devastating news to come.

"Emergency signal from Cambion!" Michael reported when Wil entered.

You have to play dumb. "What's the status?"

"They're under Bakzen attack. The planetary shield is dropping." Michael shook his head, examining the reports on the screen. "Does this have anything to do with that mystery call?"

Do they know? Wil concocted a lie, "It was a secure communication from Taelis—some vague intel about a Bakzen attack. This must be it."

Michael nodded, apparently satisfied with the response.

Wil could barely breathe. *I did this. They're all going to die because of me.* "Planetary defenses?"

"It looks like an all-out assault. The Bakzen have them completely out-gunned," Ian replied. "We'll lose Cambion without reinforcements."

It was lost before the first report. "Have the Bakzen already taken out the shield?"

"Two of the generators are offline. It'll fully collapse within the next thirty seconds," Ian stated.

"Then it's already too late. There's nothing we can do." Wil cast his gaze down, unable to witness the digital representation of the slaughter onscreen. *All those deaths are on my hands...*

The crew looked appalled. "We can't just abandon them!" Curtis cried.

Wil shook his head. "There won't be anything left by the time any reinforcements arrive." The knives twisted in his stomach.

"We have to do *something.*"

I could have, but I didn't. "We'll just lose more people and ships. We need to conserve the limited resources we have. It's a Bakzen world now." *Stars! I chose to let this happen...*

The crew continued to watch, even as they realized it was a futile fight.

Michael reviewed the reports on his console and main viewscreen. "A few ships are trying to jump out, but the Bakzen are hunting them down."

"Stars! They're bombing the planet's surface," Ian murmured.

"Four billion people..." Ethan breathed. "Isn't Tom from Cambion?"

Wil nodded. *I just killed one of my best friend's families.* "There's nothing we can do." Numbness began to replace the twisting blades in his stomach.

The crew fell silent as the remaining friendly icons on the viewscreen extinguished.

The numbness in Wil crept upward in his chest as emotional pain radiated from the crew surrounding him. It was too much. "Stay put. We proceed with the attack in the morning." *You have to pull yourself together.* "I'll be in the Strategy Room until Saera's on board."

Wil barely held his composure until he was in the privacy of the conference room. The moment the door was closed, he dropped to his knees and sobbed. He held nothing back, trying to expel his guilt for making such a selfish decision. *I thought losing her would break me. Will I be able to recover from this, either?*

He remained on his knees and elbows for what seemed like an eternity. Eventually, the sobs subsided, replaced by numbness in his core. It was the only way to cope—to purge his emotions. He wouldn't have to face his guilt that way, but he would also lose the love that motivated him to keep going through the worst moments.

"Where are you?" he called out to Saera. He needed her, more than he'd ever needed anything.

"About to dock," she replied. He could sense her, so close.

Wil reached up to wipe his face. He pulled out his tinted glasses from his pocket to hide his eyes that must surely still be red. With a deep breath, he left the Strategy Room and headed for the hangar below.

After the brief lift ride, he darted down the hall to the hangar. When the door opened, Saera's transport ship was powering down. She was safe.

The door in the side of the ship opened with a hiss, and Saera hopped out.

Wil's heart leaped when he saw her. *There's still some of me left... for now.* He needed to feel her again before he felt nothing at all.

He rushed to her, cupping her face with his hand. With his arms wrapped around her, he pulled her into a passionate kiss— channeling everything that remained of himself into one more intimate moment while he could still feel their connection. She kissed him back for an instant, then broke away.

"Not *here.*" She glanced at the confused technicians waiting nearby.

Wil's sense of self was drifting away like sand through his fingers. "I can't wait." He brought his lips back to hers, desperate to keep the fading ember alive.

"Are you okay?" Saera asked in his mind, but he shut her out—lest she glimpse the dark secret he now harbored. He had

given them up for her... but would she understand? It wasn't a risk he could take. She was alive and all he wanted was to be with her one more time before he was revealed as the vicious, cold monster he'd always known himself to be.

He pressed her against the hull of the ship, lust staving off the cold slowly consuming him from within. Saera responded to his touch, a low moan of desire escaping her lips.

Out of the corner of his eye, Wil saw the technicians silently retreat from the hangar. They were now alone.

With the assurance of relative privacy, Wil released Saera from the shuttle to strip off his jacket. He fanned it out on the floor and embraced Saera once more. "I love you," he murmured into her ear, the words carrying more meaning in that moment than she might ever know.

They sank on to the jacket, entwined in passion. Wil savored every detail, imprinting her in his mind. Even if he could never feel such love again, he would at least have that one last memory.

CHAPTER 19

"FOK, WHAT HAPPENED?" Taelis paced across Banks' viewscreen, more openly distraught than Banks had ever seen him.

"You've said yourself that loss is inevitable," Banks replied, hearing the hollowness in his own words. *This wasn't just a remote colony. Cambion was a major world.*

"All those people…" Taelis massaged his eyes with his thumb and index finger. "We've never had a loss on that scale."

"I can't even fully grasp it." Losing tens of thousands of people in a single Bakzen attack had unfortunately become a fact of the war, but to have billions of lives extinguished in a matter of minutes was too atrocious to fathom. Worlds like Cambion were protected by redundant shields and enough artillery to put up a substantial fight. Since the planetary shield had been brought down from the inside, that meant the Priesthood hadn't deployed the counteragent to the neurotoxin in time—if that was ever even their intention. Regardless, the Bakzen had demonstrated that they were capable of executing a large-scale attack with enough swiftness and precision that no world was safe.

The other High Commander gathered himself. "There's nothing we can do about their deaths now. The immediate concern is maintaining supply distribution to the frontlines. We're at a critical juncture."

"I know," Banks agreed, turning his focus to business. *When did we become so cold?* "I already reached out to some civilian contacts. A shipment will be arriving to the Prisaris shipyard in the morning. We can use the facility as a new staging ground."

Taelis nodded. "That'll help, thank you. But it doesn't change how this attack unfolded. Wil didn't even send the fleet to assist."

"What could more ships have possibly done by that point? The world was lost within the first minute of the attack."

"Not all of its inhabitants," Taelis protested.

"It was a calculated decision. We've always coached Wil to look toward long-term outcomes. Losing ships in a counterattack wouldn't have increased our ultimate position."

"That's true," Taelis conceded, "but this isn't the first time he's shown such disregard for casualties. In his CR exam—"

Banks scoffed. "Do you really want to question Wil's judgement now? We gave him a job to do, and he's doing it. I never expected everything to be all clean and pretty. The fact is, we molded someone to commit genocide. We can't expect there won't be any other casualties along the way."

"But a whole planet!"

"We're in no position to question him. We lost that right when we made him the center of all our plans."

Taelis paused. "I never thought we'd have to worry about him coming through for us."

"I have no concerns about that," Banks countered. "He'll find a way—but I have no illusions about it being a way we like. We've forced one person to make all of those tough decisions on our behalf, so we have to live with the consequences. I have no doubt that he will always do what is best in the moment and will drive us toward victory in the war. We'll pick up the shattered pieces once the fighting is over."

After a moment of reflection, Taelis nodded. "You're right. All we can do for now is stand back and let Wil do what we've asked."

"I didn't anticipate how much this war would change me," Banks murmured. "Weighing the worth of lives, treating people like resources—it's the very way of thinking I always tried to avoid."

"We change so that others can maintain their innocence. It's the burden of our station."

The sacrifices hidden in shadow... Banks bobbed his head with grim determination. "At least it will be over soon."

"I used to think that would be a day of cheers and fanfare. Now I'm not so sure."

"Either way, we'll finally be able to rest easy," Banks said.

"That will be a good day."

— — —

Tom wiped his eyes only to find that the tears had already dried. *I can't believe they're gone...*

The news about Cambion's capture seemed too surreal to be true. Such a large world with so many defenses—it was too much to have been wiped out in a matter of minutes. Though ten percent of the population had managed to flee after the initial assault, Tom's uncle was the only surviving member of his family. The rest had died in the initial firebombing, or—he couldn't bring himself to think about the alternatives.

It had been years since he'd seen his family in person. Occasional video chats had done little to make up for the years apart. There were so many things he wished he'd been able to tell his parents, jokes he'd wanted to tell in good-natured teasing with his little sister, all the adventures he'd never get to have with his childhood friends. While the Primus Elites had become his family away from home, Tom had always taken comfort in knowing that there were others loving him from afar. Now, those around him were all he had left.

After a night to let the reality of his loss sink in, Tom found that his initial grief had transformed into an inner fury. The Bakzen had taken those that held a special place in his heart. His hands clenched into fists, his cheeks flushed and eyes narrow. Justice would be served.

The door to his cabin on the *Conquest* hissed open. Sander popped his head in. "How are you holding up?"

Tom shrugged, releasing his fists.

"I'm so sorry for your loss," his friend murmured for the dozenth time.

"There's nothing we can do now but beat the Bakzen to a pulp. They'll foking pay for this."

Sander nodded, grim. "Are you sure you're up for flying today?"

"There's nothing you could do to keep me out of battle now."

"All right." Sander headed for the door. "Let's go get some revenge."

—   —   —

A simulated sunrise woke Wil in his quarters on the *Conquest*. Next to him, Saera stirred.

He inched away. *I can't be near her. She'll know what I did… Know how truly terrible I am.*

His actions may have been to save her, but that didn't change the fact that he'd allowed billions of people to die due to his decision. That wasn't forgivable, and it certainly didn't make him worthy of her love.

Besides, she couldn't be an anchor and confidant anymore. He wouldn't be able to open himself to her like he always did before—like he needed to be able to do with anyone in that role. There had never been any secrets or barriers between them, but now he'd have to remain guarded at all times. The longer she stayed with him, the more suspicious she would become of what secret he was keeping.

Tek was right—this was how to destroy me. His heart raced with panic. *The guilt will eat away…*

No, he couldn't let the Bakzen get into his head. There had to be a way to block it out, to maintain focus. Maybe, with some time, he could wall off all the memories that implicated him in Cambion's destruction. Except, he needed an immediate solution.

He watched Saera's chest rise and fall in her peaceful sleep. *I can't possibly explain any of this.*

They were too close for him to only partially pull away—to gain the distance he'd need to erect a fortress around his secret. He could hide it from the others for the interim, perhaps, but not from her. He'd never be able to make the mental barrier secure if she was around to serve as a constant reminder of what he'd done, creating cracks in the walls that would already be so difficult to construct. Moreover, if she stayed with him, she'd eventually find out how he traded her life for so many others and would never forgive him for making her guilty by extension.

Just a little time apart—until I can come to terms. Sending her away was a risk, but he saw no other choice. Wil expected more heartache with the decision, but the numbness that had been spreading through him since the previous night had dulled his senses.

Wil watched her sleep for just a moment more, memorizing the peacefulness of her sleeping face. He knew he was about to unintentionally hurt her, and she wouldn't understand. Maybe, one day, he could make things right again, but only cold realities were in his near future.

Saera blinked and stretched her arms above her head. "Hey, you're awake."

"Hi." He couldn't bring himself to wish her good morning, not with what was coming next.

She sat up in bed. "How'd you sleep?"

"Well enough," he lied. There was no sense prolonging the inevitable. "Saera, you should go back to Headquarters."

Saera laughed off the statement, rubbing the sleep from her eyes. "Don't be ridiculous. It's too early to mess with me."

"I'm serious."

Her face dropped. "Wil, that's crazy. In all the training, I've always been here with you."

I can't let her into my mind again. Not until the walls are secure. "We'll find a way to adjust without you."

She shook her head. "Right before an attack? No way."

"I can't have you here right now," Wil pleaded.

Saera pulled the sheet up to her chin, brow knitted. "Why? Did I do something…?"

"No." Wil shook his head. "Stars, Saera… Please, just wait at home where it's safe."

"Are you afraid I'll get hurt? Is that it?"

"No. Yes…" Wil clutched his head. The final dying moments of Cambion replayed within Saera's pupils. "You can't be here."

"Wil—" she tried to reach out to him.

He clamored out of the bed, unable to face her. "Wait here. You'll transport back to Headquarters after the skirmish." Blocking out her continued protests, Wil finished dressing and then quickly slipped out the door. A day before, he would have shared her heartbreak over the thought of being separated. Now, there was nothing left of himself to lose.

—   —   —

Saera sat in stunned silence until well after Wil had gone. *Sending me back to Headquarters?* He hadn't even looked her in the eye as he said it.

Based on their reunion the previous night, it seemed impossible for him to have changed his attitude so suddenly. There was never any lack of passion in their relationship, but she had somehow felt even closer to him over that night together. At the time, she'd thought it was making up for their separation while she tended to the navigation coding. In retrospect, maybe it was something far darker.

Was he saying goodbye?

That didn't make any sense. They were partners. Through all the challenges over the years, their bond had never wavered. She was mystified about what could have possibly happened within the span of three days to alter their relationship.

There was no way she'd go that easily. If he was that distressed, it was all the more reason for her to be around. She had pledged to be a supportive partner, and whatever was wrong, it was her duty to help him.

—   —   —

Michael braced against the chair across from his podium in the Command Center to stretch, trying to loosen up in advance of the hours he was about to spend in telepathic communication.

As he finished up his final series of stretches, Wil walked in—strangely, alone.

"Did Saera decide to take an extra-long shower this morning?" Michael joked.

"She won't be stationed on the *Conquest* anymore," Wil replied, his voice flat.

"Wh—"

"It's not up for discussion," Wil cut him off.

Even as others entered the Command Center, Wil remained equally reticent about Saera's sudden absence. Michael suppressed his concern for the sake of their battle coordination, but deep down he knew something was seriously wrong.

"Get ready," Wil instructed.

Michael sensed the beginning of simultaneous observation. "Without Saera, how will you remain anchored?" he asked.

"The ship is enough," Wil shot back, bite in the words.

"What's wrong?" Michael asked him privately.

Without responding, Wil closed his mind to future questions.

Something was definitely wrong—and their operations were far too delicate for anyone to be off their game, especially their leader. *"We should postpone the fight,"* Michael said to Ian, Ethan, and Curtis.

"Did something happen with Wil and Saera?" Ethan asked.

"He won't tell me, but clearly there's an issue." Michael ended the private conversation. "Wil, maybe we should rethink the attack this morning."

"We proceed as planned," Wil replied.

"But—"

"But nothing," Wil cut him off. "That's an order." He grabbed his handholds and began slipping into a state of simultaneous observation.

I guess I'll have to be his backup, then. Michael hurriedly followed Wil, reaching out for him.

Rather than the normal openness, Michael met only a wall around Wil's consciousness. He tried to grasp on, but there was no way to maintain his hold. "Wil, wait!" he begged. Without a telepathic tether other than the ship, there was no telling if Wil would be able to find his way back to his physical self.

Wil didn't listen, drifting further and further until Michael barely had him in sight.

"*He's going too far,*" Michael alerted the other officers.

Immediately, he sensed Ian, Ethan, and Curtis coming to his aid. The four of them linked and set out after Wil. With their chain, the four of them were able to catch up to where Wil had ventured—as far as they dared go without potentially losing themselves.

"*Come back!*" Michael urged.

"*I know what I'm doing,*" Wil replied, drifting even further away.

"*It's too risky,*" Michael countered.

He held firm as an anchor while the other Captains lassoed Wil within a telepathic net. Wil resisted, trying to break free.

"*You aren't allowed to leave us like this.*" Michael strained to pull his four friends back in, stretching himself to his limits. So much power, such strength—it was more than he could contain.

The other Captains extended tendrils back to hold onto Michael while doing everything they could to contain Wil.

Why is he resisting us? Michael gave everything he could. They had to bring him back.

At last, Wil gave in.

Michael reeled him back, releasing the anchor when everyone was connected with their physical selves again. He let go of the handholds and leaned back in his chair. "What were you doing?" he demanded, glaring at Wil.

"My job. Why did you stop me?" Wil shot back.

"You can't go that far without a tether."

Wil's eyes narrowed. "You're in no position to tell me my limits."

Michael glanced over at a very confused-looking Rianne, but it was already too late to care about what she may think. "What's going on with you? First you tell me Saera's heading back to Headquarters, and now you're trying to run off to lose yourself in subspace?"

"I always go out that far," Wil insisted.

"That doesn't answer my question."

"Hey, gentleman," Ethan cut in. "Why don't we calm down for a minute."

Wil groaned. "We're late for our meeting with the fleet. We have an attack to command."

Shit. It's not fair of him to put me in this position. "I don't think you're in the best mental state to lead that attack right now."

"You don't have the authority to make that call," Wil retorted.

"Actually, with Saera gone, that makes me your second-in-command. So, I do."

Wil took a deep breath, closing his eyes for a moment. "I'm sorry." He paused. "You're right, I'm not in top form this morning. It was a tough decision to send Saera back home, but after Cambion, I just can't have her on the frontlines anymore."

Michael took a calming breath. "Maybe it's not the right decision if it has you this upset."

"No, this is the only way," Wil insisted. "You're right, though. It's interfering."

Ian glanced around the circle. "We can handle the coordination on this one, if you want to take some time."

Wil shook his head. "No, it's a complicated plan and we'll need the insights from my observation. I'll hold it together—no more risky moves, I promise."

Michael reached out to Wil's mind and found it guarded, but on the surface the words were sincere. And Wil was right: they did need simultaneous observation. He wasn't completely comfortable having Wil in the battle in his current state, but the fleet would be too badly off if they backed out now. "Okay, let's proceed."

True to his word, Wil did what he needed to do in the battle. If anything, Michael found that he actually played it safe compared to normal. Despite making it through the battle without incident, there was still an underlying issue that needed to be addressed.

As soon as the post-battle fleet reports were in, Michael excused himself on the pretense of taking a nap before the next assault. Really, he needed to talk to Saera and get her side of it.

He jogged through the empty halls to the captain's quarters and pressed the buzzer. After a moment, the door slid open. Saera's face was tense and her exposed eyes were reddened.

"What's going on?" Michael asked through the open

doorway. "I heard you're heading back to Headquarters."

"That's what Wil thinks."

Michael frowned, sensing a mixture of hurt and confusion emanating from his friend. "Why is he trying to send you away?"

Saera shook her head, causing a segment of hair to slip from behind her ear. "He won't talk to me—he's completely shut me out." She crossed her arms. "I'm frustrated and annoyed, but more than that, it terrifies me what could have happened to make him withdraw like that."

"I know he's upset about Cambion last night, but we all are."

"I think it's about me." Saera set her jaw and re-tucked her hair behind her ear.

"He's under a lot of stress," Michael replied. "I'm sure it's just an overreaction driven by worry about your safety out here."

"I know him too well. That's not all of it."

Michael tilted his head. "If he's already made up his mind, arguing won't get you anywhere."

Saera swallowed, her expression grim. "I have to try. He'll let this war consume him if there isn't someone to hold him back from that dark path. I can't leave him now."

"What will—"

"Why are you still here, Saera?" Wil barked from down the hall, interrupting Michael. He stormed toward them.

Michael placed himself between his two friends. "I think we should talk this through."

"Don't get involved," Wil shot back.

"Too late for that," Michael replied. "You've been acting erratically all day. Take some time to cool off, or whatever you need."

"What I need is for Saera to go back to Headquarters like I ordered."

"Don't treat me like a first-year Trainee!" Saera retorted. "I'm your First Officer and your wife. You can't order me around."

"I tried asking you earlier as your husband, and you refused. What other option do I have than to pull rank?" Wil spat back.

Saera crossed her arms. "Maybe try *discussing it* like civilized adults?"

Michael took a step back from Wil toward Saera. *This is*

escalating way too quickly. "I don't want to pick sides here, but as a senior officer, I have to express my concern. I don't think sending Saera away—"

"Your concern is noted," Wil interrupted. "Saera, I need you to go back to Headquarters now. Don't make me call a security detail."

She opened her mouth to respond, but Michael cut in, "I'll escort her out."

Saera gaped at him, lip quivering. "How can you go along with this?" Tears welled in her eyes. *"I thought you were on my side."*

"Do you really want to be dragged off by armed Militia guards?" Michael asked her. *"What would that do for crew morale? Let's just do what he's asked and give it a couple of days to settle. I'm sure you'll be back here in no time."*

After a moment, she nodded. "I still don't like this, but fine. I'll go." She headed for the bedroom. "Let me grab my things."

Wil stood in stoic silence for a few moments. He took a deep breath and released it slowly. "I can feel you silently judging me," he murmured to Michael.

"I'm just really confused about what's going on."

"I wish I could offer you a deeper explanation, but I can't get into it. Believe me when I say I'll be more focused without her here."

Michael frowned. "In the past five years, it's always been the opposite."

"Circumstances change." Wil met Michael's gaze, his exposed eyes pleading. "Please, just trust me on this."

How can I trust him when he's so obviously making a huge mistake? Despite his misgivings, Michael nodded. *I need to stay in his good graces so I can keep an eye on him.*

Saera returned to the living room with a travel bag slung over her shoulder. "All right." She came to meet Michael by the door, but focused on Wil. "Good luck. Let me know if you need anything."

Wil gnawed on his lip, then stepped forward and embraced her. "Thank you."

They parted from the hug, and Wil rushed off in the direction of the Command Center without another word.

Saera took a moment to gather herself, releasing a slow breath. "Let's go."

Michael walked with her in silence down to the hangar. *This isn't right. We need her here.*

He hated feeling so helpless. More than witnessing his commander make a terrible strategic decision, he was unnerved to witness cracks in a relationship that he had never seen falter. Everyone relied on Wil to be level-headed and calm, but this decision gave a very different impression. Michael shuddered to think what the sudden change might mean for Wil's overall state of mind. For the time being, Michael decided that the best he could do was damage control to quell any rumors that might compromise Wil's authority. *We can't give up on him. We have nowhere else to turn.*

When they arrived at the hangar entrance, Saera bit her lip. "Look after him, okay?"

"I always have his back. You know that."

Saera swallowed. "He's further down that dark path than I realized."

Having already witnessed a taste of that earlier in the morning, Michael was torn. "Maybe you *should* stay. Go to the *Vanquish...*"

"He'd know, and I don't want to make things worse." She looked down. "Besides, it seems like I'm part of the problem. If that's the case, then maybe some time away will help him get over it faster."

"Or," Michael realized, "maybe this is just an overreaction to Cambion and he's worried about you being here in a warzone—that his concern will become a distraction." *This ship is the Bakzen's top target, and I wouldn't want someone I cared about here, either. I hadn't thought about it that way until now.*

Saera nodded. "That's how he tried to justify it at first, but there's something else he isn't saying. Regardless, there was desperation in his tone—like me leaving was a last resort option."

"I caught that, too. How do we help him if he won't tell us what's wrong?"

She shook her head. "I wouldn't be being escorted off this

ship if I knew the answer."

Everything we've worked for could unravel if we're not careful.
"I'll keep watch. I promise."

"Okay." Saera gave Michael a hug. "Thank you for always being there for us."

"Hey, someone has to be the dutiful sidekick, right?" He pulled away and chuckled in spite of the tension. "Remember when we used to play Alien Invaders in my backyard? I never thought we'd actually be out saving the galaxy one day."

She let out a pained laugh. "Go figure."

Michael placed a gentle hand on her shoulder. "We'll get through this," he assured her. As Saera boarded the shuttle, Michael sent a quick note to Elise on his handheld: >>Saera's coming home. Wil isn't himself. Hopefully, it's temporary, but Saera will need your support.<<

A response came back almost immediately: >>I'm on it. Does this have anything to do with Cambion? It's all over the Taran news.<<

>>I don't know what's going on between Wil and Saera,<< Michael wrote back. >>The whole fleet is talking about Cambion, too, but we need to stay focused on the frontlines.<<

>>Understood. I'll keep an eye on Saera. Take care.<<

>>You too.<< But if Wil was cracking, there was no guarantee that any of them were safe.

—   —   —

In his wildest speculation, Haersen had never imagined that Wil would choose one person over an entire planet. All the same, he couldn't be more pleased with the decision.

Tek's top advisors were gathered around the conference table, each sporting a grin that unnaturally stretched their coarse skin over their heavy cheekbones. Their red eyes shone with exuberance—they had achieved a major victory worthy of celebration and weren't afraid to gloat.

"How much of the population survived the initial bombardment?" General Gerek asked.

"Approximately ten percent," General Komatra replied, "but more importantly, we were able to confirm distribution of our neuro control agent to two hundred million of those survivors. That gives us more than enough drones to take Tararia."

"All that we have to do now is get them to the planet," General Iko stated.

Gerek's smile faded. "That's a huge population to relocate."

"We can't move them ourselves," Komatra clarified. "The entire point is to have them as sleeper drones. At most, we can implant a subtle message to direct them toward Tararia, but the journey there must be on their own terms."

"It could take weeks or months for enough of them to gather," Iko objected.

"Then so be it," Tek stated.

The other officers fell silent, turning to their commander for guidance.

"Those plans are for future endeavors. Today we celebrate," Tek continued. "We have dealt a significant blow to not only Tarans and the TSS, but also directly to their leader. I looked into his eyes and saw defeat."

"The TSS' lost resources on Cambion are only a temporary setback," Gerek pointed out.

Tek nodded. "Yes, but the emotional damage will run much deeper, I'm told." He glanced at Haersen. "We have tied Cambion's devastation to a loved one, and thereby inserted a wedge that will continue to drive the TSS' trusted leader away from his support team well after the initial loss of the planet wears off. As soldiers, we tend to think in terms of physical combat as the greatest measure of victory, but we have to think like our enemy. We have targeted the fragile Taran heart and mind—if we can't attack directly, we'll just let them destroy themselves from within."

"An attack on… emotions?" Komatra raised his brow with skepticism.

"Don't worry," Tek replied to his officer. "Have no doubt— the Dragon has been weakened. Only time will tell by how much."

CHAPTER 20

JUST ONE BATTLE at a time. I can do this... Wil's pep-talk to himself didn't produce the result he'd hoped.

Since Saera's departure a week prior, he was finding it difficult to concentrate and even more difficult to maintain simultaneous observation for the longer battles. Cambion's destruction was still far too raw for him to be able to separate Saera from that horrific scene in his mind. Until that was possible, she couldn't be anywhere near him, lest he reveal what he'd done.

Despite his attempts to close off all emotion, he missed Saera—her companionship, counsel, love. But experiencing that connection would come with the price of looking into her eyes and seeing what he had traded in return. His difficulty with concentration was more than missing Saera, though. There was the guilt—a festering wound deep in his soul that grew more burdensome with every death in battle.

To make matters worse, constant chatter about Cambion's decimation filled the TSS communications network between active battles, spreading reports that mass panic was threatening to send the general population on other worlds into riots. For once, it was clear that the Taran public sensed the danger of war coming to their own doorsteps. Losing a remote colony was one thing, but the capture of a major Taran world had far-reaching ripple effects.

Yet, Wil and his team had to concentrate on the frontlines. They couldn't take their eyes off the end goal, or the future losses might be even more devastating.

"Wil?"

Michael's voice returned Wil to the present in the *Conquest*'s Strategy Room. The fleet was awaiting his orders for the next coordinated strike.

"Right, so we need a simultaneous strike on both bases," Wil said, trying to remember what he'd been saying before his mind began to wander.

"Yes. And the collector complexes…" Michael prompted.

"We need to keep it quick and stealthy," Wil continued, remembering his place. "Disrupting the power grid at both sites simultaneously will allow us to bring down the Defense Barrier."

"That's not a certainty," Curtis interjected. "Yes, the simulations show that those are the two main power stations for the grid, but it's impossible to know if there are backup systems or how the internal structure works."

"I need to go on the information in front of me, and all the data indicates that this is our best bet toward eliminating one of the biggest obstacles standing in our way before we can take the Bakzen homeworld," Wil stated. "We need to eliminate those sensors if we want any chance of a surprise strike—otherwise, they'll see us coming, even with a subspace jump."

"I'm not arguing that point, just your proposed methods," Curtis clarified.

Wil folded his hands on the tabletop. "I'm open to suggestions."

"Well…" Curtis stared at the sleek tabletop. "I don't know what to recommend."

I understand his hesitation. It is a crazy plan. Wil activated the holographic diagram of the two Bakzen bases again.

Sutan and Haelo were star systems at either end of the Defense Barrier in relation to Tararia. What appeared to be solar collector installations were erected near the stars, which supported the theory behind the Defense Barrier's power source. The problem was that the equipment around such collector installations was highly reactive—they couldn't go in blasters blazing like any other firefight. One stray weapons discharge and the resulting explosion from the collectors would take out the whole fleet within the star system.

It would have to be a small, precision strike—in and out as quickly as possible, jumping away before detonation. By any measure, dividing up the Primus Squad was a perfect solution. Except, they always worked in a team of four and the mission was extremely risky. Two fighters wouldn't stand a chance against the Bakzen defenses if they were caught, given a warship and two cruisers were stationed at each facility. The Primus pilots would have speed, agility, and stealth on their side, but sometimes sheer numbers and brute strength were the better advantage.

"Okay, so two members of the Primus Squad at each location," Ian said. "Is that enough?"

"For that kind of precision strike? Absolutely," Ethan confirmed. "But they'd be totally foked if everything doesn't go exactly as planned. They'll need to jump away before they can confirm a strike in order to avoid the explosion. If they hang back…"

"We'd be out our best pilots and lose some of our closest friends," Wil vocalized the statement they were all dancing around. "I know the risks, but they're the best chance of pulling it off, and it's the most efficient way to bring down the Defense Barrier."

Eventually, all the officers murmured their agreement.

"All right, I'll relay the plan," Ethan agreed. "Let's hope it works."

—   —   —

Tom studied the details of the Primus Squad's latest orders alongside his fellow pilots. "Are they insane?" he said when he finished reading the brief.

"That's my conclusion." Sander waved his hand to return the brief to its starting point, showing a holographic projection of the solar collector facility at Sutan.

Andy crossed his arms. "It's one thing to send in a whole fleet against the odds, but relying on just two fighters... There's no room for error."

"May as well be a suicide run," Ray scoffed.

"Wil wouldn't do that to us," Tom told them. "We're the best, remember? We can do this, no problem." *This is the chance to make a real impact. This can be revenge for my family.*

"Are we looking at the same diagram?" Ray asked, incredulous. "Because I see a one-meter-wide target that would need to be hit from a range of three kilometers, and we'd have to jump before confirming impact."

"Not to mention," Andy added, "that if our aim is off and we need to take a second shot, the whole star system explodes before we can jump away. Or, if we go within the three kilometer radius of the detection grid and they fire on us, the resulting firefight may—again—lead to the whole star system exploding with us still in it."

Sander let out a sarcastic laugh. "At least the mission would succeed either way, since the facility would be destroyed, so it's all okay."

"We knew our lives would be on the line when we agreed to be on this team," Tom reminded them. *My parents and sister weren't supposed to be the ones in danger. I couldn't protect them on Cambion, but we can make sure the Bakzen won't hurt anyone else.*

"It's one thing to risk our lives in the line of service and duty," Ray replied. "This is a shite plan. There's a difference."

"So... what? We run it up the chain?" Tom asked, not sure how to address the team's resistance.

"Ethan can't be on board with this," Sander muttered.

A moment later, Tom detected a telepathic link beckoning at the edge of his mind. He opened his consciousness to the communication.

"We have some concerns about the brief," Sander relayed through the link to Ethan.

"Were the orders unclear?" their Captain replied.

"No, but—" Ray started to protest.

Ethan cut in, *"Then you'll make the necessary arrangements and proceed."*

"Was this your idea?" Tom asked.

"No," Ethan replied. *"Straight from Wil. There's no talking him out of it. You guys can do it, don't worry."* He disconnected from the link before anyone could voice additional protests.

"That was super helpful," Andy huffed.

Tom headed toward his locker. "You heard him. Let's go."

Reluctantly, the others followed.

"Andy and I will take Sutan. Sander and Ray, you're on Haelo," Tom instructed as he pulled his flight suit and helmet engraved with his name from the locker.

They acknowledged the orders with a curt nod and retrieved their own suits and helmets.

Once dressed, they headed across the hangar to their waiting IT-1 fighters.

Tom's fighter powered up as he approached, detecting his telepathic presence. After months of coordinated maneuvering together, he and the fighter were fully in sync. The telepathic link with the fighter automatically solidified as he climbed up the side handholds leading to the cockpit. He dropped down into the molded seat and secured the oxygen connection and flight harness. When he was settled, the transparent dome slid closed above him. He initiated the pre-flight check.

"Comm check," Sander's voice came through the speaker in Tom's helmet.

"Check," Tom replied, echoed by the two other pilots.

"Primus team check," Tom initiated the telepathic link, reaching out to Ethan as their connection to the central command structure.

"Check," Ethan and the others replied simultaneously. After a moment, Ethan continued, *"Head out when ready."*

Tom released a slow breath. "Here we go."

The four fighters taxied toward the door of the hangar along an open central path. Technicians moved off to the side to clear the way for them to pass.

Each fighter's engine revved on the final straight-away to the door, gaining enough momentum to break through the force field separating the hangar from space.

Once free, Tom and Andy arced to the left while Sander and

Ray headed to the right.

"See you on the other side," Sander called out as he vanished into subspace with Ray.

"Jump coordinates confirmed," Andy said. *"Ready?"*

Tom initiated the jump. *"Let's go."*

After two minutes, the two fighters emerged from the blue-green cloud of subspace just beyond the outside edge of the invisible proximity detection grid.

Three kilometers away in front of them, a warship and two cruisers were stationed in defensive positions around the target complex. The solar collector station glistened in the starlight—a golden sail floating in the emptiness, with four wings fanned outward from a central hub. It was that hub, through a narrow hatch leading to a vent tube, they needed to strike. Unfortunately, the hub rotated around a central axis, and the hatch was out of their current line of sight.

"Shite! There's no way to make the shot from here," Tom relayed to Andy and Ethan.

"We can't wait for it to rotate…" Andy replied through their near-instantaneous communications.

Detection grid or not, they were still vulnerable to visual recognition. *"Reposition. We have no choice."* Without hesitation, Tom envisioned his destination seventy-degrees from his present vantage, which would align him with the hatch and, hopefully, still place him outside the threshold of the detection grid. The ship hummed in response to his silent command, sending a flash across his vision to confirm the jump coordinates.

The fighter slipped through subspace toward the destination. When he emerged, he'd have virtually no time to line up the shot. *Let's hope I come out in the right place…*

Normal space re-solidified around him. The hatch was in sight, but a warning lit up on the head-up display. He'd misjudged the distance without any visual reference points—he was within the three kilometer sensor zone. *Shite.*

"Fire!" Andy shouted in his mind.

Tom sensed the location of the hatch and lined it up. Purely following instinct, he took the shot.

The energy blasts from their ships careened through open

space. He held his breath, waiting for impact.

"*Fall back!*" Andy's shuttle slipped into subspace.

Tom waited—duty and his commitment to avenge his family driving him to make sure they had accomplished their mission. He magnified the target on the head-up display. The hatch blew apart as the blast connected; it would reach the inner target in any moment.

A shockwave fanned out from the hub, racing toward Tom's position. He slipped the ship into subspace—but a moment too late.

The fighter jolted backward as it caught the front end of the shockwave just as he entered subspace. His head hit the back of the seat hard, dazing him. Agonizing seconds passed with his ears buzzing and vision blurred, trying to regain his senses in time for the exit at the rendezvous with the *Conquest*.

The cloud of subspace lifted. Tom struggled to focus. "*I'm hit,*" he relayed to the others.

Red flashed in the corner of his vision, indicating damage to the ship. *How bad was it?*

All the controls were sluggish, and the starboard thrusters were completely non-responsive. He reached out telekinetically to assess the external damage to the ship—the entire front maneuvering array and half the nose of the fighter were completely gone. *I'm foked...*

Under the best circumstances, it would be a rough landing. Far worse was the fact that he was only separated from the cold vacuum of space by a single, fragile interior wall barely thick enough to maintain the pressure. While his flight suit would protect him, a rapid depressurization would throw the fighter off-course during landing.

"*I'm going to need guidance assistance,*" he alerted Andy. Telekinetic lead lines should help him land safely. It was his best—and only—shot.

"*I've got you,*" Andy acknowledged.

The ship buzzed with telekinetic energy as Andy's tethers wrapped around the craft. Tom extended his own guides toward the *Conquest* to set his course and try to slow the velocity of the ship.

The *Conquest* was in sight. *Just a little further...*

His fighter wasn't slowing to landing speed. *"Pull me back!"*

"I can't—not alone."

With no way of slowing down, Tom directed all his energy to making sure he was at least lined up with the hangar door. Distance was closing fast. There was nothing more he could do. *"Help!"* he called out to Ethan, hoping the Captains on the *Conquest* could offer additional tethers, but he knew by then it was too late.

His fighter passed through the entry force field and slammed against the metal deck plates nose first.

The wall by Tom's right leg buckled. Shards of metal curled backward, slicing into his thigh down to the bone. The fighter lurched to the side, driving the twisted metal deeper.

He cried out in pain, but couldn't hear his own voice over a crescendoing buzz in his ears. Dark spots danced across his vision. Craft whirled by outside the clear dome of the fighter's canopy as he spiraled uncontrolled across the hanger.

The fighter struck the back safety net, thudding to a halt as the broken metal side panel sliced straight through his femur. Tom gasped for air through the incomprehensible pain closing in around his consciousness. *Blood... so much blood.*

Someone called to him from outside. *Andy?*

"Help!" Tom managed to croak. Telekinetically, he ripped back the cracked upper canopy of his fighter.

Have to stop the bleeding... He sent energy to his fingertips, directing searing heat at the wound above his knee. He gaped in horror as the skin cauterized—but it wasn't just a surface gash. The leg had been sliced completely off.

He gagged, using every modicum of his remaining willpower to keep from vomiting inside his helmet.

"Fok!" Andy exclaimed from above, peering over the lip of the cockpit.

"It— It's sliced straight through," Tom stammered.

"I'll get the medical team. Don't move." Andy disappeared.

Gripped with panic, Tom struggled to breathe inside his helmet. He reached toward his throat and groped blindly for the seal, his hand shaking.

Cool air rushed to his lungs as the helmet released. He gulped it in.

Footsteps echoed across the hangar.

"We'll get you out," an unfamiliar voice called up. "Stay still."

Tom waited in the pool of his own blood while the medical staff worked with the fighter maintenance crew to remove the remaining starboard side panels around the cockpit. When the final panel was thrown to the ground, the head medic was finally able to get a proper look at Tom's injury.

"It's gone, isn't it?" Tom asked her.

She nodded. "There's too much damage to salvage the limb, but we'll get you a new one."

He stared down at his severed leg. In retrospect, he realized just how much he'd taken it for granted. *It was worth it... The Bakzen won't recover from this.*

"Let's get you cleaned up," the medic said, wrapping her arm around Tom's shoulders. "You'll live to fight another day."

CHAPTER 21

WIL WAVED HIS hand to minimize the crash report above his desktop. It was miraculous they all hadn't died. Tom's fighter had nearly wiped out the other half of the Primus Squad that had already landed and a third of the maintenance crew when it crashed into the hangar. One lost leg was a minor price to pay for an otherwise successful mission, with both of the solar collectors destroyed by the two Primus pilot duos.

"How's Tom?" Wil asked.

Across the desk, Ethan's face was still lined with worry. "Drugged up on pain meds, so he's great for now."

"And the others?"

Ethan shrugged. "Shaken, but they'll pull through."

The accident had hit close to home. Wil wondered if he'd be able to shake off his concern for his friends' well-being. They were the only ones he trusted, so he sent them into the most dangerous situations, but the risks were becoming too great for him to stomach. First Saera, then the Primus Squad… His friends and his family were his weakness. *I can't allow them to be a liability any longer.* "Going forward, the Primus Squad's members will transition to ops coordination roles."

Ethan scowled. "They're never going to go for that."

"Tom's grounded for now, until Medical can grow him a new leg. I can't keep worrying about the rest of them."

"So don't. We knew about the mortal danger when we signed

up. They're the best pilots in the TSS—let them do their job," Ethan implored.

"The matter isn't up for discussion." Wil rose from his desk. "We're late for the team meeting. I just wanted you to know in advance."

Ethan nodded, but his scowl persisted.

I won't knowingly send my friends into that kind of danger anymore. As awful as it is, the anonymity of the other pilots and ship crews makes it easier... Wil headed with Ethan out from his office through the Command Center to the Strategy Room.

Michael, Ian, and Curtis were already waiting for them around the conference table.

Wil and Ethan sat down in two of the empty chairs.

"How are they?" Ian asked.

"On edge but eager to keep going," Ethan replied. "Even Tom. He said he's going to kick some Bakzen ass as soon as the temp prosthetic is calibrated."

Ian cracked a smile. "Sounds about right."

"I'll make sure he gets the best regenerative care," Wil assured them. "It'll take a couple months to regrow the limb, but he'll be okay."

"He has too much fight not to be fine," Curtis commented.

"Very true. But with one person out, I'm grounding the whole unit. My decision to break them up was what allowed the accident to happen in the first place—three tethers could have prevented the hard landing. I won't send them into battle down a person again."

"I begrudgingly agree," Ethan muttered.

Ethan would take Tom's place in the field, but I need him here. We'll find a way to work without the Primus Squad. Wil turned his attention to the real reason for the meeting. "We successfully brought down the Defense Barrier, but we still need a tangible path to finish the war once and for all."

"What we're doing already is working," Michael pointed out. "Targeted strikes. The other Primus Elites have been doing a great job of preparing each target for us."

"Yes, they have. But why prolong the war? Though we came into this expecting months or years of fighting, it doesn't have to be that way." Wil stood up and paced across the Strategy Room, arms crossed. "Stars, the Defense Barrier is down now! Let's end it while we have an opening."

"The Bakzen are still so spread out," Michael countered. "What other choice do we have than one-off battles?"

"We just need to hurt them enough so we can make a run for the homeworld. If we could make them concentrate their forces…" Wil mused.

Michael tilted his head. "What are you thinking?"

"Something that might be crazy enough to work." Wil strode over to the center viewscreen on the wall and activated the holographic projector. After some inputs on the main panel, a holographic representation of H2 appeared in midair.

His friend eyed the projection with confusion. "Are you suggesting we lure the Bakzen to H2?"

"Hear me out," Wil said. "The war with the Bakzen has been going on for hundreds of years, right? The two places that have never been directly in the conflict are the TSS base—in its various iterations over the years—and the Bakzen homeworld. Our greatest aspirations involve a direct attack on the Bakzen's home planet, so I can only imagine they'd be as eager to get their hands on H2."

"Okay, I'll buy that logic," Michael agreed. "That doesn't mean we should hand it over to them, though."

"That's not my intention." Wil manipulated the holographic image, revealing a hidden layer of armor that he had learned about in his first visit to H2 a decade before. *We just need to make it too appealing a target to resist.* "This armor is rated for five minutes of direct barrage using known weapons. That's not long, but I think it would be enough to take out the main Bakzen warships and cripple their fleet."

"If I understand you correctly, that's a huge risk to take."

"No risk, no reward," Wil countered.

Michael raised an eyebrow. "But inviting an attack? That seems a bit extreme."

"We need to make a show of weakness. By going into a lockdown mode, it'd look like we were retreating. We lure the Bakzen in for the kill, with our fleet waiting in distributed locations. Once the Bakzen converge on us, the fleet jumps back and takes them out."

His friend considered the plan. "What if they don't take the bait?"

Wil shook his head. "Tek will. He'll figure it's a trap, but his ego will drive him to take advantage of the opportunity, thinking he'll win in the end. He'll go in with enough firepower to put up a fight—and enough that it'll make a dent in Bakzen forces when we take them out. His inherent boldness means that he'll ultimately underestimate us, especially since we'll have the tactical advantage of surprise and position."

"You're seeming a bit over-confident yourself," Michael replied.

Maybe I am, but we need to try something new to end this before the Bakzen can repair the Defense Barrier. "I believe in our equipment and our training. I wouldn't recommend this kind of move if I didn't think it'd work."

Michael took a slow breath. "All right. Let's go over the details."

—   —   —

Tom winced as the medical technician sent a test signal through his temporary prosthetic leg. The energy pulse registered as a sharp pain on the right side of his calf. "Ow! Yeah, felt that, too."

"I'll turn down the sensitivity," Ruth, the technician, replied. She gave a slight wince of her own as her soft, brown eyes conveyed an apology for hurting him. "At least we know the connections took."

"How much longer will this take?" Tom asked, reclining onto the medical bed in the infirmary.

She looked over the length of Tom's temporary leg at the various servos and sensors exposed for the calibration exercise. "We should be able to get you on your feet in another half hour, or so."

Tom glanced over at the flesh-toned casing sitting on the

adjacent table, which would enclose the leg after the calibration. The technology was tried and true, but he was anxious to have a real flesh limb again—unfortunately, that took time to grow. According to his doctor on the *Conquest*, they'd already started preparations to clone his missing leg in one of the labs back on Tararia, based on the genetic code in his medical file. As soon as it was ready, he could go have it attached. *I never thought I'd need to have a spare part grown on demand.*

Ruth finished another adjustment on one of the sensors next to his knee. "How's that?"

This time, the energy pulse registered as a gentle tickle. "Perfect."

She nodded with satisfaction. "Okay. Let me set the others."

While she was working on Tom's foot, the main door to the infirmary opened and Wil stepped in. Tom waved him over.

Wil smiled as he approached. "You need to work on your landing form."

"Well, *someone* cut our training short," Tom jested back.

His commander stopped a meter from Tom and examined the prosthetic limb. "How are you feeling?"

"Like a tree that was on the wrong side of a fight with a plasma saw." Tom forced a grin. "But I'm all right."

Wil's smile faded. "Could you give us a few moments?" he asked Ruth.

She inclined her head and walked to the other side of the room.

"You've probably heard by now that I'm grounding the Primus Squad," Wil continued, taking a step closer.

Tom groaned as he sat up on the bed. "Yeah, Ethan told me." *One accident isn't a good reason to ground the best pilots in the TSS.*

"Once you're comfortable with the prosthetic, maybe we can reconsider. However, we're about to try something new. If it's successful, the war might be over very soon."

"Let me be a part of it! Ruth said I'd be back on my feet in half an hour—" Tom started.

"No, I can only imagine what kind of pain meds they have you on right now. You're not going anywhere without a clear head," his commander insisted.

"Fine, no more meds. Once the calibrations are done, I'll sober up and get back out there." *Shite! Most of my family was killed by the enemy. I can't be stuck on the sidelines, unable to do a foking thing about it!*

Wil placed a hand on his shoulder. "I understand why it's so important to you." He looked down. "Tom, I'm sorry that I haven't spoken with you since Cambion…"

A knife jabbed into Tom's heart. "Yeah, well, it's—"

"I wish things had been different," Wil interrupted.

"The Bakzen attack wasn't your fault."

Wil hesitated for a moment. "I just wanted you to know how sorry I am." Suddenly, he turned around and rushed out of the infirmary.

Tom watched him go, feeling helpless that he could do nothing more to avenge his family while he was stuck on medical leave.

Ruth inched back over. "Is everything okay, sir?"

"Yeah, just condolences." *Somehow, that felt like it was more for him than me.* Tom settled back down on the bed. *I don't envy what it must be like for Wil—being responsible for all of us. Every loss must feel like his own.* "Let's finish up these calibrations. I want to get back out there."

— — —

Weeks of digging through data archives had taken Banks to the edge of his mental fortitude. In the last thirty years, more than three hundred female TSS Agent applicants had gone missing—vanished without a trace.

With recognition technology so integrated into society, there was no way a person could completely drop out of contact so completely and inexplicably. Moreover, there was far too strong a correlation between the women's ability levels and their disappearances for it to be a coincidence. Each of them had a genetic potential that placed them in the upper Sacon Agent range—or Primus, in some cases. Not the absolutely strongest candidates, but well above average. In purely scientific terms, they were the applicants that struck the balance between leaving the TSS with the most Gifted potential soldiers while reserving the second-best for what Banks could only guess were telekinetic bloodline propagation purposes.

Where did they go? The question had been plaguing him since the beginning of the search. Each attempt to trace the last movements of the women before they went missing had only met dead ends.

To avoid drawing suspicion to his investigation, he'd resisted the urge to reach out directly to any friends or family of the missing. Fortunately, a handful of the families had filed a report with the Tararian Guard.

Unlike any other filing with the Guard, the sensitive nature of these investigations dictated security clearance. Curiously, the clearance level had been set to 10—meaning only Banks and Taelis would have access, prior to Wil's promotion. He found it intriguing that the Priesthood would modify the security level of the records rather than just deleting them, but perhaps some paper trail was necessary to avoid drawing suspicion; after all, if the family went to follow up, an administrative representative could legitimately say that the case was indefinitely open and they didn't have clearance to view the results, rather than needing to disclose that the record had vanished.

Most of the case notes from the family interviews were just gushing statements from the family about how wonderful their little girl had been and that they couldn't think of a reason why she would want to disappear. In almost every case, the young woman's last whereabouts were unknown.

Finally, though, one interview caught Banks' attention. A mother was describing her daughter and mentioned that she had a fear of open water, and how she was concerned about some upcoming travel. The last line of the interview jumped out: "She hoped that the island was big enough that she couldn't see the other side."

Traveling to an island… the Priesthood's island? There was no direct mention of the Priesthood or a specific location, so perhaps the automated review software had missed the reference.

The Priesthood would never intentionally implicate themselves, and this was a reach at best. But it was all Banks had to go on. Given the lack of details elsewhere, the other information had to have been doctored. Only the Priesthood could execute that kind of cover-up.

Banks took an unsteady breath. *Why would she be traveling to the Priesthood's island? And why wouldn't she come back?* The possibilities were chilling.

He stood up and paced the room, overcome with nerves. His recent actions on Tararia had already initiated a new plan with far-reaching implications. In so doing, he'd brought himself and his kin into the web of half-truths and secrets revolving around the Priesthood. Digging further now would place all of them at risk.

As much as he wanted to press forward with the investigation, he was in no position to do so alone. He needed Cris, or someone else with influence, working with him to broach the bigger issues of the Priesthood's absolute power. For now, he had to wait.

With a heavy heart, he placed a summary of his most recent discovery into the secured file, along with the details about his trip to Tararia. The time for that information would come in the future. For now, all he could do was remove the auto-rejection protocol from the TSS application. No more women would go missing on his watch. TSS Headquarters would be a safe haven— perhaps the only one.

CHAPTER 22

THERE WAS A fine line between crazy and brilliant. As they got closer to putting his latest battle plan into action, Wil wasn't sure on which side of the line they'd end up.

The *Conquest* floated on its own a kilometer from H2, granting full view of the facility on the viewscreen surrounding the Command Center. The spacedocks surrounding H2 were completely empty for the first time, leaving kilometers of structures barren and vulnerable. The illusion of an abandoned base was almost complete.

Wil relaxed into the chair behind his command podium, anxious for the transformation to get underway.

In front of him to the right, Michael shifted in his seat. His agreement to move forward with the plan to bait the Bakzen was tenuous at best.

Ian, Ethan, and Curtis had also voiced their support, but Wil could feel their doubts deep within. He was putting H2 at risk. Still, he stood by his decision. With dwindling resources, he needed to end the fighting as quickly as possible. That was his mandate, and he'd see it through.

Wil activated a comm link to H2. "What's your status?" he asked Laecy, who was overseeing the operation.

"All essential personnel have been relocated," she informed him. "We're ready to begin."

"Proceed," Wil ordered.

The lights on the massive H2 structure simultaneously extinguished, leaving the base illuminated only by the glow from the skeletal space docks around it. Under the eerie light, H2 began its transformation. Armored blast shields slid out from between the ring layers to cover all the viewports, encasing the entire structure in sheets of the same impact-absorbing metal that coated each TSS battleship. When the blast shields were locked in place, the ring at the center of the structure shuddered. Slowly, either half of H2 began to extend from the central ring— just enough for twelve pods around the previously seamless ring to begin swiveling ninety degrees. As the pods locked into their new perpendicular position, lights once again illuminated along the central ring. A moment later, the ring began to rotate— gaining momentum with each revolution. It gradually built up to a speed that would maintain standard Taran gravity within the outermost floors of each pod.

"I have to admit, that was pretty impressive," Ethan said, breaking the silence in the Command Center.

"I do have to hand it to the engineers," Wil agreed. "When I first saw the specs, I doubted it would really work. I'm glad they built in this feature."

"I doubt this was the original intention," Ian added.

Wil shrugged. "Well, times change."

Curtis grinned. "The kind of times where we send a 'please come attack us' message to the enemy?"

"Hey, whatever works. On that note… Michael, please send a distress message to the fleet stating that there's been a critical power failure at H2 and all ships are to report to their secondary bases," Wil instructed. "H2 will remain in lockdown with a skeleton crew until further notice."

With a heavy exhale, Michael made the entries in the console. "Message sent."

Wil nodded. "All right. Rianne, take us to the rendezvous at Kyron."

"Yes, sir," Rianne affirmed.

A blue-green subspace cloud overtook the ship, and they made the short jump to the nebula hosting a quarter of the TSS fleet until the battle began. Situated more than a jump's length from the nearest SiNavTech beacon, it was the safest place they had out of Bakzen reach while still remaining accessible enough to defend their base when the time came. If all went according to plan, they'd take out a good portion of the Bakzen fleet in the process.

Individual ships were all but invisible amid the gold and green gasses within the nebula, though their presence was indicated by ID tags floating around the viewscreen. Wil made note of the two carriers he'd redirected to the staging site. One would hang back as a reserve, but the fighters in the other would be a critical component to the opening counter-strike against the Bakzen.

So many variables. I hope this works... Wil took a slow breath to calm his rising nerves.

"What now?" Ian asked. His face was tense with anticipation for his tactical team's role in the upcoming fight. They'd no doubt face their toughest challenge yet.

Wil leaned back in his chair. "Now we wait."

—   —   —

Laecy made her final checks of the command module for the ring gyro in H2. With the artificial gravity disabled, the physical rotation was the only thing keeping her from losing her lunch. "I never thought we'd activate this protocol."

"No kidding." Nolan sighed. "I hope they know what they're doing."

"Wil wouldn't leave us here to die." At least that's what Laecy told herself. There was no room for doubt.

Nolan sealed the access hatch in the control room. "Everything looks good on our end. Time to hunker down."

"Let's hope the timing calculations are correct."

They headed for the safe room toward the center of the ring, where they'd wait with the skeleton crew remaining in H2, monitoring structural integrity on their tablets. Laecy took a deep, calming breath. *We'll make it through this. The war is almost over... Then I can finally have my time in the fields of*

Aderoth.

—   —   —

Haersen surveyed the holographic map alongside Tek. TSS forces had scattered to only a handful of remaining pockets within the Rift. Despite bringing down the Defense Barrier, the TSS seemed to be running for cover—too scared to venture into Bakzen territory. That gave the Bakzen the upper hand. All they had to do was stay on the offensive and the war would finally end.

"We almost have them," Haersen commented.

Tek grunted from the other side of the table. "We've had the TSS on the run like this before. They always find a way out."

"We need to hit them hard, before they have a chance to recover."

"Perhaps," the Bakzen leader mused, studying the map.

A rap on the door pulled them from their strategizing. The door swung open with a creak.

"Sir, I just received a new scout report from the TSS Rift base," General Komatra informed Tek from the doorway.

Haersen perked up with interest. With any luck, the report brought news of a new TSS vulnerability.

"Yes?" prompted Tek.

"It appears that the facility has entered some sort of lockdown," Komatra explained. "The fleet has dispersed, leaving the base largely unguarded."

It was too good to be true. "Sounds like a trap, sir," Haersen said with a frown.

"To what end?" Tek asked. "Why leave their command facility defenseless?"

"We sent the scout in response to an intercepted communication stating that the headquarters base was experiencing power issues," Komatra explained. "Based on the visual report, the story checks out. It looks like they might be abandoning the facility."

Haersen frowned. It wasn't like the TSS to retreat from a

main base. They were weak in many ways, but they were also stubbornly defensive of their homes.

Tek studied his two advisors. "Let's assume it is a trap. Why would they draw us to a vulnerable facility?"

"Make it easy to surround us," Haersen offered. "Hope for a quick hit to take out as many Bakzen ships as they can before we get our bearings."

"Their leadership has to know we'd expect it," Tek said.

"Maybe they think it's worth the risk?" Komatra offered.

"Perhaps," Tek agreed. "And maybe it is on both fronts—for us to call their bluff and take our chances."

Haersen crossed his arms. "As much as I'd like to see the TSS fall so quickly, there's little to gain by capturing the base."

"How so?" Tek asked. "The ships, technology records... The wealth of information would make it well worthwhile."

"Assuming they didn't activate a self-destruct protocol first," Haersen countered.

"Do you know of any such safeguard?" Tek pressed.

"I was never in H2, so I can't state for certain," Haersen admitted. "But I would anticipate that at least the Mainframe connections would be severed."

"Worst case, we scrap it for parts," Tek stated. "This presents us with an excellent opportunity, while all of their focus is on this fight." He turned his attention to Komatra. "Is the rift corridor to Earth complete?"

"It can be within the hour," Komatra replied. "We have a ship standing by with drones."

"Excellent. The TSS wants us to bring the fight to them, so we'll give them what they want. Let's see how they handle an attack on two fronts."

CHAPTER 23

"UH, MA'AM?"

Saera snapped back to attention, re-focusing on her students. "Sorry. Anyway, to express the subspace flow—"

"Class ended a minute ago," Becky continued.

"Oh." Saera checked the time on the viewscreen at the front of the classroom. "So it did. You're dismissed."

The dozen students in the advanced navigation class gathered their tablets and headed for the door.

Becky hung back from the others. "Is everything okay, ma'am?" she asked Saera as she walked by.

My husband won't talk to me for some inexplicable reason, and I'm stuck here on the sidelines while they're about to execute an insane battle plan. Things are far from okay. "That's sweet of you to ask," Saera replied. "There's nothing to worry about."

"You seem really distracted."

"Just a lot on my mind." Saera forced a smile. "I'll try to be more present for class going forward. I apologize."

"We do understand why you're distracted, you know," Becky said. "The war is in the final stages."

Saera leaned against the front desk. "Yes, it is."

"Will things change around here after it's over?"

"I don't know," Saera replied honestly. "We'll just have to see."

Becky nodded. "Anyway, I'm happy to listen if you ever need

to talk."

Saera patted her student's shoulder. "Thank you, I appreciate it. Now go on—that homework won't do itself."

Becky rolled her eyes, but a smile shined through. "See you in two days."

"Take care."

Saera let out a long breath as soon as Becky was gone. The constant tension gripping her chest was becoming too much to bear. Even Elise's support couldn't curb her frustration about being relegated to Headquarters while so much was happening on the frontlines. *Why is Wil making such reckless decisions? If only he hadn't shut me out...*

Just as she forced herself back on her feet, Saera's handheld buzzed in her pocket. She retrieved the device and saw that it was a message from Banks: >>My office. Now.<<

She groaned. *Are students filing complaints about my inattention?* As she trudged toward the door, another message came through: >>Bakzen are coming.<<

—   —   —

So many loose ends... There's no time to prepare. Banks rushed to his desk, running through a mental list of the most critical items to address.

The spatial rift forming next to Earth's moon would provide an open conduit for the Bakzen to invade the planet. Cambion was a great enough loss—he couldn't stand by and let the same thing happen on his watch. Unfortunately, the only way to prevent the spatial rift from forming completely would be a telekinetic charge stronger than anything in the TSS arsenal. *We need a bomb like the Bakzen use. I didn't think I'd have to die today.*

He was surprised how little he feared the prospect of death. Perhaps the knowledge that his death would serve a purpose made the idea more palatable. Whenever he'd thought about his own end before, he'd always hated the notion of growing old and slowly wasting away from his former self. The chance to go out in his prime was still terrifying, but there was comfort in knowing that he'd be remembered that way.

Still, for the first time in his life, he had been looking forward to a life outside the TSS. Even if it was from a distance, watching such monumental events unfold would have been a most satisfying culmination of his life's work. *At least I've made my contribution, even if I can't see the results.*

Since he wouldn't be there as a guide in the way he'd hoped, he needed to make sure that there would be a steward to protect that new vision for the future. There was no one he could trust more than Cris.

Using the genetic code of the unborn heir as the cipher, Banks hurriedly set up an encryption for all the Dainetris files. Cris would probably drive himself crazy trying to crack the code ahead of time, but it should all be clear to him as soon as the heir surfaced after he came of age and his mother passed on time-locked files given to her by Banks, per their agreement. More than anyone, Cris would know what to do with the information. The heir was only part of the equation, though—there was one message he needed to pass onto Wil, as well.

Banks barely glanced up from making the furious entries on his desktop when he heard Saera slip through the door to his office. The door clicked closed behind her. "What do you mean the Bakzen are coming?" she asked, breathless.

"The proximity alarms just detected a spatial rift forming between Headquarters and Earth," Banks replied in far too calm a tone. "We have maybe half an hour before the corridor is fully formed."

"We're completely defenseless! If they come through…"

Banks finished his entries and headed for the door.

"Where are you going?" Saera asked, panic pitching her voice.

"I need to seal the rift corridor. If we disable the nav beacon, no other ships will be able to follow. You'll be safe."

"Seal it? How—" Saera gaped at him, appalled when she realized what he was proposing. "You can't!"

"There's no other way, Saera. We might be fine here in Headquarters, if we're lucky, but Earth is completely exposed."

She clenched her fists, struggling to identify an alternative that didn't exist.

Banks took her by the shoulders. "Saera, you're the most senior Agent here. You'll be in command."

"Please, don't do this," Saera pleaded, but the urgency was already fading from her tone as she accepted the situation.

"Reseal the subspace lock as soon as I'm out," Banks instructed as he released Saera. "You'll need to set it to a rotating encryption key."

"I know the protocol."

"See? You'll be fine." Banks was about to leave, but turned and pulled Saera in for a hug. "Wil loves you more than anything. He'll always come back to you, no matter what."

Saera nodded into his shoulder. "It's been an honor serving with you."

Banks forced down the lump in his throat. "The honor was mine. Please make sure that Cris, Kate, and Wil know how much being a part of their family always meant to me."

"They know," Saera said, holding her hand to her chest. "Thank you for everything."

"Anytime." Before his resolution waned, Banks dashed to the door. The clock was ticking.

—   —   —

There was no time to waste. Saera rushed to the viewscreen on the side wall of Banks' office. "CACI, activate a Headquarters-wide communication." The computer chirped with compliance, and Saera's image appeared on the viewscreen.

"An Alpha-One lockdown is now in effect. I am in command," she stated. "All Trainees are to immediately report to their home mess hall. Initiates are to return to your quarters and prepare to access the weapon's cache in your common room. All Agents, Junior Agents, and Militia officers are to follow your designated Alpha-One orders. If an enemy breaches our walls, use any force necessary."

Saera swiped her hand sideways to end the transmission. *Is this really happening?* Her mind flashed to what Banks was about to do—the sacrifice he would make to save her world. There was no greater parting gift a person could give.

Suppressing the emotion knotting her chest, she activated the holographic projector in front of the viewscreen. A schematic of Headquarters illuminated before her, complete with the entry shaft from the moon's surface. She spotted a single elevator car making its way toward the surface, indicated by a wireframe representation. The car passed through the subspace lock, and she sprang into action.

"CACI, seal the subspace lock and secure with the following encryption." She opened a command window and began manually configuring a code. Wil might be able to crack it, but it should hold off the Bakzen long enough for everyone to get into position within Headquarters if Banks wasn't successful.

"Lock set," CACI confirmed in its synthesized female voice.

Saera tensed. *I need to tell the rest of the fleet! If we don't make it, they need to know what happened.*

—   —   —

The Command Center of the *Vanquish* was far too quiet while they waited for Wil's order to jump from their hiding place in the Kyron nebula. Cris nearly jumped at the sound of his own seat creaking as he shifted position.

"Any minute now," Kate said to break the silence. She slouched in the command chair to his right.

"I can't wait until this is over," Cris muttered. *I never dreamed we'd be instigating a battle at H2.*

A chirp sounded on the front right console a step below the central dais.

"Message coming through from Headquarters," Kari informed Cris. Her brow wrinkled. "The origin is the High Commander's office, but it's Saera's code."

"Open a channel," Cris instructed.

Saera's image appeared on the front of the curved dome. "We're under attack," she said the moment the video resolved.

Kate took a sharp breath next to him.

"Bakzen?" Cris asked, his pulse spiking.

"They're about to open a spatial rift. It's maybe ten minutes from tearing through. Banks is going to stop it. He's in a shuttle now." Saera crossed her arms around herself. "He said there's no other way."

Cris' mouth fell open with horror. "He's going to throw himself into space—"

"The Bakzen fleet just appeared at H2," Kari cut in. "Wil gave the order for our first wave to jump in."

Shite! That's us. There was no time to jump back to Headquarters and make it back for the impending battle at H2. It was one or the other. "If we…"

"The carrier is exposed without us," Kate reminded him, even though it didn't need to be said.

We can't deviate from the plan. Headquarters is on its own. Cris' gut wrenched. "Make the jump to H2, Alec."

"Aye," Alec affirmed.

"We'll be there as soon as we can, Saera," Cris told her as the *Vanquish* slipped into subspace. By then it would be over, but there was nothing more they could do. *I'm sorry, Banks.*

Kate reached across the center console and took Cris' hand in hers. *"We'll win this for him."*

—   —   —

The compact transport ship that normally served as a ferry between the spaceport and surface of the moon now felt more like a coffin. Banks cast aside the thought as he struggled to override the autopilot so he could direct the craft toward the spatial rift.

Unfortunately, the shuttle was never designed to deviate from its set course. *There's no time to go all the way to the port to get another ship. I need to make this work.*

The shuttle let out another angry buzz of disapproval as Banks' latest attempt to bypass the security safeguards failed. "Insufficient route data," CACI stated.

I know… it's a one-way trip. He let out a gruff sigh and

dislodged the main panel beneath the console. "You asked for it," he muttered as he dropped to his knees to get a better vantage. The crystalline circuitry all looked identical at first glance, but his trained eye spotted the regulating command module. He wrenched it from the console with his thumb and forefinger.

The console blanked for a moment, then refreshed with a flash. Banks tried his route input again.

"Route confirmed," CACI stated, and the shuttle lifted from the surface.

Banks set the chip on top of the console and took a deep breath. His life would be over in a matter of minutes.

What will be my legacy? War, manipulation, deceit—he could only hope to be remembered for more. Others may never know what he'd done for them over his career, but he could enter into his eternal rest knowing that he'd had a hand in changing the course of Taran history. Though for better or worse remained to be seen, at least he had followed his beliefs. The Priesthood's unchecked rule could finally end with Cris leading the charge.

The shuttle made its silent approach to the spatial rift and adjacent nav beacon. Focusing on the nav beacon, Banks gripped it with his mind and rended it apart in four directions at once. The beacon shattered in a shower of sparks, its signal disconnected. Without the beacon or the rift corridor, only a TSS ship with an independent jump drive could make the journey in any reasonable amount of time.

The emerging rift was practically invisible to the naked eye, but Banks could feel its signature. Electromagnetic sparks danced before his mind's eye as space frayed around the edge of the corridor. His surroundings sang and pulsed with an eternal chorus of ancient energy he had heard so rarely in recent years— always confined to Headquarters, performing his duties. To spend his final moment so close to the unbridled power within the rift was freeing. His mind was clear, his senses unburdened. Never had he felt so alive.

While he yearned to bask in its energy, the Bakzen were knocking on the door to his home and he had one final task to complete. He removed his tinted glasses and placed them in his inner pocket one last time.

Banks cleared his mind and began to form a spatial dislocation field around himself, creating a bubble within the shuttle. The air was still as the energy swirled around him in a shimmering orb of light. He lifted off the floor and passed through the shuttle's ceiling in that state on the brink of subspace—energized and confident.

Drawn by the immense energy of the forming rift portal, he drew himself to its center in open space. He drank in the energy, using it to feed the power coursing through his body.

It is a part of me, his consciousness called, from somewhere that was not his former self. The tendrils of the natural energy grid resonated with him, drawing him in. Twisted darkness from the Bakzen's attempts to warp the fabric of space tried to push through the natural energy web, but the light emanating from Banks held it at bay.

Banks released himself to the light. The natural grid rippled as the energy tendrils solidified into unbreakable bonds. No more could the structure be twisted. The rift corridor was sealed.

Energy swelled around the former portal, gathering along the ancient energy corridors beneath the fabric of reality. The natural grid flexed around the marring corridor that the Bakzen had started to rip through the fabric, snapping the energy pathways back into their proper forms and dislodging the Bakzen forces within to endlessly drift within subspace.

With a flash, the concentration of energy dissipated, as though nothing was ever out of place.

Only a single, empty transport shuttle floated in the blackness. One sentinel, watching over Earth below.

CHAPTER 24

WIL LEAPED TO his feet and gripped the handholds at his command pedestal. *"Jump on my mark..."* he ordered. *"Now!"*

In an instant, the first wave of TSS ships within the Kyron belt disappeared into the blue-green cloud of subspace.

The *Conquest* shuddered as the cloud lifted around them at their destination, revealing a battle already unfolding.

Eight heavily armored enemy cruisers and two carriers were positioned at great enough distances from H2 that there was no way to surround the Bakzen forces. Two cruisers occupied each quadrant around the central TSS target and the two Bakzen carriers were on the opposite side of the battlefield from the TSS carrier the *Vanquish* was escorting. Bakzen assault fighters from the cruisers and carrier swarmed around H2 in triangular formations of six—raining shots before arcing away to avoid counter-attack blasts from H2. The less nimble carriers, however, already showed signs of damage where H2's rail guns had sliced through the outer hull shielding.

Between each set of fighter attacks, the Bakzen cruisers took two rapid shots targeted at the connection point between the rotating central ring and the rest of the structure—the greatest weak point for the transformed facility. The armor was rated for five minutes of constant fire, but Wil couldn't be sure the exposed mechanical mechanisms would hold out for half that long. They needed to offer immediate relief.

Unfortunately, the Bakzen's positioning was exactly what Wil would have done, were the roles reversed. He searched for any possible weakness in the formations, but none stood out. However, inaction would get them nowhere.

Wil gripped the handholds of his pedestal and slipped into a state of simultaneous observation. A cross-section of the planes appeared around him as only ethereal echoes of the places and objects in each until he focused in on just one. With the overall image relayed through the *Conquest*'s neural interface, his officers in the Command Center had a clear image of the battle on all fronts. Their telepathic commands to the rest of the fleet flitted through Wil's mind with instantaneous precision.

"Focus your fire on each of the cruisers," Ian commanded to his tactical teams.

"Surround the Bakzen ships," Michael ordered the fleet commanders. *"Don't let any stray too far. We need to keep them contained."*

Curtis contacted the flight leaders for the fleet of TSS fighters, *"Separate the Bakzen formations and pull them out of pattern. Thin them out."*

"Gamma Squad," Ethan said, *"take out the shield on the cruiser docking bay so they have nowhere to run. Watch out for the Detno!"*

Each order was accompanied with the tactical specifics through a combination of telepathic imagery and computer inputs on their consoles. A fluid tapestry of battle plans overlaid on the rendering of the space around the *Conquest* on the Command Center's spherical viewscreen. Flight paths and targets illuminated in a rainbow of colors that would seem like complete chaos to any outsider, but all their training and drillings had been building to that moment. They were in control.

With his men focusing on the minutia, Wil extended himself to get a broader picture of the battle zone. *They were clearly expecting us. That can't be all their ships.* Then, he spotted the second wave charging on three fronts.

"Incoming!" Wil warned in the minds of his officers.

The Bakzen fleet surged forward through the Rift. On the final approach, a wave of fighters poured out of the hangers of a dozen new cruisers and three additional carriers. The fighters fanned out before winking out of view.

In response, Wil stretched himself in an elevated state of simultaneous observation so he could maintain a broad vantage across all planes. His team rallied around him, but there was hesitation without having Saera there as an extra anchor. *"We have this. Hang on,"* Wil tried to assure them as he pressed further.

The echoing forms of the overlapping planes came into view in his mind's eye. He cycled through the Rift, subspace and normal space, trying to locate all the Bakzen vessels. They were all changing planes at different times—Wil would have to keep track of all three at once.

It's too much. His vision slipped, craving the simplicity of the physical world.

Michael caught him. *"Don't give up."*

Wil took a deep breath and focused on the fighters. He studied their movements, looking for patterns across the planes. As he watched them, three groups emerged. One group was headed for H2, one was going for the main TSS carrier, and the last was headed straight for the *Conquest*.

"Curtis, send a team to intercept the group heading for H2. Michael, have the Vanquish *move into position to defend the carrier,"* Wil ordered. *"Get the rest of our fleet here!"*

His men relayed the telepathic commands to their counterparts in the field, transmitting the mental image Wil was routing through the *Conquest*. The TSS forces moved seamlessly into place through normal space, ready to strike when the moment was right.

Wil tracked the enemy forces, waiting for their flight pattern to loop back to when the greatest number of ships were all within the Rift where the Agent pilots were strongest. *"Jump!"*

The TSS fleet moved at once, opening fire even before the ships were fully clear from subspace.

Bakzen fighters banked to the side, some slipping back into subspace to avoid the stealth attack. But the TSS ships were waiting there, too.

Wil and his officers herded the Bakzen ships back toward the main fleet where the two dozen cruisers opened fire on the cornered Bakzen ships just as the TSS fighters would slip out of harm's way.

The reserve TSS contingent emerged from the subspace cloud around the Bakzen forces, immediately opening fire on the newest cruisers and carriers. Two TSS tactical warships under Ian's command made a run for a new Bakzen carrier—disabling the launch bay before any more fighters could emerge. A TSS cruiser moved into position to assist the smaller tactical vessels, overwhelming the Bakzen carrier until it buckled. The TSS ships pulled back just in time to avoid the explosive decompression blast from the ruined Bakzen carrier. Three Bakzen cruisers occupied with an assault on H2 were caught in the blast, charring their hulls and disrupting their fire.

More Bakzen fighters were destroyed with every pass of the TSS fighters looping through the battlefield, weaving through the planes using the relayed map from Wil. The damaged vessels were dealt swift deathblows, leaving a field of debris floating around the fractured former TSS space dock and scarred H2 structure.

Empowered by Wil's vision across the spatial planes, the TSS was waiting to counter every Bakzen move. For every TSS ship damaged, four Bakzen ships were completely destroyed.

Wil kept a vigilant eye on the Bakzen command ships as the battle progressed. One, in particular, was holding back. *"Are you there, Tek?"* Wil asked across the distance, not expecting a reply.

But a voice did respond. *"Well played."*

Before Wil could react, the ship jumped away—stranding all its fighters in a hopeless battle against the superior TSS forces.

He tightened his grip on the handhold, anger boiling in his chest. *Next time, I won't let him get away. All the destruction over the years, Cambion, the wedge he drove between Saera and me… Tek needs to die.*

"They're retreating!" Ian exclaimed to the group.

Another Bakzen cruiser jumped away, but seven more floated helplessly on the battlefield—their jump drives disabled in the tactical team's precision strikes.

"It's not over yet," Wil reminded his team.

He spotted a group of Bakzen fighters that were still making a desperate run for H2 through the wreckage. *"The armor can't take much more. We need to end this."*

"I'm on it," Ethan said, and began doling out commands to the fighter squadrons.

Wil watched the IT-1s weave through the planes with expert precision, corralling the Bakzen fighters before they knew they were surrounded. The IT-1s jumped into the Rift in one fluid motion, bombarding the Bakzen vessels with a deadly barrage. In an instant, the dozen enemy fighters exploded in fiery bursts that quickly extinguished in the vacuum of space.

Only one mobile Bakzen carrier remained—making a suicide run for H2.

"Take it out!" Wil ordered, even though the TSS fleet was already targeting everything they had left at the ship. Easily two-thirds the size of H2, the mass of the craft was simply too great to be shifted from its course.

"We need to do something!" Michael pleaded.

Only one other weapon remained. Wil pulled out of simultaneous observation to focus on the Rift, solidifying his connection to the ship and its systems. Around him, he felt his men following his lead, gripping their handholds tighter as they began to feed pure telekinetic energy into the neural link pathways. The energy coursed through the ship, gathering along the amplifier ring around its perimeter.

The *Conquest* buzzed with the charge, an audible hum filling the air as the energy mounted—but there was no time to wait for a complete charge. The ship was mere seconds from impact.

Wil released the energy beam, striking the front third of the Bakzen cruiser on the starboard side. The ship splintered apart in a blinding flash as a ball of energy billowed out from the impact site—nearly enveloping H2.

A feedback spark shot back through the *Conquest*'s neural relays, forcing Wil to release the handhold on his pedestal. His officers around him shook their hands with surprise as the shock reached them.

He gazed at the surrounding viewscreen to assess the damage while the energy sparks in the pedestal dissipated. Except, there wasn't anything left to see.

"Where's the carrier?" Ethan asked.

"Completely vaporized," Wil stated. Remarkably, H2 appeared unscathed aside from the blackened shielding where the first Bakzen wave had their short advantage.

"That wasn't even a full charge…" Curtis breathed.

"I guess that's what the combined force of five powerful Agents can do," Wil murmured. *Or me alone. This is one way I never wanted to use my power.*

On the viewscreen, the rest of the TSS fleet opened fire on the disabled Bakzen cruisers, erupting each into a quickly extinguished fireball as the ships decompressed.

Wil and his men smiled at each other. "We did it."

A comm chirp sounded in the Command Center.

"It's the *Vanquish*." Rianne announced.

"Accept," Wil said, looking to the front of the dome.

An image of the *Vanquish*'s Command Center appeared with his parents at the center. "Are there any more Bakzen ships waiting in subspace?" Cris asked.

"No, that was the last of them," Wil confirmed.

His father slumped in his command chair. "I guess we won the battle."

"That went a lot better than I expected," Wil admitted with a grin.

Cris didn't share his enthusiasm. "I'm afraid there was another development. I'm coming over. We need to talk."

CHAPTER 25

WIL SAT IN quiet contemplation in the *Conquest*'s Strategy Room, waiting for his father to arrive. An in-person meeting almost certainly meant his father brought bad news. *What could it be? I hope Saera—*

The door slid open with a hiss and his parents entered. Their mouths were drawn and even with their tinted glasses he could see the loss in their expressions.

"What is it?" Wil asked.

Cris and Kate walked to him, stopping an arm's length away. Wil stood.

"The Bakzen took our bait," Cris began, "but they had another plan of their own. While we were busy here, they sent another fleet for our home Headquarters."

An icy chill washed over Wil. *Earth is completely defenseless! Did they...?*

"They were constructing a spatial rift corridor," Cris continued before Wil could speak. "The sensors around Headquarters saw it forming, fortunately, so there was time to act. Banks—" his voice caught, "Banks did what any great commander would do and stopped it."

"How?" Wil stammered.

"The same way the Bakzen make the rifts," Kate said. "The power to destroy and the power to rebuild."

Wil choked on his breath as knives stabbed into his heart.

"He's gone?" *The war was never supposed to touch our home.*

Cris nodded and pulled Wil into an embrace. "But we're safe. Our home is safe."

"Saera?" Wil asked into his father's shoulder.

"She's fine. The Bakzen never made it through," Kate assured him, rubbing his back.

Wil stepped away from his father. "They'll come back."

"The nav beacon is destroyed," Cris stated. "The only way to get there is with a true independent jump drive."

Wil leaned against the conference table, his breath ragged. "I never should have left it so exposed."

"We needed every ship we had," Cris tried to comfort him. "No size fleet would have guaranteed Earth's safety. Sealing the rift corridor was the only way."

"We should have taken out the beacon sooner. Something!" Wil exclaimed.

"It's done now," his mother murmured.

I can't believe he's dead... Banks was always more family than commander. Beyond the loss of an exceptional leader, there would be a hole in Wil's life. Mentor, surrogate grandfather, protector—Banks had always looked out for Wil even through the most difficult moments of his life. As much as Wil despised the manipulation and deceit, he knew in his heart that he would have been in a far worse place were it not for Banks' guidance. No words felt fitting to express the loss, and so he remained silent.

"Saera is in command," Cris stated. "Headquarters is still in lockdown."

Wil nodded slowly. "I should call her." His parents glanced at each other, no doubt still perplexed by why Wil had sent her away in the first place.

"We have a lot of cleanup to begin," Cris said at last. "Take some time to recover."

"No." Wil stepped forward from the table. "We need to go after the Bakzen now, before they have time to regroup."

"We're in no shape—" Cris started to protest.

"We're in better shape than them for the moment," Wil countered. "We need to cut off the rest of their supply lines so they can't rebuild. We have to act fast, before they expect it."

Kate sighed. "All right. I'll get the ships that are still able to fight ready to go."

"We'll leave in an hour," Wil instructed. "They'll go for Tararia next. We'll head them off."

"Okay," Cris agreed. "And please do check in with Saera."

"Yeah." Wil took a few minutes to gather himself after his parents departed. Banks' loss would leave a deep scar.

He took a resolute breath and initiated a call to Headquarters on the viewscreen, where the communication automatically routed to Saera's location. An image of her resolved on the viewscreen against the backdrop of the High Commander's office. "Hey," he greeted.

"Hi," she replied. Her normal radiance was absent, as though she was just a shell of herself.

I did that to her. I sent her away, abandoned her. I destroyed myself to save her and then gave up the very thing I wanted to protect. His chest ached. "I'm so sorry."

"You heard about Banks?" Saera asked after a moment, her voice shaking.

"My parents just told me. Are you okay?"

"I should be asking you that. You knew him way better than me."

Wil's shoulders rounded. *This is too much to process right now.* "I thought you'd be safe there."

"Apparently, nowhere is safe from the war," Saera murmured. "I still don't understand what happened—why you sent me back here."

"I was shortsighted," Wil admitted. *I did exactly what the Bakzen wanted—played right into their hand. I should have seen all of it coming, but I lost focus.* "It's all my fault."

"We've all just been doing the best we can under the circumstances."

Wil leaned against the conference table. "I'll make things right again, Saera. Somehow." He let out a long breath. "How are you holding up?"

Saera wiped a tear from beneath her tinted glasses. "I feel like everything's falling apart."

"Not everything." Wil pushed off the table and stepped close to the viewscreen. "I'm going to end this war, and we won't have to live in fear anymore."

"I'd rather live in fear than continue being apart from you like this."

"It won't be for much longer," Wil told her, hoping it was true.

"Let me come back!" Saera pleaded. "Let me help."

Maybe if Banks were still there. "There's no time for transport now. Besides, Headquarters needs you. Make everyone feel safe. It's almost over."

"What about you?"

"I'm fine," Wil insisted.

Saera shook her head. "No, you're not. Going a week without talking to me… What's been going on?"

I can never tell her about Cambion. No one can ever know. "That's something I still can't share. Try to accept that—I can't lose you."

"Then stop pushing me away."

"I never should have," Wil said, hanging his head. *I let the enemy get to me.*

Saera bit her lower lip. "I will always be here for you. But I can't help if you don't let me."

"Right now, the best help is staying safe and looking after our home. I'll come back to you as soon as I can." *If there's anything of me left.*

"You'd better." Saera ventured a smile.

Wil smiled back through the pain. "I love you."

"Love you, too. Now go get the bad guys."

—   —   —

Cris looked over the ship manifest Kate had gathered. They were in better shape than he expected. Unfortunately, they had no indication of the Bakzen's reserve forces.

"Do you really think they'll make a run for Tararia?" Kate asked.

"That's been their goal all along," Cris replied. "Eliminate all Tarans and make the Bakzen the prominent race."

Kate examined the viewscreen. "Based on this manifest, we do have sufficient numbers to blockade each of the subspace corridors heading for Tararia."

"It'll be thin, but the Bakzen can't be in much better shape by this point," Cris agreed. "All the targets are within close jump range, so we can redistribute once we know where they're coming from."

Kate crossed her arms. "There has to be a better offensive strategy."

"If only there were a way to collapse the corridors..." Cris mused.

"Maybe there is!" Kate exclaimed. "Wil's ship. Destroying or collapsing portions of the Rift takes more energy than one person can handle and it burns them out. However, sharing the load across five people and running it through the amplifier..."

Cris lit up. "That just might work."

—   —   —

The shadow of High Commander Banks' death had left a sober mood in the *Conquest*'s Command Center, despite the former excitement of their battle victory. Michael made no effort to cheer up his comrades, knowing that everyone processed loss in their own way. The news would be kept need-to-know for the time being, but he was grateful for the certainty that Earth was safe.

As soon as he'd heard about the attack, he'd messaged Elise. She had only had time for a short reply, but it sounded like Saera was holding things together for the time being. Michael wished he could be there to comfort his friends, but they had more pressing issues to worry about in the field.

Little time remained to make repairs in preparation for the next assault. The last hour had been a flurry of communications and system checks. They were almost ready, but their leader had yet to show himself.

"Any word from Wil?" Michael asked Ian, who was working at his adjacent console.

"No. I'm surprised he isn't here," Ian replied.

"We need to talk strategy." Michael reached out with his mind, searching for Wil. It only took a moment to identify that he was in the Strategy Room. *"We're prepared to head out on your order,"* he told him. No response. Michael sighed. "I'll be right back."

Michael exited the Command Center and stepped across the hall to the Strategy Room. He hit the buzzer on the door but immediately stepped inside.

Wil was at the back of the room staring out the viewport at the salvage ships beginning to clear the scrap from the battlefield. H2 was still in its transformed state, and a series of shuttles were examining the armor plating for critical damage.

"Hi," Michael greeted. He stepped inside and the door automatically closed behind him. "Are you ready to head out?"

Wil slumped against the back bulkhead. "I'm really not, but we need to."

Michael approached the table on the opposite side from Wil. "I know you lost a close friend today, but the rest of us are counting on you. You were great in the battle—exactly how we always hoped we'd be together."

"We still lost twenty percent of our forces," Wil replied.

"And took out about ninety percent of the Bakzen. I'd say those are pretty good margins."

Wil scoffed, shaking his head.

"We're all tired, Wil. We both almost had our home destroyed. We just need to push through and end this."

"I know. Even still… I can feel myself slipping away," Wil murmured. "When we vaporized that carrier, I was reminded of the kind of destruction my power could bring—it wouldn't even take this ship as an amplifier. I have no right to decide who lives and dies, but that's exactly what I'm doing."

"It's what we're all doing. But right now, we have an opportunity to prevent even greater losses," Michael said. "Your parents had an idea."

"To use the ship to restore the rift corridors to the natural energy grid?" Wil asked.

"Yeah…"

"I've been thinking about that, too. It never occurred to me before, but I'm still not sure it'll be enough."

Michael shrugged. "We don't know until we try. It's the best shot we have right now to seal off Tararia from a Bakzen stealth attack, without sacrificing more lives."

"Or we just go straight for the Bakzen homeworld."

"That still leaves Tararia exposed." Michael placed his palms on the tabletop and leaned forward. "I don't like what we have to do, either, but running away from your abilities won't help matters. Let's just get this done, and then we can find some way to atone."

Wil swallowed. "There's no atonement for what I've done and what I'm about to do."

"Is stopping here any better?"

His friend hung his head.

"Come on," Michael said, trying to sound upbeat. "We're finally making headway. We can't stop now."

Wil took a slow breath and nodded. He silently stepped around the table toward the door.

"Look, Wil, I know things have been tough." Michael met him by the door and placed his hand on his shoulder. "We're all here for you." *Including Saera, even if it is from a distance.*

"Thanks."

They returned to the Command Center across the hall and took their stations at the pedestals.

"All right, where do we get started?" Wil said as he pulled up a star map around the domed viewscreen. He activated an overlay of the rift corridors.

"Tararia is the most logical Bakzen target," Michael suggested.

"That has always been Tek's prize. We just spat in his face and he'll be looking for payback." Wil examined the pathways around Tararia, zooming in with his hands. "Here." He pointed at three rift corridors extending almost to Tararia. "They'll use these. It follows with the rest of their strategies."

"So, we collapse the pathways?" Ethan asked.

"That's the idea, anyway," Wil confirmed. "It looks like this corridor is the main route to the nearest Bakzen base." He pointed along the pathway with his finger across the ceiling. "I say we try collapsing that one first."

"Sounds good to me," Curtis agreed with a shrug.

"Michael, are any of the cruisers able to travel yet?" Wil asked.

Michael checked the reports again and saw that eight cruisers were reporting less than five percent damage. "Several."

"Pick two and have them jump with us to…" Wil studied the map again, "…Merda."

The planet was located midway along the rift corridor, passing by two intersecting pathways. "Are you hoping for a chain reaction?" Michael asked.

"May as well try," Wil replied.

Michael selected two of the cruisers with the least damage and sent the command. "Ready."

"Rianne, take us over," Wil ordered.

"Aye," she acknowledged and activated the jump.

The *Conquest* dropped out of subspace at the outermost end of visual range from the planet Merda. Their position was at the closest intersection of the target rift corridors. Michael swallowed hard. *We should be trying a small corridor first, not a full chain reaction.*

Wil must have sensed his doubt because he glanced over at him. "Don't worry, we'll start small. I just figured this way we won't have to relocate."

Michael breathed a sigh of relief. *It must have taken hundreds of thousands of Bakzen to form the Rift over the centuries. What kind of impact can a handful of us have?* "So, what do we do?"

"I've never closed a rift before, so I really have no idea," Wil admitted. He gripped his handholds. "Time to experiment."

Grabbing his own handhold, Michael felt the now familiar surge of energy through the *Conquest*. The Captains established their positions in the telepathic connection and waited for Wil's direction.

Wil led them toward one of the smaller corridors and began assessing it—pulling at the tendrils yanked apart from the natural energy grid to open up the Rift. He directed a collective pulse of energy through the ship into the grid to test its reaction. The tendrils flickered and bent in the direction of the energy pulse, like a flower orienting toward sunlight.

"That's it," Wil said. *"We can direct the grid."*

"It will take forever moving tendril by tendril," Ian protested.

"We shouldn't go too fast. We have no idea how it will react to a greater concentration of energy," Michael cautioned the group.

"Ian is right," Wil said. *"We can't go this slowly. We need to ramp it up."* He began charging the ship for a new energy pulse, pausing when it was ten times the magnitude of the first.

The energy beam shot from the ship, directed at the center of the corridor where the smaller pulse had yielded success. Energy from the beam coalesced into an orb with spikes fanning out to the surrounding grid.

The grid shuddered as it began to warp around the new energy orb. As it fused with the surrounding grid, the orb contracted, then quickly expanded as energy poured in through the spikes—creating an even larger sphere of unchecked power.

We need to get away. Michael tugged at the minds of his comrades, but they were transfixed by the interplay of electromagnetic energy.

Wil reached out toward the forms, trying to guide the flow to repair the grid, just as he'd done before. But it was too much, moving far too quickly and still growing stronger.

Michael retreated, barely maintaining the neural link. *"Wil, stop!"* He shouted in his friend's mind.

"I can fix it!" Wil insisted. *"Let me—"*

There was no time to find out. Michael disconnected from the neural link and dove toward Wil at his pedestal. The others released their handholds with a start, their link severed.

Outside, the blue energy orb exploded outward, sending a shockwave that rocked the *Conquest*. The waves cascaded through the very fabric of space around them along the rift corridor, illuminating briefly with a spark of blue light as the shockwave traveled outward.

"What happened?" Ethan asked.

Wil shoved Michael off of him. "I wasn't finished."

"That shockwave would have incinerated us if we'd been connected," Michael shot back.

Curtis gestured to the viewing dome to bring up the map of the rift pathways. Everyone gasped when they saw the real-time readings.

"Stars! We made it worse," Wil breathed.

There had been a chain reaction, as they had hoped—but their work had only served to rip the rift pathway even closer to Tararia. So close that a ship could practically cruise right to the planet through the Rift, barely detectable. With the energy signature rippling back in the other direction, as well, they'd just sent the Bakzen an express invite to attack.

Wil gaped at the map. "We need to go for the Bakzen homeworld. Now."

CHAPTER 26

"WE'RE NOT PREPARED for a planetary invasion!" Michael exclaimed.

Wil dismissed his friend's objection. "Now is our best shot. We'll take off the head of the beast." Before anyone else could protest, he initiated a telepathic link to his officers scattered around the fleet. *"We're going for the Bakzen homeworld. All capable ships are to jump on my mark."*

"What's the plan?" Ian asked.

Wil flashed a wry grin. "Shoot the bad guys." He looked around at the concerned faces of his Command Center crew. "We have the telepathic commands down. It's just like we used to practice—making up scenarios on the fly. Follow my lead and trust your instincts. We can do this."

They took deep breaths and grabbed their handholds.

"And we need everyone," Wil continued. "Ethan, is Tom healed enough to fly?"

Ethan nodded. "He's rearing to go."

"All right, have the Primus Squad suit up. Prep the rest of the fleet to jump."

The next several minutes were a flurry of telepathic and spoken commands as the fleet prepared to mobilize.

"We're ready," Michael said at last.

"Okay. Let me scout ahead." Wil slipped into a state of simultaneous observation, tethered to the ship. He reached outward toward Bakzen territory, taking in the various inhabited outposts dotting the Rift, but those would all be easy to eliminate once the center of command was gone.

I just need to see where we're going... Wil reached out further, but his vision unexpectedly began to distort as he approached the main planet. He struggled to fight through the fog, but he couldn't make out any details about the Bakzen forces surrounding the planet in normal space or the Rift. After a full minute of trying to cut through and getting nowhere, he pulled back to his physical self. "Shite."

"What was it?" Michael asked, frowning.

"I can't get through whatever that was blocking my view. We'll have to jump in blind." Wil pulled up the command interface for the navigation network on the lower portion of the viewscreen. "This will all need to happen fast. Since we don't have a nav beacon at the destination, we'll need to feed coordinates to the ships that don't have independent jump drives. The *Conquest* will jump in and relay the rendezvous details to the rest of the fleet. We'll only have a few seconds to act and maintain the element of surprise."

"I'm standing by," Rianne assured him.

"All right. Now, I remember the Bakzen having the majority of their forces in the Rift, so we'll tackle that first and then pick off the rest in normal space. The planet is populated in normal space, just like any of ours," Wil continued. "Michael, Ian, and Ethan, I want you to clear the Rift. Curtis, assess the situation on the planet and figure out how to fence them in. I won't be able to do much else while holding both of those visuals for you. Once we clear the Rift, we'll pull into normal space and finish off the planet."

Curtis smirked. "Easy!"

"I knew you'd think so." Wil tightened his grip on his handhold. "Let's go!"

The *Conquest* vibrated with a surge of energy as it slipped into subspace. It hovered for a moment in the swirling cloud before dropping into normal space.

"Stars!" Wil breathed.

Taking up the entire front of the viewscreen, the Bakzen

planet stood out against the blackness of space as a uniform brown. The *Conquest* was situated toward the planet's dawn, and the atmosphere glowed slightly in the rays of light. Wispy white clouds swirled in the sky over the barren rust-colored landscape below. In the areas still cast in shadow, lights illuminated massive cities laid out in precise grids around a central district, like spokes on a wheel. In orbit of the planet, massive spaceports housing warships were situated in geosynchronous orbit. If it wasn't an enemy force, Wil would have been impressed with the scale and design of the structures—enough to rival the most developed Taran worlds. If the Bakzen could accomplish so much while relegated to the outskirts of society with minimal resources, he couldn't help but wonder what would have been possible if the Bakzen had been embraced by Tarans as their creators originally intended.

"Coordinates acquired!" Rianne announced. "Transmitting to the fleet now."

There was no time to waste. Wil detached from his physical self and pulled into a state of simultaneous observation. The clear image of normal space distorted as he passed through the dimensional veil. Beyond, he found the Rift. Except, it was no longer the stockpile of weaponry he had witnessed as a teenager. There were spaceports surrounding the planet, but they were only empty skeletons.

The fleet is jumping to the wrong place! Curtis' tactical team would be completely exposed on its own. *"They're not in the Rift,"* Wil hurriedly told his officers. *"Head straight for normal space."*

He shifted his attention to observing the physical plane around him, but kept the back of his consciousness connected enough to the Rift to detect any new Bakzen presence.

The planet below was fortified, but surprisingly few ships were standing guard. Then again, Tararia or any of the other planets didn't have a large-scale defense fleet, either. The fight was never supposed to come to one's front door.

A pang of guilt struck Wil. *This entire civilization is about to end.* He hated that truth, but he had no other choice. He needed to restore peace, and that would only be possible once the Bakzen were no longer a threat. Hatred for Tararia ran too deep for them to find any common ground. The outcome was decided well before he was ever born. He just needed to carry out the order.

Tek is down there, he reminded himself, to fuel his motivation for the final hunt. *The war ends today.*

The fleet emerged from subspace in one spectacular wave. As the blue-green cloud dissipated, Wil saw that only half the fleet had received the command to go to normal space rather than the Rift. They'd have to make do until the rest could make the dimensional jump.

Determined to not allow himself to become distracted by the emotional weight of what he was about to do, Wil gripped his handhold tighter and began doling out commands. *"Michael, have the fleet concentrate on the space docks first. We need to drive them to the surface. Ian, send tactical teams to begin a bombardment on the main cities. Take out the command centers so they can't mobilize."*

Wil swallowed the knot in his throat as the initial weapons fire rained from the ships on the viewscreen. *There's no other way.*

—   —   —

Another blast shook the administrative building, sending a shower of concrete dust onto Haersen's shoulders.

"We need to get down to a bunker!" he insisted to Tek again.

The Imperial Director shook his head, not taking his gaze from the display on his wall. The grid of video feeds depicted the destruction all around the planet and its surrounding ports. Once majestic cities were slowly being reduced to rubble with each passing TSS bombardment.

"If we take the tunnels to the port—" Haersen began.

"No." Tek finally tore his attention from the screen. "They won't stop until we're destroyed. All of us. I would rather die in my home than run like a coward."

"Yes, sir."

To think after all those years and finally gaining the power

Haersen had desired his whole life, the TSS would win in the end. The Bakzen were no doubt superior, but the TSS did have numbers on their side. In the end, perhaps that was enough.

The building shuddered as the adjacent plaza burst into flames.

Haersen took in his reflection against the glass of the viewport. His transformation was complete—he was one of the Bakzen, despite the odds. He had pledged to live as one of them, and so he would die as one. They had given him power and strength, but also the confidence to be himself. Though his time with them was short, it was the only opportunity he'd had to live to the fullest—the life he wanted to have. The pain, the sacrifice... every excruciating moment was worth it to have experienced the power that now coursed through him. Nothing could ever change that he had become his best self. He would rather die prematurely as a Bakzen than have lived his full life as a Taran.

"I didn't think it would end like this," Tek mused, breaking Haersen's reverie. "Tararia was always supposed to be the one to fall."

"If only Wil had died back then." That failure was on both of them.

Tek let out a slow breath, surprisingly calm despite the building crumbling around them. "If it wasn't him, then it would have been another."

That was probably true. If Tarans were anything, they were tenacious. Wil could have died years before, but it could have just delayed the inevitable. When it came down to it, the Bakzen would always be outsiders—a deviation from the natural order. They would always have had to fight for survival. It would seem the odds were too much to overcome, despite their ambitions.

"At least I had a vision," Tek continued. "I wanted more for us."

"It was a glorious vision," Haersen agreed.

"It's a shame all of this was for nothing."

"No, not nothing." Haersen stepped toward his leader, unsteady on his feet as the building lurched again. "You showed what was possible—what could be achieved when a civilization unites. You showed a glimpse of what Tarans can become. They may be too blind to see it now, but you demonstrated that path. One day, they'll thank you."

"A day I'll never get to see."

"But you will die free and unburdened knowing that you did everything you could for your people."

Tek nodded. "That I will."

The power flickered, then cut out entirely. Only light cast from the smoldering plaza outside illuminated the office.

"Come. We have one more stop to make." Tek headed for the door.

Haersen took in the office one last time—a place where he was finally respected. The place where his loyalty and dedication had granted him a role in bringing the Bakzen into a new era. That era would be the last, but it was also their greatest. He was in his true home, and for that he was eternally thankful.

—   —   —

"Don't let any of the ships jump away!" Wil commanded as the main space station in orbit of the Bakzen planet succumbed to the weapons fire.

One of the TSS cruisers from the second wave of ships emerged from the Rift and took aim at the Bakzen vessels attempting to flee. A Bakzen carrier separated itself from the fighting enough to initiate a jump, and a subspace glow formed around it.

"I've got it," Ian stated.

Fighters from Ian's lead tactical unit swooped in, targeting their shots on the Bakzen ship's jump drive. The engines exploded, and the subspace glow dissipated in an instant. With their target destroyed, the fighters headed out toward the other large ships to ensure they were also disabled. A TSS cruiser opened fire on the stranded Bakzen carrier to finish it off, first taking out the weapons and shields. In a matter of seconds, it was completely at the mercy of the TSS fleet, charred and ragged. The ship was too close to the planet by the end of the fight, and it was drawn into the gravity. It burst into a fiery mass of twisted metal as it burned through the atmosphere.

The other ships fared no better. Most were soon reduced to scrap floating across the battlefield. The carnage was too much for Wil to absorb at once, so he kept his focus on the goal. They needed to take out the planet itself.

"All available ships, target the planetary shield," Wil instructed.

"Sir, I'm getting an incoming communication," Rianne stated. "It's not one of ours."

Wil's officers glanced up with confusion for a moment, but quickly returned their attention to doling out telepathic commands to finish off the remaining Bakzen vessels.

"Put it through," Wil told Rianne.

The video feed resolved on the viewscreen. Smoke clouded the picture, but the faces of Tek and Haersen were unmistakable. The two of them took up the entire view, obscuring the background.

"Haersen," Wil said, "so you managed to worm your way right to the top with Tek."

Rianne gasped, and Wil's other officers paused their commands to stare at the viewscreen, in shock.

The Bakzen had never had a tangible face to them, Wil realized. They knew the names, but the enemy was always just a ship in the distance. Seeing that their leader was a person not too dissimilar from them changed that impression. *That's why I couldn't tell them who the Bakzen really are.*

"I've made something of myself," Haersen replied. "You do nothing but destroy."

"They're trying to distract us. Stay focused," Wil told his friends.

They returned to their commands, but eyes kept darting toward the viewscreen.

"I should have made sure you were dead," Haersen sneered.

Wil could hardly believe the transformation of the former TSS officer. His skin had completely morphed into the tough orange-tinted exterior of the Bakzen, and his eyes shone with their characteristic red glow. Even his once thin frame was now muscular and broadened. "What have they done to you?"

"They made me better, just like we could have done for all of you," Haersen spat back. "Instead, you'll eliminate us and continue on with your weak, pathetic lives."

Wil met his gaze. "What you are now isn't natural." *The Priesthood shouldn't have created a life that had no way of surviving. To make them suffer like this is too great an injustice to comprehend.*

"We were the future," Tek declared.

"No, Tek," Wil shook his head. "Your ancestors were a grasp at capturing a future that should never have been. Engineering a new way of life was never a viable answer. The physical self cannot be separated from its surrounding context. We need to evolve as a people holistically—culture driving form and function. What happened to you was wrong, but it can't be undone. You never should have been driven away, but you also shouldn't have been created in the first place. I understand why you have fought for your existence—I would have done the same—but the time for fighting has ended. If we can't live together, then our conflict must end here."

"So, you *do* know the truth," Tek murmured.

"I do. I'm sorry that the Bakzen people need to meet this end, but you led them to this juncture. And facing you... I've been waiting for this day a very long time."

Around him, Wil's officers had tuned into the conversation, trying to piece together the truth he was talking around. There was no sense in keeping it from them any longer—the war was already won.

Wil straightened in his chair. "The Priesthood will pay for their mistakes. I'll make sure the Bakzen are remembered for what you achieved, not for what we made you become."

Tek's face softened with surprising understanding. "We fought to the end."

"Your people did," Wil agreed. "But you, Tek—you don't deserve an honorable death." *He came after me, after Saera—he tried to take everything I love from me, and so now I'll do the same. He'll die knowing that everything he's built will be destroyed.*

"Sir, a volley of shuttles just launched from the surface!"

Rianne interrupted. "Intense telekinetic signatures."

More clones to detonate as bombs. Wil met Tek's cool stare.

Tek nodded. "They are so very special. It's a shame you never had a chance to meet your brothers." He stepped to the side, revealing an underground lab filled with clone maturation tanks. Their faces were eerily familiar.

They cloned me! Wil gaped in horror at the abominations. He had always wondered why the Bakzen had wanted to extract marrow from him during his initial capture. In his wildest speculation, he never imagined it was to bolster the Bakzen army. The hatred for all things Taran had seemingly run far too deep. If there was some aspect of him worth incorporating, even if it meant an adulteration of the pure Bakzen bloodlines, then he couldn't underestimate them for a moment.

"I wonder if they're as strong as you?" Tek asked.

"Take out those shuttles!" Wil ordered Rianne. *That's it... That's the pinnacle of his achievement. They will be his undoing.*

"I'm on it!" she replied, targeting the *Conquest*'s weapons on the approaching vessels.

Wil's skin tingled as telekinetic energy surged through him. "This was your aim all along—to make me a part of your perverse plan."

Tek sneered back. "Don't flatter yourself. This has always just been about the advancement of the Bakzen race, and we borrowed one little piece from you to accomplish that goal. It's the very same imperative the Priesthood programmed into us at our inception."

Not only did they try to manipulate my mind, but they used my very genetic code as a weapon! His grip tightened on the handhold, glaring into Tek's searing red eyes. *This ends now.* "I won't have any part in your future."

"You didn't have a choice," Tek replied. "And come now— you couldn't hurt these poor innocents, could you?" He swept his arm to encompass the clones in the maturation tanks. "After all, they're your brothers. They want to meet you."

"Sir!" Rianne cut in. "The shuttles have been destroyed, but the electromagnetic signature around the planet is intensifying. Our sensors can't get clear readings."

The clones... that must have been what was blocking me when I attempted to observe the planet before the attack. Wil examined the immature clones in the tanks behind Tek on the viewscreen, detecting a telekinetic link between them. Together, under Tek's direction, they could take out the whole TSS fleet. However, their abilities were also the perfect weapon to use against Tek—turning the creation against the creator, just like the Bakzen had done to the Priesthood.

Wil steeled himself for the task at hand, trying to maintain emotional distance from the abominations on screen in front of him. The clones had been aged to the equivalent of early-teens— almost the same age as Wil was when the bone marrow sample had been taken from him. Their entire purpose in life was to kill and destroy, just like Wil had been created to do. Except, they weren't a copy of him, but rather living weapons in the hands of the enemy—mindless drones being manipulated toward Tek's ends. The Bakzen could consume them alive, with no thought for them as individuals. *I won't let them suffer any longer. I won't let anyone else suffer at the Bakzen's hands.* "You say they want to meet me?" Wil asked his adversaries over the viewscreen.

Tek nodded, and Haersen smirked next to him.

Wil extended his consciousness toward the planet. As he approached, hundreds of the clones' voices filled Wil's mind, chanting a repeating mantra in unison: *"Killer! You let them die. You killed them all."* Caught by surprise, Wil released the handholds connecting him to the *Conquest* and pressed his palms over his ears, but the voices continued to taunt him. Except, the thoughts weren't from the clones. Underneath it all, Wil detected Tek and Haersen leading the chorus.

Gathering himself, Wil remembered his target. This was between him and Tek—the rest was just a distraction. *He can't control me.*

Consumed by rage, Wil summoned all his power and blocked his mind. His world went silent. In the new stillness around him, he reached across the distance to isolate Tek's mind. *"No, I didn't kill them,"* he told him. *"You did."*

Without hesitation, Wil expanded his mind to let in the clones—tapping into the parts of them that were once part of himself. He sensed a resonance as the clones recognized their kinship. *"More will die as long as Tek lives,"* he said into their blank minds. *"Kill him."*

On screen, the clones writhed in their maturation tanks, sloshing the nutrient water onto the floor. Tek ignored them at first, but then he went rigid—frozen in a telekinetic vise as the clones latched onto him with their collective minds. Next to him, Haersen's eyes widened with distress.

"I have you now, Tek." Wil sliced into his consciousness, tearing through the layers of hate and fury that had driven Tek's blind ambition to destroy Taran civilization. As Wil ripped apart his enemy's consciousness, he caught sight of Tek's childhood, growing up as the only child to have ever walked among the Bakzen. He had been weak then—he hated being weak. No one else should ever feel so helpless, so the Bakzen must become stronger. Everything in his life going forward had been dedicated to achieving that strength, through any means necessary.

As Wil stripped Tek down to his innermost self, he saw that dedication to gaining power persisted down to Tek's very core. *"You had physical prowess, Tek,"* Wil told the sliver that was left of the former Bakzen commander's consciousness, *"but you lost sight of kinship and love. In the end, no force is more powerful."*

With one final telepathic spear into his mind, Tek collapsed on the floor in the Bakzen lab beneath the planet's surface.

Haersen took a step back from the body. "This isn't over!"

"It will be soon enough." Wil reached out to the clones again. *"He tried to kill us. Don't let him get away."*

As Haersen was gripped in a telekinetic vise on screen, Wil cut the video feed. Ignoring the shocked expressions of his crew throughout the Command Center, he gripped the handhelds to fuse once again with the ship. "Tek was only their leader. We leave no survivors."

The air hummed as Wil fed telekinetic energy into the relays. After a moment, the others joined him. As the ship charged, Wil focused on his target: the planet. They had never attacked anything larger than a carrier with the telekinetic weapon, but the only way to take out the Bakzen for good would be to decimate their world.

"Don't hold back," he told his officers. He released the onslaught.

A beam of pure telekinetic energy shot from the ship toward the capital city on the planet. The ground buckled at the impact site, sending a shockwave through the surrounding landscape.

Wil continued to feed the beam, pouring more of himself through the ship's relays. At the edge of his consciousness, he sensed his officers straining to keep up. He couldn't let them hold him back. He needed to end it.

For the first time since his Course Rank test, Wil let himself go. The sweet energy of the Rift fueled him from beyond the dimensional veil as he directed the destructive force through the ship. While he focused, the crater on the planet spread under the crippling force. Around the darkened pit, the ground began to glow as the rock liquefied. Cracks jutted across the surface and fissures formed around the equator. No population could seemingly survive, but Wil had to be sure. He poured more energy through the ship, aware that his officers had withdrawn. It was better that way—they wouldn't need to bear the burden of the planet's destruction.

Wil lost himself in the energy. All the anger and bitterness about the war poured forth into the telekinetic beam burrowing through the planet. Soon it would be over. He just needed a little more...

"Evacuate the fleet!" he heard Michael order somewhere in the back of his mind.

Wil was barely aware of the ships disappearing from view around the edges of the screen. He was consumed by the energy feeding into the ship—his consciousness reaching deep into the Rift beyond the dimensional veil in a search for even greater power.

Beneath them, the entire planet was a molten mass collapsing in on itself from the impact crater. It contracted until it was a blinding point of light against the starscape. For a moment, the light dimmed.

A shockwave fanned out from the planet, hurtling molten rock that instantly turned to dust in the cold vacuum of space. The wave sped toward the *Conquest.*

Wil's officers redirect their energy to the shield. The *Conquest* hurdled backward under force from the explosion. They tumbled to the side, the artificial gravity unable to compensate.

Wil was thrown from the console. He hit the floor with his shoulder, but he barely registered the impact. Energy still surged through him. He fought to keep it in check—with nowhere to direct it, he could take out the ship. Slowly, the charge dissipated.

As he rose to his feet, everything was still.

On the viewscreen, only a dusting of debris gave any indication of where the Bakzen world used to be. It was gone, utterly and completely. Whatever Bakzen remained at outposts were the last of their kind. Soon, they, too, would be destroyed.

Cheers erupted in the Command Center and over the comms.

"We did it!" Ian exclaimed.

Ethan grinned. "That was foking spectacular!"

Michael placed a hand on Wil's shoulder. "We won."

Wil looked around at the joyous faces around him. *Don't they realize what we've just done? We exterminated a whole race. They were one of us.... We made them, cast them aside, and then killed them. All of them. How can they celebrate?*

He collapsed to his knees. The cheers around him were muted in the distance, his vision faded at the edges. Images of the planet's final moments replayed in his mind. They had won. The Bakzen were all but eliminated. Everything that had made them who they were had been extinguished by his hand. And all the others who had died along the way in the name of that singular mission to annihilate an entire people—those deaths were on his hands, his conscience.

Darkness closed in around him. *What have I done?*

CHAPTER 27

S<small>AERA HUNG HER</small> head, wishing she brought better news about her husband. "There's still no change."

Cris closed his eyes and slumped against the wall outside Wil's quarters on the *Conquest*. "I can't stand to see him like this. We have to do something."

"I don't know what we can do," Saera replied. *He'll barely even talk to me, let alone look me in the eye.* It had been that way for four days. Saera had journeyed from Headquarters as soon as the war was declared won, since Wil had immediately sequestered himself and refused to interact with anyone. If even she and Cris couldn't get through to him, it was looking like there would be no remedy other than time.

"I hate to suggest it, but do we need to be watching him more closely?" Cris asked.

Suicide watch. "I'd like to think that's not a concern... But besides, he would never stand for it. I think it would only make things worse."

"You're right." Cris sighed. "I had no idea how great the burden on him really was. Michael told me about the final call with Tek—that the Priesthood created the Bakzen."

"Wil thought it would be easier if you didn't know," Saera admitted.

Cris took a moment to reply. "I suppose I'm thankful for that. All the same, I hate that Wil had to bear that alone."

"He told me," Saera pointed out.

"That's true."

"But then he shut me out, so I guess that's not the best example." She placed her back against the wall next to Cris and slid down to sit on the floor, overtaken with emotional and physical exhaustion. The end of the war was supposed to be a celebration. Instead, it seemed like her entire world was collapsing.

"Relationships are complicated enough without all the added stress of command. He'll come around," Cris told her.

There was more to it than that, she had no doubt. For years Wil had treated her as a confidant, sharing things he didn't dare utter to anyone else. If he had shut her out so completely, it wasn't because of stress or lack of trust. It was because whatever he was hiding related to her in some way—that much was clear. Whatever it was seemed to be compounding the guilt she knew he felt about the war. It was enough to have put him over the edge.

Why won't he just talk to me? She jumped back up to her feet, too frustrated and agitated to sit still. "I'm going for a walk."

"Okay. I'll hang around," Cris replied.

Saera headed down the hall toward the other officers' quarters. The Primus Elites had been taking turns with rift corridor repairs, only coming back to the *Conquest* to sleep for a few hours at a time. Their experiences with Wil made them uniquely qualified to guide others in the repairs, once they figured out how to work in tandem without an amplifier like the *Conquest*—keeping it slow and steady to avoid any tears or burning themselves out. It was exhausting work, but they were making progress. She didn't know if any of them would be around in the common area, let alone feeling up for socializing, but she needed to get away from the cloud hanging over Wil's quarters; she couldn't even think of it as their shared space anymore.

As Saera approached the common area outside the sleeping chambers, she saw Michael sitting in one of the plush chairs by the back viewport while he reviewed something on his handheld. He roused as she neared. "How is he?"

She shrugged.

"I keep wondering if I could have done anything differently toward the end to prevent this," Michael murmured.

"Whatever is going on with Wil right now, I don't think any of us could have prevented it," Saera replied. *He never thought he would make it through the war. Is he just fulfilling his own dire expectation?*

"Still…"

Saera leaned against the chair across from him. "I know what you mean."

"In better news, I think we've perfected the system for repairing the Rift, with three or four Agents working in tandem. It takes a lot longer than the ways we were doing it before, but it's much more effective. The other ways left space prone to tearing when we used a jump drive nearby."

"That is good to hear," Saera replied, her mind still elsewhere.

"We could use some extra help, if you want to get out for a bit," Michael offered.

"I might take you up on that. My presence here isn't helping any."

"Don't underestimate yourself."

Saera shrugged. "Or maybe I should just go back to Headquarters to attend to the students."

"No rush. Elise said she's having fun playing High Commander, though I guess it must be pretty empty back there if she's the most senior Agent."

"You've been talking with Elise?" Saera was caught off-guard.

"I mean, yes. Almost all available Agents have been sent to repair the rift corridors around the Taran worlds and to pick off the scattered Bakzen survivors. It's going to take a long time to get everything back to how it should be."

"It will," Michael agreed. He paused. "And yes, we've become good friends over the last few months. It was nice to have someone to talk to about everything that was going on."

"She's always been a good listener."

He examined her. "Are you okay with us—"

"Of course! Why wouldn't I be?" Saera responded too forcefully.

"I'll always be your friend, Saera," Michael said after a moment.

"I know." Tears stung Saera's eyes. *Why are you crying?* She turned away.

Michael rose and wrapped his arms around her before she could protest. The once familiar embrace stripped away her defenses, and she sobbed into his chest.

She was surrounded by people who cared for her, and yet she felt completely alone. Wil was her partner—her world. Friends and family were no substitute for that companionship. But moreover, she felt his pain through their bond. It gnawed at the edges of her mind as she sensed it slowly consuming him. She hated not knowing what was causing it, and for being defenseless against its darkness. Seeking comfort from an old friend didn't stop its advance, but it did make it temporarily easier to bear.

"Wil is going to rally, don't worry," Michael murmured into her hair.

"He better hurry up and do it already." Saera wiped her cheeks with the back of her hand. "Thanks for the hug. I needed that."

"Anytime."

"You know, I think I will go out with you tomorrow. I'd like to help with the rebuilding." *At least the Rift is one thing I can fix.*

—   —   —

"All right, just a little more," Tom urged the other members of the Primus Squad as they manipulated the energy grid around the edge of the Rift.

Each of the four men stared out the viewport in the lounge of their assigned transport ship, concentrating on an agreed upon patch of space two hundred meters away. They stood in a line, directing telekinetic energy into one unified beam to repair the Rift torn by the Bakzen over the last several hundred years. The frayed pathways that had been yanked apart to form the Rift drifted back into place within the natural grid as the team sent a steady stream of healing telekinetic energy toward the wound.

The repair process was painstakingly slow-going, but they'd been warned about what had happened to Wil's team when they had tried to do too much, too fast. They kept feeding the trickle of energy to redirect the broken spatial pathways, and eventually, the Rift was a tiny measure smaller.

Tom released his telekinetic beam when the repairs in the target zone were complete. He itched the connection point between his thigh and his temporary prosthetic leg, fatigued from hours of concentration on the numerous zones they'd visited so far that day. "I don't see how we'll ever seal the whole Rift at this pace."

"Don't think in those terms," Ray replied. "We take care of our portion each day, and the other teams do their part. In aggregate, we'll start to see measurable results in no time."

"Still, this isn't what I had in mind for a post-war assignment," Tom muttered. *There are still Bakzen out there we need to hunt down.*

Andy shrugged. "Until I have other orders, I'll do what I'm told. The Rift is too dangerous to leave unchecked."

"I'm with you," Sander agreed.

Tom sighed. "Okay, you win. No more complaints from me." He stepped over to the viewscreen in the lounge to consult the map of their assignments for the day. "Let's see... I guess we should head over here next—"

A communications chirp interrupted him just as he was about to point to the map.

"Alert! We have a situation with an occupied Bakzen outpost in the adjacent system. You're the closest Agents. Please respond," Helen, their contact in fleet command, informed them.

Sander frowned. "Isn't there anyone else?"

"Sir, a Militia team has tried to access the facility, but there is a telekinetic shield around one of the rooms," Helen explained. "The combat group requires Agent intervention."

Tom muted the comm channel. "I, for one, would like to go face-to-face with the Bakzen for a change."

"It was easy to shoot down a fighter, but exterminating them in person..." Andy trailed off.

Tom nodded. "My point, exactly." *Finally, I can take out some*

Bakzen like they did to my family.

"I don't share your enthusiasm, but we can't ignore a request for backup," Ray chimed in.

Sander nodded.

"Then it's settled." Tom unmuted the comm channel. "Send us the coordinates. We're on our way."

The destination was a short jump further into former Bakzen territory, on a rock moon around a planet with a red, gaseous atmosphere. A surface port on the moon had already been captured by a team of TSS Militia soldiers, but an underground chamber was inaccessible.

After landing the transport ship at the port using a universal docking coupling installed by the Militia team, the Primus Squad was escorted to the edge of the telekinetic shield underground. The plain concrete corridor was pressurized and equipped with artificial gravity, so they didn't need suits. However, wearing only his normal Agent uniform, Tom's skin crawled under the dim lights illuminating the dreary space.

The group approached the end of a hall, which terminated in a steel door. A meter in front of the door, Tom detected the edge of the telekinetic shield that had caused the Militia officers to turn back.

"I can see the problem," he commented as he assessed the barrier.

"This isn't mechanically generated," Sander observed as he performed his own evaluation. "There could be a whole army of Bakzen soldiers in there."

Tom sent a low-intensity counter pulse against the shield to see if it flexed. There did seem to be a little give. "I think the four of us could break through. It's just a matter of what we'll find on the other side."

"I think we should call in some reinforcements," Andy suggested.

"The other ground teams haven't experienced resistance from the Bakzen, have they?" Tom asked. "Once we break through the shield, they'll probably surrender." *And then I can get some proper revenge.*

"I don't like it," Ray insisted. "Let's get a couple more Agents here, just in case." He pulled out his handheld and headed back to the surface to get in touch with central ops while the others waited for instruction. After a minute, he returned. "We're in luck. Michael, Ethan, and Saera are heading over."

"Since when is Saera doing Rift repairs?" Andy asked.

"First I've heard of it," Tom replied.

Sander crossed his arms. "I guess that means Wil is still sequestering himself."

"What's up with that, anyway?" questioned Andy. "We won the war."

"How'd you feel if you came across a bunch of hybrid clones?" replied Ray. "We don't know if that batch on the homeworld was all of them. I wouldn't want to be out in the field, either, if there was a chance of accidentally wandering into a room with an enemy version of myself."

"Based on what Ethan said, it was a pretty gruesome scene," Sander said with a shiver.

"Not to mention everything else," Ray continued. "I haven't even started to process all the deaths. TSS officers, Cambion, the other border worlds... I don't blame him for needing to disconnect from reality for a while."

I don't want to accept my new reality, either. Tom anxiously milled around in the empty concrete hall while they waited for their backup to arrive.

After fifteen minutes, three sets of footsteps echoed from down the hall.

"Finally!" Sander breathed, pushing off from the wall he'd been leaning against during the wait.

Michael, Ethan, and Saera rounded a bend in the hall and waved at the group.

"Good to see you!" Tom called out. "Couldn't have asked for better backup."

"Great timing," Ethan replied. "It was about time I checked up on you to make sure you were actually working." He flashed them a grin.

"Very funny," Tom retorted.

Andy ignored the exchange and focused on Saera. "How are you?"

She smiled back, but it seemed half-hearted. "Relieved to be anywhere other than Headquarters."

"And how's Wil?" Ray asked.

"About the same." Her smiled faded. "So, the telekinetic shield…"

"It extends about a meter out from the door," Tom replied, gesturing toward the end of the hall.

Saera glanced at Michael. "What's the mystery behind Door Number 1?"

He gave her a knowing smile. "Let's find out."

The seven Agents gathered two meters from the shield, facing the end of the hall. Due to the relatively narrow width of the corridor, they had to stand shoulder-to-shoulder two rows deep, with three in the front and four in the back. Saera took front and center with Michael to her left, and Tom bumped Ethan to the back row so he could be in the front right—wanting the first possible opportunity to face whatever Bakzen waited for them on the other side of the door head-on.

In a similar fashion to Tom's test pulse, the Agents simultaneously directed a dispersed wave of energy at the field. With the augmented support, Tom realized that the shield was composed of several separate telekinetic signatures, though he perceived them to be more like echoes of the same voice than unique individuals.

Saera was the first to pull back from the assessment, and the others withdrew, as well. Her brow knitted. "I think it's just some drone soldiers maintaining the shield. The question is, what are they guarding?"

Michael tensed. "It's something important, or they would have surrendered by now, like the others."

"There aren't that many of them," Ethan said as he eyed the door. "I counted six distinct signatures. We can easily take them."

"Let's just do it, already!" Tom urged.

"All right," Saera agreed. "Punch through at the door, and then we should be able to collapse the shield from there."

Following Saera's lead, Tom sent a steady stream of energy at the shield directly in front of the door. The shield flashed in his mind's eye, glistening with silver sparks as it absorbed the initial blast. Soon, though, the light intensified as the shield was overwhelmed by the Agents' assault. With a shimmering wave, the telekinetic bubble collapsed.

"I don't suppose it's unlocked," Saera said as she stepped toward the door. She pressed her palms on the smooth metal surface, but it didn't budge. There didn't appear to be a control panel. "Of course not. That would have been too easy."

"I'll take care of it," Tom offered.

Saera nodded and stepped back behind him with the others.

Tom focused on the edges of the metal door and yanked it away from the surrounding concrete structure, sending a shower of dust to the floor. He propped the door on the side of the hall, leaving enough room for two people to walk side-by-side. As the concrete dust cleared, he peered into the dim room beyond.

Six Bakzen soldiers stepped forward to block the doorway. Their hands were at their sides, seemingly not posing a physical threat, and there were no auras of telekinetic exertion now that the shield was down.

Tom examined their sickly orange-tinted skin and angular features. Everything about them conveyed a warlike nature, designed and bred for combat. Yet, there was no malice in their gaze. The anger that had fueled Tom's thirst for revenge wavered as he looked his enemy in the eye. *They know they've lost. They're not going to fight.*

"You kill us, too," one of the Bakzen soldiers stated in broken New Taran.

Tom faltered. "The war is over."

Saera brushed past him, addressing the Bakzen soldier who'd spoken, "What are you protecting?"

The soldier shook his head. "They not ready yet. We failed."

A guttural cry sounded from within the room.

Tom instinctively raised a telekinetic shield around himself and felt the other Agents do the same.

"What's in there?" Saera demanded.

The Bakzen soldier cocked his head as though the answer were obvious. "The future."

"*Pin them,*" Saera commanded telepathically to the other Agents.

Tom instantly grappled the Bakzen soldier closest to him, throwing the broad figure onto his back. The other Agents each secured one of the other Bakzen soldiers, leaving Saera free to investigate.

She approached the doorway and peered inside. "I don't detect any telekinetic traps, but there's definitely someone else with abilities nearby."

"So close," the Bakzen soldier Tom was pinning murmured.

"What's close?" Saera demanded.

Another cry of anguish reverberated down the hall.

"Hold them. Stay together," Saera instructed as she entered the room with a telekinetic shield raised.

Still maintaining his hold on the Bakzen soldier, Tom followed her inside.

The limits of the room were in shadow, with only a row of lights leading inward from the door. To either side of a central walkway, person-sized tanks filled with a translucent reddish liquid were arranged at one-meter intervals. Tom exchanged a worried glance with Saera before they stepped further into the room.

Several meters from the door, Tom caught sight of a figure huddled behind one of the tanks. *"Over here!"* he alerted Saera.

Cautiously, she approached the tank. She recoiled with a gasp.

"What is it?" Michael asked, rushing over.

Tom ran to see for himself while he kept the Bakzen soldier pinned. Behind the tank, the crouching figure had patchy, dark hair and her skin was coarse and peeling. "Stars!" he breathed, trying to wrap his mind around what he was seeing.

"You're Taran, aren't you?" Saera said, crouching down near the disfigured woman.

The woman nodded. "They won't let us die," she stammered. "Please, kill me!"

Saera took a slow breath. "What did they do to you?"

"Experiments," the woman, replied, her hands shaking. "They took us from Kaldern—started injecting us with something. They... They said that they were going to make us better. Like them."

"Changing Tarans into Bakzen..." Michael murmured.

Saera stood back up. "Just like Haersen. Except, it looks like it took years for him to change… It's only been a few months since Kaldern was captured."

Tom studied the woman, sensing a faint aura around her. *"She has abilities,"* he said to the other Agents.

"Have you always had telekinetic skill?" Saera asked the woman.

Her eyes widened. "What? Never! I…" She trailed off, staring at her peeling hands.

Saera backed away. *"The mind control neurotoxin was just the first step. The Bakzen must have been trying to transform the population—and they figured out a new, accelerated process."*

"Can we reverse it?" Michael asked.

"I have no idea." Saera turned back to the woman. "You said 'us'. Where are the others?"

The woman pointed with a shaking hand toward the back of the room.

"It's okay!" Saera called out. "We're here to help."

Slowly, a dozen people edged out of the shadows, some even more twisted than the first woman.

"You can't help us," a man said in a gruff voice, his head completely bald and eyes with a sorrel tint. "The pain… it won't stop! Don't make us live like this…"

"Please, let me die!" another cried.

Soon every one of the mutilated Tarans had joined the pleas for death.

In shock, the other Agents standing guard over the Bakzen soldiers watched the unfolding scene.

"No, we'll take you to the nearest medical facility, and—" Saera cut off as the throng of Tarans lunged for the Bakzen soldiers pinned to the ground by the Agents.

They began clawing and kicking at the immobilized soldiers like wild animals, teeth bared and eyes wide.

Tom dodged the crazed mass as he dashed for the door. "What do we do?" he asked no one in particular.

"This isn't our outcome to decide," Saera replied as she, too, ran for the door. "We let it play out."

As soon as they were out of the room, the Agents released

their hold on the Bakzen soldiers.

Tom turned for one last look before he rounded the bend in the hallway, seeing that the Bakzen had formed a telekinetic chain. Energy was swirling around them. "They're going to blow the facility!" he warned the others.

With renewed urgency, the Agents sprinted for the surface.

"Evacuate!" Michael called out to the Militia soldiers standing guard at the port.

"What?" the Militia captain started to question, but he jumped to attention as soon as he saw the Agents running at full speed.

The eight Militia soldiers joined the Agents in their sprint for the concourse.

"Our engine is still warm," Saera shouted as they ran. "Everyone follow us."

Michael and Ethan surged ahead with her toward their ship. It would be a tight fit for everyone on the vessel, but there wouldn't be time to get another ship prepped from a cold start.

The group ran up the gangway, with Ethan darting ahead to the controls to start up the ship.

Tom checked that all the Militia soldiers had made it on, then sealed the door. "Clear!"

Moments later, Ethan had the ship in the air. At only a kilometer elevation, a telekinetic shockwave blasted out from the port, rocking the craft as it continued to gain altitude.

"Shite! It took out the whole port," Sander observed out the viewport.

Tom peered over his shoulder, taking in the destruction for himself. The location of the former port was now a round crater, perfectly scooped out from the rock. No one could have survived the telekinetic detonation.

Saera took a shaky breath. "When I agreed to come into the field today, I wasn't expecting this."

Michael's face was drawn. "None of us were."

"What happened?" the Militia captain asked.

"We encountered Bakzen hostiles," Saera replied. She gazed out at the crater in the side of the moon and swallowed, then focused just on the Agents. *"I'll file an official report, but I think it's best if we don't talk about what we saw here. In the future, if anyone comes across a telekinetic shield like that, I'll make sure there's a standing order for the entire facility to be destroyed without entry."*

"Agreed," Michael said, his face still pale.

Tom and the others nodded their understanding. *There are fates worse than a swift death. Knowing that, I can put my family to rest now.*

—   —   —

H2 was barely recognizable from the place where Laecy had spent the majority of her TSS career. Though the facility's blast shields had been raised and she could once again look out the viewports, the surrounding sight bore no resemblance to the concentrated hub of TSS power that had always been her reality.

Most of the spacedock had been destroyed in the Bakzen ambush outside H2, leaving charred stubs of mangled concourses fanning out from the core space station like branches on a lightning-struck tree. The fleet was distributed throughout the Rift as Agents began the tedious process of repairing the Rift the Bakzen had created. It would be years before the Rift was fully healed—possibly decades—but at least the recovery had begun.

Laecy returned her attention to inside her engineering lab. The space was now only a relic from a war-torn past. She could move on.

Nolan and Becca were in the process of reviewing the final fleet manifest to decide which ships to decommission and which the TSS should keep in service for future peacekeeping missions.

"How goes it?" Laecy asked them.

Nolan glanced up from his work. "I think we're just about done with the recommendations."

"It's strange," Becca added, "talking about decommissioning these warships. Up until a week ago, we would have been brainstorming every possible way to keep them flying."

"I know, I'm not sure I can make that mental shift," Laecy admitted.

"What's next, after we're done with this inventory?" Nolan asked.

Laecy shrugged. "I guess you find other assignments, if you want."

"What are you doing?" inquired Becca, likely looking for a chance to keep the team together.

"You'd both be at the top of my list for my next leadership post," Laecy replied to the underlying question. "But I'm retiring. I said I'd see the war through, and I have." *Now I have to live the future that Jack will never get the chance to share with me, in his memory.*

Nolan scrunched up his nose. "I can't picture you retired. You like solving problems too much."

Laecy smiled. "I'm sure I can find something to keep me occupied. Maybe learning to relax will be my first challenge to overcome."

"I don't see myself leaving the TSS for a long time," Nolan said. "I'd like to be a part of the rebuilding."

"Me too," Becca agreed.

"There'll be plenty of work to go around," Laecy told them. "You'll each get a glowing recommendation from me."

"Can we just stay here?" asked Becca.

"I think the plan is to decommission H2," responded Laecy. "Not sure when, but if they're closing the Rift, then this structure will eventually have to be dismantled and moved piece-by-piece into normal space."

The young engineers exchanged glances.

"I hadn't thought about that," Nolan said. "It makes sense, but…"

"This headquarters was always such a fixture in the war. It's hard to imagine it not being here anymore," Becca murmured.

"Talk about a huge undertaking to move it." Nolan shook his head, letting out a slow breath.

"Looks like you've figured out a new challenge of your own." Laecy beamed at them.

Nolan chuckled. "Suddenly, I understand why you're getting out while you can. They'd never let you go once that project is underway."

Becca's eyes widened with feigned distress. "They'd be forced to promote us. We'll have our whole careers mapped out on a road to everlasting glory."

"Receiving endless praise for how amazing we are," Nolan added with a grin.

"I think you two will be just fine without me." *I'll miss them all the same. It was tough, but we also had some good times.* Laecy took in her lab, remembering what it was like at the height of her time as the Lead Engineer for a fleet fighting an impossible war. "The future of H2 is in your hands now. My time here is done."

CHAPTER 28

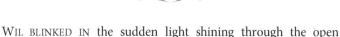

WIL BLINKED IN the sudden light shining through the open doorway. *What do they want now?* He set down his tablet next to him on the bed in his quarters on the *Conquest.*

His father and wife stepped into the room. They closed the door.

"Wil, it's been a week since you last left this room. It's time to go home," Saera said.

I can't just continue on with my life like nothing happened. Wil laid back down and rolled away from the unwelcome visitors.

"Wil…" Saera sat down on the edge of the bed behind him. She reached out to rub his back.

He flinched under her touch. *How can she still want to be near me after everything I've done?*

"The Rift repairs are underway, and we're needed back at Headquarters. We have a lot of people that need new assignments," Cris said.

"Have fun with that," Wil muttered.

"You're coming with us," his father continued. "Maybe some familiar surroundings will break you out of this funk."

Wil shot up in bed. "A 'funk'. You really think that's what this is?" He rolled to his feet off the far side of the bed. "You don't have a clue."

"If you'd talk to us—" Saera began.

"I have nothing to say," Wil shot back. He dropped to a

crouch against the wall in the corner.

"If you don't want to talk, then you'll just have to listen," Cris said as he squatted across from Wil. "I recognize that you've been through a lot—more than the rest of us. You were placed in an impossible position and had to make decisions that would leave anyone with regrets. The Bakzen were created and used by the Priesthood just like we were, and it's hard not to feel a little sympathetic to their plight. Despite all that, you can't let your role in the war define the rest of your life. You made it through. Now, you have lots of friends and a wife who can't wait to start living life with you outside of the war and all this awfulness we've been wrapped up in for the last decade. Push past it and let's start over."

Wil shook his head. "I can't let it go so effortlessly. The power I felt while destroying the Bakzen's world… It was exhilarating, but I also realized what I can do and it terrifies me. There's already been so much destruction, so many deaths. I feel responsible for all of it."

"We've done things, too, Wil," Saera said. "Now that I've seen the Bakzen's twisted methods up close, I feel confident that ending the war the way we did needed to be done."

Cris nodded. "We all gave kill orders as commanders. We share that burden."

"That was a handful of individuals compared to me. I killed billions." *Cambion, the Bakzen homeworld… It's too many to count.*

"It'll be difficult to come to terms with everything we've been through, but dwelling on it here isn't helping," Saera said.

Can I ever forgive myself for what I've done? Wil searched the faces of the two people closest to him, seeing their eagerness for him to be the person he was before. *I can't be that same person again, but I owe it to them to try to find a way to live with this new reality—to find a new purpose for my life.* "Okay, we'll go home."

Cris nodded. "Good, because there's also the matter of a new High Commander."

Wil shook his head. "No, I can't."

"I'm willing to step up as interim High Commander, until you're ready to assume the position," Cris offered.

Wil rose to his feet. "It's yours. At this rate, I never want another command."

"Okay, I'll keep the chair warm for you." Cris attempted a smile.

"When can we leave?" Wil asked.

Cris and Saera exchanged glances. "I guess we could take one of the smaller ships and head out now," Cris said.

"All right, then let's go."

— — —

To Michael's surprise, their return home wasn't met with even a Militia guard reception. As he walked down the spacedock concourse with Wil, Saera, and Wil's parents, he felt none of the joyous return home he'd always envisioned. The TSS spaceport was devoid of life, and the subdued energy of normal space made everything dim after experiencing regular exposure to the Rift.

They made their way down to the moon's surface and boarded the central elevator. The five of them stood in silence as the elevator descended through the shaft to the heart of the moon. With the facility leaderless after Banks' death, they were the chosen few to reassemble the broken pieces of the TSS. Michael wished in some ways that he'd been able to stay in the Rift with the other Elites to help tend to the aftermath of the war, but Cris had requested his presence at Headquarters to lend emotional support to Wil and Saera. While Michael doubted he'd be much help on that front, it was an excuse to see Elise sooner.

As they rode in the elevator, Michael glanced over at Wil, who was staring sullenly at the floor in much the same manner he had during the journey home. *I hope being back here does him some good.*

A thud outside the elevator signaled that they were entering the subspace bubble around Headquarters. The dampening effect on Michael's abilities took effect immediately—as though he were reaching out to grasp at smoke.

"I guess there's not a need for the subspace shell anymore," Cris commented.

No more Bakzen to protect against. Michael nodded but chose not to reply when he saw Wil's grimace deepen.

"It does keep the trainees in check," Kate said.

"Limiting exposure to abilities doesn't help with training, though," Saera pointed out. "I'd support bringing the facility into normal space."

Cris cracked a smile. "That'd be quite a feat if we could pull it off. Transitioning the whole facility from one plane to another…"

Kate placed her hand on his arm. "Let's take it one step at a time. We have a lot of other transitions to make before then."

Somberness quieted them yet again.

Eventually, the elevator slowed and the doors opened to Level 1.

Elise was waiting for them in the lobby. She lit up when she saw Michael, but quickly turned her attention to Cris. "Sir, welcome back."

"Thank you for keeping everything in order," Cris replied. "Anything to report?"

Elise shook her head. "No, sir. It's been quiet since Saera left."

"All right, I guess we'll get settled in." Cris took his wife's hand. "Wil, did you want to go over any of the staffing?"

"No, it's up to you," Wil mumbled.

Cris and Kate stepped out of the elevator.

Elise hesitated in the lobby. "Sir, did you need anything else from me?"

"Not right now," Cris replied. "I'll give you a call if I have any questions."

"Of course, sir. Anytime." Elise darted onto the elevator, flashing a coy smile to Michael. *"Hi,"* she greeted in his mind.

"Hi," he greeted back. *"It's good to see you."*

"You too." Elise threw her arms around Saera. "Welcome home! Next time I won't let you leave me behind."

Saera hugged her back. "I won't, promise." She released her friend. "We'll catch up soon, but I need a little down time first."

Elise glanced at Michael again. "Of course, take your time."

Cris and Kate waved goodbye as the elevator doors closed.

Saera selected Level 2 on the control panel next to the door. "Residential wing okay?" she asked Elise.

"Works for me."

They exited into the residential corridor on Level 2, and Saera escorted Wil toward their quarters. Elise hung back with Michael, waiting for their friends to round a bend in the hallway.

Michael was overcome with an unexpected wave of nerves as he found himself alone with her. "How are you?" he asked when Wil and Saera had disappeared from view.

Elise stepped forward and embraced him. "I'm so glad you made it home safely."

He wrapped his arms around her, savoring her warmth. "I was one of the lucky ones out of the thick of battle, for the most part."

Elise pulled back slightly, her dark eyes searching his. "I think being on the lead command team qualifies as being in the thick of it."

"Not as much as some people."

"You mean your friend... who was hurt?"

Michael took a deep breath. "Tom and the rest of them were the ones who made a real difference. I had it easy."

"You made a difference as far as I'm concerned." Suddenly, she stretched up on her toes and gave him a quick kiss.

His heart leaped as her lips brushed against his—soft and inviting. He stood in shock for a moment after the unexpected advance.

"I'd like to give us a shot," Elise stated matter-of-factly.

A happy tingle spread through Michael's core. He took her hand. *"I'd like that."*

"All right." Elise grinned. "Now, let's go find you some proper Agent quarters."

— — —

Cris stepped into the vacant High Commander's office. *Banks' office...*

His heart ached from the loss of his longtime friend and mentor. Though their relationship had been rocky at times, Banks was always more of a father to him than his own blood relation. He had been with Cris along every step of his career in the TSS, had filled in as a surrogate grandfather for Wil. Even though Banks was fulfilling his responsibilities to the Priesthood, that didn't change the fact that there was genuine affection between them. More than a friend, he was part of the family. The loss left a void that could never be filled.

"I guess this is yours now," Kate said from behind him.

"Wil said he didn't want it," Cris replied. "I'm not sure I do, either."

Kate came forward and slipped her hand into his. "Everyone needs a leader right now—a familiar face to offer some consistency. You're the best person for the job."

"Maybe Taelis will want to take over."

Kate raised an eyebrow. "Are you inviting mutiny?"

"Good point," Cris smirked. "Besides, he'll probably want to retire. I can't imagine going back to administrative tedium after spending four decades in a warzone. All of those people in the Jotun division deserve a break."

"I'd say we do, too, but we haven't had it nearly as bad."

"I think I have a few years left in me." Cris' handheld chirped in his pocket. The call was from Taelis.

"Nice timing. I'll leave you to it." Kate gave him a quick kiss and showed herself out of the office.

Cris directed the call up to the main viewscreen. "Hello, sir."

"Hi, Cris. You left in a hurry," Taelis' image said from the screen.

"We were able to convince Wil to travel back here. Needed to keep the momentum while we had it."

"Hopefully, that's a sign of improvement," Taelis said.

"I'm trying to be optimistic."

The High Commander nodded slowly. He seemed to take in Cris' surroundings. "Is that the High Commander's office?"

"It is. I was just making sure everything was in order."

Taelis drew a deep breath. "I still can't believe he's gone."

"Me either." Cris hung his head. "We'll arrange for a memorial service here. I think that's most fitting."

"Yes, good," Taelis replied. "I take it you're in charge at the moment?"

"Wil's in no position to command right now, so I've stepped up as interim High Commander."

Taelis' tilted his head. "I didn't expect him to break like this."

"He led the destruction of an entire people."

"They were the enemy!" the High Commander shot back.

"They were innocent. The Priesthood is the real enemy. They created the Bakzen, then decided that it was a mistake. Wil was also created. Used. He empathized with them, I think. The Bakzen were only trying to survive."

Taelis scoffed. "Do you know how many of us they killed?"

"At least we survived. The Bakzen are all but extinct now, thanks to us."

"They never should have been created in the first place."

He is a pawn of the Priesthood. I can't reveal my intentions yet. "At least the war is over now."

"It is," the High Commander agreed. He released a slow breath. "It will take a while to change my mindset."

"What are your plans?" Cris asked.

"There is no longer a need for H2 or the Jotun division. I would like to live out my remaining days in some quiet corner of the galaxy. I just have a few remaining details related to fleet decommissioning to attend to. There's also the matter of Aram Laensir."

"Oh, right," Cris muttered, remembering the would-be Bakzen sympathizer they'd apprehended in H2. "May as well let him go. There are plenty of other people who hate those with telekinetic abilities—he can't defect to the Bakzen now."

"My thoughts, as well." Taelis sighed. "I hope we can begin the process of unification."

That's my new mission. "Indeed. I'll look after things here as best I can," Cris told him.

"I have no doubt." Taelis paused. "I'll make sure all the important information gets transferred to your account."

"Thank you, sir."

"And Cris… I've come to understand why Banks was so fond of you. I trust you'll make sure we never end up in a position like this again."

Maybe he's not such a pawn after all. "Yes, sir."

Taelis inclined his head. "Take care. The TSS is in good hands." He ended the transmission.

Cris took a moment to let the words settle in. Banks had always talked about Taelis as though he was completely aligned with the Priesthood, but perhaps that was not the case. He might be a resource to help fill in some of the missing information about the Priesthood's involvement in the Bakzen's creation, but if Cris was wrong about his loyalties, he'd place himself in a dangerous position. It was a matter to investigate further when everything else was settled.

Turning to more pressing matters, he logged into the Mainframe to check the latest messages and reports that had gone to Banks' account, since no routing had been set up to a new contact yet. Only 1,357 unread messages, all marked as high-priority. *The next few days are going to be great.*

He closed out of the email application. The screen defaulted to a desktop view, and one of the icons caught his attention. It was simply titled: 'For Cris'.

Banks knew he was going to his death. Were these his final wishes? Reluctantly, Cris opened the file. It read:

> Dear Cris,
>
> You're reading this because I'm dead. I was never much of one for theories around time dilation, but maybe these sorts of letters are a loophole.
>
> I wish I could have said goodbye properly, except the bomaxed war had to get in the way. I spent my whole career preparing for other people to enter the fight, so I suppose it's fitting that I go out this way defending our home. I hope it worked—but then again, you wouldn't be reading this if it hadn't.
>
> I want you to know that you were the only son I ever knew. You were my family and despite all the secrets I had to keep from you, you were always my most trusted friend. I hope that the coming peace is every bit as wonderful as we've dreamed it to be. Enjoy every moment

you share with your loved ones and cherish those times. Learn from my mistakes and live with no regrets.

Life is complicated. I didn't always know what the correct action was, but I'm confident you'll figure it out. I have sealed some information for you that will unlock when the time is right. I entrust you to the safekeeping of my legacy.

Give Wil, Kate, and Saera my regards. Perhaps we will all meet again in another lifetime.

- Jason

By the end, Cris' vision was clouded and his throat tight. His path may have been designed by the Priesthood, but Banks had made the TSS Cris' genuine family. *Whatever you want me to do, I'll do it. I owe you my life.*

CHAPTER 29

"WIL, PLEASE SAY something," Saera pleaded from the doorway of their bedroom.

Her husband didn't so much as glance up from writing on his tablet as he sat cross-legged on the bed. He'd been furiously typing for days with no indication about the nature of the project.

Whatever person Wil used to be was buried somewhere deep. On the rare occasion he did look at her, she sensed only pain and sadness in his gaze. Gone was the love, the desire, the excitement to be in each other's presence. It would be easier to live with a stranger than to watch him deteriorate without explanation.

"What are you working on?" she asked again, expecting silence.

"Someone else needs to know," Wil replied.

Surprised, she almost choked on her own breath. "Know what?"

"The truth about the Bakzen."

Very few people knew yet about the Priesthood's involvement. The members of Wil's Command Center crew were the first to put the pieces together after the final battle of the war. They'd gone to Cris as the most senior officer, but Saera was the only one with the insights to fill in the missing pieces when they asked; by that point, she had no reason to deny anything. The war was already over. No sentiments of the morality of their actions would change the outcome.

Even as word spread within segments of the TSS, there was an unspoken understanding that the information was sensitive. In particular regard to those who'd spent their whole careers—given their lives—to the Jotun division, divulging that all the fighting had essentially been a civil war against their divergent Taran kin would only result in heartache. There were too many nuances to explain or justify. All that mattered for the present was that Tarans could begin to recover. No more resources dedicated to endless fights, no more raids and threats of attack. They could begin rebuilding, and hopefully make it a better future.

"What are you saying about the Bakzen?" Saera asked.

Wil paused his writing. "The facts, or as close to fact as records indicate. I suspect the Priesthood will attempt another data purge. I don't want the rest getting lost."

"We won't let it."

He stared at his hands. "I don't know if I'll be able to see it through myself."

At the risk of him shying away from her as he had since he first sent her away, Saera moved to her husband and sat on the edge of the bed next to him. Up close, he was noticeably thinner and pale compared to his usual self—worn from lack of sleep and a poor appetite.

Cautiously, she reached out her hand toward his. To her relief, he allowed her to take it. A spark passed between them. Her heart leaped; their connection was still there, even if he was ignoring it.

"I would do anything for you," Saera murmured.

"I would for you, too." Wil looked away again.

"Come back to me."

He shook his head. "It's not that simple."

"So, explain it to me!" she urged. "Did I do something wrong?"

"No, Saera, you're perfect. You've given me far more than I deserve."

"After what you've been through? You deserve anything you damn well please!"

He scoffed. "You have no idea what I've done."

"You won the war, just like they wanted." She rubbed his

hand. "You're a hero."

"Do you know how many people died because of me? I've been trying to add it all up—"

"No, don't even go there," Saera interrupted. "That is not a line of thinking worth pursuing."

"I need to tell the whole story. I need to put it in perspective," Wil insisted.

"What good will any of that do? It won't bring them back."

"At least they won't be forgotten."

"They won't be," Saera assured him. "Word of the war is going to spread whether or not people know the whole truth. To move forward, they don't need depressing details about the past that can't be changed—they need leadership and inspiration. They need someone to show them a new future where we can be united rather than divided—where leaders put others before themselves."

"I'm not that person, if that's what you're getting at."

"You are!"

Wil scowled. "I'm far too selfish."

"After giving your whole life to others?" Saera asked, incredulous.

"There are some things I could never give up." He paused, taking her other hand in his. "I could never put anyone else before you."

For an instant, his hard façade opened and the love in his touch was there again. Saera reached out to him through their bond—tantalizingly close to the fulfillment she'd been thirsting for since he'd first shut her out. But the wall was already back. "What about yourself?"

"What do you mean?"

"Would you put yourself before me?" she clarified.

"I would try not to."

All the bitterness within Saera rose to the surface in one unstoppable wave. "Then maybe you should start thinking about my feelings rather than wallowing in whatever misery you've brought down on yourself. You promised to be there for me, so get over whatever issues you're having and start being my partner again!"

Wil sat in stunned silence.

"I'm sorry," Saera hastily added. "I didn't mean—"

"No, you did," Wil cut in. "And you're right."

"I—"

Wil retracted his hands. "Let me finish this up." He went back to work on his tablet.

I'm not sure if I got through to him or just pissed him off. Saera rose from the bed and headed toward the door. "Are you going to Banks' service tonight?"

Her husband took a slow breath. "Yes, I'll be there."

"I'll see you then." She left him to his writing.

— — —

Dressed in his TSS formal uniform, Wil made his way up to the TSS spaceport for Banks' memorial service. There were few events that could have pulled him from his quarters, but honoring his lifelong friend topped the list. *With any luck, I can sneak in unnoticed.*

His plan for a stealthy entry was dashed the moment he stepped out of the elevator to the surface port, where he found Saera waiting for him.

"Good, you're here," she said. "Your father decided to have the service on one of the transport ships, so we could be near his resting place. There'll just be twenty or so of us, and we'll broadcast to the rest of the TSS."

"I wasn't expecting something so intimate."

Saera gave him a faint smile. "Do you really think he'd want us to make a big fuss over him?"

Wil shook his head. "No. This is more fitting, you're right."

They took a shuttle up to the main spaceport and then walked in silence to the transport vessel.

Cris, also dressed in his formal uniform, greeted them at the top of the gangway. "Wil, I'm glad you came."

"I wouldn't miss it." *At least, for once, loss will be on everyone else's minds, too.*

Twenty other Agents were already gathered in the main cabin

of the small ship, seated with two on either side of the center aisle.

Kate, seated next to Scott Wincowski, beckoned Wil and Saera to two empty seats on the other side of the aisle from her in the front row. She gave Wil's hand a light squeeze as he passed by, concern evident on her face as she looked him over.

"I'm okay," he murmured to dismiss her silent inquiry, and then quickly slipped into the window seat.

Saera sat down next to him and took in the crowd behind them, exchanging a respectful nod with Taelis and the Agents who were old friends or past mentors. "Looks like many of the senior Agents are taking a break from the field to be here."

Wil stared out the viewport at the nearly empty spaceport. "Banks touched a lot of people's lives. Repairing the Rift can wait."

Two minutes later, a low rumble resonated through the floor as the transport ship headed to the place where Banks had sacrificed himself to save Headquarters and Earth. Wil's chest constricted as they approached the location, sensing a faint trace of energy still lingering from the rift corridor. *Banks gave his life to the war, yet here I am alive and doing nothing. It should have been the other way around.*

Thrusters maneuvered the ship into position, and the rumble ceased when the engine cut out. Earth was visible out Wil's viewport, and the moon dominated the view out the opposite side of the craft. It all seemed so peaceful now that the threat had passed.

Cris walked to the front of the ship along the center aisle and turned to face the group, fixing his gaze on a camera at the back center of the cabin. "Thank you all for joining us as we pay our respects to Jason Banks, our longtime High Commander and friend. I'll keep this brief, but I wanted to take a few moments to reflect on not only this one death, but the many losses we have suffered in the war. Banks was more than just a friend to me—he was truly family. More than anything, when I hear people discuss the TSS, they reflect on the fact that the TSS community is one big family of individuals working toward a common goal. When we lose one of our own, we have lost a part of ourselves. But we are still united, and together we have shown that we can make it through anything.

"While engaged together in the fight against the Bakzen, we each needed to do things that pushed us to our physical and emotional limits, but we can be thankful that we made it through alive. I think it's important to recognize that those actions we took during the war do not reflect on who we are as individuals—or as a community—but rather were the result of necessity.

"Now, with our shared goal of defeating the Bakzen completed, we have the opportunity to reimagine the TSS as an organization where Agents' abilities aren't used for combat, but rather for peace. That is the future we have all envisioned at one point or another, whether it was ever verbalized or not. We were fighting with the hope that an era would arrive when we could live without fear of attack or persecution. We're halfway there, but even with the Bakzen threat eliminated, we still have a long way to go before we can consider ourselves to be on equal footing with the rest of Tarans. There has long been a divide between those with abilities and those without, but my hope is that in the peacetime to come, we can begin a reintegration.

"So, let us not dwell on what we have lost in the war, but rather what those sacrifices will enable us to achieve in the future. We have been given a great gift: the chance to start over and shape our own destinies. To honor all of those who have fallen, we must make the most of that opportunity. It is our duty to make sure that those lives weren't given in vain.

"As I address you now as a new High Commander of the TSS, I give you my word that I will work toward that new goal of peace across the Taran worlds, where those with abilities no longer need to hide." Cris paused and swept his gaze across all of those in the room, lingering on Kate. She nodded. "To begin that process," Cris continued, "I will state for the record a fact that has been danced around since I first joined the TSS three decades ago. If you were watching the advancement ceremony for my son, Wil, to Supreme Commander, you heard him introduced as Williame Sietinen. So, let there be no mistake: I am Cristoph Sietinen, heir to the Sietinen Dynasty. My wife, Katrine Vaenetri, and I have committed our lives to serving Tararia. For now, that is through our roles in the TSS. I hope to lead by example and show that those from all walks of life can be united and walk together as equals. That is the future we were fighting for in the war, and by achieving that goal, Banks and all of our fallen comrades will live on through that enduring peace."

Applause filled the small craft, but Wil was too absorbed in his own thoughts to hear the follow-on comments. He doubted anyone in the shuttle would be surprised by the formal announcement of his family's lineage, but it would certainly be a popular topic of conversation within the TSS in the coming weeks.

As soon as the shuttle docked with the port, Wil returned to his quarters while the others stayed behind to swap memories over drinks. He sat in quiet contemplation, reflecting on his father's words and the future at hand. Eventually, Saera returned and went to bed for the night. Though Wil joined her in bed, sleep was elusive.

He stared up at the ceiling in the dark, listening to the sounds of Saera's soft breathing next to him as she slept.

Words from Banks' funeral replayed in his mind. *Duty and honor… I can't be a leader and just allow myself to waste away. I owe it to Saera—to all of them—to get through this.*

Yet, guilt was consuming him from within. It gnawed at him during every waking moment and brought nightmares when he did manage to sleep. TSS soldiers, Cambion, the Bakzen, the hybrid clones—there was too much loss to process, and he had a hand in it all. Moving past it seemed like an impossible task from his current vantage. Except somehow, he had to. He needed to try to be the leader everyone saw him to be. His father was right: the fight wasn't over yet.

The war didn't kill me—not all the way. I need to reconnect with what's left of myself. He took a deep breath. The problem was, there was no way he could possibly come to terms in his present surroundings.

So many memories filled TSS Headquarters. Even the bedroom that had once been a sanctuary for Wil was now a prison. Everywhere were the smiling faces of those who thought him an infallible champion. Every time he had to put on the mask hiding the dark truth of what he'd sacrificed, a little more of him died inside. *No one can know what I did at Cambion. Especially not Saera.*

To permanently suppress his hurt and guilt, he would need to make a new reality for himself—one where he truly believed himself to be the good person everyone else saw him to be. Somewhere deep within, perhaps there was the strength to start again, where he could be a husband and partner and leader in all the ways he needed to be in order to see his loved ones through the coming trials.

I need to get out of here. The compulsion was overwhelming. It was his only chance to recover. A fleeting hope, but maybe— just maybe—he could recapture enough of himself to pull through.

He slipped from the bed and began to pack. He wouldn't need much, just a few changes of clothes and some rations; he could get those on the way, perhaps from a supply station. A faint smile touched his lips—it wasn't unlike when his father had left Tararia so many years before.

When his travel bag was ready, Wil crouched down next to Saera's side of the bed and brushed her temple with his fingertips.

She awoke with a start, her glowing jade eyes blinking with surprise. "Wil...? Wait, why are you dressed?"

"I need to leave."

His wife bolted upright. "Where are you going?"

"I'm not sure yet," he replied truthfully.

She frowned.

Wil grasped her hands. "I can never recover in a place with so many memories, and with everyone watching. I need to be alone so I can find myself—really find myself. I've never had the chance to do that before. I've always been told who to be, what to do. Not once did I have any say over my own pursuits."

Saera took a shaky breath. "Let me go with you."

"Not this time. If I'm to have any chance of being a worthy partner to you, then I need to do this on my own."

After a moment, she nodded. "Come back soon."

"I'll try." Wil swallowed. "If you haven't heard from me within four months, then you should assume I'm never coming back."

"No…" Tears glistened in the subtle light cast from her eyes.

"It won't come to that, if I can help it."

Wil sensed her reach out to him through their bond, feeling his pain and confusion and experiencing it as her own. She withdrew. "I understand."

He brushed away a tear on her cheek. "I could have never made it this far without you."

She placed her hand over his against her face. "I can't imagine a future without you. But I'll fulfill my duty even if you aren't here, if it's necessary."

Wil leaned in and brushed his lips against hers before pulling away. "You always were the strongest one."

—   —   —

Saera reached over and felt the cool space on the bed where Wil should be. Even when he was withdrawn, his presence was a reminder of their partnership. With him gone, she just felt empty.

She got dressed for the day slowly, trying to delay the conversations that were to come. Once dressed, she took some time to gather herself, but eventually she could delay no longer. She crossed the hall to Cris and Kate's quarters.

Steeling herself, Saera pressed the buzzer at the door.

Cris answered. "Hi, Saera. How are you?" Kate came up behind him.

"I'm…" She looked to the side, unable to meet his gaze. "Wil has gone away."

Cris' eyes widened with alarm. "Where did he go?"

I wish I were with him. "I don't know. But he needed to. He couldn't recover here."

Cris took a slow breath. "We'll just have to trust him, I suppose."

"Part of me wanted to bar him from leaving, but this was no way to live our lives. It's been weeks of decline. I'm glad he finally took some action." *He was wasting away, and he would have taken the rest of us with him eventually.*

"Did he say anything else about his intentions?" Kate asked.

"That he needs time to himself. He said if he's not back in four months then he's never coming back."

Cris nodded. "Let's hope it's not that long."

I'm not ready to lose my husband—my best friend, my confidant... my everything. "I want him to find peace. I've been feeling the echo of torment within him for all this time, and I can't even begin to imagine what he must be experiencing himself."

"That's all I've ever wanted for him, too." Cris paused. "We should tell the Primus Elites he's gone away."

Saera nodded.

"I'll go with you, if you want," Cris offered.

"No, I'll tell Michael first. He'll know the best way to handle that communication." *They'll want to hear it from one of their own.*

"Okay." Cris exhaled slowly. "We need to be here for each other. Know our door is always open."

"Thanks." Saera's breath caught in her throat. Tears burned the corners of her eyes, but she managed to keep them at bay. *I need to be strong.* She was about to retreat to her quarters when Cris pulled her in for a hug. She leaned against him, grateful for someone to comfort her.

Kate rubbed Saera's back. "You're family, no matter what."

When the knot in her chest had eased, Saera pulled away. *I can't dwell on some imagined loss. I need to believe that Wil will come back healed.* "Hey, I could use a distraction," she said to Cris. "Do you need any help with your new administrative duties?"

Cris' eyebrows raised with surprise. "Is that a genuine offer?"

"I'm going to drive myself crazy waiting for Wil if I don't keep busy," Saera admitted.

"Well, I haven't officially selected a new Lead Agent. I didn't think you'd be interested, but you have a higher CR than anyone else so you get first right of refusal. The position is yours, if you want it."

If that can't fill up my time, nothing will. Saera nodded. "I'd be honored."

"All right. Consider it done." Cris gave her the hint of a smile. "You can start tomorrow."

"Thanks." She tucked a loose strand of hair behind her ear, thankful to have a new sense of direction. "I appreciate it."

Cris' smile touched his eyes this time. "You'll be way better at the job than I ever was."

They parted with another hug. Feeling temporarily in control of her emotions, Saera decided to get the conversation with Michael out of the way. She headed down the hall of Primus Agents' quarters.

Under other circumstances, receiving such a significant career promotion would have elated her, but in her present mental state, it was just enough to counter the emotional torment emanating from Wil through their bond. The weeks of vicariously experiencing his pain had worn her down, but she was determined to not succumb. As long as she had her friends' support, she could find her way until Wil returned. Michael, in particular, had always been there for her over the years. He could give her the perspective she needed, and he would know how to tell their other friends that Wil had gone.

Saera hit the buzzer next to Michael's new Agent quarters. She waited, but there was no answer. *He should be home at this hour.* She pressed the buzzer again.

Another minute passed, then the lock finally clicked open and the door slid to the side, just a crack. Michael peered out from inside, pants on but shirtless.

"Good morning," Saera greeted. "May I come in?"

Michael shifted on his feet. "This isn't really a good time."

"I have some news."

"Can it wait?"

"Maybe, but…" Saera's heart was heavy as she thought about what to say regarding Wil.

"Who is it?" a familiar voice asked from within.

Saera staggered backward a step as Elise came into view. "You two…?"

"Saera! I was going to tell you—" Elise started.

Michael swallowed, visibly uncomfortable in his position

between them. "We wanted to make sure it was real before we said anything."

Two of my best friends… I should be happy for them. Except at the present, celebrating the new couple was the last thing on her mind. "I didn't realize you were…"

"It's new," Elise replied. "Once the war ended, we realized— Wait, Saera, what's wrong?"

The fragile threads allowing Saera to maintain composure started to unravel. Everyone else had their own lives to live—she couldn't expect anyone to be there for her. With Wil gone, she was on her own. *I promised Wil that I would carry on without him, but I don't want to. I want my best friend back.* Overcome with a sudden sense of isolation, she sobbed into her hands.

At the edge of her consciousness, Saera sensed Michael's and Elise's hands on her back, gently guiding her inside and to the couch. She followed their direction, still in a daze of uncertainty about the future ahead. Elise sat down and pulled Saera's face to her shoulder. Saera heartily accepted the gesture, thankful for any physical comfort.

"What is it?" Elise asked when Saera's breathing had evened.

"Wil left," Saera said, the words not seeming real.

"He Left!" Elise exclaimed.

"No," Saera hastily corrected, realizing that her phrasing gave the wrong impression. The Taran custom of elderly individuals or couples Leaving to die quietly on their own terms in a remote location was distinct, but in some ways the present circumstances might not be too different. "He's traveling."

"Oh." Elise relaxed.

"I don't know where," Saera continued. "I hate that he made me stay behind."

Elise hugged her. "Don't worry."

"Taking some time away for private introspection isn't a bad thing," Michael added. "I'm sure he won't be away for long."

"That's what I keep telling myself," Saera murmured, pulling away from her friend. "All the same, we should probably tell the other Elites."

"Yeah, I agree." Michael shifted on his feet, seeming to remember he was still only half-dressed. "Just give me a few minutes to get ready and we can go call them from a conference room. I'll come find you soon."

Right, I interrupted them. Saera hastily stood up. "Sorry for intruding."

"Not at all. You're welcome to wait here—" Elise started.

One glance toward Michael's uncomfortable expression told Saera to ignore Elise's offer. Michael would always be a good friend, but there were boundaries, and this visit had crossed the line. "It's okay. I'll be in my quarters. No rush," Saera said and headed for the door.

Elise nodded with compassion. "We're here if you need anything."

Michael showed her out. "He'll be back soon. I have no doubt."

Saera nodded, though she wasn't yet sure she genuinely believed the statement. "I'm really happy for you."

He glanced back at Elise. "Me too."

Without another word, Saera headed back to her quarters. *Wil has to come back. We have so much left to do.*

— — —

The High Commander's office would always belong to Banks in Cris' mind, but he would have to find a way to make it his own. Especially with Wil gone for an indeterminate time, the TSS was in his hands. He'd made his stand as a dynastic heir helming the TSS, and he needed to own that new position.

Cris closed out of the latest reports about progress repairing the Rift. *I hope the administrative tedium doesn't drive me crazy. At least it will be fun having Saera as Lead Agent.*

As he leaned back in the desk chair to take a quick break, a chirp from the desktop returned him to attention.

The source of the communication was completely masked, but a star was displayed next to the caller, indicating prior communications. *Is this my new boss checking in on me?*

"CACI, accept call on the main viewscreen," Cris instructed, walking over to face the display.

The broad viewscreen on the side wall briefly illuminated with the TSS logo, then transitioned to an image of a single figure robed in black.

"Hello," Cris greeted, instantly on edge.

"Cristoph Sietinen," the figure stated in a low male voice. "Sietinen heir, and now acting High Commander. So much power for one so volatile."

Cris crossed his arms. "Volatile? I think I've been a pretty reliable officer."

"You claim to serve the TSS, but still you think of other matters. You have never learned your place."

"My place is in service to the Taran Empire."

The figure shook his head, face concealed in shadow. "You think only of what will improve the lives of those like you, not the will of the people."

I can only assume this is one of the Priesthood's leaders. What is he trying to get from me? "I have vowed to do what I think is in the best interest of all Tarans."

"That is not your decision to make!" the figure bellowed.

"Is it yours?" Cris asked, trying to appear unruffled. *If this is what Banks was dealing with all those years, no wonder he always kept quiet.*

"You answer to the Priesthood, now and always."

That was all the confirmation Cris needed. "Yes. As I said, I serve the Taran people."

"Understand your role."

"And what is that, exactly? You're speaking in vague generalizations—threats, maybe. I mean, you call yourself a leader, but you won't show your face, or even share your name. In my experience, that's not a great way to win over followers."

"I am a Priest. That is all you need to know."

So that makes him deserving of authority? I think not. "We won your war for you. Things are going to be different going forward."

The Priest leaned closer to the camera. "You'll do exactly what you're told to do."

Cris cocked his head. "You know, I think these little check-ins between the TSS and Priesthood are over. I call the shots around here now."

"The TSS will wither without our support," the Priest retorted. "The Priesthood provides your primary source of funding."

"Really, you're threatening to cut off our funding?" Cris laughed. "Now that we don't have a war to sponsor, I can easily cover normal TSS operating costs for training and fleet upkeep on my SiNavTech royalties alone. Considering the TSS is now basically an undirected group of battle-hardened telekinetic soldiers, I don't think that's a fight you want to start."

The Priest was silent for a moment, then red eyes flashed beneath his hood—eyes like Cris had only ever seen on a Bakzen. "Enjoy the TSS while you can. It won't remain a sanctuary forever." He ended the transmission.

Cris leaned against the desk, letting out a slow breath. *I hope I know what I'm doing.*

CHAPTER 30

WAVES LAPPED AT the rocky shore of the tiny island. Wil sat on the ground with his bare feet in the sand, watching the water ebb and flow just out of reach from his toes, just as he'd done every day for the last month.

The island was the smallest land mass on the planet of Orino, where he had spent his Junior Agent internship in what felt like a previous lifetime. It would be easy for a passing boat to miss, with barely any elevation and only a few dozen meters in diameter— just large enough to support his shuttle, which was stocked with several months of rations. He had once come to terms with his inner self and purpose on Orino, so he could think of no better place to hopefully find himself again.

As he watched the dark green water along the horizon, it was hard for him to believe how much had transpired since he had last looked upon the ocean. His relationship with Saera had still been new back then, their bond fresh and untested. The war with the Bakzen had still been a distant future that seemed possible to alter. He had still had a sense of self that didn't revolve around death and destruction—with hope for a future beyond the war.

Wil burrowed into the beach pebbles with his toes. The empty hole in his chest was too much to bear.

So many died because of me. Why should I live? There was a logical answer to the question. He was a Sietinen heir, uniquely positioned to bridge Taran politics and those with telekinetic abilities within the TSS. He had the tools to make life better for those like him, so others with abilities would no longer be treated as outcasts.

There were plenty of excuses for why he shouldn't be held responsible for what happened in the war. He didn't start the fighting, but it was his duty to end it. By following through, he had fulfilled his purpose. The consequences of those actions weren't his to bear, but rather the Priesthood's for bringing about the war in the first place—for engineering Wil to clean up their mess. With no thanks or admission of wrongdoing, the Priesthood remained unchecked. Wil was in a position to set things right, once and for all.

Yet, no future application of his life seemed like enough.

The genocide of the Bakzen had justification, perhaps, but that was not his only transgression. What happened to Cambion was solely on his hands. For those billions of lives, there was no way to make amends. To continue on with his own life as if nothing had happened would only insult their memory. *How can I be happy when so many others have lost their lives entirely? When their friends and family continue to suffer from the loss?*

Wil kicked the pebbles aside and lurched to his feet, stiff from sitting for so long on the hard ground.

Walking into the water to be freed from his burden would be so simple. He could be washed away, existing only in memory. No one would have to know what he'd done.

He approached the edge of the surf, as he'd done in the days before, and let the waves lap at his toes. Only a few steps forward and he could plunge into the depths and be released. It would be all too easy, but he had never been one to take the easy way out.

The water chilled him as it eddied around his ankles, soaking the cuff of his pants. He wished for release—to no longer bear the weight of guilt and loss. He had fulfilled his role and it had consumed him, just as he expected. The shreds of his former self needed to be reassembled, but he didn't know how.

As Wil took another step forward into the cold to temporarily numb his pain, he gazed out at the endless waters. And then he saw the boat.

It glided over the gently rolling water, carried on the strong easterly breeze. A single sail billowed on the central mast, the details still indistinct at that distance.

Wil remained in the water while the boat approached, numb from his knees down. As the vessel neared, the rusted hull came into focus. Only a single person occupied the deck. A hundred meters out, the tall, slim figure waved to him—nearly jumping with excitement. Wil strained to make out the face masked by the shadow of the sail.

Mila? The spark of recognition brought the scene into focus. His lips parted with surprise as he took in the sight of his old friend and travel companion from his internship on Orino nearly a decade before. She had matured from the girl he'd known into a woman, though her longer hair was the biggest change.

"You're back!" she exclaimed, running to the railing to grab the anchor.

"What are you doing here?" Wil shouted back over the water.

"Coming to see you, of course!" Mila replied and dropped the anchor into the ocean. Before Wil had time to respond, she dove from her vessel and began swimming toward the shore.

Two meters from Wil, Mila found her footing. The water came up to her waist, and she wrapped her arms around herself to stave off the chill. "You didn't have to come into the water to meet me, silly."

"I was already out here."

"You came to the wrong planet if you wanted to play around in the ocean." She waded toward him, examining his face. "What's wrong? I thought you'd be happy to see me."

"You shouldn't have come," Wil murmured. *I came here to be alone.*

Mila evaluated his scowl. "Now I'm especially glad I did." She gestured toward the shore. "Come on, let's talk."

Wil allowed her to lead him from the water back to the campsite he had erected next to the shuttle. A chair was situated next to a compact thermal unit functioning as a heater and food warmer, and a solar collector rested on the ground to power Wil's handheld in the event it was needed. He'd tried to step fully away from the ties to his life back home, but the tether was there in the event he could find his way back. Maybe, with Mila's help, that would be possible.

Mila set Wil down in the folding chair by the heater. "I don't suppose you have a second seat?"

"I wasn't expecting company."

Mila nodded, her oval face soft with understanding. She surveyed the campsite and spotted one of the crates containing the meal rations he'd procured from a space station en route. Without hesitation, she dragged it across the black rock and sat down to face Wil. "Something tells me you weren't about to go on a recreational swim."

Wil dropped his head, not wanting to meet her searching eyes.

"Wil..." Mila placed her hand on his knee, radiating surprising warmth despite her wet clothes and the cool air.

"I'm not the same person you knew before."

Mila frowned. "What did they do to you?"

What did I do to myself? "I can't even begin to explain what I've been through over the last several years. It feels like five lifetimes. I'm tired. I don't want to carry this weight anymore."

"You came all the way here to drown yourself in the ocean?" Mila raised an eyebrow.

"No... I needed to escape."

"Escape what?"

Myself. Except, there's nowhere to go. "I just had to get away. My whole life I've had others telling me who I needed to be. I wanted to find out who I am without all that."

Mila shrugged. "Okay... But that doesn't explain why you were contemplating drowning yourself in the ocean."

"I wasn't trying to drown myself." *I feel like I'm already drowning, even on land...*

"I ask," she continued, "because that doesn't seem like a very reliable way of offing yourself. If you were serious about it, I'd think you'd throw yourself out an airlock. You were born in space, may as well die that way, too."

The bluntness of her statement caught Wil by surprise. *That's true, I could—use my power to begin repairing the Rift the Bakzen created. But I didn't...* "That's not what I want."

"As you keep insisting, but your actions say otherwise. Why

the inner conflict?"

"I did something unforgivable."

"I'm sure most people who've been through a war would say the same thing."

Wil shook his head. "Not like this."

"So, you want to punish yourself?" Mila asked, ducking her head in an attempt to look him in the eye.

"It's complicated."

She smirked. "Of course, isn't it always?"

Wil crossed his arms and leaned back in the chair, careful to avoid eye contact. *There's no way she could possibly understand. Can't I just be left alone?*

"I'm not going to let you off that easily."

He groaned. "Why are you even here? I didn't invite you."

"I saw your ship fly over and came looking for you. The winds didn't pick up until last week so it took a while to set out."

"How did you know it was me?"

"I didn't, but I had a hunch." Mila crossed her legs and propped her arms back on the crate. "I'm afraid you're stuck with me now."

"How's that?"

"There's no way I'm leaving you alone in this state. I'm not going anywhere until you're in your right mind again."

"My well-being isn't your concern."

She made a sweeping survey of the barren surroundings from her seat. "I don't see anyone else around to keep watch. That leaves me."

"I don't need a babysitter."

"You're right, what you need is counseling with an elder. Except, I'm the only one around so you'll have to make do." Mila flashed a determined smile.

"Thanks for the offer, but I'm fine."

"Considering I found you knee-deep in the water and you could have been about to dive in, I'm not buying it."

Wil let out an exasperated sigh. "Mila, please. This is something I need to work through on my own."

"Nope, still not buying it," she shot back. "You could have landed here without anyone being the wiser. I mean, stars! I never even knew this little island was here and I've lived a two-weeks' sail away from it my whole life. Yet, you did a little flyby where there was a good chance of one of your old friends seeing you. I think you wanted company out here."

"I would have brought a second chair, if that were the case."

"But this crate is so comfy!" She leaned forward, placing her forearms on her thighs. "Come on, Wil. Just admit that maybe you don't want to be alone right now."

The best he could manage was a shrug.

Mila tilted her head. "All right, I'll take it. Now, what drove you to abandon civilization and take up residence on this deserted rock for the last month?"

"I had a lot of thinking to do. I wanted to go somewhere where I wouldn't be bothered."

She barely batted an eye at his accusing glare. "So, think out loud. What's on your mind?"

Wil groaned. "Don't you have somewhere better to be? What about Tiro?"

Mila slumped. "Sometimes things don't work out how you imagine."

Oh... Wil gave her a moment to gather herself. "What happened?"

She picked at one of her fingernails. "When it came down to it, we wanted different things. He wanted a family, I wanted adventure."

"I'm sorry."

She shrugged. "Don't be. We enjoyed our time together. It is what it is." She let out a slow breath. "What about you? Did you and your girl fare any better?"

"We've been married for almost three years," Wil replied.

"Why isn't she here with you?"

"I needed to work through this on my own." *Can I ever come to terms with my actions so I can look at her without seeing the ruins of Cambion?*

"Do you still love her?"

"Of course."

Mila eyed him. "Then what's the problem?"

Wil shook his head in silence, unable to put his actions into words.

"Tell me, Wil," Mila pressed.

"I—" He searched for what to say. "I had an impossible decision to make, and I chose her."

"Okay… Still not seeing the problem."

Wil took a ragged breath. "I allowed others to die so that she might live." As he heard the admission in his own voice, the destruction of Cambion replayed in his mind, vivid and visceral. Cries of pain, the stench of smoke, a pounding heart—his senses overwhelmed with his own personal nightmare of how the planet's final moments may have played out.

Then, everything became quiet and still. Even in vague terms, he had revealed his deepest secret, taking the first step to pry the weights from his conscience.

Mila let the words sink in. "She means a lot to you."

"Everything."

"I'm willing to bet she thinks about you the same way."

Wil hugged himself, reflecting on the tender moments he'd shared with Saera over the years. There was no question how she felt about him. "She does."

"You said you let others die in exchange for her life… But what kind of life could it possibly be for her if you're not in it?"

The words cut deep. *Saera's innocent in all this. I can't possibly ask her to accept me after what I've done. It's not fair to her.* "She deserves better than me."

"I don't know her, so it's not my place to say what she deserves. But speaking as someone who's been in love, I can tell you that it's infuriating to have anyone else tell you who you should or shouldn't be with. If she wants you, then you need to be there for her."

Wil shook his head. "It doesn't feel right. Not after what I've done."

"Then you need to find a way to deal with the guilt, or whatever it is that you're feeling right now."

"It's not that simple."

Mila's eyes narrowed. "Don't diminish the sacrifice of others. If you chose her life, then make it count. Her living life to the fullest is the closest you can ever come to atoning. How could she even begin to find happiness without her favorite person by her side?"

She's right. Wil wilted, burying his face in his hands. He had been so wrapped up in his own feelings that he'd lost sight of the bigger picture. There was no undoing his decision—the only path forward was to embrace all that the decision allowed—for Saera to live, for them to be together and have the life outside the TSS that they'd always dreamed of having.

He couldn't return the lives of those who'd died, but their death could still have meaning. In honor of their memory, he could bring justice to those that had started the war in the first place. He could make sure no one would have to suffer again. "I want to be better. For her."

Mila leaned forward and took his hand. "You can be."

Wil took a deep breath. "I don't know where to begin."

"We'll figure it out together."

He finally met her gaze. "How can you be so kind to me after what I've done?"

"Because you helped me when I needed it most. It's the least I can do."

She took one life. I took billions. "I'll never be who I was before the war."

"Then reinvent yourself," Mila replied, venturing a smile. "Your friends and family want you back—even if it's a different version of you."

"What if they don't like the new me?"

"Impossible. Real friends want you to grow."

I need to pull through—for Saera, and everyone else who's believed in me. At last, the darkness swirling in his mind began to recede. "Thank you."

Mila chuckled. "Don't thank me yet! You're still all mopey."

"But you've given me genuine hope. I was having difficulty seeing a way forward before, and now I think it's possible."

"Hey, what are friends for?" she quipped.

"I've been a pretty poor friend since I was here last time."

"Meh." Mila shrugged. "I know you were busy. Still, you could have written."

Wil cracked a smile. "What, and delivered it by seagull?"

She grinned. "I think there's more of you left than you believe."

"I guess I just have to find it."

"We will." She jumped to her feet, excitement in her eyes. "Now, you have to show me around the shuttle. I've never been in a spaceship!"

CHAPTER 31

AFTER THREE MONTHS in the role of Lead Agent, Saera understood why Cris had added the 'if you want it' qualifier to his job offer. The administrative side of the TSS was a mess following the war, and she'd been keeping busy with Cris as they started to envision a new structure for the TSS without the Jotun division. However, the distraction was just what she needed while Wil was away.

There still hadn't been any word from Wil since he left, and there was only one month left before the expiration date of his timeline to return. Yet, she had felt a change over the recent weeks. The darkness eating away at her core through her bond with Wil had long since faded to the background. Either it was just the passage of time that made their bond less distinct, or his emotional state was improving.

However, for the first time since Wil initially departed on the vague mission to find himself, Saera found herself questioning whether he would, in fact, come back. Three months… that was far longer than she ever anticipated for him to be away. If he really was recovering, as her connection to him seemed to indicate, then it didn't make sense that he hadn't returned yet.

She had already made up her mind to go looking for him after the four months were up, if he hadn't come back on his own; there was no way she'd let him just disappear without explanation. Until that time, though, she'd promised to give him space. So, she'd thrown herself into her new position as Lead Agent and tried to block out everything else.

Cris and Kate had helped keep her grounded, but otherwise she was isolated compared to the previous years within the TSS. In particular, the budding relationship between Michael and Elise had distanced her from the two longtime friends and confidants she'd always relied on in the past. While she was pleased to see her friends find happiness, she couldn't help feeling a little resentful about the timing. Just when she was on her own and needed them most, they had become absorbed in each other. She knew it was selfish to think in those terms, but it was pointless to lie to herself—she craved to have things back the way they were before the war, surrounded by friends and with Wil at her side. Being named Lead Agent and advancing in her career just wasn't the same without being able to share it with others.

Saera tried to swallow a lump in her throat as she climbed in bed alone for the night. If the person closest to her could leave without any meaningful explanation, there was no reason to expect anyone else to stick around. All the relationships she thought she could rely on were, in the end, disposable. The only person she could count on was herself.

Except, she didn't want to be a unit of one. Being in a partnership, on a team, felt right. Her other half was missing. Still, she put on a mask of optimism every day when she was out of her quarters. At home alone, though—there she could admit that she was scared Wil would never return, that she would have to raise a child on her own to fulfill the obligation she made to the Sietinen Dynasty.

She took a slow breath to ease the knot in her chest. *No, I promised that I would rather have a few years with Wil than no time at all. I meant it then, and I still mean it now.*

Letting out another long breath, she nestled into her pillow. Her chest was still tight, but the burden on her heart was lifted, at least for a moment.

Saera was just on the verge of sleep when she was suddenly roused by the sound of the front door opening out in the living room. No one should be there at that hour, let alone have access without permission. She bolted upright in bed, readying a telekinetic shield.

Then, she felt him. The steady, calming presence of Wil—the old Wil, before the darkness had consumed him from within.

The bedroom door cracked open. Wil stood there, watching her in silence in the dark.

Her heart leaped. They were frozen, eyes locked on each other.

He smiled. "Hey."

Saera lunged forward across the bed, meeting Wil in an embrace at the foot of the mattress. She buried her face in his shoulder, speechless from joy and relief.

He cradled her close, opening himself to her—feeding their bond that had atrophied in the long months apart.

She pivoted to gaze up at him, braced for it to be a fantasy that would evaporate into thin air. But there he was—real and solid, looking back at her with the same adoration she felt for him.

Their lips met, sending a warm spark all the way down to Saera's toes. She pressed against him. It had been far too long since she had felt such affection or desire.

Wil pulled back slightly to catch his breath. "Saera, I'm so sorry."

She found her voice. "You were gone for so long! Where have you been?"

"Orino."

"Where you had your internship?"

He stroked the side of her face. "Yes. I found a small island and watched the waves."

"For three months?" she asked, incredulous.

"Mostly. Mila came to visit me."

Saera bristled. "What kind of visit?"

"We just talked," he assured her.

"Oh, really? So, you'll talk with her and not me? Yeah, I'm sure that's all you did—"

Wil looked her squarely in the eye. "I'd never do that to you."

Saera swallowed the misplaced anger. *He's telling the truth... But why couldn't he talk with me?* She sat back on her heels. "You opened up to her, of all people?"

He eased onto the bed next to her. "I know it seems strange, but she got to know a different side of me when we were younger. I needed that outside perspective while I reflected on the war. She helped me come to terms with a lot of things."

Saera was about to launch another protest, but decided that it ultimately didn't matter—they were back together, and nothing else was more important than that. *I need to let the past go in order for us to move forward.* With the internal resolution, the resentment began to evaporate. "I was starting to wonder if you'd ever come back."

Wil took her hands. "I'm sorry to make you wait for so long. I wanted to make sure that I was really ready to be back here."

She looked down, eyes stinging. "I thought I'd lost you."

Wil wrapped his arms around her. "I lost myself for a while, but I'm back now. I'll never leave you again."

She hugged him tighter. "You better not!"

He chuckled and pulled back, cupping her face in his hand as he searched her eyes. "Stars, I missed you."

"Me too." She leaned in and gave him a kiss. "How are you feeling?"

Wil worked his mouth, seemingly searching for the right words. "I'm still rebuilding. After what we went through... those experiences change a person. But I'm on a good path now, I think. I don't feel like I'm drowning anymore."

Saera ran her fingertips down the side of his face. "It means everything to have you back."

"It'll be an adjustment being here again, but I couldn't stand to be away from you any longer." He gazed into her eyes. "How have you been? I know I've been a terrible partner to you recently."

Saera swallowed. "It was pretty rough for a while..." She perked up. "But hey, I'm Lead Agent now!"

Wil smiled. "I can't think of anyone more qualified. Congratulations!"

"It's been good. Your dad and I have started hatching some big plans for the TSS."

"That doesn't surprise me in the least," Wil said, stroking her hair with one hand. "I can't wait to hear all about it."

She reclined him on the bed with her, snuggling up with her head against his chest. "It's a fresh start. We can really begin our lives together."

"No more war hanging over our heads."

"We could even start a family."

Wil swiveled around to face her. "Saera, I'm still a pretty long way off from being ready for that. I finally have enough of a grasp on myself to be a husband to you again, but 'parent' is too much to throw into the mix right now. I've never had the opportunity before to figure out what I truly enjoy. It's all been about the TSS, or SiNavTech, or whatever else the higher-ups have thrown at me. For once, I'd like to be able to study music, or art—something that isn't about business, or politics, or war."

"There's no rush." Saera ran her fingers through his hair. "It would be nice to see you use your intellect for something beyond ship engineering or battle strategy."

"Besides, this is our chance to just be a couple and enjoy each other."

"Now *that* I completely endorse." She shifted to give him a kiss, lingering with her face nuzzled against his. "Welcome home."

"I couldn't stay away. Here with you—this will always be where I belong."

—   —   —

Waking up in his own bed with his wife in his arms, Wil found himself in a supremely satisfied state of contentment. His guilt about Cambion and the destruction of the Bakzen would always linger in the back of his mind, but he was in control again. Those secrets about the war would be his alone to bear.

While he was tempted to stay in bed with Saera all day, he was anxious to see the friends and family he'd pushed away before his departure. There were relationships to mend and questions to answer.

He unfurled himself from Saera. "Time to get up. I should go see everyone else."

Saera yawned. "I'm actually surprised your parents haven't already rushed over. I think your dad had an alert set up for your credentials at the spaceport security gates."

Wil smirked. "I figured as much, which is why I designed a fake ID to use instead."

"You're too smart for your own good."

"I just wanted to get some time alone with you before being bombarded by demands to explain myself."

"I'm glad you did." Saera sat up and rubbed the sleep from her eyes. "I'll go shower." She slid out of bed and headed for the bathroom.

Wil rolled off the other side of the bed and grabbed his tablet from the charging pad on the desk. He'd completely neglected his email communications for most of the war and all the months since. *I'm going to guess.... ten thousand unread messages.* He wasn't far off: 9,237. With a heavy sigh, he started sorting through the messages, discarding anything that was clearly time-sensitive for a window long since passed.

On the fourteenth page of messages, one from Banks caught his attention—sent within an hour of his death. Simply titled 'Farewell', it read:

> *Wil,*
>
> *It's been an honor to watch you grow up and to be a part of your life. I'm sorry for everything I kept from you over the years. I hope one day you'll understand why.*
>
> *By the time you read this, hopefully the war is over and you're looking toward a brighter future. Maybe you should have a daughter—you Sietinen men always seem to get into trouble.*
>
> *Take care,*
> *Banks*

Wil stared at the message, reliving his final conversations with the High Commander and wishing that he hadn't ever doubted Banks' commitment to him or his family. There was a deeper meaning to the message, he was sure—what that was eluded him for the time being.

Saera emerged from the bathroom and stopped in the

doorway when she saw Wil's expression. "Is everything okay? You look like you've seen a ghost."

"I just did, in a way." He set down the tablet and moved across the room to embrace Saera. "Come here," he murmured, wrapping his arms around her. "I need to remember what's real."

"A lot has changed in the past year, but I'll always love you," Saera replied. "You can count on that."

He held her for another minute and then went to shower himself.

Once dressed, Wil braced himself for the upcoming reunion with his TSS family. He took Saera's hand and they headed into the hall.

The corridors were still relatively empty, to Wil's surprise. "Are most of the Agents still in the Rift?" he asked.

Saera nodded. "It's going to take a long time to fix the damage, but it's healing. Slowly."

"I'm glad it's working."

"All the Primus Elites except for Michael are still there," Saera continued. "I'm sure they'd love to hear from you, when you're ready."

"I'll get in touch."

They paused at the entry to the Primus mess hall. Then, hand-in-hand, they passed through the doorway. The room fell silent as all eyes turned to Wil.

"Stars!" Cris exclaimed from a table up front, breaking the silence. He ran to Wil and embraced him. Kate was only steps behind.

He hugged his parents back. "I'm sorry for leaving."

"The important thing is you're home now," his mother replied, pulling away to look at him.

"How are you?" Cris asked, searching Wil's face.

Wil smiled. "Getting better."

"Welcome back," Michael said from behind.

Wil turned to see Michael approaching with Elise, walking far closer together than the casual acquaintances he'd always thought them to be.

"Well, look at you two!" Wil exclaimed.

Elise blushed. "A lot can change in a few months."

Michael flashed a sheepish grin and placed his hand on the small of Elise's back. "Now that the war is over, we needed something new to look forward to."

Wil took in the happy faces of his friends around him. Despite the trials from the last several years, they had made it through. "We're not completely done yet. The Bakzen War may be finished, but as long as things stay the same, there could be another."

"That kind of change—it's not going to be easy," Cris cautioned.

We can't turn back now. Wil squeezed Saera's hand. "Nothing worth fighting for ever is."

—   —   —

High Priest Quadris strolled down the airy corridor of the administrative building on the northern coast of the Priesthood's isle, his black robe billowing around him. A breeze blew off the surrounding sea, bringing a briskness to the otherwise temperate summer weather. He breathed in the salty air and admired the rolling waves in the distance as he walked.

Deep within the island below, the newest experiment was progressing nicely. While the Bakzen had been a nuisance for far too long, at least the Priesthood would gain enduring benefits from the Bakzen's advances in remote mind-control, thanks to the information relayed by the TSS. Using the counteragent developed by the TSS, soon the Priesthood would be able to reverse engineer the Bakzen's original neurotoxin and command codes. Not only would the Priesthood then be able to activate the neurotoxin already within the Taran survivors of past Bakzen attacks, but it would only be a simple matter of manufacturing and distributing more of the neurotoxin to any worlds that demonstrated a risk of getting out of line—such an elegant solution to the growing political unrest. Despite the bold claims of Cristoph Sietinen, the TSS would never stand a chance in gaining influence over all the Taran worlds. The Priesthood's continued reign was secure.

When Quadris arrived in his office at the corner of the main administrative building, he accessed his workstation. Waiting for him was a message marked with the highest transmission priority, but there was no subject line or return address. The sender was identified only as 'Cadicle'. Sending such a message would require the utmost skill and knowledge of Taran communications infrastructure.

Quadris glared at the message, having no doubt about whom it was from. It read: >>I'll come for you one day, and there's nothing you can do to stop me.<<

CONTINUE THE STORY...

Volume 6: Path of Justice

In the years since the Bakzen War, Wil and Saera have raised a family on Earth outside the purview of the High Dynasties and Priesthood. Except, it's almost time for their teenage twins, Raena and Jason, to begin telekinesis training and they have no idea such abilities even exist. With the Bakzen threat eliminated, Wil hopes the TSS can offer them training without the need to commit to a lifetime of military service.

Just as the twins come to understand the life on Tararia that was kept from them as children, the family discovers that there's always another layer of secrets guiding their lives.

Path of Justice is the sixth installment in the Cadicle series. This novel lays the foundation for the plan to finally bring down the Priesthood.

OTHER CADICLE UNIVERSE BOOKS

CADICLE SERIES
Volume 1: Architects of Destiny (in *Shadows of Empire*)
Volume 2: Veil of Reality (in *Shadows of Empire*)
Volume 3: Bonds of Resolve (in *Shadows of Empire*)
Volume 4: Web of Truth
Volume 5: Crossroads of Fate
Volume 6: Path of Justice
Volume 7: Scions of Change

MINDSPACE
Book 1: Infiltration
Book 2: Conspiracy
Book 3: Offensive
Book 4: Endgame

VERITY CHRONICLES *with T.S. Valmond*
Book 1: Exile
Book 2: Divided Loyalties
Book 3: On the Run

SHADOWED SPACE *with Lucinda Pebre*
Book 1: Shadow Behind the Stars
Book 2: Shadow Rising
Book 3: Shadow Beyond the Reach

IN DARKNESS DWELLS *with James Fox*

TARAN EMPIRE SAGA
Book 1: Empire Reborn
Book 2: Empire Uprising
Book 3: Empire Defied
Book 4: Empire United

ACKNOWLEDGEMENTS

In early 2015, I never would have imagined I'd have published five books by September 2016. Considering that I started working on this series around 1997, it's been a whirlwind year and a half to finally have the books release out into the world in such a short span!

When I first started conceiving the Cadicle series, this fifth book was, in many ways, the original story I set out to write. I had read "Ender's Game" in fourth grade, which ignited my love for science fiction. One of my early thoughts was, "What if Ender had known that it wasn't a simulated game, and, right from the beginning of his training, he knew what he was going to eventually do?" Being the daughter of a therapist, I couldn't help but think through the psychological impacts of that knowledge. As I began crafting my own story, I knew that inner struggle was something that I wanted to explore with Wil. Many details of the Cadicle series have evolved over the years, but that balance of duty and morality has been a steady theme.

It's been an exciting challenge to bring those early concepts to fruition, and to watch the story grow as I've been shaped by experiences in my own life. I am indebted to my beta readers—Eric, Kurt, Katy, Julie, Liz, Cassie, and Bryan—for their tireless evaluations and candid feedback. Without them, this book wouldn't have become what it is today.

As always, I am especially thankful for the support from my husband and my parents for helping make this writing dream become a reality. I am incredibly lucky.

GLOSSARY

Aesir - A mysterious group of people known to be of Taran descent that live on the outskirts of explored space, engaging in metaphysical pursuits.

Agent - A class of officer within the TSS reserved for those with telekinetic and telepathic gifts. There are three levels of Agent based on level of ability: Primus, Sacon and Trion.

Ateron – An element that oscillates between normal space and subspace, facilitating high levels of telekinetic energy transfer.

Baellas - A corporation run by the Baellas Dynasty, producing housewares, clothing, furniture, and other textiles for use across the Taran civilization. Additional specialty lines managed by other smaller corporations are licensed to Baellas for distribution.

Bakzen - A militaristic race living beyond the outer colonies. All Bakzen are clones, with individuals differentiated by war scars. Officers are highly intelligent and possess extensive telekinetic abilities. Drones are conditioned to follow orders but still possess moderate telekinetic capabilities.

Cadicle - The definition of individual perfection in the Priesthood's founding ideology, with emergence of the Cadicle heralding the start to the next stage of evolution for the Taran race.

Course Rank (CR) - The official measurement of an Agent's ability level, taken at the end of their training immediately before graduation from Junior Agent to Agent. The Course Rank Test is a multi-phase examination, including direct focusing of telekinetic energy into a testing sphere. The magnitude of energy focused during the exercise is the primary factor dictating the Agent's CR.

Dainetris Dynasty - Formerly a seventh High Dynasty, the

Dainetris Dynasty was responsible for ship manufacturing before its fall from power.

Earth - A planet occupied by Humans, a divergent race of Tarans. Considered a "lost colony," Earth is not recognized as part of the Taran government.

H2 - The nickname for the TSS headquarters in the rift. The facility was created to serve as a base of operations for the Bakzen War.

High Commander - The officer responsible for the administration of the TSS. Always an Agent from the Primus class.

High Dynasties - Six families on Tararia that control the corporations critical to the functioning of Taran society. The "Big Six" each have a designated Region on Tararia, which is the seat of their power. The Dynasties in aggregate form an oligarchical government for the Taran colonies. In descending order of recognized influence, the Dynasties are: Sietinen, Vaenetri, Makaris, Monsari, Talsari, and Baellas.

Independent Jump Drive - A jump drive that does not rely on the SiNavTech beacon network for navigation, instead using a mathematical formula to calculate jump positions through normal space and the Rift.

Initiate - The second stage of the TSS training program for Agents. A trainee will typically remain at the Initiate stage for two or three years.

Jotun - The codename assigned to the division of the TSS dedicated to the war in the rift, based in H2.

Jump Drive - The engine system for travel through subspace. Conventional jump drives require an interface with the SiNavTech navigation system and subspace navigation beacons.

Junior Agent - The third stage of the TSS training program for

Agents. A trainee will typically remain at the Junior Agent stage for three to five years.

Lead Agent - The highest ranking Agent and second in command to the High Commander. The Lead Agent is responsible for overseeing the Agent training program and frequently serves as a liaison for TSS business with Taran colonies.

Lower Dynasties - There are 247 recognized Lower Dynasties in Taran society. Many of these families have a presence on Tararia, but some are residents of the other inner colonies.

Makaris Corp - A corporation run by the Makaris High Dynasty responsible for the distribution of food, water filters, and other necessary supplies to Taran colonies without diverse natural resources.

Monsari Power Solutions (MPS) - A corporation run by the Monsari Dynasty, responsible for power generation systems for the Taran worlds, including geothermal generators, portable generators, and reactors to power spacecraft.

Rift - A habitable pocket between normal space and subspace.

Sacon - The middle tier of TSS Agents. Typically, Sacon Agents will score a CR between 6 and 7.9.

Simultaneous Observation - The act of separating one's consciousness from the physical self in order to observe multiple spatial planes (i.e., normal space, subspace, and the rift) at the same time.

SiNavTech - A corporation run by the Sietinen High Dynasty, which controls and maintains the subspace navigation network used by Taran civilians and the TSS.

Spatial Dislocation - The act of physically transitioning from normal space to the brink of subspace, either by means of a jump drive or telekinetic abilities.

Starstone – An extremely rare gem. Only ten such gem veins are known anywhere in the galaxy, and each of the six High Dynasties has claim to one. Only enough material for one set of wedding rings is produced by each vein every generation. Starstones emit a luminescent resonance when positioned near other stones cut from the same vein.

TalEx - A corporation run by the Talsari Dynasty, managing mining operations and ore processing across Taran territories.

Tarans - The general term for all individuals with genetic relation to Tararian ancestry. Several divergent races are recognized by their planet or system.

Tararia - The home planet for the Taran race and seat of the central government.

Tararian Selective Service (TSS) - A military organization with two divisions: (1) Agent Class, and (2) Militia Class. Agents possess telekinetic and telepathic abilities; the TSS is the only place where individuals with such gifts can gain official training. The Militia class offers a formal training program for those without telekinetic abilities, providing tactical and administrative support to Agents. The Headquarters is located inside the moon of the planet Earth. Additional Militia training facilities are located throughout the Taran colonies.

Trainee - The generic term for a student of the TSS, and also the term for first year Agent students (when capitalized Trainee). Students are not fully "initiated" into the TSS until their second year.

Trion - The lowest tier of TSS Agents. Typically, Trion Agents will score a CR below 5.9.

Priesthood of the Cadicle - A formerly theological institution responsible for oversight of all governmental affairs and the flow of information throughout the Taran colonies. The Priesthood has jurisdiction over even the High Dynasties and provides a tiebreaking vote on new initiatives proposed by the High Dynasty oligarchy.

Primus - The highest of three Agent classes within the TSS, reserved for those with the strongest telekinetic abilities. Typically, Primus Agents will score a CR above 8.

Primus Elite - A new classification of Agent above Primus signifying an exceptional level of ability.

VComm – A telecommunications corporation owned and operated by the Vaenetri Dynasty.

ABOUT THE AUTHOR

Award-winning author A.K. (Amy) DuBoff has always loved science fiction in all its forms—books, movies, shows, and games. If it involves outer space, even better! She is a Nebula Award finalist and *USA Today* bestselling author most known for her Cadicle Universe, but she's also written a variety of space fantasy and comedic sci-fi. Now a full-time author, Amy can frequently be found traveling the world. When she's not writing, she enjoys wine tasting, binge-watching TV series, and playing epic strategy board games.

www.amyduboff.com

Made in the USA
Las Vegas, NV
03 July 2025

24391934R00194